A FIELD OF INNOCENCE

JACK ESTES

WARNER BOOKS

A Warner Communications Company

You can write to the author at the following address:

17780 Overlook Circle
Lake Oswego, Oregon 97034

WARNER BOOKS EDITION

This Warner Books Edition is published by arrangement with the author.

Cover photo by Jack Estes
Cover design by Don Puckey

Warner Books, Inc.
666 Fifth Avenue
New York, N.Y. 10103

A Warner Communications Company

Printed in the United States of America

First Warner Books Printing: August 1990

10 9 8 7 6 5 4 3 2 1

To my beautiful Irish lass...
and to my friend and editor
David Morgan

A FIELD OF INNOCENCE

One

IT WAS STILL DARK but the rain had stopped as we stood on a quiet corner and held onto each other. Occasionally a car would drive by, breaking the silence and splashing gutters full of rain on empty sidewalks, but otherwise, the city was sleeping.

It was that time of year when the mornings are cold and gray and lonely. Gone were holiday memories, once hanging in store windows or standing on crowded street corners in red suits ringing bells. It was February 1968 and the snow had melted weeks ago.

"Kristen, I have to go now," I said, cradling her face in my hands. "I love you. Don't cry. Things will be all right." Then I turned and walked up the block to the Armed Services Recruiting Station.

Leaving wasn't easy, but I didn't see a choice. I didn't have a job, was fast flunking out of college and Kristen was carrying our child. I was barely in a position to take care of myself, let alone a family of three. So I ran.

I left that day believing that by enlisting I could avoid the responsibility of being an adult and at the same time grow up. It seemed to be the answer. As a Marine, I would come home and somehow be important. Not so much a hero, but at least I would elevate my self-esteem. I would come back better than I had left. I could postpone my reality and maybe after two years Kristen and I would have a chance to make a life together.

Before long I was standing with a group of other boys in front of a pock-faced young lieutenant, being sworn in. As a child I had always been introspective and searching. But in this moment I wasn't trying to understand what I was feeling. I let my thoughts run through me, poetic, sentimental and fluid. I thought about being a father at eighteen and how scared Kristen must be. I, too, was scared. Scared for our future. And scared because I really didn't know what to do. I was in that period between child and man, buying time, as most of us standing there were.

While growing up I had not been instilled with a great sense of patriotic duty. Nor was I caught up in a fervor over the war in Vietnam. I wasn't dreaming of God and country and a red badge of courage. And I was too young to have been influenced by the Kennedy mystique of "Ask not what your country can do for you..."

The Korean Conflict and World War II were just comic books and John Wayne movies to me. The closest I came to comprehending war was when my father and my Uncle Chuck would get drunk and ramble on, bragging about "Killing all them Germans... we just plumb blew their ass away," they used to say. "When we came home, we were heroes. Got free drinks in damn near every bar."

When joining I really didn't think much about Vietnam. I was just too worried about my pregnant girlfriend to consider the consequences of war. I had no visual images of being shot, only ones of being strong and brave and poster-perfect in my Marine dress blues.

The lieutenant rambled on monotonously. Not smiling; seemingly bored, as if his speech were a preamble to college freshman orientation and not the first step toward fighting in Vietnam.

I don't think any of us standing there being sworn in were emotionally swept up by the lieutenant's speech about freedom, liberty or justice, nor were we choked up with emotion over the thought of defending our country. In fact, the lieutenant's chatter seemed to fly by us like old fencing outside the window of a fast moving car. The moment was memorable only because of its lack of emotion. Like most seventeen- and eighteen-year-old kids, I didn't even know where Vietnam was, let alone what we were fighting for.

The lieutenant talked on and on as I thought of my home.... I thought about when I was a little boy, before my parents were divorced, and how I used to lie awake at night listening to them fight in the next room. And then the next morning my dad would open up the door and shout, "Rise and shine, Jackson. Rise and shine, my boy, it's time to go to school," as if nothing had happened the night before.

My family was middle class, living from paycheck to paycheck, and burdened with more than its share of internal problems. I had a father who was an alcoholic, a mother who suffered through ten years of menopause, two mental breakdowns, and my father's drunken stupors. My older sister was always getting married and divorced, and my younger brother just stayed quiet and high all the time. As I grew up, each of us dissolved into different, disconnected realities.

There were good times, to be sure. Moments when I excelled in sports and my parents would brag to their friends about me. But my memory still held fast the all-night alcoholic brawls and my father falling drunk into our Christmas tree.

As the lieutenant continued, he began to blush and the holes in his face seemed more pronounced. It was as if the words were tightening in his throat, trying hard not to come out. His speech announced exalted virtues of country and glory, more like he was selling used cars than ideals, while I drifted into thoughts and images of Kristen. I pictured Kristen and me making love for the first time and how clumsy and frightened we were. I could see her mouth and recall the taste of her skin and the feel of her underneath me. I knew her with an intensity that was powerful and good, and when we made love it was shattering.

While the lieutenant stood beside his flag and spoke of pride, I thought of her naked body and how a spiritual bond seemed to envelop us. We had magic; innocent, simple and pure. God, it was magic.

Following the lieutenant's protracted dissertation, we were given orders to "stand by." We were informed that we would be flying to Camp Pendleton, California, in a few hours. With some time to waste, I called Kristen and said goodbye all over again,.Then I walked into the recreation room and stood against a wall and watched a game of pool being played by two wild looking characters who obviously had no talent for the game. They each had huge cigars planted in their mouths, ear-to-ear smart-ass grins, and talked like cowboys, through clenched teeth. At six feet, I was nearly a head taller than either of them. Short-sleeved and blue-jeaned, they looked like small town tough guys on their first trip to the big city. One had massive shoulders, wore a beat-up cowboy hat and was shooting a left-handed stick. He was also sporting a nasty scab running from his left elbow to his wrist. It was about an inch wide and appeared to be a few days old. His opponent was a little shorter, hatless, and not as powerfully built.

They circled the table like roosters in a cock fight, sizing up each position as if they really understood the game, exchanging jokes and trading missed shots. They were a curious pair, so unaffected by where we were and where we were going, but I thought I would like them and wanted to know them.

The game continued for several minutes until the one with the scab on his arm scratched on the eight-ball.

"Damn, if that ain't pathetic! Well, partner, I guess you're up," he said, placing the cue on the rack on the wall that was next to me.

"No, thank you, I'm terrible at pool," I answered.

He was friendly, kind of a down home, 'how ya doin'?' country cowboy. He probably did steer roping and barrel racing at county fairs.

"Well, partner, how about a ci-gar?" he asked, reaching into his shirt pocket and shoving one in my face.

"No, I'm sorry, I don't smoke."

"You don't smoke and you don't play pool. Next you're gonna tell me you don't drink or diddle. How you ever expect to become a real-l-l Marine?" Then he paused and looked around the room as if to make sure no one was eavesdropping. "Come on. Tell me straight," he said, motioning me to lean down so he could tell me a secret. "You ever eat pussy?"

I felt amused and embarrassed and quickly tried to change the subject. "That's an awfully ugly scab," I said, pointing to his arm. "How'd it happen?"

He lifted his cigar with his tongue to the corner of his mouth and spoke like his mouth was wired shut.

"Oh, this little scratch? Well, pal, I tell 'ya. Last Saturday night a bunch of us got drunked up playing cards and someone bet me five bucks I couldn't burn a cigarette down the length of my arm. Didn't hurt," he said proudly. "Hell, I was too drunk to feel it anyway! You from Portland?"

"Yes," I replied, "how about you?"

"I'm from Whitefish, near Ontario, in eastern Oregon. We're about ready to get electricity any day now," he joked. "My friends call me 'P.J.', but you can call me 'sir'." With that he laughed, said he was only kidding and thrust out his hand, shaking mine with a firm, strong grip. It was easy to understand where the strength in his handshake came from. He was built like a short weight lifter, with broad shoulders, no waist and stubby legs. "And that little douche bag over there is Jarvis," he said, pointing to the winner of their pool game.

Every time P.J. spoke, his round, red face rolled into a grin and nearly broke into a full teeth-showing smile, but not quite. His grin reminded me of a twelve-year-old kid who had just been caught smoking behind the barn or peeking at dirty magazines.

We hung out for awhile then we ate lunch across the street from the recruiting station but were soon back waiting for our orders. Several hours later the lieutenant addressed us.

"Gentlemen, your time has come. The bus is waiting."

I felt nervous and unsure as we were bussed to the airport and took off in darkness. The plane was quiet except for P.J., who wandered around the cabin talking to whoever would listen, or chatting up the stewardesses.

I sat alone and looked out of the plane's windows at the lights on the tip of the wing and noticed my reflection looking

5

back at me. I missed Kristen, and felt afraid and alone. I wanted someone to comfort me and tell me that I was doing the right thing. I wanted my father to put his arm around my shoulder and say, "Son, it will be all right. Son, it'll be OK." I wanted something he never gave me.

In the plane's darkness, a foreboding sense of uncertainty seemed to haunt us, as young boys' voices spoke of home and hope and when they'd see their girls again.

"Say, Jackson?" P.J. said, settling into the empty seat next to me.

"What?"

"You scared?" he asked, tentatively.

"No," I said, lying, "how 'bout you?"

"Me? No way! I'll skate this cartoon. I just wondered if you were worried or anything."

I sat in the dark of the airplane listening to P.J. breathe deeply as he slept. I was so afraid that leaving was wrong. I wanted to be with Kristen and hold her. I wanted to let her know we would be all right. I found strength in my love for her. She was my friend, lover and now mother of my child. She was everything to me. Everything.

We landed at the Camp Pendleton Airport, home of the United States Marine Corps. There were about fifty of us raw recruits nervously waiting. We were greeted inside the vast terminal by a couple of Marine Corps sergeants. Both were very deliberate and erect as they approached us in their freshly pressed khakis. One was very thin, while the other looked as if he had been eating too much pasta. He had a light complexion and, with no visible neck, appeared to be almost square. He had a slight roll hanging over his belt, huge shoulders and arms that would look fitting on an NFL lineman. His chest was thick like a hanging side of beef and seemed to arrive before the rest of his body.

"Ladies." The heavy-set sergeant spoke as the thin one stood by. "Get out that door and line up outside. Let's move it, girls!" he ordered, reminding me of a gruff football coach.

I could feel the tension building as we were directed away from the terminal toward a dimly lit area next to a large trash container. We stood alone for several minutes until the last kid in our group showed up. On his heels was the heavy-set sergeant, pushing him angrily from behind.

"MOVE YOUR ASS, YOU SISSY FUCK!" he screamed, and at the same time he pushed the kid violently to the ground and kicked him hard in the side. "GET UP, YOU PIECE AH SHIT, BEFORE I KICK YOUR FUCKING ASS." His voice was like a blast furnace as the kid scrambled to his feet, more scared than hurt and rushed into our group, trying to hide. I stood frozen like the rest of us, shocked by the attack. Then the sergeant's tirade swept over the entire group.

"FALL IN, YOU STUPID MOTHERFUCKERS, FALL IN!" The heavy-set sergeant roared. "YA BEST GET YOUR SWEET ASSES IN LINE, GIRLS," he bellowed, shoving and slapping us into formation. "I'M TALKIN' TA YOU, SCUMBAG!"

"Me?" I thought out loud.

"YEAH, YOU, MOTHERFUCKER!" he was screaming in my face and poking his finger hard against my chest. "YOU SMILE AT ME, SWEETHEART, AND I'LL KNOCK YER DICK STIFF." I could see clear to the back of his mouth and felt like I was face to face with a violent barking dog. I knew he was going to bite my face. I could almost feel his teeth tear into my mouth and nose, as his scream grew louder. "EYES FRONT, SCUMBAG," his finger was jabbing at my Adam's apple. Jesus Christ, I thought, what the hell is going on?

Just as quickly as he was on me, he was off and going down the line, striking terror into the hearts of each and every one of us. He was screaming and yelling, at us to "SUCK IT IN, MAGGOTS, SUCK IT IN! YOU PUKES BEST FALL IN LINE OR I'M GONNA KICK THE SHIT OUTA EVER' SWINGIN' DICK."

As quickly as his verbal barrage began, it ended. He marched to the front of our formation. With his back to us, he placed his right foot behind his left, did a half pirouette, and came to attention. Then, placing his hands on his hips, he stood to face us. I felt like I'd been mugged and now the mugger was in front of me and there was nothing I could do. I watched the sergeant closely, trying to figure out what I'd gotten myself into.

His brown rimmed Smokey the Bear hat was tilted slightly over his face, covering most of his eyes from our view. When he spoke, we could see his bulbous nose and full cheeks and mouth. He stood alone, but his presence was menacing and powerful. He slowly panned our rag-tag formation of frightened kids, then stopped. In a voice rough and worn from years of screaming, and laced with hints of sadistic, mad pleasure, he introduced himself. "My name is Sergeant Whitehead and I have been sent here to torture you!" No one moved and no one spoke a word, and the night was gravely quiet except for the thunderous sound of my own heartbeat.

My God, I thought, this guy's a psycho!

In the fear of the moment, our group seemed to take on an identity, like we were lambs hovering together. The moment ended.

"LET'S MOVE IT! GET YOUR FUCKIN' ASSES ON THAT BUS! MOVE IT MOVE IT MOVE IT!"

We were then pushed, amidst more shouting, shoving and cursing, into a green military bus, where, crowded and cramped we sat, three to a two-man seat, dazed and scared. We were being transported to our new home, the United States Marine Corps Recruiting Depot, San Diego, California.

As the bus left the lights of the air terminal behind, I felt a sense of deep regret and uncertainty. I knew I was changing and that I'd never be a boy again.

Two

IT WAS ONE O'CLOCK in the morning when the bus rolled to a stop in front of Camp Pendleton's receiving barracks. The doors opened and as we poured out onto the blacktop, the tirade began again. "ON THE ROOADD! ON THE ROOADD!" It was Whitehead. "ON THE ROOADD YOU LAME MOTHER-FUCKERS. ON THE ROOADD! NOW FALL INTO FORMATION," he bellowed, pointing to several rows of neatly formed foot-prints, painted yellow, with heels together and toes pointed out. "And get yer asses at attention! You, puke bucket," he was close, barking in some kid's face. "You best square yer ass away!"

"You dick lickin' pussy suckin' faggots," Whitehead was in back of the formation. "Listen up!" His shouting had subsided. "You ladies are in the Corps," he said, clipping off the last word of each sentence for added impact.

"You girls is in MY home! Yer MY little girls! I promise 'ya. If you fuck up, I WILL torture you!" What he said sounded true and real and were words and phrases of vulgarity I had not heard before. He began to work himself into a quick wild frenzy. "YOU DUMB SONS OF BITCHES, YOU BEST GRAB THE BACK OF THE PANTS OF THE ONE IN FRONT OF YOU!" Then like a parade of the blind, we held onto each other's pants and moved to the receiving station.

The receiving station looked like the Alamo. Like John Wayne should be riding out at any moment. It was a massive

Spanish structure with stucco walls, a tile roof, lots of pillars, and an assortment of curved archways. This was where Drill Instructor Garcia first graced our lives. He stepped out of the shadows of an archway and crossed quickly to us.

Garcia, the Mexican Madman, as we eventually called him, looked like a wild-eyed rat, hungry to kill. He was all spit and polish in his fresh-pressed khakis, black-rimmed glasses, and thin dark moustache. He was about 150 pounds of shoe leather tough. His lips curled back and exposed his yellow teeth as he spoke. And when he looked at you his whole body would tighten and you could sense he was close to rage. What soon became the trademark of the Mexican Madman was the riding crop he held in his right hand.

"Well, ladies," Garcia said, with a sinister smile while rhythmically slapping the crop into his left hand. "Welcome to Platoon 328." Then he walked back and forth in front of us as if he were stalking, his crop always slapping. Finally he stopped and kind of reared his back before he spoke. "I know there are several Communists among you scumbags that have been sent here to IN-FIL-TRATE my Marine Corps, but you will not succeed." His jaw tightened. "I will seek you out and place hand and foot on your body." Again, his jaw tightened and his intensity heightened. "YOU COMMUNIST SWEETPEAS WILL NOT IN-FIL-TRATE MY MARINE CORPS!" he shouted, his words running together, as he slapped the crop against his leg. "You will not fuck me up. GOD DAMN YOU GOD DAMN YOU!" he fired at us through clenched teeth, with machine-gun rapidity. "You Communist sweetpeas! I will seek you out and destroy your young asses. GOD DAMN YOU GOD DAMN YOU!"

Whitehead walked up, stood next to Garcia, and addressed the platoon with controlled rage. "Hogs, I want you to file in squad formation inside the receiving station." The glaring lights made me squint and I felt like an idiot for ever leaving Portland as we moved from night to light. Inside there were several rows of large wooden boxes.

"Get your sweet asses behind one of those bins," Garcia ordered, his words flying out fast and furious. We moved as if the building was on fire. "Now take those faggot clothes off. I mean everything!" he said, not slowing to take a breath. We stripped to bare asses, revealing an assortment of bodies, fat and skinny, short and tall, lining the room, each behind a box.

Garcia walked wildly around and slapped asses with his crop while Whitehead stood in the only doorway with his massive arms crossed and a scowl on his face like a guard hoping an inmate would get out of line so he would have an excuse to kick some ass.

"Look at this little peter," Garcia said, touching P.J.'s penis with his crop. I believe this faggot's little dick's at attention. Get outa my face and stand in that corner!" he yelled, as P.J. hurried naked across the room to face the corner.

"Fuck that wall, bitch!" P.J. didn't move.

"I know this faggot's a queer," Garcia said, standing right behind him. "The only fuckin' you're gonna get is in your mind! Now get back, Dickhead!" And P.J. returned to his bin, covering himself, obviously humiliated.

As I cautiously scanned the room, each boy's face looked the same — innocent, frightened and dazed. It was like we were trapped in a collective time warp, devoid of individual history. Our identities were fading, our histories gone. There was only now, and, if we were lucky, perhaps tomorrow. We placed our clothes in cardboard boxes to be mailed home, were issued green fatigues and black boots, and were back on the road again, victims of an instant metamorphosis from civilians to new recruits, dressed in military green.

Following another short speech about how incorrigible we were, we groveled off, holding onto the backs of each other's pants, to a row of quonset huts and then we were split up, twenty to a hut.

We were assigned to a bunk bed without sheets or blankets and ordered by the Madman, "Ready, sleep!"

I was numb, still not believing what had transpired. I felt as if I had stepped into a world of incomprehensible madness. A world of nonsensical screaming. I felt as though I had made the biggest mistake of my life and would be paying for it for two years. Finally, despite the strain, my mind cleared and I thought of Kristen. I thought of how just one night ago, Kristen and I were in her bed, loving and holding each other. I thought of all our dreams of children, and when everything would be all right. I could escape this place through thoughts of her. She would be my retreat. I would draw strength from her and be settled by thoughts of her. Like when I broke my leg in football and she came to me at the hospital and told me to "be strong," that the "world isn't over." That I would "play again."

Tired, I closed my eyes to the darkness of the bizarre and brutal reality and fell into a deep, dreamless sleep. Suddenly, out of nowhere, there was screaming again. "ON THE ROOADD! ON THE ROOADD!" belted out in cadence. "ON THE ROOADD!"

The door of the quonset hut burst open. A garbage can flew in and banged, rattled and careened off rows of deep-sleeping bunks. I thought it must be a dream. It couldn't be real. It had only been moments since I had shut my eyes. Through tiny windows I could see that it was still dark outside.

"GET YER SWEET ASSES OUT OF THE RACK AND OUT-SIDE ON MY MARINE CORPS ROAD!" The voice was real, all right, it was unmistakably that of Whitehead. We flew out of our racks stumbling, falling, grabbing pants and shirts as we rushed for the door. No one knew what to do, except move.

"SHAKE THOSE ASSES! GOD DAMN YOU GOD DAMN YOU!" came Garcia's command as he circled around us, snapping his crop.

"Arm's length apart, scumbags!" Whitehead blasted. "PUKES! I SAID ARM'S LENGTH APART!". We shuffled in the damp, dark morning air. All of us desperate to please, trying to line up straight.

"What's your name, peter puffer?" Garcia said, just inches away from a skinny kid's face.

"Clapshaw, sir."

"Clapshaw?" Garcia asked in disbelief. "Clapshaw?" he continued. "That sounds like Clapshit to me." His voice rang with pride at his joke. "Clapshit, I think you're a goddamn

Communist sent to IN-FIL-TRATE my Marine Corps. God damn you God damn you!" he said, teeth snarling.

"No, sir!" the frightened Marine replied.

Garcia studied Clapshaw carefully, inches from his face, obviously not pleased. "I'm keeping an eye on you, Clapshit. If you ain't a Communist, then you're a goddamn queer! You want to suck my peter, sweet lips?" he said, bumping Clapshaw's forehead with the rim of his hat. "I'm talking to you, boy," he said as their foreheads nearly touched.

"Yes, sir, I... mean, no, sir," he stammered. I imagined Clapshaw would have answered anything just to be rid of the Mexican Madman. "You want to lick my dick, Pussy?" Clapshaw froze, speechless.

Sergeant Garcia reeled around and rubbed Clapshaw's ass, rolled his eyes skyward, smiled wildly and then moved to the front of the platoon by Sergeant Whitehead, who was facing us.

I had suspected Clapshaw was in for trouble the minute I saw him at the recruiting station. Ridiculously bohemian, he was straight out of Haight-Ashbury and sleeping in Golden Gate Park. Tall and skinny with long, dirty dark hair, he dressed in a jeans jacket, Indian beads and ragged bell-bottom pants. He looked like he should have been standing along some road with a pack on his back, hitchhiking to spiritual enlightenment. He was perfect, a prime target for Garcia's crazed form of discipline.

We stood in the dark at attention, heels together, toes pointing out, clutching the sides of our trousers with thumb and forefinger. Half-dressed, in baggy uniforms, looking sloppy and rag-tag, I could not imagine us ever being poster-perfect, tall and erect, with granite jaw and a sense of pride radiating from our faces. I was tired, I couldn't picture much of anything.

We stood there waiting. That's all. Waiting. Waiting in the cool night air that was soon to be morning. Waiting. Just waiting. All of us, P.J., Little Jarvis, Clapshaw, boys from the farm and boys from the city, trying to stand at attention, silent and waiting. The Madman who sought out Communist infiltrators and Whitehead, who had come to torture us, they too were at attention. Glaring at us. Waiting.

Then someone emerged from the shadow of the quonset hut as the last moments of night melted into morning. In long, slow, powerful strides, he crossed to face us. Light from the outside lamppost drew down upon him as a hunter might on a proud, powerful elk, or a spotlight on Hamlet in one of his famous soliloquies.

He stood in front of us as the sweet smell of daybreak filled the air. He had to be the biggest black man I had ever seen. He was Satan, carved from dark, heavy stone. I could see the volcanic strength and definition almost rupture from his body. He stood tall, hands on his hips, feet shoulder width apart. His head was slightly tilted down. The brim of his brown smokey covered his eyes and added greatly to his overpowering appearance. He was menacing and riveting.

When he spoke, his words were slow and fluent, articulate and alarming. They came in deep whispers of unequaled resonance. "You're nothing but a bunch of low life niggers and white trash! I'm terrible bad... I'm your worst nightmare... I *will* hurt you." And he paused. No one dared to move. "I'm six-four, two hundred and twenty pounds of twisted steel, and bitches... you-best-not-do-me-wrong!" He paused again and stared for over a minute. "For you slow-witted individuals I'll attempt to make this simple. Your ass is MINE!"

We were paralyzed. I never knew his age, but he might have been thirty-five or twenty-five. Whatever age he wanted to be was fine with me.

Again he spoke. "I'll break this down to monosyllabic words even the dumbest of the dumb will understand.... I want the baddest bitch to come up front and fuck with me." No one moved. "I want five hard ass cunts up front and in my face." A long pause. No one moved. Then another long pause. A moment to reconsider, but again no one moved.

"My name is Gunnery Sergeant Lewis. From now on you will refer to me as your Platoon Commander." His voice was rich and powerful as it rolled slowly from his mouth. "From now on your dick don't get hard without asking me." I tried to memorize each sentence and felt as if I were waiting for one to end so that the next could begin. As words flowed from his mouth, his teeth took the form of two solid chunks of white ivory biting down and through each word. His stare was cold and piercing.

"The first word out of your mouths when you speak will be 'Sir' and the last word out of your mouths will be 'Sir.' Is that understood, girls?"

We all responded with a hearty, "Sir, yes sir." But it wasn't loud enough.

"I can't hear you," he stated, not raising his voice above a strong whisper.

"Sir, yes sir!" Louder this time.

"I still can't hear you," was again his quiet reply.

"SIR, YES SIR!" We were all together and louder.

"From this day forward, you amoeba brains will address Sergeant Whitehead and Sergeant Garcia as 'Drill Instructor.' Is that understood?"

"SIR, YES SIR!" We were gaining in volume, if not in confidence.

"It makes me sick to look at you. You're repugnant, clumsy and obviously unintelligent. I seriously doubt if any of you will ever make it through the next twelve weeks. I'll leave you with Sergeants Whitehead and Garcia before I puke!" And then he left.

From that day on, every time Lewis spoke it was quiet and methodical. He didn't need to scream to get his point across; or to get us to respond. He was above that. Yet, he could whip us into a frenzy of fear and awe with his compelling presence and forceful manner. He carried himself with intelligence, pride, inner strength and power. He was controlled rage, a black panther, a fluid mass of disciplined energy to be feared and yet admired. His philosophy was, "We can only go as fast as the slowest private." And, "If one fails, you all fail."

When we as a platoon were not marching quite right, or were performing incorrectly, he would punish us without raising his voice. The words he spoke seemed to flow elegantly from his mouth before impacting on us like a sledge hammer of remorse. Before coming to Camp Pendleton we had taken aptitude tests. We were scored in categories, One to

Four. Four was the lowest. Lewis always referred to us in our moments of stupidity as "Cat-Fours", for Category Four intelligence.

"What we have here are a few Cat-Fours that can't get with the program," Lewis said, referring to whoever made the mistakes that day, "and they are trying to disrupt the integrity of my Marine Corps. Which means... you ALL have to pay."

Then he would say the words we learned to dread, "Cat-Fours, get down," the command for all of us to get down into a push-up position. Our punishment was based on how badly we had "disrupted his Marine Corps" or how badly we "malfunctioned."

His cadence for calling out our punishment was directly related to the severity of our crime. If we had been very disruptive, he would call out the cadence in a very slow and deliberate manner, "Down... Up... Down... Up." The more slowly he counted the harder it became to do the push-ups. While we "assumed the front leaning position," as Lewis liked to call it, he would chastise us about our wrongdoings.

"Down," a long pause, "You know that you insufferable morons perplex me? Up. You're garbage and bring discredit to my Marine Corps! Down. Are you trying to dishonor my Marine Corps?" he would whisper.

And we would scream out, "SIR, NO SIR!"

"Are you trying to destroy our country?"

"SIR, NO SIR!"

"Up... Down... Up... Down."

As he continued, my arms would shake and cramps would run down my back until I felt like I was going to throw up.

"You Cat-Fours have got to shake years of slime from your otherwise empty heads! Down! You Cat-Fours are the dumbest of the dumb. Up! But I will not allow you to discredit my Marine Corps!"

And if Lewis were especially angry with us for committing an unpardonable sin like talking in the shower, he would make us "Get up on 'em!" which meant we had to do push-ups on our knuckles. The pain would intensify tremendously.

A chorus of "SIR, YES SIR!" would ring out.

"Cat-Fours, shake your heads." And we'd shake our heads furiously. "Shake that civilian garbage right out of your heads."

"Up," he'd finally say, as my arms began to lose all strength and knuckles ached under my body's weight and sometimes began to bleed. We thought it was hell; Lewis called it "a dose of motivation."

"Down. I don't like malfunctioning in my Marine Corps. Up."

If we were extremely unfortunate, Sergeants Garcia or Whitehead might be present, walking amongst us, kicking or screaming at us. It would go on for what seemed like hours, commander saying, "Down" and the commanded saying, "SIR, YES SIR!"

The first few days of boot camp were a blur.

Our hair was sheared to a mere stubble by an assembly line of barbers. "Butcher Barber", the sign above their door said, "We guarantee to make hair short." Then, we were issued more clothes and Marine Corps gear, M-14 rifles, a little red book covering Marine Corps history and General Orders. We were always rushing to the next place of business and then waiting.

Quickness was essential in boot camp. We never walked. It was either military march or double time wherever we went. If we were slow of foot, or hand, we would have to do whatever it was that we were ordered to do again, and again, until it was right. Or we faced the threat of Lewis' "Get down!"

Those first days I stole a few moments during our nightly platoon shower to speak with P.J. about his life in a small town in eastern Oregon.

"I tell you, Jackson, we did some heavy duty partying," he'd whisper under the running water. "Used to cruise the main drag drinkin' rocket fuel...you know, beer and wine mixed. Anyway, we'd drink and hang B.A.'s out the window or try to cause some trouble."

"Why did you join the Corps?"

"I stole a totem pole."

"What?"

"Listen, late one night we got tanked up and ripped off this old 75-foot handcarved totem pole that used to sit in front of the Wigwam Restaurant. It took eight of us to lift the damn

17

thing onto the back of a flatbed truck. Our plan was to paint it pink and lay it in front of the Mayor's house with a sign that said, 'World's Biggest Dildo'."

"But I got busted. Cops found the totem pole in my back yard and hit me with Grand Larceny. I had to go to court and the judge, who was an ex-jarhead, said, 'Boy, it's the Marine Corps or you're going to jail.' No humor, my man."

"How was I to know the damn thing was worth almost twenty grand? Jackson, small towns just don't take any shit when you mess with their pride and joy."

Another night just before lights out, P.J. and I were sitting on his rack. "P.J., what's that scar on your belly about?"

"Oh, that," he said, sitting there looking down at his bare stomach as he ran his fingers the length of the old wound. "That happened when I was sixteen. A bunch of my old buddies and I went to stay overnight at my granddad's cabin up in the mountains near Whitefish."

"Well, what happened?"

"We all got drunk on rocket fuel. I mean all kinds of fucked up. And the next thing I knew, I woke up in the morning with a hole in my belly," he said with great pride. Then the lights went out, leaving us sitting in the darkness and me visualizing his wound.

"After awhile, everybody else got up and we finally figured out I'd been shot," he continued. "My buddies took my stupid ass back down the mountain in the rear of my dad's truck to the county hospital. Later, I was placed in an alcoholic ward for thirty days." Then he paused, as if to think back, and his voice softened. "My dad was an alcoholic but quit drinking the day I got shot." Months later P.J. revealed to me that when he was ten he found his mother on their kitchen floor lying in a pool of blood with the top half of her head blown away.

"Why? Why?" he mumbled to me, trying not to cry. "I mean, why?"

I never talked to him about his mother again. Just as I had never asked him who shot him that night when he was sixteen. It was more or less understood that it was a special secret we shared.

From that night on, P.J. and I were so close that the others were just casual friends.

Clapshaw was as I had pictured him to be. He was from the city, had taken LSD before, and wanted someday to be a musician. I think he played the guitar. I remember thinking he was quiet and much too passive to be a Marine, but I admired the way he handled Garcia's almost daily taunts of "God damn Communist."

And Jarvis! I never knew much about him except that he was in superb physical condition. He could do more pull-ups than anyone I had ever seen. I suppose it's just as well we hadn't become good friends. I heard he was killed his first week in Nam. He got hit by a light machine gun, and that little body just couldn't take all those slugs as they tore him apart. But boy, at seventeen, could he do pull-ups!

Dearest Kristen,

This is the first real chance that I've had to write you. We've been so busy, going to classes, marching, and exercising. We wake up about five a.m. and start the same routine all over again.

How are you feeling? I'll send some money home as soon as I get paid. It won't be much. There are a few things I have to buy at the PX, or I would send it all.

I miss you so much. Sometimes it seems like I'm in a dream and I think any minute I'll wake. And then I'd come over and pick you up. Maybe we'd go cruising downtown or go to one of those crowded smoky coffee houses where the singers think they're Bob Dylan and always play such bad harmonica. God, I miss you.

When will you tell your parents about our baby? It will all work out. When I get leave, I'll come home and we will get married. I'll even get paid more then, and you can use the PX up in Washington. We can save up money and get a car, and find a nice apartment when I get out.

Don't worry about me. I'll be all right. I might not even have to go to Vietnam. The war could end in a couple of months, you know. Or maybe I can get on a military athletic team, play football, or baseball, and never have to leave the United States. I heard about one guy who spent his two years in Hawaii playing softball.

Well, honey, I had better run. I'm writing this letter after lights are supposed to be out. I'm underneath my blanket with a little flashlight and if I get caught, I'll be doing push-ups forever. I love you, and miss you so much. When the lights go out, the picture of you in my heart glows bright.

Love forever,
Jack

P.S. By the way, they showed us where Vietnam is on the map today. It's not very big, that's for sure.

P.P.S.S. I've thought of a great nickname for my beautiful pregnant lady. 'Momma Belly.'

Three

THE DAYS AND WEEKS of boot camp continued to run into each other, interrupted only by Kristen's letters. In her last letter she wrote and said, "My tummy's getting bigger, so I'm wearing a pair of your old sweats. There are no secrets in our house any more. Mom and Dad both know." She closed by saying, "I hate working at Arctic Circle, but I love you, Daddy Jack."

Her letters were important. I worried about her and needed to know that she worried about me. The letters came often and added to my strength.

Each day was the same constant routine of exercising in the morning, cleaning up, classes, and countless hours of marching on the parade deck learning drill formations. "Teaches you discipline, ladies," Garcia would say.

Of course, the screaming barrage of Garcia and Whitehead stayed with us like a nagging earache. If we weren't being yelled at or threatened, we were being jabbed and poked, or struck with Garcia's riding crop.

There were times when Whitehead did torture us, like grabbing us by the throat or making forty of us strip down naked, and forcing us to exercise under cold showers in a room big enough for only twenty. Or Garcia's favorite: "Fall out, God damn you. We will exercise until I'm tired," then he would sit in front of us in a folding chair and count cadence. "I'm not tired, sweetpeas, are you?"

Between Lewis, Garcia, and Whitehead, we never had a break. As a platoon we were always in trouble. One day after a rifle inspection that didn't go well, Lewis addressed us: "Cat-Fours messed up, now you're in the pool." Fifty to sixty of us were marched over to a sand pit located not far from the barracks. It was called "going swimming." We would have to lie down and pretend we were in a swimming pool, and do the free-style across the pit. After about twenty minutes of this, Lewis would say, "All right, ladies, backstroke!" then we would flip over like a platoon of seals out of water and under the blazing sun, throw handfuls of sand into the air and let it scatter all over us. The rest of the day was spent with sand in our shirts and pants.

The biggest fear in boot camp was Motivation School. If you were caught fighting, stealing, or just generally "malfunctioning," you were sent there to be motivated. Those privates who had the misfortune to end up in the Motivation Platoon could be seen at the sand pit daily with buckets and shovels, digging craters in the sand and filling up their buckets. The buckets were dumped forming one small mountain of sand. When the mountain of sand was large enough, the D.I. would bark, "Well, ladies, I like the size, but I don't like the location. Ready, move it!" Then, pointing about thirty or forty yards in another direction, the shoveling and carrying of sand began all over again. This went on for hours until the privates were motivated.

For most of us tboot camp was very trying, and for a few it proved to be unbearable. One recruit was found slumped over in the shower, back against the wall with a razor in one hand, staring at his blood-soaked arm as his life pumped out onto the concrete floor.

But in the middle of all this madness, I could see us changing. We were being programmed, losing our individuality and being taught to work together like a football team. Often we were humiliated, but paradoxically a foundation of great pride and accomplishment was being born. We looked better, we were stronger and on our way to becoming Marines.

As the days dragged on, each one became a test of mental and physical toughness which our platoon seemed to enjoy overcoming. Occasionally, P.J.'s reassertion of his unique personality interrupted our daily grind.

One afternoon we were marched by Sergeants Whitehead and Garcia to a wooded area several miles from our quonset huts. I felt comforted by the change of scenery. It reminded me of the woods not far from my home where I used to go when I needed to be alone. Nestled among a collection of various trees was a white building. It looked like a large, windowless chicken coop, I thought. Soon some tired old farmer would walk out with a basket of eggs or tell us to "get off my property."

"All right, scumbags," Whitehead bellowed. "Today we are going to let you ladies sing." I was puzzled, and wondered what the madman and fat man had in store for us. As we stood feet spread shoulder width apart and hands clasped behind our backs, at the position of parade rest, I was confident that whatever happened it couldn't be worse than "going swimming" at the sand pit.

With his usual sinister aplomb and rat-like grin, Sergeant Garcia took over. "God damn you! You sweet-singing hummingbirds. We is gonna make you sing and cry and puke all over the place. We is gonna make you wish you was dead." Then he laughed deep and slapped the side of his pants with his riding crop and laughed again. "You tight-butted mothers are gonna get gassed." He laughed wildly. "Each one of you Communist sweetpeas is gonna sing in the gas house. Sing like the sweetpeas you are." His laugh was growing increasingly loud and demonic.

A group of ten of us were rounded up and led inside the single wide door of the building. After a few minutes those of us still outside could hear strong clear singing of the Marine Corps Hymn coming from inside the gas house. Then as quickly as it began, the singing waned and was replaced by fits of coughing. Suddenly, the door flew open, and the first group fought to get out. Each one of them was reeling, coughing, stumbling, bent over gasping for breath or puking. The posters down at the Post Office never showed any of this.

"Come on, scum," Sergeant Whitehead commanded, pointing the next group of us in. P.J. was smiling typically, round-faced and wide, entering just before me. With great reluctance, I followed.

The inside of the building was very dark, with only faint hints of light creeping through slight cracks in the walls. Heavy traces of tear gas were lingering in the air, wetting my eyes, while what sounded like the drone of a vacuum or fan could be heard in the background. Two Marines, with gas masks on, quickly passed out additional masks and gave brief instructions on how to use them. Once the mask was on, I breathed deeply, thankful that the mask worked. More tear gas was dropped from an opening in the wall and mushroomed out in a thick, enveloping haze.

"All right, ladies," one of the Marines shouted through his mask, "Take it off and sing to me." Slowly, anxiously, with tremendous reservation, we peeled the masks away and placed them on the floor. "From the halls of Montezuma" rang out loud and clear, "to the shores of — cough-cough-cough — Tripoli." "Breathe deep, ladies. Suck it up, girls," the two masked Marines shouted. The tear gas had stifled all singing. My eyes and nose and throat were on fire. "Leave those masks on the floor, girls. What's wrong, ladies?" one of the Marines asked sadistically. I was just about to lose my lunch when, mercifully, the door was opened. "Outside, ladies, bring the next herd in."

I staggered out, coughing and spitting up in uncontrollable convulsions, bumping into the rest of my group. We threw up and staggered and complained, "Jesus, this sucks!"

"Yeah, right, man."

"Hey, dude, move yer ass over, you's spitting on my boot."

Then we lined up and waited, watching the next ten, and the next, until all of us had a chance to experience getting gassed. As each successive group reeled out the door, gasping for breath, I developed a deep appreciation for the gas mask.

Then Garcia moved to the front of the still gagging platoon. "All right, sweetpeas, you're lucky today!" A lump quickly grew in my throat. I was sure we were going to have to go back in. "Yeah, you commie faggots are lucky today. Is there anyone here that wants to go back in?" He smiled. "If so, get your sweet ass up here on the double."

There was dead silence. No one dared move. No one, that is, except P.J., who suddenly broke from ranks. "Sir, the private loves the gas house," P.J. blurted out, with a nonsensical look on his face and deadly serious tone in his voice.

Garcia and Whitehead were stunned. They broke from character, like actors forgetting lines. "Sir, the private loves the gas house," P.J. added again and then ran back inside, leaving us all in a state of total disbelief.

His voice sang out from inside the gas house, as Whitehead and Garcia stood outside, shaking their heads, amazed, as we all were. A few minutes later, P.J. came out, coughing and spitting, still smiling, his face carrying an illuminated, incorrigible grin. Once again he had become more eccentric than the moment we were living.

"Sir, the private loves the gas house."

Dear Kristen,

Boot camp is moving along a little faster now, soon we will be graduating. Please don't send any more sticks of gum in your letters. Sergeant Garcia always passes out our mail and feels the letters for "communist contraband." He found the last piece of gum you sent and let me chew it — with the paper and foil still on it. Poor P.J. got a package sent to him that had four chocolate Hershey bars in it. He had to stuff all four (without the wrapping) in his mouth at once and stand at attention and recite the general orders. Then Garcia gave him two minutes to eat and swallow them.

That Garcia is nuts. Today I was standing at attention in line outside the mess hall, waiting to go in. Garcia was walking up and down our squad formation and telling us, "We're going to have duck for dinner, sweetpeas. You're gonna duck in and duck out." And then he'd laugh. Well, I was standing there, trying hard not to smile, when he came up and started screaming, "You communist, God damn you, God damn you." Then he bit me on the ear. I'm not kidding. He bit me on the ear. He said, "Your ears are moving out of order, private. You'd best get them back at attention."

Listen, babe, when you do send me my chocolate chip cookies and brownies, please, please mail them just a couple of days before boot camp graduation.

I'm sending you some money. I know it's not much, but it's all I have.

Love you
Jack

P.S. Goodnight Momma Belly

One night, just after our shower, we were told to fall out. We dropped everything and hit the door of our quonset hut in a rush of half-dressed bodies. Back on the road, we spaced ourselves military neat and waited for the word. It came not from the Madman or Whitehead in waves of oceanic screams, but from Lewis, in soft whispers, more frightening than all of our real or imagined nightmares.

"Gentlemen." That was a first. "Today was a major malfunction. You cheated not me, but yourselves." I assumed he was talking about those few who had fallen asleep for a moment in class, or dogged it on the obstacle course. He continued, "I want you to understand that there are young men like yourselves fighting and dying in Vietnam as I stand before you. They're from farms and cities as you are," he said slowly, quietly, and somehow sadly. And as he spoke, I could feel a deep silence fall over us and suddenly I felt small and afraid.

"They are dying," Lewis said, pausing. The silence became deafening. "They are dying. As you sleep or eat, they are dying. And, as you stand here, they are dying." The words were numbing. "Some," and there was a long pause, "are dying because they are unlucky and some because they are unprepared."

I was swallowing his words, trying to keep them inside of me, trying to hold onto them, knowing they were important.

"What I am attempting to eliminate in these next few days are those who are unprepared." He stood there for long minutes, saying nothing, until finally we heard a weak "dismissed." No one spoke a word as we filed off, back to our metal homes. There were no glances, smirks, or smiles. We all hung our heads, making sure that no one saw a break in each other's toughness.

When the lights went out that night, I lay back in silence, rethinking Lewis' words. For the next few moments, I tried hard to be a Marine, but through gentle sobs, I could feel tears run down my cheeks. I'd never thought about dying.

In the darkness, I cried softly and I could hear that I was not alone.

Four

I HAD EXPECTED that at the conclusion of boot camp I would be issued leave and return to Kristen, but the fighting in Vietnam had escalated tremendously, creating an immediate need for replacements. Leaves were not issued and the training took on a different physical and psychological dimension. We were no longer referred to as "pukes" and "scum," but as Marines preparing for war.

P.J. and I were assigned to I.T.R. (Infantry Training Regiment) for advanced infantry training. I had hoped Kristen would be able to come to California so that we could be married, but that would have to wait.

Lewis, Garcia, and Whitehead were left behind and replaced by Sergeant O'Callahan, a huge worn-out looking lifer who spoke slowly and to the point like a losing football coach might speak to his team. "Boys. I done three tours in the Nam...it's a mind fuck. And I tell 'ya, boys. Some day soon you'll be walking across a rice paddy, or humping in the bush and you'll take fire. Your best buddy'll get hit in the face and his head'll explode and all you'll think is: 'better him than me.'"

The training went on and on with little time to consider how to be with Kristen.

We were taught to fire machine guns, flame throwers, anti-tank weapons and how to toss hand grenades. We learned basic field strategies and how to set ambushes and what to do if we walked into one. We learned how to tie off wounds and inject

29

tubes of morphine to numb the pain. We learned of fields of fire and killing zones and booby traps.

"Boys, you best listen up. You get your heads right or you'll go home in pieces."

The weeks were long and hot and terrible. Boot camp had been wild and repetitive while the combat training was intensive, with much to ingest and so little time to do it in. Letters from Kristen were welcomed, and yet sad with talk of how complicated her life was becoming. She was beginning to show our unborn child and it was difficult for her to have me gone. "I know you love me," she wrote, "but I'm scared. I need you next to me."

We decided that she should come to California and stay with her older brother until I could get leave. I had little freedom, but at night I would sneak out and call her from an isolated phone booth. Our conversations were short and tearful.

"I can't get off base, baby. I'm sorry, I can't. Maybe next week," I said, hopefully.

"Why can't you just quit? Other guys have. We could even go to Canada or somewhere," she suggested naively.

"I have to hang up now. They'll never let me off base if they catch me on the phone."

"Don't," she'd cry.

"I love you honey, really I do. But I gotta go. Someone's coming."

Then I'd hang up and walk back to my billet, trying to figure out what to do. Neither of our parents were supportive, and had even suggested an abortion at one time. But we wanted this child. We knew we had a thousand things going against us, but we were crazy for each other and wanted to have our baby.

One night I went to P.J.'s rack and woke him up.

"Hey, dude, what's up? You crazy, waking me in the middle of my wet dream? I was dreaming and sceming 'bout tits and pussy and...."

"Knock it off," I whispered. "Listen, I'm gonna sneak out and catch a bus and go see Kristen. We're going to get married tomorrow."

"You're crazy. You'll get busted."

"To what? I can't get any lower than private. Listen, I want you to come with me and be my best man."

"You're crazy. You're outa your fuckin' mind.... Oh, hell. Let's go! Besides, I been hornier than a three-peckered toad. There might be some pussy out there askin' for it, beggin' for it, and maybe even willin' to pay for it!"

We snuck off together and caught a midnight bus. Kristen picked us up and drove us to her brother's modest house. We slept on the couch, with P.J. snoring, curled up on the floor in a sleeping bag across the room. I felt Kristen's swollen belly and marveled at the internal pad of unborn feet. It was an amazing feeling. Touching her belly made me feel good and clean and responsible for that little kick. I loved that child. As P.J. snored in the darkness, we made love quietly and fell asleep.

The next morning we were married in a little church with sunlight flowing through chapel windows of baby Jesus and Mary. Kristen was happy and round as her brother gave her away while P.J. was my beaming best man. I wasn't really nervous standing there in front of the minister. I was kind of in shock or in a daze. It just didn't seem real. But when I said, "I do," I meant it and felt my commitment.

Kristen's brother took a picture of us with a little camera and his wife gave us flowers. I gave Kristen the ring I had bought at the PX the week before for $29.95. It was a good day and I was glad to be married.

"Well, Papa Bear," Kristen said as we stood outside the church, "the easy part is over. Now we have to try hard to make this marriage work."

We spent the afternoon in a motel while P.J. hung out at the pool, drinking Cokes because we were too young to buy champagne.

That night when P.J. and I got back to base we were reprimanded by O'Callahan, but excused with only extra guard duty as punishment.

"Fuck it. You guys'll be dead in a coupla months anyway."

I was given a twenty-day leave after I.T.R. and caught a plane to Portland. Kristen and I stayed in a motel with rooms that could be rented by the week, complete with kitchens. She'd cook me macaroni and cheese and then we'd go on walks by our old high school and sit on the bank that overlooked the track and football field and hold hands until dark.

"Jackson, I'm so scared about having this baby. I wish you could be there."

"So do I, sweetheart, so do I."

My twenty days at home went quickly. I painted my mother's house while she complained that I was "too young to be married." I saw my dad and he said he was "gonna stop drinkin'" and then he gave me a Bowie knife he "used on them damn Krauts." Later he gave me twenty bucks to take Kristen to dinner. We spent the money and I left the knife with my brother.

I drove past my high school one last time and recalled the hit I got in the State Baseball Playoffs and thought about how quickly those years had gone by.

At the airport Kristen said, "You come back to us, Papa Bear."

I rubbed her round tummy and said, "I will."

I arrived back at Camp Pendleton during the last week of June for ten days of staging before being shipped overseas. Most of the guys I went through boot camp with were assigned to other units, but fortunately, P.J. and I had been issued the same orders and were still together.

When staging ended our troop movement was almost instantaneous. One moment P.J. and I were drunk, riding in teacups at Disneyland, the next day we were in full combat gear in the belly of a C-140 transport plane on our way to the Nam. There was no time to adjust to the unknown, and there was no unity or pride. We traveled as a collection of anonymous men who, upon arriving in Vietnam, would be assigned in groups of three or four to new units.

On the plane there was a sense of anticipation, not knowing what to expect or where we were going. Vietnam had always been just a word, a place referred to in the six o'clock news, but unsubstantiated by experience. None of us had ever even seen a Vietnamese. Were they "crazed slant eyes" like my father said, that "don't give a damn if they live or die"? I felt like I knew nothing about Vietnam and even less about how I would react. No one talked or joked or even wrote letters. We just sat there in a state of pronounced numbness. No one smiled, outside of P.J., who always had a mischievous grin.

We had left quietly and landed a day later in Okinawa. After shots, a shower, and a few hours' sleep, we were back on the plane.

From Okinawa, the tension mounted. Fear was gripping me. All I could think about was "What will it be like? Will I lose an arm or a leg or half my face? Will my cock and balls be taken, ripped off, or blown away in some forgotten rice paddy? Will I come home in a wheelchair and never walk or run again? Will I be afraid? Will I freeze just at the moment when I need to be brave? God, what if we get hit and they are coming at us and my rifle jams? Jesus, what would I do?" My thoughts raced through my mind in an endless circle.

P.J. and I exchanged glances from across the plane, little looks of friendship and a sharing of fear. I felt a morbid empty stillness. We were a plane full of kids, trying to be brave.

When the plane began its descent toward Vietnam, a baby-faced officer in charge stood up. "Load your weapons," he said, in a not-too-sure-of-anything kind of way. And we all did, just like on the rifle range at Camp Pendleton. Only we had M-16s instead of M-14s and we were the targets this time around. My heart was pounding. I could hear it echoing in my head: louder and louder, faster and louder.

Boot camp was racing through my mind. I could see P.J. running into the gas house and hear O'Callahan say, "You'll be dead in two months anyway." I drew pictures of Kristen and our baby and I saw myself being shot in the face. I imagined sucking chest wounds and waves of satanic Vietnamese coming at me, firing and screaming in a language I had never heard before.

I grew tense and was sweating, but I was ready to fight. I was excited and scared, thrilled at the chance, and I wanted to get sick. The whole plane shifted anxiously, but we were ready. I was in shape and I was ready. P.J. and I made a pact of sorts, that if one of us were to die, the other would try to go home with his body. We were as ready to confront death as any eighteen-year-old could be. Only I didn't feel like being a hero or saving my country. I remembered my high school football coach, and how he used to yell at us in practice to "punish yourself, push yourselves. Come on, men. Push yourselves." I always thought it curious to be called men. I wanted to be a man but I felt like a boy. I could see in my mind the scar running down my coach's face as he yelled, "Punish yourselves, men!" The scar was his private Badge of Courage from the "Big One." If only I could postpone manhood. I wanted home. I wanted my Kristen.

"Be sure and spread it out when we touch ground," the same officer said. This time there was a ring of spirit in his voice. The plane hit and we all half-drew a breath, adrenaline pumping and hearts beating.

After taxiing we came to a stop and the rear of the plane opened, unfolding onto our first glance of Vietnam light. We had reached our destination, Da Nang, in the Republic of Vietnam.

Poised for the assault, I noticed P.J. not smiling. I followed the rush out of the plane and onto the runway.

There were no mortars or fire fights. No waves of screaming enemy, only a blast of incredible heat. It shot up from the corrugated steel runway in white snakes of hot air. In the distance I could hear music. It was a radio playing an old Beatles song. It was like back home, cruising Broadway and listening to tunes on the radio.

But Jesus, it was hot. All I cared about was getting out of the awful bright light and into some cool shade. Sweat began dripping from my body. It was a kind of suffocating heat I'd never felt before. It seemed to suck my breath away. We milled and breathed hard while pools of wet salt formed under our arms and across our backs. The heat and humidity were unbelievable.

We were confused, but quickly gathered in line formation and marched over to what appeared to be the airport terminal, where we were told to put down our gear and prepare for a briefing.

The inside of the terminal looked like an old bus depot with cement floors, wooden benches and signs on the walls that would never be remembered. It was packed with Vietnamese civilians and American soldiers. Diminutive women in white blouses and baggy black pants, some wearing conical hats, hovered in clusters over excited children, but it was the American soldiers just arriving or finally leaving Vietnam, who were most prevalent. It was easy to tell who was who. The ones leaving looked very tanned, very tired and very old. They looked at us with pity in their eyes, flashing thumbs up or saying, "So long, suckers."

As I scanned the room, my attention focused on a huge figure deep in the corner against a far wall, standing with his back to me. His clothes looked faded from Marine Corps green to a light brown, which soon took on the appearance of plain dirt. Curious, I walked toward him. To his left stood an equally large German shepherd, held in place by a leather leash. The straps of a shoulder holster crisscrossed the soldier's back and made his already formidable presence appear even more striking. I was sure he had killed many Viet Cong. "Excuse me," I said, and he turned around like an annoyed bear. In his hand was a half-eaten ice cream bar.

I had interrupted him just as he was about to stick the ice cream into his mouth. Ice cream? I thought all I'd ever eat over here was C-rations or rice. That's if I ever got a chance to eat between the mortars and hand-to-hand combat. But ice cream!

I was amazed, shocked, curious and pleased, but most of all amazed. Here was this massive, heavy-set Marine with six days' growth of beard, in a uniform caked and crusted with several days of dirt and what looked like dried blood, eating an Eskimo Pie.

"Love 'em," he exclaimed, as he held up the uneaten portion, smiling through gapped teeth. I haven't had one of these motherfuckers for weeks. Nixon loves 'em too." Then he reached down toward his dog and the Eskimo Pie was soon history.

"Ice cream in the middle of a war," I stammered, still not believing what I was seeing. "That's incredible! Are Eskimo Pies common around here?"

"Fuck, no!" he said. That sounded more like it. "They usually have Dixie Cups." And with that he said a quick "Hello, how you doing, nice to meet you, so long, Boot. I gotta run," and he was gone, probably to kill off a few enemy soldiers with his bare hands, or at least a couple more Eskimo Pies with his dog, Nixon.

Nixon was our president candidate.

I felt confused, and that bothered me for days.

Dear Kristen,

My first day in Vietnam is almost over. I can tell it's not going to be nearly as bad over here as I had thought. The heat is unbearable, however, and I could sure use some lemonade. Remember the lemonade you used to make? God, it was good.

As you know, I've been assigned to the Third Marine Corps Division, the Ninth Regiment. Today, I found out that I will be with Kilo Company. So my letters should be sent to 3/9 Kilo Co., Third Platoon.

I sure am missing you.

I've talked with a few guys around here and they seem to think that the worst fighting for the year is over. I guess the monsoon rains will soon start and any combat is on a small scale.

Looks like a couple months from now I'll be a daddy. I thought I'd be playing baseball now, with you in the stands watching me throw strikes. Last summer, that's how it was. Last summer seems like years ago.

Well, honey, I will go for now. Tomorrow, P.J. and I will be sent to Quang Tri, which is the rear for 3/9, so I had better get some sleep. Good night. I love you more than anything.

Jack
June 1968

That first night P.J. and I stayed in a two-story transit hut that was circled with sandbagged trenches. We grabbed empty bunks and talked with wild-eyed tired guys who were going home or on R & R.

"While you boots are humping in the boonies, I'll be humping some slick-lookin' bitch in Bangkok," one guy said.

"Right," his buddy replied. "And you'll be back with a double dose ah drippy dick."

"Well, I won't be back," said another, smoking a joint and passed it around. "And that's for damn sure. I'm so short I'll be highside stateside before you dudes take your first dump."

"Keep low, that's all I gotta say."

I slept restlessly in the crowded little room until a loud explosion came.

"Incoming! Incoming!" someone screamed, and I awoke instantly. I rolled from my top bunk, hit the floor with both feet and grabbed my shirt on the way, all in one frightened motion. The small room I was sharing with P.J. and six others was engulfed in total darkness and alive with bodies flying out the door, down the stairs, and shoving to get outside.

"Incoming! Incoming!" Again the shouts, and a new screaming I hadn't heard before. From out of the night came a high, shrill whine, like the first screeches from a police siren, followed by a sudden, loud and violent explosion of beautiful bright light and an outward spray of jagged steel. It was the Fourth of July fireworks on the ground.

"Those gook motherfuckers!" someone yelled.

I was terrified as I moved among the mass of silhouettes, running, falling, pulling up pants, and finally diving and stumbling into a long, wide sandbagged trench. I hit the hole, and pushing and shoving, tried to suck the earth. I wanted to burrow beneath the ground. P.J. landed next to me.

"Damn gooks," P.J. complained. "I was dreaming I had this big titted...."

"Shut up, P.J.," I said, amazed at the way his mind worked.

The loud whine and explosions kept coming. I wanted to burrow so deep that nothing could get me. "God help me," I cried to myself, wanting to be brave in front of P.J. "Don't let it land on me!"

The screeching came again and again, with explosions of light and two buildings in the darkness now a mass of flames. Another screech, louder and much closer, came and the darkness ripped open with light. A body flew through the air like a giant rag doll not fifty feet away.

I was a lunatic now! Drugged up; loaded on fear. Why couldn't the trench be deeper? My left leg shook uncontrollably. I covered my head and held fast to the earth.

Suddenly it was quiet. No one moved; more quiet, ears listening.

Then someone placed a hand on my shoulder. "Hey, brothers, it's all right. Those rounds was an accident. They's a couple hundred yards off target." I looked up from my protective crouch in the flame-flickering light, cowering like a frightened child. He was tall, and black, with lots of teeth.

"You's new b's. This bullshit be happenin' ever night." His words were tempered and calm. "Gooks don't wan' us! They's aiming for the ammo dump." Then he took his hand from my shoulder and told me, "It's cool, dude, happen to us all."

"It's over," came another shout. Just as suddenly as the hole filled with troops, it emptied. "Fuckin' rockets!" a voice said.

"Yeah," said another.

"Fucking gooks hit the damn mess hall."

Rockets? I thought. They never mentioned anything about rockets in boot camp. What the hell were rockets? I looked around in the darkness at the burning mess hall and felt overpowered by the night and the sounds of rockets and the images that had followed.

The black guy left and so did the silhouettes. Oh, God, I thought, if this happens all the time, I'm gonna lose my mind.

"They're crazy," I said to P.J., "I'm not about to get out of this hole, just to be blasted out of my bunk by mortars or rockets or whatever. They're out of their minds! They're nuts! I'm not leaving! I'll stay in this damn hole for the rest of my tour if I have to."

"Well, I guess it's just you and me in this hole, Jackson," P.J. said, lying down. "You won't take advantage of me, will you?"

We probably would have stayed there for the duration of the war if someone hadn't awakened us and said, "You still in that hole? It's morning, time for chow." And so we climbed out, a little embarrassed, and walked to the remains of the mess hall to begin our second day in the Nam.

It was noon when several trucks from a convoy staggered to a stop on the road in front of last night's rocket madness.

"Hey, numb nuts!" a kid on the back of the truck hollered, "throw your shit topside!" The sun beat down as P.J. and I picked up our rifles and seabags and climbed in back. We were the only two from the flight over who were assigned to Kilo. We were like brothers as we settled on top of a layer of sandbags, feeling naive and alone. The sandbags covered the truck's bed and were there to protect us from being blown off if we rolled over a land mine.

"Jackson — great weather for a tan, don't you think? But damn, I need some butt, some sweeet bootie for the kid," P.J. declared, rubbing between his legs.

"Cool down, P.J., enjoy the ride."

From the back of the open bed truck, we ate the thick dust of the road and watched the Da Nang billets and battered mess hall grow small, fade, and finally disappear. At the front of the bed stood the ragged-looking kid who yelled at us. Eighteen, maybe. He was tall and slender, with a Tom Sawyer freckled face. However, his oversized helmet and flak jacket just didn't belong. He would have looked much more at home bare-chested and shoeless, goin' fishin' rather than standing there looking out over the top of the cab with his .30 Cal, ready to lock and load.

"Y'all's boots, ain't ya now?" the kid said, in a southern drawl, turning from the front and glancing at us over his shoulder.

"That's it," I said. And the kid turned back.

"How long you been in country?" P.J. asked, feeling proud of his new terminology.

"I ain't no boot, if that's what ya mean," the kid said, turning all the way around to face us, I think for dramatic effect. "Been here for two months and a Purple." Then he turned back to the front.

P.J. just sat there with a dumb grin. We both looked at each other and shrugged. Hell, what could we say, we were two days new to the Nam.

The breeze felt good as the truck sped down the dusty, jarring road. Potholes made by land mines bumped the truck and knocked off our helmets as we fought to stay on board.

We rumbled past neat rows of military tents and plywood buildings surrounded by sandbagged trenches and small bunkers. Standing by were jeeps, trucks and an occasional tank or lonely basketball hoop. There were scores of Marines walking along with rifles and packs and helmets kicking up puffs of red clay dirt as they moved, covering everything.

On the outskirts of the Da Nang base, we passed miles of shacks made from cardboard and corrugated tin, strung together like one long shanty town. They were government supported Vietnamese Refugee camps. Each camp was separated from the road by eight-foot-high cyclone fencing. As we drove by, skinny brown kids, ragged and wide-eyed, would rush the fence shouting "Marine gimme chow! Marine gimme chow!" or "Marine souvenir me cigarette." Then P.J. or I, or the Marines in the trucks in front of us would toss cans of chow or C-rat candy bars over the fence. The minute the prize hit there would be a mad scramble and fight for possessions.

There were hundreds of kids standing in the backwash of our dirt. All of them were begging or smoking and some of them were on crutches, waving as we drove by.

The mamasans squatted next to the children, like busy nervous squirrels. They were dressed in gaily colored clothing now faded and torn. Some wore conical hats and were chewing and spitting through red lips and black stained teeth while they nursed their babies whose heads were full of scabs and running sores. I could see, smell, and almost taste the filth that pocketed their lives. They were like animals, hungry little animals grown accustomed to despair. It was stark and depressing, unlike anything I'd seen before.

I was glad when the convoy moved on and we finally left sight of the shanties and pushed out into the countryside. I felt glad to be an American, and wondered why there was such poverty.

The kid on the gun told P.J. and me to stay alert, to watch for snipers from the wide expanse of rice paddy fields on both sides of us. There was a section up the road that had drawn fire in recent weeks. We both swallowed deep and let out a heavy sigh, trying to see into and behind each and every bush, mud dike, banana tree or broad leafed plant that came into view.

Once past the sniper danger, I relaxed and studied my new country. On each side of the road were acres of rice fields, outlined by neat rows of eighteen- to twenty-four-inch high connecting mud dikes. From the air, the fields would look like flat Oregon farm land with skimpy paths outlining the countryside like squares on a chess board. In front and to the side on every few acres sat small huts made of bamboo and grass with thatch roofs to keep out the monsoon rains. The homes were built up higher than the fields on several layers of dirt to withstand flooding, I assumed. Occasionally, I would see a concrete home with a grass roof or tin roof or a religious temple or pagoda. As our column pushed on, I noticed almost exclusively women or children or very old men were tending the fields or walking the big black water buffalo.

I asked the kid on the gun where the young men were. "They're mostly over there," he replied, pointing to a little section of farmland that was now a graveyard, "or they're Cong." I felt a sudden remorse, a sense of doom, like I too would end up dead in a field somewhere.

Behind the rice paddies and huts, in the distance rose majestic green mountains, full of deep untamed jungle. They reminded me of Oregon and of the rich, beautiful trees and mountains that banked the Columbia River Gorge. I recalled standing at Lookout Point with Kristen and looking down into the huge gaping gorge and feeling almost overwhelmed by the power and beauty of it. But these mountains had been spoiled. Huge craters could be seen from the road. There were wide sections of mountainside that had been violently destroyed, pocked with great ruptures of bomb-pitted earth.

When I looked at these mountains I felt terribly sad. Having been raised in Oregon, I had developed an appreciation of trees washing together in a sea of undisturbed green. The mountains I knew were alive with deer and elk and fresh-water streams, not huge crevices so wide and deep that they could never be filled.

We drove alongside a river where several burned-out and blown away huts with still-smoldering fires looked down upon the water.

I began to feel as if we were in a time warp, passing by miles of rice paddies and nearly empty fields where life had been reduced to aimless moving. Then, suddenly, there would be no one, nothing but traces of violent destruction. But the convoy didn't stop, and it was always the same.

We reached Quang Tri just before dusk, tired, hungry, and a little more than happy to get off that damn truck. I wasn't sure where Quang Tri was in relationship to the large cities or the DMZ. It could have been located ten miles from Bangkok, Thailand, for all I know. But after chow and checking our sea bags for storage, P.J. and I found a map and figured out where we were. We were a few miles south of a small city called Don Ha. A few miles north of Don Ha lay the DMZ. Well, we wouldn't have to worry until morning, we were in the rear, which means we had a tent to sleep in, and an outhouse for convenience. What more could we ask?

Tomorrow was the big day. Tomorrow we would draw the rest of our combat gear, and be choppered out to Kilo Company. They could use us. They needed a few good men. We saw several of them wrapped up in body bags by the side of the road as our convoy came in. They were waiting, waiting to go home.

Five

WHAP, WHAP, WHAP, whap, whap. The noise was thundering in our ears. Whap, whap, whap, whap, whap. P.J. and I were being choppered out to Kilo Company in a double-rotored Chinook C-40. I couldn't see the faces of the two pilots from where I sat, but they seemed at ease, very businesslike, as if they were on a pleasure trip. From my webbed bench seat I could see the backs of their flight helmets, the corners of their dark glasses, their green headsets and the tops of their matching flight jackets. I watched them point at the jungle below, adjust gauges and their headsets. They kept looking out from side to side, mouthing words I couldn't hear.

The door gunner was dressed like their twin, except I could see all of him and a row of not-so-white teeth flashing occasionally from beneath his moustache. The gunner was just a few feet in front of me, leaning with incredible nonchalance on his mounted M-60. He looked ridiculously at ease, scanning the jungle and now the rice paddies below. On the back of his flak jacket, written in big black letters, were the words, "Widow Maker"! It gave him a horrendous, fitting power. But I felt unsafe. Like the chopper could bank hard and I would fall out of the open rear loading ramp. Or we could take fire and there would be nowhere to hide.

As we flew over rice paddies, and remote villages, back up into the mountains and over the top, and then down into a valley, I felt small and insignificant. I wondered what difference my being here could make. I wasn't horrified, only anxious, and as we passed over the jungle below the war seemed so very far away.

I enjoyed the wind whipping as the copter's blades moved and cooled the air. It was a relief from the constant glaring of a sun that didn't understand mercy. Finally the chopper made its approach to the small camp.

Kilo Company's perimeter was located on top of a small, yellow, treeless hill. From the air I could see the troops gathered or walking around mortar pits and foxholes with plastic tents erected next to them. Surrounded by rich green mountains and valleys, the yellow hill looked desolate and out of place.

When we landed and unloaded and the bird left us in a fury of flying dirt and debris, the barren isolation became evident. There was no cover, no way to escape the remorseless rays, except by hiding under plastic ponchos made up like poor beach umbrellas. Three black Marines, shirtless with green hand towels draped on their heads like desert soldiers were cleaning their rifles, while listening to a transistor radio play "Puff, the Magic Dragon, lives by the sea and frolics in the...." They slowly pushed rods down the barrels and pulled them out while other Marines lay sleeping, or writing, or sitting on the edges of their holes looking detached, drained and burned out.

Without the breeze from the chopper the heat began to work on me. My temperature seemed to soar as sweat ran from my forehead down into my eyes, along my back, and under my arms. Just standing there with P.J. was an effort. We stood in the sun for a couple of minutes listening to "Puff" on the radio and watching the black Marines.

"That Puff kicks some ass. It's bad for a fat man," one of them said.

"Yeah, Puff be ah mutherfuck."

I had no idea what they were talking about. Puff kicking ass? What fat man?

I felt out of place and unsure of myself. Everyone looked older and hardened, or used up. Our coming in seemed so unremarkable to them.

"You guys didn't bring mail?" a tall, unshaven trooper said. "Well, God damn it. It's been three fuckin' days. What the hell are those assholes in the rear doing?" he asked, scolding us. I didn't know what to say.

"Well, shit. OK, men. I'm your Platoon Commander, Lieutenant Neal." We started to salute. He grabbed my arm. "Don't! When you're in the brush, don't ever salute officers. You'll draw sniper fire, dumb shit!" P.J. and I looked at each other, sharing stupidity.

Neal wore a floppy bush cover that had "Don't shoot, I'm short" written on it. As he looked at us his eyes would dart in quick glances and his face would twitch nervously. He reminded me of a boxer who'd been beat up so many times that he'd gone slightly punch drunk.

"This is Ski, your squad leader," the lieutenant said, eyes darkening, face twitching, as he pointed to a shirtless, tanned kid. "He'll get you settled." Then he left quickly and resumed whatever he had been doing before we came. P.J. and I tried to shake hands with Ski, but blew the ritual hand movement.

"Glad to see some fresh meat," Ski said. The remark drew a weird look of puzzlement from P.J. Then we followed Ski across the small, flat dirt helipad and down the side of the small knoll. We passed more foxholes, Marines, machine gun implacements, and several guys listening to the radio sing the start of the Beach Boys' "Surfin' U.S.A." and I felt an eerie sense of preordained doom, like everything was out of whack. "Drop your packs here," Ski said, matter-of-factly, "and dig yourselves a hole. I'll be back later." Then he left us, shouting back over his shoulder, "I'll be back most rickety-tick, and we'll get some for a fat man!"

"Man, this place is heavy duty," P.J. said. "We're about as important as a sack of shit. And who the hell is that 'fat man'?"

"I don't know, must be someone in our platoon."

I took out my entrenching tool from the back of my pack. It took awhile to get used to the little two-foot long shovel I'd never used before, but I dug through the soft earth and felt glad that P.J. was with me. From where my hole would face, I could see down into the floor of the valley some one hundred yards away. There were signs of vegetation and small trees, unlike our naked hill. The farther you looked into the valley, the thicker the growth became. The valley was bordered with green mountains shooting up on each side, making the small knoll we were on appear even smaller. The base of the mountains was five hundred yards from where we were set in. Each mountain had been ravaged by the war, with huge bomb pits and rended earth like sudden ugly clear cutting. At the end of the valley, the terrain leveled off, breaking into flat ground. Suddenly I heard planes high overhead moving toward the other side of the mountains we faced, and shortly came the rumble of thunder in the distance.

"B-52s dropping bombs," P.J. said.

"Oh, shit!" and the ground we were on started to shake. All along our little hillside came cheers and clapping and shouts of "Eat shit, Charlie! Fuck ya!" or "Get some BIG for a fat man!"

I was in awe as I shoveled and dug and took off my shirt and wiped the sweat from my eyes. God, we had some fire power. Then I unpacked my poncho and Snoopy blanket and heard another rumble, the ground shook and more cheers were heard. Wrapped up inside my blanket was an 8 by 10 color high school graduation picture of Kristen. She looked incredibly beautiful. Her face was clean and white and her eyes seemed to look at me as if alive, and aware that I was holding her.

High school seemed so far away, and such a long time ago. Back home I had been expected to get a job or go to college. But I didn't want to grow up and end up doing something I didn't like for the next thirty years. I wanted to play baseball, I wanted to get half drunk with my cousin Rich and take out our girls on Saturday night. I wanted to be home, or anyplace but Vietnam.

As I unpacked, I thought about the first time I got drunk. I was feeling bad about a fight my father and mother had just had and how I had to break it up by knocking my dad to the ground. Hitting his face, I had screamed and cried. I would have pounded on him all night if Rich hadn't been there and pulled me off. It wasn't like I hated him, but rather like I was trying to say, "Can't you understand how much it hurts me to see you do this to mom and to yourself?"

Later I went to a wedding reception and got really drunk. I tore up the party and hammered a few people. I don't suppose any of them understood that it wasn't them I was beating, but my dad. Kristen took care of me that night. She took me home, cleaned me up, and listened to me cry. From then on, like a cared-for, wounded animal, I had an undying faith and tremendous love for her.

I looked at her picture and thought about that night and how she took care of me, and how I was here and she was an ocean and what seemed like light years away from me. I began to believe that to survive Vietnam, I must remain in constant thought of her and our unborn child. And, if I did, God would watch over me. He would allow me to survive to go home to my Kristen.

"Hey, air head." I looked up and Ski was smiling at me from behind his thin moustache. "I've been watching you stare at that picture for ten minutes. Didn't you hear me?"

"No, I'm sorry. I was just looking at a picture of my wife, Kristen."

"You married? You're really out to lunch," he said, making me feel like I was a stupid kid. I explained how we had gotten married a few weeks before I was shipped over.

"Let me see this broad. Geeze, she must be blind," he joked, handing the picture back. "Well, listen. Your hole better be a little deeper. We'll probably get some incoming tonight. Nothing big. Just mortars." He appeared calmer, almost gentle now, and yet disturbingly unemotional as he spoke.

"How long have you been in country?"

"Ten months, twenty-two days and a purple. I'm an old man. Be twenty in a week," he said, pulling a cigarette from behind his ear and placing it in his mouth. "Then I'll slide out these last few weeks and be highside back to the world. Be home!" he grinned. "Guys," he continued, "we gotta dig in good. The gooks are all over this place lookin' to kick ass."

P.J. stopped digging and looked up from his hole. "No kidding? This place looks dead."

"You'll be dead if you think like that. A couple weeks ago we were set in five or six clicks up the valley."

"What's a click?" I interrupted.

"What are you, Question Man? A click's a thousand yards. Anyway, we were hit with mortars and machine guns just before dawn," he continued, sucking but not lighting his cigarette. "The North Vietnamese Army was comin' outta the bush, rushin' toward us. We'd shoot the little fuckers, knock 'em down, and they'd get up and we'd knock 'em down again." His words were making me want to go home immediately.

"It sure scared the hell out of us," he said. "Was some bad news, dudes, worse than the bullets. But then they brought in gunships and Puff to kick ass."

"Puff the magic dragon?" I asked.

"Right. Anyway, that old C-130 was laying about 6,000 rounds a minute on Charles. From the air they worked over the gooks until Charlie hauled ass back into the brush, leaving behind twenty-six dead and three or four wounded. Some of them slope-heads had their pressure points tied off with bamboo and had little cloth bags with syringes and small amounts of heroin or opium. Apparently they were suicide squads, hopped up and tied off so they could absorb more rounds in their bodies. It was unreal," he added, sucking once again on his unlit cigarette, but not acting like his story was any more frightening than describing a punch-out in some bar. "We kicked ass for a fat man," he added, bringing up again the term that puzzled me. I guess anything good and in abundance was "for a fat man."

"During the fire fight, the barrel of one of my squad's machine guns was working out so much, that it heated up, turned red, and you could see the rounds inside the barrel pass through, shooting out. It was some bad shit. We had seven KIAs and a whole bunch of wounded."

Ski's words were frightening and difficult to comprehend. Boot camp and I.T.R. never mentioned or prepared us for this. I wondered how long it would be before I would be pumping rounds into suicidal "slant-eyes". I felt stupid and scared and realized that what I had imagined Vietnam was like was so very wrong. I knew nothing about where I was or what we were doing. I knew nothing about killing or war, and yet here I was, about to go hunting, and I had never hunted anything in my entire life, let alone other men.

"Say happenin'?" a voice called as Ski turned to greet a group of five Marines who were walking up to us. He reached out to slap the outstretched hand of a tall guy with big ears and a wide Mickey Mouse grin, who looked like a hard twenty.

"It ALL be happenin'," Ski replied, turning his hand palm-up for the tall kid's slap. They slapped hands, grabbed hands, shook hands, bumped fists, hit their chests, and said, "Get some!"

"Are these the new b's, Ski, DOWNNN?" the new arrival shot back.

"This is Rat," Ski said to P.J. and me, referring to the kid with the big ears. "He was John Wayne last fire fight. Rat's up for a bronze medal."

"I'll take a ride home instead," Rat countered.

Ski continued introducing P.J. and me to the rest of the squad. They were a ragged looking group, dressed in green fatigue pants, tee shirts or no shirts, and flak jackets, with their dog tags stuck in the laces of their jungle boots. Each Marine had on a canteen belt with pouches and green plastic canteens and each one carried an M-16, except for a big angry looking guy who had an M-60 balanced on his massive shoulder. He held the machine gun at the barrel like a hobo would carry his bed roll, and had machine gun ammo criss-crossing his chest, which added to his menacing presence.

"This here is Tiny, our squad's gunner," Ski pointed to the big guy, "and Pig Pen, his ammo man." Tagging along next to Tiny was a skinny, goofy-looking kid weighted down by ammo belts and strapped-on little boxes of machine gun ammunition. He was much dirtier than the rest, and looked like the high school chump everyone picked on. Both names seemed fitting.

"That's Smitty. The little guy with the big mouth," he said, grinning and pointing to a short guy who looked a little older than the rest and whose uniform was way too big. "He's the bloop man. Carries the M-79."

"Yeah, well, fuck you! This little guy'll rip off your head and shit it! Ski, I'm sick ah this shit. I want out," Smitty retorted angrily, half to himself and half to the rest of us. Then he tossed his oversized helmet on the ground, and stood there in his baggy pants, looking frustrated.

"Yeah. Shit! These turkeys want us to do all the shit work," Smitty complained, twisting his angry face into a frown. "I'm fed up. I'm sick of the heat, I'm sick of the filth, and I'm sick of the lifers," he added, throwing off the sack of M-79 rounds and his overly large flak jacket. "They got us by the balls."

"Cool down, pal," the last guy coming up said, placing his arm around the little guy's shoulder. "Cool down, Smitty, or your brain's gonna pop. Somebody's got to do the dirt."

"Buddy, you big ox, get your arm off me. You dumb pachyderms drive me crazy," he said, pushing back. "So you're the new guys, here to get us blown away?" Smitty asked.

"Cool it, Smitty!" Ski demanded.

"P.J., Jackson, this is Buddy."

"Where you burr-heads from?" Buddy asked, extending a hand to get a slap.

"Oregon," P.J. responded. "He's from Portland, I'm from a little town called Whitefish."

"Or-gon! Cowboy town!" Buddy laughed as he slapped hands and helped us through a protracted handshake.

Buddy seemed different from the rest. He was big like Tiny, but in better shape and he seemed brighter, more educated. He was blonde and had a smile much like a blown up version of P.J. I could tell he had been an athlete in high school, just by the way he moved, fluid and confidently. He was also much cleaner than the rest. He was exactly the opposite of Pig Pen.

"Welcome to the Third Herd," Buddy said. "We may not be bad. But then the bad don't fuck with us." Then he sat down on his helmet. "Ski, it's 'bout brew time, isn't it?" he asked, as the others started to scatter.

"Naw. No beer. Chopper loaded down took a nose dive," Ski answered.

"Get hit?"

"Guess so. The other squads are gonna recon it out," Ski replied as he lay down.

"Yeah. That's right. Those damn lifers will get a few more killed for a case of beer!" Smitty interjected between tugs on his canteen. "They don't give a rat's ass."

"Smitty, you better cool it, your brain's on overload," Buddy said. "Don't mind him, Jackson. Listen, you guys have a good war. I'm catching some Z's." Then Buddy stood up and sauntered over to his hole and crawled beneath the cover of his plastic hooch.

P.J. and I spent the rest of the day trying to build a tent to hide from the sun. We met more people, heard stories, and learned how to build little cooking stoves from empty C-ration cans. As daylight began to fall I started to worry. I thought of rockets and enemy sneaking around trying to get me, as if I were singled out because I was new. I felt so useless — naive. I couldn't remember anything I learned in training, and I didn't even know if my rifle worked.

As darkness came, Ski divided our squad into two holes for watch. P.J. and I were split up. They didn't want two new guys together, one was a big enough liability. I was with Buddy, Smitty, Tiny, and Ski. P.J. and the rest of the squad were over to our left about ten yards, with Rat supervising. As darkness crept in we sat there talking about home and the Nam, with Tiny and Buddy jockeying for position in the conversation, each trying to outdo the other with a story funnier or more frightening. "Sheett Jim," Tiny said, spitting through his teeth. Tiny always began a sentence with the same two words, no matter what your name was, or who he was talking about. "They used to call my last unit, 'Bravo 1/9, the Walking Dead'. Sheett Jim, I tell ya," spit, spit, "they was all kinds ah fucked up," he said. "We was always gettin' hit and gettin' our shit blown away." I was listening intently now. "When 1/9 first got over here, they was so fucked up, they was goin' out on night patrols with flashlights."

"That ain't nothing," Buddy said, forcing his way into the conversation. "I heard 1/9 used to get in fire fights and throw

51

grenades uphill and have 'em roll back down and blow up in their face."

Ski soon divided the night watch up into four shifts. While one man stood alert, the other three slept. Being a boot to the Nam, I was on the first shift. "Ski," I said, rather embarrassed, "before I go on watch, where can I go to the bathroom?" There was never any mention in boot camp about the procedure of how it was done at night in a combat situation.

"There ain't no bathroom, fool. Tell someone you're going out, then go out in front of the lines," Ski said. "But be sure to let whoever is on watch know, or you'll get your ass in a sling."

I went outside our perimeter with my rifle on full automatic, scared to death. I imagined suddenly coming under fire or some North Vietnamese crawling up on me with a knife clenched between his teeth, trying to slit my throat, and me caught there with my pants down. I resolved never to let this happen at night again. I was done in a hurry!

"Ski," I asked when I was back, "how do you keep from falling asleep on watch?" I felt dumb, asking questions.

"It's easy." He went over to his pack and came back with a hand grenade. Pulling the pin and handing it to me very cautiously, he said, "Hold on to it, and don't let the spoon fly. If you do, three seconds later you're history."

"Great one. That's all I need. If the gooks don't kill me, I'll kill myself."

It would be impossible to fall asleep with this grenade in my hand. Sitting by my hole, I stared into the darkness, clenching with great determination the grenade that kept me awake. I concentrated... aware of the darkness and aware of the grenade, trying to see them before they saw me. My mind and eyes played tricks on me. Shadows were gooks, gooks were shadows. The wind was "them" whispering. I began to sweat. I stepped down into my hole, thinking I would be a much smaller target for the snipers. I heard something! Over there! I turned to the noise. My senses quickened. I was more alert than I had ever been in my entire life. The sound moved. No, it was over there! I jerked my head. No. Wait! I was confused. It was so dark. Where were they? My heart was beating now. Louder and louder. I could hear brush breaking. They were coming. The tension was unbearable. I knew they were out there, and I knew they could hear my heart thumping louder and louder. My hand was tired from gripping the grenade.

"Hey, boot." I jumped, startled. It was Ski again. "Take it easy," he said. "I just thought I would relieve you of my toy." He took the grenade from my hand, let the spoon fly, and I dropped to the bottom of the hole. "It's cool," he said, tapping me on the back and quietly laughing. "This is only a dummy grenade. I do this to all the boots. You don't think I'm fool enough to give you a live one, do you? Anyway, I'm on watch now," he said.

I went back to my private foxhole, feeling humiliated and knowing in my heart that it was going to be a long war.

Six

THE NEXT MORNING the word was passed that we were to fill in our holes and get ready to move out. Ski came over as I was packing up.

"I noticed all the gear they gave you guys back in the rear," he said, pointing to P.J. and me and the extra bandoliers of ammunition we were carrying. "We gotta lighten you boots up. With all this extra shit you won't even be able to move your ass, and anyway, you both gotta carry a mortar round. Here, let me show you what's happenin'. You don't need this," he said, tossing my gas mask in my foxhole. "No one carries them. 'Sides, the gooks don't use gas. It's sort of an understanding."

"Jesus," he said, shaking his head as he took the extra boots we brought from our pack. "Shitcan this. And this," he said, tossing two bandoliers of ammo into the hole along with the boots, and then quickly covering it all up with dirt. "And here, take these," he said as he handed us each one more canteen of water.

"But I already have two," I protested.

"Listen, my man, TWO ain't gonna get it. In this heat I always carry at least four. Some dudes carry six or eight. The heat's gonna suck your ass dry. Trust me."

From what I understood we were the third platoon in a company of four. Ski gathered us together and told us that our platoon of about thirty men would be first off the hill and that our squad would be running third in the platoon as we moved off and down into the valley. "It's going to be a short hump today. About four clicks over easy terrain," he said, pointing to a spot on a plastic fold-up map. The spot meant nothing to me. I couldn't even read a map. I mean, it wasn't like he was pointing out a small town in Florida.

I put my pack on with the mortar round on top and worried that an enemy rifle shot might hit it and blow me into a million pieces. Or that I would fall down, crack the mortar tube and explode the round inside. The pack was heavy and the weight and construction of the flak jackets and helmets acted like a sweatsuit, and trapped my body's heat. Sweat was dripping into my eyes and we hadn't even moved out yet.

"Say, P.J., don't zip up your flak jacket. Are you crazy?" Ski warned. "If you get gut shot or hit in the chest, and a round goes through the zipper, we couldn't unzip it and you'd be stone cold dead by the time we cut your damn jacket off. I hate these jackets. The flak makes the fuckin' jacket so heavy that some grunts, like me, cut the flak out. When the shit hits, I'm up and moving. Don't want this damn thing holding me down." I cringed. I had thought I was safe in my jacket. I followed P.J. and quickly unzipped.

P.J. and I buried the mask, ammo and boots and, the briefing completed, we sat and waited with the rest of our squad for our turn off the dusty hill.

"Ski, where the hell are we?" P.J. asked, turning to Ski who was sitting on the ground next to us. "I mean, I know we're in some damn valley, but is there a name for it?"

"Yeah. Booby Trap Hill."

"Booby Trap, huh? That's what we call brassieres back home, big booby traps," laughed P.J., trying to make a joke.

I wanted to tell him to shut up because I was scared as hell, but I tried not to show concern. P.J. seemed so unaffected. He was constantly amazing me with his ability to deal with frightening information. Occasionally he would display a semblance of concern, but it would pass quickly and he would be back to his normal state of insanity.

"You won't think this is funny when your balls get blown off!" Ski said, irritated with P.J.'s remark. His young face and moustache seemed to tighten as he stood up and blasted P.J. "This ain't no cartoon, penis brain. The traps are terrible bad."

"Real quick now, both you guys listen up," he continued sternly, looking down on us like children. "This ain't boot camp. You fuck up here, you're dead, or worse, you kill somebody."

"One, you got toe-poppers made outa C-rat cans," he said, counting on his fingers. "They'll blow off your foot," and he kicked P.J.'s foot. "Then you got Bouncing Bettys. They'll pop up after you step on 'em and blow your dick off. And trip wires that can cut you in half."

I glanced at P.J. whose face had grown sullen.

"But they ain't nothin' next to daisy chains. Now, daisy chains are a row of explosions meant for a platoon or company. Are you listening?" We nodded. "Now some gook hides in the bush, waitin' for us. When we waltz by, he blows off artillery shells buried next to the road and then you're trapped. If you run one direction, he blows another one. It's crazy, man. So keep your head outta your ass and open your eyes or you could both be dead by lunch."

P.J. and I looked at the ground away from Ski, not speaking. I couldn't believe what was happening. I really could be dead by lunch.

We moved off and down the yellow parched hill, toward the valley. Our company of almost a hundred men hit the valley and pushed our way through razor sharp elephant grass that sometimes towered over our heads and limited visibility to the backside of the Marine in front of me.

My pack was heavy and the heat was unbearable as the sun rose higher in the sky. Sweat dripped into my eyes and languished on the corners of my parched mouth. I licked my lips as they dried and cracked. I fumbled my canteens awkwardly, trying to drink quickly, afraid that I'd hit a booby trap or lose Rat in front of me.

"Easy on the water," Rat said, turning back to check on me. "Don't sweat it, you'll make it to lunch," he added, grinning, like Mickey would to Minnie.

The T-shirt I had on was soaked with sweat and sticking to my back, irritating my armpits. My back ached and my forearms began to bleed from tiny cuts as we pushed on through the tall grass. The weight and cumbersome feeling of my pack sucked my energy and made me feel afraid that I wouldn't be able to move fast enough if we got hit. I worried about daisy chains and toe-poppers and an enemy I had yet to see. I tripped and fell but stood up quickly, hoping the others hadn't seen what a fool I was. I had to pee, but was afraid to stop. I could see myself getting shot in the face by a sniper while trying to piss. I fell again, struggled up, and knew I'd trip a wire and kill everyone. Soon my canteens were empty.

We had eaten up the clicks and the valley, and as the sun peaked to punish us, we crossed out of the tall grass and reached the flatlands. My throat was so dry I couldn't swallow, but finally we settled in, next to a trickling stream.

"Dig in," Ski ordered, swinging his pack form his shoulders to the ground. "We're settin' in." Soon our squad was joined by the others, forming a circular perimeter, digging foxholes, and pitching ponchos.

I filled my canteens and opened a can of fruit cocktail, ate quickly, poured water on my head, and started to dig my hole.

I had flashed on all sorts of debilitating injuries. I wasn't as concerned about dying as I was about killing someone in my squad, or being maimed, or disfigured. Back home, I had seen older people in wheelchairs, their legs missing. Probably lost in heroic battles defending God and country, I used to think. None of them ever looked like heroes, though, and I'm sure I wouldn't either.

"Great way to spend a day, huh, Big Jack?" P.J. said as he dug on our hole. The sweat ran off his shirtless body, as I thought of his scar and his mom and that he was my best friend.

"Hey, boots," Ski yelled, "our platoon is on patrol, so you and P.J. get your shirts on and saddle up. Here, Jackson, you got the PRIC," he said, handing me the radio. I was excited and proud. Proud because I had only been "in country" a few days and already they had recognized how sharp I was by giving me the responsibility of carrying the radio. I knew P.J. would envy me. I quickly imagined being a hero, with legs, calling in rockets and gunships and low, fast swooping jet fighters to wreak havoc on scores of faceless enemy. But then I realized I had never really talked on the radio before.

"Sheett, Jim," Tiny said, spitting twice as he walked toward me. I woke up again. "It's a bitch carrying the PRIC. I know! We hit the shit, you be wantin' to shitcan that radio."

"What are you talking about?"

"Sheett, have an idea! The gooks can't get brass, they shoot at whoever gots the PRIC-25. Who wants an extra ten or fifteen fuckin' pounds on their back?" he added, looking at me like I was a curiosity, then he shook his head, mumbled, "Sheett," and turned away, forgetting to spit.

"Hey, Bro, sorry," P.J. said, consoling me with a pat on my shoulder. "But that's life in the big city."

"Thanks, P.J., you're a big help. If we get hit I'll just start saluting you," I said, and he grinned.

I threw the radio with the whip antenna over my jacket, tied a bandolier of magazines around my waist on top of my canteens, picked up my 16 and followed Tiny and the rest of the squad out of the perimeter. We linked up with portions of our platoon and began moving across rice paddy fields that were dried up and looked like they had not yielded crops for quite some time. It was easier to move without the packs, but the radio was heavy and the heat was still sweltering as we circled across more barren ground.

The single file patrol of twenty was forever cursing, drawing on canteens and passing the word, "Spread it out. Come on, spread it out," or "Not so far. Close it up. Close it up."

I was tiring from the heat and hoping we wouldn't get hit. I had never really understood how to work the radio, and wouldn't know what to do or who to call if we did get hit. Maybe I would cost somebody their life because of my stupidity. I flicked the switch on the grip of my rifle to "on" and flicked it off again. I wanted Kristen. I wanted home.

I was in the middle of the column, following a tall well-built black kid from another squad. When we stopped to rest, we talked.

"Hey, dude, you's boot to the Nam, ain't you?" he said, sitting with his helmet off.

"Just got in country a few days ago."

"Where you from?" he asked. He sounded like he was from Chicago or Philadelphia or maybe New York. I really hadn't met anyone from the east coast. In fact, my biggest trip away from home was when I went to boot camp.

"I'm from Portland, Oregon."

"Or-gone! Ain't nobody from Or-gone," he said, laughing and smiling with a mouth full of white. "Or-gone, aint' nuthin' but chuck dudes and cowboys from Or-gone."

"Well, I did ride a horse to school," I lied.

"No shit?"

"No shit!"

"Damn!" He slapped his leg and laughed, a big toothy grin. And I liked him.

"Jimmy from Chi-town," he said, extending his hand for a slap. But I blew the handshake as he shook his head, smiled, and said, "Hang in there."

He wasn't a boot. His jungle fatigues and his flak jacket told me that; dirty, torn, with the months of the year written on the back in two black columns, and the words, "God walks point for the 3/9."

We pressed on, quietly slicing through the countryside that made me feel like someone was watching us. We checked out a dead water buffalo lying on its side, legs stiff with rigor mortis, a few isolated old huts, some touched by the war and some not. But we never really stopped, we just sort of moved on searching and I slowly found myself losing some of the fear I had felt earlier. Soon we were walking along a well traveled path that linked several of the abandoned huts like back alleys.

"Spread it out. Spread it out. Close it up." And we moved on. From my position in the column I could see Jimmy and several others in front of me. As the path would curve, occasionally Jimmy would lose sight of the man in front of him and hurry to catch up. The patrol passed a small collection of burned-out huts, and up around a grove of banana trees and thick vegetation. Realizing that he was losing sight of the squad ahead, Jimmy hurried up to the fork in the narrow path we were traveling. He jogged to the left. From where I was, I thought the men ahead had gone right.

KaBOOM. An explosion in front of me and I fell to the ground, shaking. Dust was flying and Jimmy was running in the dust and as he started to fall, he screamed, "I'm hit! I'm hit!"

"Incoming! Incoming!" someone yelled.

I could see Jimmy clearly, about ten yards to the left of me, off the path, lying on his back, his chest heaving spasmodically. I lay there numbed with shock, watching him sitting up, grasping his pant leg, distorting his face, then falling back again, fisting his hands into his temples, and rocking from side to side, moaning. "I'M HIT. OH, JESUS. FUCK. I'M HIT." Louder this time.

Ski and Tiny rushed over next to him. Bending down, they tried to calm him. I followed hesitantly. There were no more sounds. There was no incoming. Jimmy had picked the wrong path. He had hit a booby trap and quickly brought to me my first glimpse of what heroes look like. It was as if someone had taken a sledgehammer and hammered just above his right ankle. It was like someone had taken a full swing and then pounded and pounded and hammered on his foot, crushing the bone, splintering it, tearing the flesh and ripping it from his leg. Someone had done this to Jimmy from Chi-town. They had amputated his foot. Not smooth and clean like a swiftly skilled surgeon, but brutally in one savage explosion.

"Here it is! Here it is!" P.J. said, bending over, almost heaving, looking at Jimmy's foot lying separate from his body. It was no use. They couldn't tape it on. They couldn't put him back together again. This wasn't a fairy tale. This was reality. There was his foot and there he was, and he would never be the same. Here was a bona fide red, white and blue, all-American boy frothing like a madman.

"Oh, God, Oh, God." I gagged and vomited.

Jimmy lay there, twisting in pain, clenching his temples, screaming to God or anyone. "Oh, Jesus, fuck. KILL ME. Jesus,

PLEASE kill me." Twisting and crying, "Oh, shit. Oh, God. PLEASE, please kill me, Jesus, kill me, please."

Lieutenant Neal ran up and yelled in my face, "Wake up! Snap out of it, boy!" I was dazed and shocked. "Boy, get a hold of yourself."

Jimmy was crying in soft sobs. Shot up with morphine. "Oh, God. Oh, Jesus." His leg was all mangled and broken-boned, and covered with thick slabs of blood and full of little holes. Each heartbeat brought spurts of blood from his leg that soaked the ground like punctures in a water hose.

The lieutenant was at me again. He had to get a Medivac. "GIVE ME THAT RADIO!" he screamed, grabbing the handset from me while I stood there, dazed, wiping puke from my mouth and looking at Jimmy.

I was so sick I could scream. Jimmy the hero. He should have been home playing basketball now, or tailback on his high school football team. Instead he was lying here, fighting with death. He wasn't a hero, he was just fucked up. And he's not going to limp from the field while thousands in the stands cheer his great courage. No coaches or teammates will greet him on the sideline, slapping hands and saying, "You was great out there, my man. You were really cooking." Or, "We'll get even. We'll kick ass next time." No, Jimmy would never get even. Never. Never in a million years would Jimmy be even.

If he was lucky, he would live and go home, and there might even be moments when he would forget about losing his foot in some place he couldn't understand.

"Dust off coming!" the lieutenant yelled.

The chopper came quickly, touched down, and Jimmy and his foot were loaded up. Then he was gone.

But he'd be nobody's hero. Not even his own.

    Dear Kristen,
        I'm too tired to write. I'm OK, but God, it's hot.
                I love you,
                July 1968

Seven

A FEW DAYS AFTER Jimmy took the wrong path our company was choppered farther up into the mountains and began setting up a temporary firebase.

Everything was temporary in Vietnam.

It was fascinating to watch a firebase grow overnight from isolated Vietnamese jungle into a small American fortress. It was a concentrated effort of hundreds of men and dozens of double-bladed Chinooks and single-prop Hueys choppering in artillery, ammunition, supplies, pallets stacked high with warm beer, C-rations and green five-gallon cans filled with our water supply. It was a feverish effort of digging holes and parapets, chopping or blowing down trees, and sandbagging machine gun emplacements and stringing row after row of concertina wire around the outside of our perimeter.

As I dug and shoveled out my hole, I could not imagine, even in my wildest hallucinations, how we could ever be defeated. With all this firepower, with this wealth of military might, with Puff and jets and B-52s on call, I suspected we could win the war in a week if we wanted. But such thoughts soon evaporated as I began to learn about "reality" and how to survive from members of my squad. Each day in the bush was an education, with my squad being the indoctrinators of survival and soothsayers of despair. Each squad member shared singular nightmares of experience that cling to the memory like napalm to a burning child.

We ran day patrols and night ambushes from our perimeter and made little contact. Occasionally at night, when we set in alongside clear trails, two or three NVA would wander into our bush, probably lost or on their way to a hidden rice cache. It would be over in several seconds and was good for morale, as was the changing weather. The heat that was so suffocating during the day had been replaced by a constant drizzle that cooled and cleaned everything. It wasn't monsoon rain; it was more like the type of wet weather that would rain out the second game of a baseball double header. We all seemed to enjoy the change.

"Since you're from Oregon, you must love this wet shit," Buddy said to P.J. and me one pitch dark night as he and Tiny sat with us huddled under a couple of strung-out ponchos. It was colder than usual, and the collective body heat felt good.

"I don't mind it," I replied.

"Yeah, we're just a couple of ducks with rubber asses," P.J. joked.

"Well, sheett, Jim," Tiny said, "I don't mind this rain, but when it's this dark, man, fucks with my head. Reminds me ah my old unit."

"Christ, I heard this story about ninety times," Buddy complained.

"Cut some slack, dude, these turds haven't," Tiny said, referring to P.J. and me.

"Come on, Tiny, tell us," P.J. pleaded. "If you do, I won't art."

"Do it, Tiny! Tell him! Anything's better than that!"

"Sheett, Jim, it was a muther. We was set in and it was dark d cold and wet as hell. The gooks started with mortars d B-40s. They hits the wire with bangalore torpedos and gged-up sappers. We popped flares and damned near lit up place like the Fourth of July. Then the sappers would dive the wire, blow themselves up, dead as hell; then their lies would haul ass in, throwing satchel charges or firing "

w many you get?" P.J. asked anxiously.

"We killed a shitload of those bastards, and with Puff dropping light and miniguns kicking ass, we finally turned 'em back. But it was a muther," he said, as his voice lowered and I could almost see him shaking his big head. "Took us all day to gather up and bury the bodies." Then he paused for a long time, and though it was too dark to see, I could tell he was looking down at his hands. "Ya know, sometimes I still smell their blood on me."

"I can dig it, my man, but I tell you, the biggest mindfuck about the Nam," Buddy said with anger in his voice, "is that there's so damned many ways to die." He spooned a bite of peaches, I think, and sort of thought for a minute and then spoke.

"Jackson, P.J., not only will the NVA and VC men, women and children kill you, but in addition, so will this cluster-fuck of incompetent leaders. And, to make matters worse, half the time you got some new idiot in the hole next to you that has a tumor for a brain." He seemed to reflect on that for a moment, enjoying his own words, not realizing we were new guys.

"It happens all the time. The Nam's full of shitheads," he said disgustedly. Then he belched and said, "Boot officers are always calling artillery or gunships in on us. I forgot how many times artillery from our own guns was misdirected. And those new b's boot to the Nam, accidentally blowing themselves or someone else away. One time I was on a night bush with my old unit and a Marine patrol stumbles into us. We opened up and by the time we realized it was Marines, a couple were history. I'm talking dead, brother! I'm telling you guys there's just too many ways to get bagged. You know what I mean?"

Of course P.J. and I didn't know what he meant yet. We were really still "boots to the Nam." We were working on a month in country and had only touched on what the old timers had seen. But later that same night I got up to move, and Rat fired on me, thinking I was an enemy in front of the lines. It was my fault for moving out front without telling him.

Nothing much happened during the next couple of weeks. P.J., as usual, was crazed, eating live lizards and tree frogs, but for the most part, life was boring. The rain stopped and the heat began as patrols were sent out but no contact. 106s fired nightly, with no particular target in mind, simply to harass and intimidate suspected enemy positions. P.J. kind of got off on it, though, he liked the flash and sounds of explosion going out and the inevitable distant impact, and he would always volunteer the next day for the patrol the rest of us would want to avoid.

I liked P.J. so much, but God, I thought he was crazy. However, I thought I was crazy too. Crazy to be stuck here in the middle of a war I knew so little about.

My Dearest Kristen,

The last few days have been uneventful, and, as always, lonely and empty without you. I don't mind the days so much. I'm usually busy doing something. It's the nights I can't take. Those long minutes that run into hours and make my not being with you almost unbearable. There are times when I lay back and close my eyes or hold your picture that I can see and feel and smell you next to me.

Without the thought of coming home to you and our soon to be born child, I'd go nuts over here. Even now I can see you waiting for me when I get off that plane, coming home.

I can see you running to hold me in your arms. Like back in high school when I won the District Wrestling Championship, and the crowd went crazy and stormed me, slapping me on the back, and you rushed across the mat and jumped into my arms. Remember, for a few moments, I was a hero. Over here I'm nothing.

God, I wish we were together back home, living our lives like we should be. Just before we were to be sent overseas, I remember standing under an archway at Camp Pendleton, that had the message, "Welcome to the Gateway of the Pacific" written across the top in bold red letters. I remember standing under that archway and realizing for the first time that I was going to a war.

I remember thinking that I wouldn't be home to be with you when you had our baby, and I felt so lonely and so afraid. Oh, honey, I'll make it home, and we will soon forget about this lost year.

Tomorrow we will be choppered out of here and over to L.Z. Stud. Quang Tri is 3/9's rear, if that makes any sense. My squad leader said it's located just a few miles outside a city called Da Nang. I guess it's got showers and stuff. I could use one. It's been weeks. Anyway, we will rest up and get resupplied.

It's incredible, babe, I'm writing this letter by the moonlight. It's beautiful and calm tonight... all I need is you.

> Love you,
> Jack
> August 1968

At night
Alone, my heart sings
Knowing that I love you
Beyond

> Tenderly.

To My Unborn Child:

I think it's time I write you and tell you where I am and what I'm doing. Some day when you grow up I want you to know how important you were to me and how I thought of you so much when I was here.

I'm in a war in a little country called Vietnam. I'm here because our country says we're needed. I don't understand it all, and maybe I never will. But our lieutenant says maybe someday our being here will be important. I don't know. I do know it's hot and hard and scary and sad sometimes. And I do know I love and miss your mother very much.

I'm a young dad (well, almost) and that's kind of scary too. But I'll get to grow up with you, I guess.

I know how hard it is on your mom. And I would give anything to be there when you are born. But when I come home, I'll never leave you again.

I love you, my child.

Your Dad
August 1968

Eight

IT WAS MIDMORNING on a cloudless day as the Chinook made its descent into the Valley, did a wide bank to the left, drew back and followed a straight line descending gradually toward LZ Stud. We were only a couple of miles out, and from the nose of the chopper we could see the lines of the perimeter snaking their way across the green valley like links of pasture fences. P.J. and I were seated directly opposite each other, along with twenty others, and all of us filthy, caked with several weeks of digging, eating, and sleeping in the bush. We were very tired, and very happy to be going to Stud to rest and resupply.

"You got a smoke?" Rat asked, with a silly grin on his face.

"Rat, you know I don't smoke."

He looked disappointed, punched me gently on the arm and then sarcastically added, "Right, boot. You don't now... but you will!" Then he faced front while the wind seemed to catch his big ears as it whipped through the chopper windows, bullet holes, and doors, rustling our pant legs and helmetless hair.

From the air, Stud was a maze of reddish dirt roads, lying in flat figure eights, crisscrossing fields of green and sun-scorched yellow brown. Clusters of large cream-colored tents sagging from too much weather and too much use formed little beehives of constant activity. There were swarming jeeps, trucks, tanks and men working around sand-bagged bunkers with sand-bagged roofs, connected by sand-bagged waist-deep trenches. In the middle of it all, next to the artillery, but not far from the road, standing proud, stationary and tall, was an outdoor movie screen.

"We skated this ride in," the door gunner said as the chopper touched down. The back door opened and we scrambled off, bent over, ducking under the blades' wash, carrying rifles in one hand, while holding helmets on our heads with the other. We rushed to get clear of the swirling dust and rested on our packs about fifty yards from where we were dropped.

Buddy lit a cigarette and took a long drag, holding the smoke in his lungs and then slowly exhaling like he was smoking dope. "We're going to get allll fucked up!" he said, smiling.

When the rest of our platoon landed we picked up our gear and took off for our assigned area. We were in the center of the circular perimeter, just a short distance from the movie screen. Once there, we dropped our packs and rifles, dug holes to hide from incoming, and threw up quick-poncho tents. Having completed these tasks, the rest of the day was ours.

"Say, Jackson, my man, let's go toke up," Buddy said.

"No thanks, I'm going down by the river and hit the shower."

"That's cool, fool, we'll catch yer act later," he said, going off to get stoned with most of the remaining squad members.

I was sitting next to my tent daydreaming about a shower as I made some hot chocolate. Tiny and Pigpen were still putting up their plastic home next to me and arguing about location like two married people, when P.J. walked up.

"Come on, Jackson, you dog dick. Let's go do a number with the guys."

"No, man. I think I'll walk around or write the old lady."

"If you write her, could you do me a favor?" P.J. inquired in an unusually serious tone.

"What?"

"Ask her to send me a pair of her panties," he said laughing.

"Get out of here, you pervert."

This being my first trip to LZ Stud, I wanted to explore on my own.

LZ Stud was more than a firebase, it was a huge sprawling fortress surrounded by mountainous terrain. It was overflowing with artillery, tanks, trucks and men. Between operations, companies or battalions would come here to rest and recuperate. It was a place to relax and try to forget about the bush and the war, which was oftentimes impossible, with almost daily shellings or sniper fire. But it wasn't really as intense as the bush and it made me feel good being surrounded by such heavy firepower. It would take hell to get us out. And besides, it was such a sprawling complex, I felt safe, knowing there was always a bunker to hide in, or a tank to duck behind. If you were in a grunt unit, it was also one of the few places you could come to and feel secure smoking dope.

I left Pigpen and Tiny still fussing over their little home and wandered around looking for nothing in particular, until I stumbled onto the showers.

Bordering a shallow, slow-running river, the showers resembled what you might run cattle through in a slaughterhouse. Made from iron tubing, they resembled farming field sprinklers mounted upside down. A large long black hose was set open-mouthed in the water and led back up the river bank to a pump. From there the water was pumped to the showers. The water was always cold, but the weather was always hot, so despite their lack of visual appeal, the showers were a great hit and wildly appreciated. For the grunts coming in from the bush, there was another area set up for exchanging old uniforms for new.

As I approached, there were about thirty to forty naked Marines standing together, wetting themselves down and lathering up. It had been several weeks since I had last bathed, so being clean would be a welcome experience.

Suddenly from behind me, I heard, "Hey, Sweetpea, surprise. I ripped off a couple of doobies and thought I'd join you." Turning, I saw P.J. staggering toward me, obviously already high. We stripped naked and tossed our old fatigues into a bin, placed our clean new uniforms in neat piles, then jumped into the shower.

"P.J., this is outstanding," I said, as water splashed over me.

"Jackson, this is better than some sweet thing tugging on my carrot."

The water felt so cool and refreshing that we could have stayed there all day, but there were others waiting quietly, or shouting chants of "Hurry up, I got a hot one waiting to cool off," or "'Bout time, the fuckin' river's gettin' low."

Reluctantly we stepped out, hurried to dress, and began our shuffling from one intrigue to the next. As we walked by some troops who had yet to shower, I could smell them twenty feet away.

"Damn, Jackson, we didn't smell that bad, did we?" P.J. asked.

"Probably worse."

We talked to a couple of shirtless Marines sitting on a tank, wearing dark sunglasses with peace medallions hanging from their necks, who said, "Party tonight in Bunker 5 by the guns." Then we checked out the movie screen.

"Blows my mind, Jackson," P.J. said, marveling at the screen, "Blows my fuckin' mind. Now if I can only find some sweet little lady to blow my..."

"Come on, P.J., I thought that shower would cool you down."

P.J. and I walked back toward our area.

"What do you think, Jackson? You wanna hit Bunker 5 tonight and do a trip on your head?"

"I'll go, but I'm not smoking that shit."

"Don't you want to get twisted?" he said, rolling his eyes in his round cherub face and then crossing them for effect.

"I'm already twisted. I must be. I'm hanging out with your crazy ass."

Then he playfully threw a punch at me and reached up and wrapped his arm around my shoulder and neck as we walked.

We crossed through the center of the perimeter past bunkers and tents back to our area where several Marines were now cooking on barbeques made out of empty 50-gallon drums, split in half and lying sideways. Marines were drinking warm Pabst or Black Label in clusters of four or five as Sly and the Family Stone rocked loudly from a tape deck. "Higher. Gonna take you higher."

A group of blacks dressed in shorts and bush covers and sunglasses were singing and dancing in a tight circle, shouting along with Sly and his family.

"Higher. Gonna take you higher. Baby, baby, baby..."

It was late afternoon and the heat was still sweltering. A truck pulled up and more cases of beer were tossed out. P.J. and I grabbed a few and tried to catch up with Sly. We chewed on tough, dry-tasting meat and sucked beers, enjoying the party. The music was loud and the beer was great, as my mind began to dull.

Buddy, Smitty and Ski staggered up to P.J. and me as we sat drinking beer on a row of sandbags about twenty yards from the beer-tossing truck.

"These two boys is ripped... I mean ripped!" Smitty said, smiling and pointing his thumbs back over his shoulders at Buddy and Ski. Smitty was grinning a smile bigger than a guy just paroled, and laughing at the off-kiltered walk of his two buddies. "Hell, they is three or four kinds of fucked up!"

They were smashed on a combination of the best pot you could smoke, and the warmest beer you could drink.

"Now, I ask you, is that any way for our fearless leader to act?" I asked, making note of Ski's extremely inebriated condition.

"Listen, scumbags," Ski said in a very slow, deliberate laid-back manner. "I'm," and he paused and tried to collect his wits. "I'm just gettin' primed... in time for the flick."

"What's showing?" P.J. asked, his attention heightened. "I hope it's something hot and nasty!" he added, rubbing his crotch and hanging his tongue out.

"I DON'T GIVE A FLYING FUCK. I'm just gettin' tuned up," Ski added, heavy-eyed with a kind of 'drunk and pissed off for nothing' look. He carefully sat down on the ground, lay back and covered his face with his bush cover.

As Ski bit the dust, dozing into a place the mind occupies when on a drug-induced overload, Rat walked up, looking like Mickey again in his new grunt uniform. "Hey, who punched out this chump's lights?" he asked, kicking Ski playfully in the side and looking down.

"He's just a weak tit!" P.J. said. "A boot! Can't handle the smoke." Then, reaching down, P.J. and Rat lifted Ski by the arms and tried to stand him up.

"Wake up, you chump dude. Come on, hero, you're missing the war," Rat said, steadying Ski.

"Hey, Dumbo, I need some Z's," Ski protested, shaking off Rat.

"Eat the big one. We're heading towards dark. We're gonna haul your stupid ass over to the screen and catch the flick," Rat ordered.

"Jackson," Rat said, "you and P.J. help this worthless fuck of a squad leader over to the flick. I'll see if Tiny and Pigpen are still playing house."

"We saw Tiny about an hour or so ago down by the shitters," P.J. offered. "He's probably still in there pounding his pud."

We headed ragged ass and out of formation over to the screen as darkness began smothering the day.

"Hey, shitbirds, sit your funky asses down over here." It was Tiny. However, he was obviously in a world of hurt. Sitting next to Pigpen, he tried to stand up, but fell back down and quickly gave up on that idea.

"Sheett, I'm all kinds of fucked up. Now sit your ass down," he said, slapping the ground. We obeyed. A couple of platoons of grunts, most of them stoned or on their way to being drunk, sat huddled in the trampled grass and dirt. Beers were being tipped, a couple of transistors were rocking, and as it grew dark, joints were being fired up and passed discreetly from man to man. Getting lit wasn't the worry. But fear of the C.O.'s finding you getting high was always on everyone's mind.

"Want a hit, brother?" someone said. "Hey, all right," said another.

"Gimme that shit," a black voice said.

"Over here, man," another voice shouted from somewhere.

"Sorry, it's my last toke."

"Well, kiss my ass, if you ain't a sorry motherfucker," the same black voice said, unseen in the darkness.

"My main man is on tooooonight!" Tiny said.

"What you talkin' about, man?" Little Smitty had to bitch a-bout something.

"I'm talkin' about the baddest dude outside of me!!"

"Buddy ain't here yet," I interjected. A bad joke.

"Shit, Jim, I'm talking about Clint Eastwood."

"All *right*, all *right!*" We were visibly impressed.

Smitty was the most excited. "Oh, man! Oh, man! Come on now, you jerking us around?"

"That's the story, morning glory," Buddy said, sneaking up on us from behind. "Just talked to the dude on the projector. And if we don't catch any stray rounds, we'll be into "The Good, The Bad and The Ugly."

"All right! All right!" The crowd was getting restless.

"Turn on the flick!" a voice yelled.

"Crank that baby up."

"Hey, wake this boy up," P.J. said, punching Ski, who had passed out despite the news of Clint Eastwood. "Wake your ass up. We're gettin' hit, we're gettin' hit!" he said with some meaning.

"Huh? What? Huh? Where?" Ski started to snap to. "What the fuck are you talking about? We ain't being hit." He realized he had been had. He was all business now, and a little annoyed at the joke, and our laughter. "What'sa matter with you airheads? Huh? Huh?"

"You see that fool?" Buddy asked, referring to Ski's battle to wake up quickly and survey the situation. "Corporal Ski gonna save our ass," Buddy said, mocking the now alert Ski. Again we all laughed, and Ski forced a smile.

"Well, take a bite!" he said.

A voice from the crowd yelled out, "It's on!" and a chorus of cheers went up as we all settled in, concentrating on the screen.

The movie progressed smoothly with shouts from the crowd of "Turn it up! Turn it up!" or "Move your ass outta the way," or "Get some for a fat man!"

"Man, I love Eastwood," Buddy said, sitting next to me. "He's good therapy for minds that need a rest."

"You know, Jackson," Buddy whispered again. "World War II

vets had their John Wayne. We got Eastwood. He's our Super-man. His strength is that he doesn't need anyone. Just like us. I mean, he's a cold motherfucker. At least on the outside. And every time he blows another Mexican or bad guy away, he's won. He's survived. It's a personal victory, and you know, pal, that's the way it is with us."

But as the flick progressed, I thought instead of Jimmy and the mortars and the rockets, and the Vietnamese kids begging "Gimme chow. Gimme chow." And I drifted to Kristen, and how it felt to be with her. I thought how bizarre it was to be sitting here watching a movie. But then the movie ended pre-maturely. A fight had broken out up front, near the screen and some crazed marine stood up and emptied his 16 into Eastwood and the Mexicans, killing a couple of Marines unfortunate enough to be in the way.

Dear Kristen,

It's been so long since I made love to you... I'm go-ing crazy again. We are at LZ Stud now, and will be here a few more days. I have seen some strange things since I have arrived, but none of them harder to take than being without you.

You know, we still haven't decided on a name for our baby. I like the name Chad for a boy or Jenny for a girl. Chad. Jenny. You know, I have never met a Jenny I didn't like.

Chad. Now I really like the way that sounds. I can see it now. Our Chad, outstanding athlete. And I'll al-ways be there. "Hey, Chad, why don't you get your old man and we'll play catch with the football," one of his friends might say. Or, "Chad, you have the great-est dad."

I wish I could have had that with my dad. You know, babe, my dad means well, it's just that his drinking controls him. I'll never get drunk in front of our kids. They will never see us scream or fill our voices with hate. We'll love them, take care of them, and they'll always be proud.

I can see it now. He'll be a great high school quarterback. "Chad's got the ball, he fades back, the linemen are almost on him, he eludes one, and then another, he's scrambling. Look, he's spotted a receiver in the end zone. It's a long pass. The end leaps up. Perfect. Touchdown! The game's over. He won the game. He's a hero!" He'll be a great kid and I'll be a great dad.

Oh, Babe, I love and miss you so much.

Tomorrow we go on an Operation. I'll write again soon.

Jack

August 1968

P.S. P.J. says Hi. He wants to know if you can line him up with a well endowed nymphomaniac?

P.S.S. I just had a thought. Champ sounds good, or Chad. I don't know. I do know I miss you more than you will ever know. I know it's hard for you, being pregnant and having to work at that hamburger joint all day. And I'm sure it's kind of awkward around your house. But hang in there. You're my champion girl. The best in the world. I love you, baby.

We stayed drunk and screwed up at Stud for a couple more days, exchanging stories of boot camp and how P.J. had made a name for himself with his outrageous behavior. Once when we were in advanced training, we had weekend liberty. We went in to Oceanside and then on to Anaheim. There was P.J., and me and two or three other guys trying to maintain an inebriated state and cause a little trouble.

As we were walking down Motel Row across from Disneyland, P.J. stopped and did an about face and marched into a pet store we had just passed. He walked around with everybody following and wondering what he would do. He stopped at the cage stocked with lizards and chameleons.

"Can I help you?" the storekeeper asked.

"Yes, I believe I'll have one of those," P.J. said in a very serious and polite manner. Then he opened the lid and reached inside and pulled out a small lizard and followed the store-keeper up to the cash register.

"Would you like a little box for him, or a small wire cage?" the shopkeeper asked.

"No, thank you," P.J. replied, handing him the money. "I'll have him here!" Then he bit off the lizard's head, spit it into a garbage can by the register, and, placing the lizard in his mouth with the hind legs and tail hanging out, walked out of the store.

After relaxing for several days, we were about to be choppered out, up into the mountains to set up another firebase to run patrol from. The sun was still on its rise as P.J., Ski and I and the rest of the squad scrambled on board.

"I sure hope we aren't headed towards Mother's Ridge," Ski said, sitting next to me and shouting above the chopper's noise. "We got hit there on Valentine's Day. Ambushed our battalion. Had 28 KIAs. It was so bad, dudes were running on the back of Medivacs that were flying out wounded. Jesus, it was bad!" he kept saying, shaking his head. "I shit you not. It was bad, dude."

We were flying high, trying to stay out of the range of small arms. It didn't work. The rounds came and rattled through the Chinook, hitting no one. The gunner yelled, "Grab your balls! We got a hot LZ!" and opened fire with his .60, spraying the jungle.

My right leg shook uncontrollably. I wondered if I'd ever get used to this.

The Chinook swooped down and hovered over the ground for a few long seconds, kicking up dirt and fallen limbs from blown apart, broken trees. Rounds twanged and whacked and whizzed by. The door gunner fired on, spraying randomly and casually as if he were watering a garden. The Chinook dropped, then settled down. "The nose is at twelve o'clock," Ski shouted, standing up. "Spread out and set your asses in from one to six." The back ramp opened and we swarmed out. There was an explosion about 25 yards away, blowing up dirt, followed by a steady stream of rounds slashing from the jungle.

P.J. and I dove into rough heavy thicket to avoid the invisible enemy. P.J.'s helmet flew off and rolled in front of him, just as he was opening up. "Oh, shit!" he said, "I just blew a hole in my goddamn helmet." I started to laugh, forgetting to be scared. The Chinook lifted off, kicking up dirt and whipping us with its wash, leaving us behind.

Our squad crawled into position, forming a makeshift perimeter, and started firing. A few frags were tossed and we continued firing, at nothing. Choppers flew wide circles above, waiting for green smoke to signal that we were secured as we continued to recon by fire. It felt good to empty a couple of magazines into the trees and jungle. I felt power surging through me. Throw a frag, duck, then blow the hell out of the jungle. It was such a high to be dishing it out. To be firing and emptying magazines. It was a powerful undeniable sensation to open up and not receive return fire. It was like I was controlling a game. Like playing war as a kid. I enjoyed the rifle's kick and the smell of rounds cooking and the feel of snapping a magazine in place. It was a high and I was getting off on it.

Our firing subsided as choppers came in, dropped off troops and supplies, and lifted away to pick up more.

With the enemy contact broken, a patrol was sent out to recon the area and immediately the process of carving out another firebase began. We were faced with dense, steep mountainous jungle with no sign of villages or rice paddies.

Artillery was going to be dropped in a few hours so additional working parties were formed to dig parapets. Ten men would shovel furiously for ten minutes then rest as another ten troopers dug deeper until their turn to rest. The building of our fire base was extremely well orchestrated. Each man had a specific job as holes were dug, concertina wire strung, mortars set and machine guns placed.

"Hurry up. Dig in, men," the C.O. shouted, "or we'll have hell tonight."

The firebase was constructed in three flat tiers. The 105s occupied the highest level. They were choppered in, hanging from long slings attached to the bellies of the giant Chinooks. As the guns were lowered they would swing like pendulums until they settled into the freshly dug parapets. The second level consisted of mortars and the command post, and on the third level was our landing zone. Wire was strung around the entire three tiers, while inside the wire we dug our holes. As the day drifted toward night, the last piece of heavy artillery was dropped and our perimeter was completed.

The sky was falling fast as clouds rolled in on dark gloomy waves suggesting the ominous approach of heavy monsoons. As the weather changed I felt like the universe was sucking in, closing us off. I felt uneasy, like a hurricane or a tornado was about to hit. All the mountains and miles of jungle seemed quiet as if waiting.

Our last-minute digging and building of hooches was frantic and isolated, like the only life, the only living being done, was here on our three-level mountain.

Our firebase was becoming a separate world, surrounded and enveloped by a tormenting calm.

P.J., crazed as usual, volunteered for a listening post for the night, so Buddy and I pitched ponchos together. As the sky fell we quickly cleared and hollowed out the earth, making a flat bed of dirt to sleep on. We formed a retaining wall and dug a ditch to keep the water from seeping in and soaking us. We strung our ponchos above our bed and then tied them between two trees and anchored them at four corners to the ground. We were proud of the tent we had constructed. Our work was detailed and meticulous. Our house was strong and should protect us from the expected monsoon rain. If the NVA attacked, we could slide from our two-man tent into our deep hole and blow a claymore or throw frags down the mountain's steep side. It felt good to be ready.

Then the rain came. Suddenly. Not in drizzles or showers or downpours. It came in floods of wet wind blowing powerful and cold. The sky became huge balloons of black; bursting and showering us with waterfalls. The Nam was kicking ass, knocking down tents, blowing Snoopys away or soaking them thick and wringing wet. The storm came in sudden waves of apocalyptic rain and darkness. It was ripping, ravaging and slapping through the jungle. It came and went and came again, stronger and louder, howling like a monstrous beast. Tiny and Pigpen battled and lost their tent to swooping gusts of wind. Tidal waves poured from the sky as more tents flew and were torn from the ground.

Then suddenly, the storm was gone. It was quiet and it was gone.

All around us, Ski, Rat, Smitty, Tiny and Pigpen were cursing the gods and frantically trying to strike another home; to build another tent before the rains came back, before the shadow of night wrapped around us and ended our sight.

Parts of our dirt floor were wet from the rain blowing in the open front. But we were dry. The trenches we had dug to catch the spilloff had done their job. The water was flowing freely down them, away from our two-man tent. Our tent had held. Barely. But it held.

The dark was on us now as Buddy and I sat up, our heads touching the roof of our plastic home. The rain began again in gentle tappings, trickling off our ponchos, dripping loudly. No one moved, the tents were once again secure. It was quiet, soothing, and calm. We sat for awhile not speaking.

"Jackson," Buddy said, interrupting the silence. "This Nam is a son-of-a-bitch." It was so dark I could barely see Buddy's face, even though he was sitting next to me. But I could sense a tired urgency in his voice. For the past few days he had been quieter than usual and now he was talking slowly, as if he were drained of all energy.

"I'm getting worn out by this war."

"I hear ya, Bud."

"And, well, like tonight."

"What about it?"

"Well... this night reminds me," he said, dropping off, not completing his sentence.

"Of what?"

"Oh, I know this sounds weird, but tonight reminds me of the night before my first patrol."

I could sense he needed to talk, so I listened hard, like that one night in boot camp when Lewis made us cry. I listened, knowing somehow it would be important.

"I had only been in the Nam a couple of weeks. Not long enough to see the shit," he said, his voice laced with depression. "It rained that night before the patrol, and even though it wasn't a bad storm, and even though we weren't in the mountains, it was like tonight. It sounded and felt like tonight. You know what I'm saying?" I was absorbed, hanging on to his words. "Anyhow, the night before, we had sent out a four-man fire team to patrol near a ville and set up an ambush. They got hit just as the rain started and we lost radio contact with them. I knew it was bad, you understand? It was bad." His voice dropped to a whisper. I could feel his words grabbing hold of me. I was a kid now, listening to a frightening story.

"There was a lot of firing and explosions," he went on. "By the time the firefight had stopped, the rain and wind was going full blast. The C.O. couldn't send out another squad under those conditions and risk losing more men. So, we had to wait until first light. When morning came, we moved out. We passed by an open area of rice paddies and on into a tree line." His voice grew weak and childlike. "I was sweatin' it. I thought we were about to get hit. Anyhow, we could tell that's where our guys got it. But there were no bodies, nothing. Only trails of blood and empty cartridges." His words seemed to crawl inside of me and become the memories I never had. I could feel his fear as my stomach tightened and the images became clear.

He stopped and paused as if he were a long way off, thinking. "We reached the ville, but it was empty, so we began searching." Again, he paused, only longer, his voice a whining whisper.

"I found 'em," he said, trying not to cry. "I found 'em," he sobbed. "I found the fire team inside a grass hut." He didn't say anything for a few minutes, but when he spoke again, his voice sounded haunted and had aged a thousand years. "They had been butchered... they were naked, hanging upside down from the ceiling." He stopped for what seemed like minutes. "They were slit open, like deer, man, like animals! Their guts hanging in their faces and their balls and cocks... Jesus, their balls and cocks were cut off and stuffed in their mouths!" he cried.

My stomach contracted as if to puke.

"A black corporal from Texas I had just met, I mean I just met the dude," he pleaded. "Didn't have no head! The fucker didn't have no head!" Buddy began to cry harder. "I know I act like a bad ass, but Jesus, man, sometimes I can't stand it anymore!" His cries were deep and without regard. "I've just been here too long."

I couldn't listen to him any longer. I couldn't stand it. His words punished me and beat me. I tried to forget. I wanted to be home. I wanted to forget. I wanted to lose myself in thoughts of Kristen. But his images were strong. They wouldn't leave me. I saw the fire team. I saw them hanging, and I couldn't stand it.

Why did he tell me? Why did it happen? Why was I here? I wanted to scream and cry and hold Buddy. I was caught up and lost in colors of red and blood, cocks and balls. And I was angry. Why weren't there more men on the night patrol? Why couldn't the others leave to help them? Why had the fire team walked into the tree line? What the fuck was going on? My head swirled and I held Buddy tight. Oh, Kristen, Kristen, Kristen.

Finally the images dissolved, and I listened to the rain and thought of how it sounded as it hit and rolled off the plastic roof and out onto the ground.

I remembered that sound now. And I started to drift back to Kristen. I faded into the past and lost myself in her and the sound of the rain. I was floating outside myself. Drifting. I wasn't in Vietnam. I was seventeen, in high school and in love. I listened to the rain and remembered it and remembered her. It was coming back to me. I was there. I remembered it now. I remember.

It was midnight, and I'd climbed up on top of her family's porch to her bedroom window. I was going to wait right there by her window until she came home. We had argued earlier in the day. I knew she was out with some other guy, and I would wait right there until she came home. Then I would jump off the porch and kick his ass and tell her we were through.

I wanted her to be just mine. I wanted her to understand how important that was. But she was out with some guy. I'd show her.

It was raining, but that didn't bother me. And it was cold, but I didn't care. It kept getting later and later, and the rain came down harder. I was confused and hurt. Where were they? I never had her out this late. And she told me she loved me!

It was raining hard when the window to Kristen's bedroom opened, and she leaned out. "Are you still there?" she asked. "I got home hours ago. Come on in." I crawled through her window. She told me she didn't really have a date with anyone else. She loved me and was sorry we had fought the day before. I felt like a fool and I needed her. I took off my clothes and climbed into bed. We held each other. I remembered now, how she felt... so warm, so good. I touched her gently, carefully. I kissed her mouth and neck and took her breast. Soon I was inside her, breathing heavy, melting, loving her strong.

"Jackson?" Buddy asked, shaking me from my thoughts.

"What, Bud?" I asked.

"Please don't tell anyone I cried."

"I won't Buddy, I won't."

Several nights later, word was passed from the C.P. "Jackson," P.J. said, "Lieutenant Neal wants you."

I thought I was in trouble now. But for what? Hell, I didn't know. It was very dark. I made my way up to the C.P. "You called for me, Lieutenant?" I whispered, crouching in the darkness, making sure not to raise my voice.

"Got some news for you. The Red Cross just called, and your wife had a baby."

"A baby?" I shouted, amazed and much too loud.

"Yep. You expected maybe a gook begging for chow?"

"How big?" I beamed.

"Six pounds, eight ounces."

"Gosh, thanks!" I was smiling so big I thought my face would crack. I started to leave.

"Jackson."

"Yes, sir." I stopped.

"It's a girl. Jenine, I think they said."

"Yes, sir. Thanks, sir." Then I made my way in the dark back to my hole and dug it a little deeper.

Dear Kristen,

I'm still stuck here on this damn firebase. It's been raining for the last two weeks. We are really socked in, haven't been resupplied for over a week because of the weather. The sky is dark and overcast and the wind and rain so strong that they can't get choppers in. It's really miserable.

I'm hungry. We've been out of food for days and people are starting to get edgy. Just a couple of hours ago a fight broke out over a can of crackers. One guy pulled his 16 and said he was going to blow the other guy away. Hunger can really do things to your morale.

This is a real low point, hon, but things will have changed by the time you read this letter.

We have been running patrols off the firebase daily, but have seen little contact. It's a lot quieter during the monsoon season, so maybe the rain is a blessing in disguise. I sure hate it, though. I know this sounds terrible, but I came in off an L.P. last night so wet and cold and tired, that when I laid down to sleep, I pissed on myself to keep warm.

I know all this is depressing. Forgive me, hon.

How's our baby Jenine? I received the picture you sent of her. I'm looking at her now. She's so beautiful. I can hardly wait until we're together again. In a couple of months I can put in for my R & R and Hawaii will be ours.

I forgot to mention that the night I heard you had Jenine, little Smitty got so lonesome for his wife and kids and afraid that he wouldn't make it back to the world that he asked me to break the fingers on his right hand so he could go back to the rear. I didn't want to, but he was so scared something would happen to him and he'd never see home. So, I grabbed his first two fingers and snapped them real quick. He screamed and went to the C.P. and said he fell down.

The doc said they were broken, and he was Medivac'd the next morning. He was so happy. He was a friend, and I know he'd do it for me.

Well, I'll run now. Love you so much.

Jack

September 1968

P.S. Send me something to read, will you? When the weather clears we are going back to Stud and I'll have some more free time.

On my nineteenth birthday, I was Medivac'd back to LZ Stud. It was two weeks after the birth of our daughter, Jenine. I had ringworm over 80% of my body, and with all the rain there was absolutely no chance of arresting or curing it in the bush. The ringworm was annoying, but anything was better than the bush.

I spent the next few days on work details filling sandbags, burning shitters or standing guard duty. The rain was still constant and monotonous, but it curbed enemy probes and rocket attacks. With the mud and adverse weather, movement around Stud was greatly diminished, so sagging tents full of card games and getting high were the big highlights.

Most of my time was spent writing to Kristen and worrying if she was all right, if she had enough money, and how she was adjusting to my absence now that she had our baby. I dreamed about how things should have been; how I should have been with her when Jenine was born.

Our life was difficult, but I never doubted we'd be together again. The one thought that dominated my mind was coming home and having Kristen there to hold me, to know that it was all finally over.

My Baby Kristen,

I'm so tired. Morning is nearly here. I have a poem for you written while standing watch in an old sandbag bunker.

Alone,
by an emberless fire
staring out at a jungle sea,
dawn breaks
as my heart does.
Another night wasted
without you.

I love and miss you. I'm so proud of you and our baby. I'll be a good dad. I'll be a dad Jenine will be proud of.

Love, Jack

September 1968

P.S. If I can get promoted soon, I could make $26.00 more a month.

Nine

I WAS STILL at Stud sitting in my little plastic home, reading and listening to the rain pop against the poncho roof. I was warm and dry, and a far cry from the soaking bush. I had built a wooden floor for my hooch from two wooden pallets that I had ripped off from the supply area. I was actually enjoying myself. Just sitting there, reading, listening to the rain and finishing off the last of a cup of hot cocoa, when the choppers started coming in. I dropped *Hamlet,* tossed aside my now finished cup of cocoa, put on my boots and made a mad dash for the LZ.

"Hey, you skating mother, what's happening?" It was Buddy, with P.J. next to him, and the rest of the squad in hot pursuit. They ducked under the rotors and ran clear of its noise and wind-swirling wash.

"Hey, what's the story, morning glory?" P.J. asked, grinning and giving me a brother handshake. "Skate, we thought the old ringworm ate your ass alive," P.J. added, kicking me in the butt and gesturing up the hill. "Let's go up to the armpit and out of this fuckin' rain."

"Wait up for the rest of us ladies," Ski yelled, hurrying to catch up. The rest of the squad was soon off the back of the Chinook and we headed up to the platoon's campsite.

It had only been a few days since I last saw my buds, but it seemed like weeks and it was good to see their skinny faces again. P.J. moved into my place right off, saying "Fuck you" to the rest of the squad. And then, gesturing toward me, while throwing his pack inside my hooch, said, "Me and my bitch is back together again," and he crawled inside.

Later that day we added a couple more ponchos and wooden pallets to our hooch so that we could share the company of Rat and Buddy. That night Buddy bought a "party pack" of eleven joints from some dude down by the showers. He came back to my hooch and got loaded with Rat and P.J. I was the only one who didn't smoke.

"Come on, you big bitch, take a hit of this joint," P.J. said to me, extending his arm and handing me the roach. "Listen, partner, this is *double deadly!*"

I pushed it away. "If I wanted to lose my mind, all I'd have to do is listen to you jerks for an hour or two." I had a secret fear of getting too stoned and not being able to respond correctly in a tight situation. I had a wife and newborn baby to worry about, and had to make it home for them.

We sat in our grown-up fort that night, with two candles lit, listening to a small tape deck play some Bob Dylan while we talked about home and food and dope and whatever else popped into our minds.

"I'm gonna ship me back a truckload of this Mary Jane," P.J. said, taking a long drag and holding the smoke deep in his lungs, then exhaling in a loud blast of air. "I'm gonna make money sellin' this rag weed to all those long-hair hippie faggots that are skating back in the world."

"It's good dope, that's for sure," Buddy said, holding the smoke in, then finally exhaling. "Say, P.J., you got something to eat?" he asked, stony-eyed and slow.

"Just C-rats."

Buddy was temporarily transfixed by the flickering candle light and the slow melting of the wax before he responded like a drunk coming to. "Man, come on. You must have something to eat," he said, as he picked up a candle to observe it more closely. He faded, then came back. "Come on, your aunt or some shit sends you chocolate chip cookies, and I'm sooo hungry. Come on, don't hold out on your buds."

"No cookies, but you want to chew on this?" P.J. responded,

as he grabbed his crotch.

"Ain't nothing but baby food," Buddy laughed.

The next morning those wonderful words were called out. "Mail call, mail call," and people began appearing out from under their dirty little tents, eagerly gathering around. Whoever had the mailbag and was passing it out was that day's Santa, dressed in green.

"Rat, P.J., Tiny," the names came and we reached out eagerly, like kids for Christmas cookies. "Buddy, Rat, P.J., Jackson."

Next to his rifle, mail was the single most important thing in a grunt's life. Mail brought dreams and hope or sometimes bad news about "Jody." Jody was the generic name given to the guy back home who takes your girl from you.

"He be gettin' tight with your lady, dude. Slippin' her the long one while you're gettin' your ass shot off."

Sometimes after a 'Dear John' letter came, the recipient would go crazy, "I'll kill that Jody motherfucker, I'll stick a BB in his ear and blow it out his ass. He'll wish he'd never had a dick." And then for the next few days, the marine would do crazy things as if life meant nothing anymore. One time a kid from the second platoon got a Dear John. When he went on R & R to Bangkok, he never came back. Rumor was he somehow got stateside and wasted a Jody, then shot himself.

Mail was a lifeline for me. It was an almost spiritual infusion. A letter from Kristen about how the "baby kicks so much, hon, I'm sure she'll be a rally queen," to "I miss how you used to pick me up in your arms and rock me like a little girl" could turn even the worst of days around. And when mail didn't come I felt helpless, like there was a problem I couldn't touch.

"Hey, look at this. Look at these assholes," P.J. said, showing everyone the front page of a "Stars & Stripes" newspaper. In full color was a picture of Jane Fonda, sharing food with two North Vietnamese Army soldiers who were sitting at an anti-aircraft gun in North Vietnam. The soldiers were eating and laughing with Jane. The caption underneath read, "Jane Fonda breaks bread with the people." A long article followed about an anti-war rally that had taken place in San Francisco's Golden Gate Park. The story outlined how several thousand anti-war protesters had gone to the park to listen to Jane Fonda denounce our participation in an immoral war. Flyers with her sharing food were passed out. Evidently there was quite a turnout. There were also a lot of drugs, alcohol, rock bands and a special guest appearance by Joan Baez.

All of this information was disturbing to us. We were far from being in tune with what public mood and sentiment was, yet we realized there were some Americans who thought being here was incorrect. But the picture was devastating. It made me hate. "What's wrong with that bitch?" I said. "She makes out like we're the bad guys and the gooks are right-eous. Jane should see those Marines Buddy saw strung up like dead deer and gutted open. Maybe that would straighten out her act."

The last portion of the article described some of the signs being carried: "Kill a baby today, join the Marines," "Stop the War," "Off the Pigs," and "Make Love, not War." The final sign given detail was "U.S. Soldiers Rape Vietnamese Land and Women." That was quite amusing. We had been up in the mountains and hadn't seen a Vietnamese woman for several months.

"Those assholes are out partying while we're stuck in this shit," P.J. said, reading over my shoulder. "I'd like to waste that lame bitch," he continued, incensed. "What the fuck does that cunt think she is? Jesus, I can't believe it!"

Like P.J., I was especially hurt by the lack of compassion and understanding Fonda and her political groupies had for the individual soldier over here. We were here because our country, our president, our political leaders said we were needed, not because we wanted to kill babies.

"You know, if Jane Fonda or Joan Baez, or any of those longhairs partying wanted to help," Buddy said, "they would shut the fuck up and expend some energy sending us letters and packages. Support us, we're not the dispassionate killers. Let's just say, for the sake of argument, that the Government is completely wrong for sending us over here," he went on, realizing he now had a captive audience. "If those fucksticks were really into us and what we thought, and felt, instead of something they didn't have the slightest idea about, they wouldn't be branding us as crazed killers. They would show us sympathy, not contempt," Buddy continued, asserting himself, voicing his convictions and capturing the others' interest. "Jesus, that's all we need. We go through all of this, then go home and get shit on. They act like Fonda's some heroic figure to be honored and followed, and they act like we're chumps or maniacs."

I turned to another page and there was a picture of Fonda standing on a platform addressing a crowd and flashing a peace sign. Next to her were two signs saying, "Stop killing innocent Vietnamese," "Ho Chi Minh for President."

"I'd like to kick that bitch's ass," P.J. said, voicing the anger of us all.

"Sheettt, Jim," Tiny said slowly, with little emotion. "Victor Charles don't give a fuck 'bout no political BUULL-SHIT," Tiny added, spitting as he spoke. "You flash at Victor and he just blow your ass away."

We were growing restless. Two weeks back at Stud this time, and we were getting tired of burning shitters and standing guard duty. Sometimes just for the hell of it, when P.J. and I were on watch, P.J. would shoot off a couple of pop-ups and we would watch the parachutes with flares gently cut and sizzle through the night, illuminating the darkness. If things were really slow, we would toss a few frags or open up with the .60. It was like our own private light show. A personal altercation with boredom.

Smitty had been long gone by now, so we received a replacement named Rodeski from another squad. He was immediately nicknamed "Rodo." Rodo had just returned from R & R, so he had about four months left to do. A blond kid of about twenty, he was drafted into the crotch when he flunked out of a small college in California. He seemed like a nice kid, quiet, sensitive, and bright. He had an infectious smile and was everyone's friend. We spent quite a bit of time together and he talked about his home in Santa Barbara, his girl, surfing, and how he wanted to go back to college and become a professional student. That's all. Just go to college, surf, and get loaded like all his friends did at the student anti-war demonstrations. "Peace rallies are the 'in' thing, and they are really getting big in California," he told us, "And the anti-war rallies are blowouts. Outstanding dope, wine and great jams. It's bullshit and political, but PARTY? Get down 'n party hardy," he added gleefully. "Hey, if no one knows you're a jarhead, it's a place to belong."

A couple of days later the word was passed that we would be moving out the next morning on a big Operation. From scuttlebutt, we learned that it was going to be an ass-kicker. To make matters worse, it was battalion size, which meant we'd be out a long time. And if that wasn't bad enough, Killer Kilo would be up front, with the Third Herd leading the way and our squad at the point.

That night before the big Op, we gathered together as a squad with our radio to try and contact other grunts in the area. By switching frequency and using phony call signs we picked up others talking.

It was a truly beautiful, peaceful night as we sat around and tried to raise someone on another frequency. It hadn't rained for several days and there was a moon so bright that we could read or write letters by it. The air was fresh and clean, and the sky was so clear you could count the stars and never lose track. Sitting on a row of sandbags, I was coasting in a separate entity then, daydreaming. There was no war, and tomorrow's big Op was light years away. I was losing myself in Kristen again. Escaping. Drifting back. Back in time to Kristen. Eyes opened, looking at the stars, the war stopped, and I was there, back home again.

It was the last weekend we had together before I went into the service. We caught a bus in downtown Portland and headed for the snow and mountains. We brought along a thermos full of hot chocolate and rum that I'd bought from a drunk in front of a liquor store, some Snickers candy bars, and forty-one dollars. We had a room at Timberline Lodge on snowcapped Mt. Hood. It came complete with fireplace and view. On the ride up we sat in the back of the bus, drinking out of the thermos, sipping from one cup, caught up in each other with our eyes.

"I love you so much," I said close to her face, holding the cup with two hands as she sipped from it.

The bus wound through the mountains and up into the snow. "Timberline Lodge," the driver said. "Everybody out."

It was cold, clear and crisp. Little puffs of steam rolled from our mouths when we spoke. "It's a new snowfall," she said, taking my hand and walking toward the lodge. The earth was blanketed with miles of white and pocked with footprints and ski trails. It was an unusually clear day, and the sky was the bluest blue I had ever seen. Skiers slashed across the mountain as we tossed snow and laughed at each other. She looked so beautiful, bundled up, blue jeans tucked into her boots. She wore a white wool sweater with a red scarf and matching red stocking cap. She was my beautiful Kristen. We rented a toboggan and went sliding down the hills and through the people for hours. We slid and fell and rolled through snow so cold our teeth hurt, and held each other in our arms as if nobody else were there.

As twilight neared, we went back to the Lodge, tired and wet. Our room was like the interior of an old log cabin: clean and neat but sparsely furnished with a table, two chairs, a bed and couch. We were sitting in front of a warm crackling fire, eating cheese, and touching each other gently as we talked.

"It won't be so long. I'll be out of boot camp in a few weeks and then we can get married," I said, trying to comfort Kristen as best I could. "We'll have a small wedding, and spend a few days by ourselves. Just you and me and our little tiger in there," I added, playfully patting her belly.

"But what if you have to go to Vietnam? Honey, I'm so scared. I want to spend my life with you." Tears filled her eyes. "I'm afraid you'll get hurt. Or I could lose you forever."

"Oh, babe, don't worry. Heck, I might not even have to go..."

She started to relax. "Really?" You think there's a chance you might not have to go?"

"Sure, babe, sure," I said, holding her close. "And the military will pay for the hospital cost for our tiger and then when I get home we'll have the GI Bill to help us get started."

It was a sad but beautiful moment. The kind of moment that etched its way into my memory and could never be dissolved by time.

Standing up, we undressed, running our hands tenderly over each others' bodies. The darkened room was awash with firelight, and our shadows danced and flickered on the wall. We touched and kissed and held each other tight. "If I took all of the good qualities of everyone I've ever known," I said, pushing her hair back from her face, "and put them all together, what I'd have would still be less than you." We kissed each other deeply, breathing each other's breath.

"Say, Jackson."

I snapped to from my reverie.

"We got the radio tuned in to a different frequency and are talking to some other dudes at another firebase," P.J. was saying. "What's the word, turd? Quit day dreamin' and come on over and listen up."

"All right now, y'all listen up," Tiny hollered into the radio handset. "This is the baddest muther ever come outa Kentucky talkin'. Iny Kentucky mountain boys out thar?" he asked, greatly exaggerating his mountain twang.

"I hear ya talkin'," a voice answered. "Ain't got no Kentucky boys here. We're all from the U.S. of A." The radio answered. We all laughed, but Tiny didn't think it was funny.

"Gimme that, come on, gimme that," P.J. said, grabbing the receiver out of Tiny's hand. "Hey, all you jarheads, this is Mr. P.J. I'm a high hooker, a good looker, a lover, a fighter, a wild bull rider. I got a hard-on a yard long, and I'm looking for some-thing to start on."

"Hey, Mr. P.J.," the voice said, "you'd better spit that hard-on out, 'cause it shore don't belong to you," which made us laugh our asses off. The radio was funny tonight. Full of comedians.

"Who am I talkin' to?" P.J. asked.

"You got Chi-town, Philly and Or-gon on the horn," came the answer.

"Hold it, we got two Or-gon boys here," P.J. said and handed the radio over to me.

"This is Portland, Oregon, Number 2, coming live and not so direct from the Stud," I said.

The radio spoke back, "No shit, Portland, huh?"

"That's affirm. Been in country about four months," I said, lying a little.

"Sheett, you's a boot. I'm rotating next week," the radio answered.

His words made me realize how little time I really had spent in country. I felt depressed, so I handed over the receiver and let the other crazies run the show.

I walked over to Rodo, who was sitting by himself on a couple of old sandbags, making hot cocoa in a C-ration can. He carefully picked the can up off the little C-rat stove, which still glowed in the night like a can full of fireflies. Holding his cocoa carefully by the bent-back lid, making sure not to spill it, he said, "It's a beautiful night. Can you dig the stars? Makes you wanta just kick back and head trip." Then he took a sip. "Grab a seat, huh? Needs to be a little bit hotter." He reached into his pack and pulled out a bar of C-4 explosives, pinched off a small white chunk and placed it carefully in the fire. A quick flash followed. A moment later his cocoa was ready to drink. "This C-4 is a heck of a lot better for cooking than those heat tabs they issue us."

"I hear you talking," I said. "And they don't smell so damn bad, either. The only thing that smells worse is P.J.'s rotten farts." He laughed. "Well, tomorrow is the big Op. I guess we're headed back to the Ah Shau Valley. It's gonna be an ass kick, you can bet on that."

"No shit," he replied, sipping from his can. "It will be my third trip back there. I was there at Mother's Ridge. It was a bear."

We sat there drinking cocoa, talking comfortably about little things like sounds and smells and then about back home.

"You'll never believe what I did on my R & R, when I got to Hawaii," Rodo said, lightness in his voice.

"I give."

"I changed into civvies and hopped a plane to Santa Barbara. I met my old lady there and we drove to Reno and got married.

We partied all the way over and all the way back." Then he paused as if to add depth to his next sentence. "And I'm telling you, it was a bitch leavin' her to come back to this armpit. We even went to an anti-war rally at the University of California," he concluded as an afterthought.

"You're shittin' me!" I exclaimed as the light from the moon cast down on him, making him appear almost angelic, like an altar boy.

Then his voice began to change. "And listen to this, we didn't tell anyone we got married. We didn't even tell our folks." He let his head fall back slowly and closed his eyes. "I wish I was home."

I knew in his mind, he was.

"I'm scared," he said, whispering while bringing his head back and gradually opening his eyes. "I know it's going to be bad. I know it is." His voice became halting. "We never know where we're going, how long we'll be gone, or if we're ever coming back." He grew despondent, broken. He looked like a lost, frightened child now. "You know, I'm... I'm... just scared." The moon was lighting up his young face clearly and I could see tears trying hard not to fall. "Oh, God, I wish I was home."

He let go. His voice cracked, and the tears didn't win. He leaned his elbows on his knees and buried his face in his hands. I felt like I was intruding, but thought I should stay. Then he looked up, wiping his eyes and breathing deeply. "I'm sorry, man. I'm sorry. I'm just scared about tomorrow."

The next morning we tore down our poncho tents, gathered up our gear, threw last-minute letters into the outgoing mailbag and got saddled up, ready to move out. It was quieter than usual. The sky was washed over with thick, gloomy gray, and a thin, moist fog hung heavy in the air. The fog was enveloping us and seemed to slow us down. There were no smiles. Talk was in loud whispers or not at all. It was a graveyard come to life. It was as if depression and doom were handed out like hunks of cheese, then mouthed, swallowed and now a part of us. We looked at each other, not speaking, knowing in our hearts only one truth: before we were finished, some of us would die.

There were hundreds of us there, loaded up heavy, like mules. We were standing, sitting or lying down, our packs overflowing, with E-tools on top. Each man carried several bandoliers of magazines and ammo crisscrossed on his chest like a Mexican bandit. We toted frags and a mortar or belts of M-60 machine gun rounds.

And we waited.

There were radio men with antennas whipping and officers strapped with 45s, and dozens and dozens of helmets with bands across the top holding plastic bottles of insect repellent and white battle dressings. There were radios, machine guns, mortars, and LAWmen. We had M-79s for each platoon, and their carriers heavy-bagged with dozens of rounds. We had Corpsmen, and at the end, near the last of the long column, was a chaplain. I suppose the generals who were in the rear monitoring our movement on maps thought it nice to bring a man of God into a Godless war.

Suddenly Chinooks filled the air like seven-year locusts. The Operation was beginning.

In those few moments before the choppers landed to carry us to war, I lost what thoughts I'd once had of democracy and freedom and liberty. I forgot about being upset over Jane Fonda feeding the enemy, and I didn't hum the Marine Corps Hymn. I began to feel very frightened again. Afraid of what I couldn't control.

I thought briefly about Kristen and my new baby. That's all, and wanting very much to go home.

"Jackson," Ski said, walking over to me. "Rat's walking point, Rodo's back-up, then P.J., and you'll be the LAWman. No sweat. I'll be right behind you," he added, attempting to be reassuring.

Great, I thought, I have to carry those damn awkward LAWs. They're just more weight, and besides, those things don't fire half the time. They were supposed to be the ultimate in modern warfare. A collapsible one-shot bazooka. They were a pain in the ass to me.

Our platoon was the first one out. Then came another and another until dozens were on choppers filling the air and leaving Stud behind.

We flew through valleys with miles and miles of thick jungled mountains on both sides, pocked and cratered from B-52 strikes. We banked past Mother's Ridge, site of the Valentine's Day Massacre where Ski and Rodo were heroes, and down into Ah Shau Valley. The eerie gray mist grew thicker as we circled, banked left, made a sharp descent, and finally touched down in a clearing at the base of a huge mountain. Quickly we filed out, down the ramp, out and away from the prop wash, trampling through thick waist-high grass as we ran and formed a half circle.

The other choppers came, dropping troops again and again until we had one platoon, then two, then another and another. Then we gathered up in a long single file, each man six or seven yards from the next. We were ready now. Our squad was up front as we moved out. We moved slowly and methodically, under the weight of the full packs. Rat was point, acting as the eyes and ears of 3/9. Rodo was close behind, followed by P.J., then me, then Ski and Buddy and the others. Rodo was covering Rat while Rat looked for trip wires and booby traps along the trail and Rodo looked to the flanks for enemy dug in, waiting to ambush us. Being in the first squad made us the most vulnerable, and therefore the tension was almost unbearable. Point squad was switched often but for now we were it.

Our plan was to attack and overrun a large NVA base camp. The resistance was expected to be heavy. We were prepared for the worst. We found a well-traveled trail. Reconnaissance reports had indicated its location, but the trail had been much easier to locate than anticipated. The dirt trail zig-zagged up through heavy jungle. A thick canopy of trees and foliage covered us. The NVA would have been impossible to spot from the air. In places sparse with overhead cover, thin trees had been bent across the trail and tied with bamboo strips to other trees. The NVA had worked hard to conceal their trail.

As the path grew steeper, so did the trail's sophistication. In some places, rows of steps were dug out and lengths of tree-formed handrails had been constructed to make travel easier. At one point we passed what looked like a religious altar made from bamboo with two wooden bowls holding rice.

We were quiet. Alert. Each of us was searching, trying to see deep into the bush, peering left, straining right. Bending, breathing hard, my heart pounded in my throat and seemed to echo out my mouth. The signs were clear. We were nearing an NVA camp.

Suddenly Rat stopped up ahead. Holding his arm up for us to halt, he dropped to one knee. We all did the same. Then he waved us to move. It was OK. The column sighed. We struggled on, passing by a decomposed body on the trail. A North Vietnamese soldier, his body slumped, bloated and decaying, probably killed by the recon team. I shuddered. I was frightened as I fingered the semi-automatic switch. My M-16 was now an extension of my body.

We crept on, climbing up into the mountain. We stopped and started, with Rat always searching, bent over, senses tuned and in control. It took a very special kind of man to walk point. You had no time for thoughts of home or a bullet splashing in your face. No time to dream or cry. On point, at any time, that special stillness may erupt. Fear is always there, and yet it isn't.

Rat's eyes were on the trail up ahead. Rodo's fixed on the short flanks and extended sides. They moved as one. We were the body, following them closely. We pushed on and as we did I felt a morbid kind of déjà vu. I felt as if I had no history or future, only now and only here in this jungle, in this squad, at the front of hundreds, walking into my destiny. Thoughts of Kristen were gone.

We stopped... No one spoke... but we listened. We moved higher and deeper into the jungle, our heartbeats thundering. We knew we were getting close.

Suddenly the bush up ahead and on the right flank erupted with the crack of AKs and 16s and sounds of chi-coms exploding.

KABOOM... CRACK. CRACK. CRACK. I sucked the earth. Rounds were dancing, kicking up or slicing through the trees overhead in high-pitched TA-WANG TA-WANG CRACK. CRACK. CRACK.

"I'm hit, I'm hit," someone shouted in front. "Oh, God," came a cry from the back. The rounds were pouring from the jungle. Somewhere in front was a machine gun, laying fire. Or maybe it was off to the side. I couldn't tell.

More explosions followed and then an R.P.G. whistled overhead until shattering a tree. I found a log to hide behind as rounds impacted into it. I could see P.J. in front of me, shaking, clawing at the ground on his belly, small, trying to hug the earth as bullets impacted next to him.

Bullets slashed overhead. Ski came up next to me, bent over, laying rounds into the smoking trees. P.J. was now hidden from my view, around the bend in the trail.

I heard P.J. yell, "He's gone."

CRACK. CRACK. CRACK. The AKs opened up, keeping us low. Then suddenly we rose up, firing over the fallen tree, one, then two magazines. Ski and I were tearing ass... pumping rounds in bursts and sprays.

"Frag those motherfuckers!" Ski screamed, "frag those motherfuckers!"

Ducking below the log, I dropped my pack and pulled a grenade from my flak jacket pouch. The area we were firing on was about thirty yards to our front and off to the right. It was a long throw, but not impossible. I pulled the pin and flipped it over my head and listened as it passed through limbs and trees. KABOOM! It was short, but just barely. I threw another longer and better placed. KABOOM!

"Listen," Ski said, shaking as much as I was. "I'll pop a green smoke for cover and lay some fire and you crawl up and see what the fuck is going on up front."

Fuck you, I thought. Goddamn smoke ain't bulletproof. I liked the tree I was behind. From there I couldn't be hit. Oh, Jesus, I said to myself, no time to think. This is it! He threw the smoke. I left the tree, crawling on my belly toward P.J. He was lying on his side, trying to pull magazines off Rodo's body.

"He's dead. He's dead," P.J. said. Rodo was lying on his back, his head toward us. His eyes were open and empty. His mouth was wide, his face twisted into a blank stare of disbelief.

There was very little blood showing, just a small hole in his neck with something white hanging out. But the ground beneath the back of his neck was red and wet. He was already turning cold and pale. I tried not to gag. He was dead. That was it, and that's the way it would always be.

"P.J., he's gone. There's nothing we can do. Leave him," I said, flat and unfeeling as if I were an old soldier who had been in war all my life and had seen hundreds of nineteen-year-old boys lying dead.

"How's Rat, P.J.?" I yelled. He didn't answer, but his face told me. The firing was slow as P.J. and I crawled up the hill toward Rat, leaving Ski behind.

Rat didn't move. He was on his stomach. The big ears and smile were gone. Half of his head was blown off and particles of his brain were hanging out, splattering the bushes and lying in the mud. Three fingers on his right hand were shot off, but he still was holding his 16.

In front of him and off to one side of the trail were two more bodies, dressed in light brown. They didn't move. We didn't take a chance. P.J. and I emptied a magazine into them. It felt good.

We started to crawl back when rounds began tearing through the bush again, reminding us to stay low. P.J. and I dragged Rodo along to Ski and the safety of the fallen tree. We took his canteens, drank his water, took his ammo and his food and covered him up with his poncho. P.J. was quiet.

CRACK... CRACK... CRACK. More fire. We kissed the ground. The three of us were in love with the log, riding close. "We'll have to leave Rat 'til later," I said, taking another sip of water. "There's still a couple of gooks dug in. Maybe three or four."

"Yeah, I know," Ski said, cool and in control. "We'll get a bloop up here and blow up the place. And if that don't work, maybe we'll have the LAWman come to town."

He was crazy. It was too close, I thought. And besides, to fire the damn thing I'd have to get up from behind the tree and expose myself. No, that idea sucked. No more chances. I had had my share of crawling and John Wayneing it. I'm just fine behind this tree. I'll let ol' Luke the Gook come after me. I've got a family. No, I'm sittin' tight right behind this big old log.

Buddy crawled up the trail to our log to join P.J., Ski and me. Sweat was pouring from him. He was breathing hard, almost gasping for air. He'd always seemed calm and self-confident, but now his face was shadowed with fear.

"What the fuck is going on?" he gasped. "The Luey from the second platoon was blown away. Wouldn't get his ass down. I yelled at the boot to get down. And he took a round in the head and fell on top of me." His voice was cracking as if he were about to break down. "God damn him. I told him to get down. I told him."

"Hey, hold on, now. Hold on," Ski said, trying to calm him.

"I told him to get down. I told him to get down."

"Shut up, just shut the fuck up," Ski said, slapping Buddy's face. Buddy calmed down, his breathing slowed.

"Now listen. Rodo and Rat bought it. But Rat took a couple of gooks with him."

Buddy's face took on an aura of sick depression and then he suddenly burst into a violent rage. "I can't stand it!" Then he rose to his knees, well above the trees and started pumping rounds into the bush, yelling, "Motherfuckers, Motherfuckers!"

Ski grabbed him from behind and pulled him down hard behind the fallen log, and then screamed, inches from his face, "You dumb son-of-a-bitch! You idiot! You're going to get your ass shot off. Now shut the fuck up!"

We sat there, tense, waiting for the AKs but they didn't come. Buddy was calm again. "Sorry I blew it for a minute. Ski, got a cigarette?"

"Sure, no problem. Here, keep 'em."

It was starting to get dark. The firing had stopped. A black dude carrying an M-79 from the squad behind us came up just short of our tree and planted three or four rounds into the general area. He waited and was answered with several misplaced shots, but no machine gun fire. He tried again. More waiting, and then again a few scattered cracks hitting nothing. It was a game now. They could see us, knew where we were, but couldn't penetrate our tree. Every time the black marine with the 79 moved into position to fire, the gooks would crawl deep into the safety of their holes. They would wait for the firing to stop and then, to show us they were still around, come out and fire a few rounds.

"They've dug in just off to the right of the trail about thirty to forty yards ahead," Ski said. "They knew we were coming. Rat and Rodo just walked into them. All it is is a handful of slant-eyes, I bet, and they've got the whole fuckin' company pinned down." Ski took off his helmet, wiping his brow with his hand. "If we stay put, we're all right. If we move back we're all right. But if we move up, we might as well kiss our asses goodbye."

The only thing between us and our enemy was thirty to forty yards, some thick underbrush, and the fallen log. Our wall of protection was about two feet high and maybe fifteen feet long. We were on a slope, which helped to keep us lower than their fire. "When darkness hits, it's the Lawman up front, got it?" Ski said, and then put on his helmet and went back down the trail to grab a radio and let the rest of the platoon know what was happening.

"This is bullshit," P.J. remarked. "I could be pounding on my pud on watch instead of waitin' for Mr. Victor Charles to move his skinny little ass out that hole he's dug in. This night shit is for the birds."

We were in heavy darkness as Ski made his way back to the fallen log. "I explained the situation to Lt. Neal. He's sliding back down the hill and talking to the C.O. When he gets the scoop, he'll let us know. Apparently the whole battalion is strung out and digging in. I think we'll probably just stay put until morning. Anyway, let's dig some holes and hope the C.O. doesn't dream up some suicide shit."

Trying to stay low and out of range, we lay on our sides and dug in, close to the log. It was a dark, moonless night. It was a night I knew I would remember no matter how hard I tried to forget.

Fear began to edge its way into my mind and manifest itself in physical reactions. I started to shake as if cold, and breathe quickly as if out of breath. It would come in waves and then I would push the fear away. I had to be stronger.

We lay lined up in a neat row; Rodo, lying dead with a poncho covering him, me three feet away, cold, and P.J., with Buddy shivering noticeably next to him. When Ski came back up the trail there were five of us shadowed by the log. The black kid with the M-79 was yards farther down the path, digging in next to another tree. Tiny and Pigpen must be somewhere down the path shoveling silently, I thought.

The wind began to blow and crackle through the trees, each gust triggering imaginations and fostering new anxieties.

"Listen, what was that?" I whispered, low and heavy. A noise came up the path and to the left somewhere in the jungle.

"I don't know," P.J. said.

"Frag it."

He did. We hit our holes. KABOOM. Shrapnel ripped through the jungle, tearing and whipping overhead. We waited. And waited. The noise was still there, but then so was the wind.

"Those zipperheads ain't dumb, partner," P.J. said sounding like a salt. "They're just sitting there, waiting for us to move. When we do, it's all over but the crying. Yeah, they're just sitting there drugged up and waiting for us to show our sweet asses. Well, I'll tell you, I'm about pissed," he added in a statement so understated I almost laughed.

"Well, we got no protection from the left side," Ski whispered. "What do you suggest we do?"

"Let's put a claymore out there," P.J. said. "We'll string a welcome out for Victor and blow his little dick off."

"Be my guest," I said, amazed that he would even consider crawling through the jungle at night in pitch darkness. "Yeah, you just crawl your ass out there and you'll be in a world of hurt."

"Fuck it. I think I'll pass."

Life was everything. I wasn't giving it away. It wasn't brave or courageous to die, I was thinking, but unfortunate, sad and incredibly unlucky. Yes, things were becoming so clear and defined in my mind. To survive was the important thing. To live and go home to my wife and baby. Stay on this side and live, on the other side I die. Yes, I loved this log. This big tree is here, I thought, here for me to live. Rodo. Rodo. Now he's dead. But I'm alive. I could never help him, but he could help me. He was lying just to the side of my freshly dug hole. I would use Rodo to help me live. Kneeling in my hole, I reached out with two hands, grabbed underneath the poncho and tugged and pulled him over to the edge of my hole.

Now I had two logs. One thick and strong, made of wood. The other one, Rodo. Surely his body could stop a few rounds, I thought. Yes, I was lucky. I had life and I had two logs.

A new system of priorities, a revelation of understanding survival was born.

I could hear a voice talking in my head, a voice no one else could hear. My thoughts came at me loud and quick and clean like a prophet or evangelist.

To die isn't important, at least not here. Not in this armpit. If I die, it won't help anyone. The war won't suddenly conclude with my death. History won't be made over the death of my body. And I won't pass on to mankind some great ideal. I'll just be dead. So the most important thing is to live, to survive.

I felt crazed, but sure that I was making sense. I sorted out my thoughts, and by doing so, I came across a psychological approach to survival. I knew it would work.

I would remove myself from caring about anyone here but me. In doing so, the only death that was important, the only death that mattered, was my own. I believed this. It must be true. I must be raving mad, the voice within me was shouting now. My new belief would carry me through. My new belief and the old one of loving Kristen and my child. I wanted to tell P.J. and Buddy. I wanted to tell them all. I would feel no death but my own.

I would not be touched by others dying. I would not cry or feel sick. And as my brain poured out thoughts, another pop-up lit the night. I could do it! I knew it! I believed this as the flare lit the sky. I believed this, right up until I slid the poncho from Rodo's face. I believed my thoughts until I saw his dead face looking up at me. I believed this until I touched the little bubble of blood that formed on his lips. I believed this,

Rodo, right up until the moment I really saw you dead. And as I looked at him, I wanted to break down and cry and scream and go absolutely crazy in my mind.

My mind howled as Ski came up the path in the darkness, crawling on all fours. He dropped his pack at the end of the log that was farthest from me, opposite Rodo, making sure to stay low. He propped a radio up against the back of the dead tree, pulled up the antenna, and motioned us to crawl closer. We huddled together on our bellies, P.J., Buddy and I.

"Listen up," Ski said. "I went down there and talked to the C.O. They're sitting fat about one hundred yards or so down the street, trying to figure which way is up. Anyway, those dumb fucks want to hit the gooks with some 105s. I told him he's nuts to try to pull that shit off in the dark and with us so close. So that's cool. Then they want us rushin' the position?"

"Buuuulshit," I whispered low. "We already got two KIAs, not counting the Luey."

"I know, I know," he said. In the dark I was sure he was nodding his head. "So here it is. We're sitting tight until morning. In the morning we'll blow those slant-eyes outta the water. We're supposed to call in every thirty minutes and let 'em know how everything is going. And just to keep Charlie on his toes, we'll be fragging his ass all night. Oh yeah, 50 percent alert. Shit, how the fuck you going to sleep in this bullshit, anyway?"

"I can't believe this," Buddy said. "I ain't sitting here on death row all night waiting for Victor. I'm down the road." He raised up to all fours and started to head down the trail.

"Keep it down," Ski yelled in a clenched teeth whisper, grabbing Buddy's arm and holding him fast. "There's no room and there ain't no cover."

"But, God damn, I..."

"Shut up," Ski said angrily. "No more talking. Buddy, you and I got first watch. You guys try to catch some Z's. And, here, I got some more frags." He emptied a dozen on the ground, and the long night began as we checked in with the C.O. over the radio every thirty minutes.

"Kilo 3/9er, this is Kilo L.P., it's cool here," we whispered into the handset. "Fire in the hole." Ski or whoever, would pull the pin and flip a live one. An explosion, a flash of light and shrapnel slashing through the night. Then, silence and waiting. Darkness... Silence and waiting.

Again, in low whispers, "Kilo 3/9er, this is Kilo L.P. It's cool. Fire in the hole." KABOOM, Light. Ripping. Silence and waiting. Waiting. "It's cool, fire in the hole." KABOOM. Light. Ripping. Silence. Waiting.

CRACK. CRACK. CRACK. The darkness erupted. Rounds began washing at the log. Long bursts and short explosions. RAT A TAT... TAT. Lines of green tracers flew overhead. A scream somewhere down the trail behind us. "I'm hit!" Someone wasn't lower than the tree.

Quiet... dark... quiet. I loved the tree and tossed a frag. Explosion, light, dark, quiet... quiet.

Then, a voice came out of the night that I would remember and carry with me for the rest of my life. It was a terrifying demonic bellow.

"Ma-reeen. Ma-reeen. You die."

It was monstrous and mocking, thundering and slicing through my head. "MA-REEEN... MA-REEEN..." I felt crazy with fear as if the voice was shouting just at me. I couldn't stand it anymore.

"FUCK YOU!" I screamed as loud as I could, forgetting P.J., Buddy and Ski, forgetting Kristen and home. "FUCK YOU!" I threw a frag and so did the others.

It was a daisy chain of explosions, deafening and brilliant. A shocking rending of earth. I was shaking in my hole. Time was speeding up. Minutes moved like seconds and seconds were no time at all.

"Pop a LAW. Pop a LAW," Ski shouted, desperately. "We'll blow that asshole to hell!"

"I can't!" I screamed. "I can't!" the jungle was full of explosions and hysterical screams and I had to stay behind my tree. Ski quickly picked up a LAW, pulled the pin in back and fired.

"Look out! EAT THIS, SLOPE!" he screamed.

Nothing happened.

"Son of a bitch." He threw it like a baseball bat toward them and picked up another LAW.

This time his effort was met with an ear-splitting, radiant blast pouring out in flashing heat waves from the front and back of the tube. The round hit and exploded directly and immediately, some forty yards to our front.

A moan came out of the darkness from where the round had impacted. Then fire came back, so we rose up over the log, propped on our knees, and fired volumes and volumes of rounds with red tracers into the area. We combed it, worked it, four of us crazily firing in flashes and tracers. And in my mind, Rodo cheering, mute beyond the grave. And Rat, too. I could feel them both ranting and raving as muzzles flashed. Grenades flew. The kid with the 79 moved up and popped off a rapid THUNK, THUNK, THUNK. Round after round. It was perfect. Overpowering. A superb orchestration of small arms.

The radio squawked at us. "L.P., what the fuck is going on? L.P.? L.P.?" It was begging now. "What's happening? What's happening?" It was afraid. We stopped and ducked behind our wooden wall, laughing at the radio.

"L.P.!? L.P.!?" It was frantic.

We laughed carefully and not too loudly. Ski put down his rifle and picked up the radio receiver. "Kilo 3/9er, it's cool. We just had some voices and movement. Over."

"Jesus Christ, we thought you were getting hit by a battalion. Over," the radio said.

"That's a negative. We just got some rounds and thought they were trying to move. It's all clear on this end. L.P. Over."

"O.K. Take it easy. You got the C.O. shittin' Christmas turkeys. This is 3/9er over and out."

"We sure scared the pee out of those donkeys," P.J. said, referring to the C.O. "What they need is some time up here behind this funky log."

The rest of the night was spent in sleepless quiet, wishing death to the voice that shouted, "Ma-reen. Ma-reen."

Finally I could sense daybreak, just as I could sense Rodo, in the waning darkness, lying next to me. Both were cold, motionless and quiet. In those few moments, a settling took place. A peaceful calm emerged to wash away the nightmare of just hours ago. As the sun rose through the jungle's canopy, all of night came alive again, except for the dead.

It was cold and damp. The chilly morning dew had settled in and soaked through our utility shirts, while the sun was still hidden by the sky's deep gray. It was a typical black and white Vietnam morning. A slow motion, one-dimensional morning. Even the bush looked dim and dreadful.

The only color was a thin stream of red that ran from under Rodo's poncho and into my hole. I wiped the dirt, trying to erase him from my memory.

"Well, what do you think, Jackson? You think those slopes are still dug in?" P.J. asked. "Did we get some, or what?" he was probing, anxiously, as I just stared at Rodo's feet sticking out from under his poncho. "I know we busted some ass!"

"Hey, guys," Ski interrupted, "I'll get the C.O., or whoever, on the horn."

Ski talked to the radio for awhile before he finally got off, rolled over, and faced us. "Well, sweethearts, the C.O. informs me that we are going to skate," and his voice took on a mock tone of authority. "Another squad is coming up to commence occupying the enemy position," he said, mimicking the C.O.'s voice and diction.

"Great one," Buddy said vehemently. "Great one. Someone else can go John Wayneing it up there and get their ass shot off. Shit, it's better him than me."

He'd spoken my thoughts. Ripped off my words.

"By the way, we got to put some covering fire out," Ski added. "And P.J., my man, you got to unload with a 72."

"Buuuuulshit. Check it out! The C.O. wants a LAWman firing, let him be a LAWman. No. Ain't no way. I'm sure as shit not leaving my log. We're just getting tight. Let the 79 work out, he's got more cover."

"Don't give me no heat! You and Jackson are the LAWman this time, sweetheart."

That ended the discussion. It had been a long night; we had not slept, we were tired, we had not eaten, and we were hungry. I had relieved myself in my hole during the night and the stench, along with the smell emanating from Rodo, had become nearly intolerable.

After what seemed like a long time, the squad that was to begin the assault came slowly up the trail, their packs left behind so they could move freely. They moved cautiously, bent over, faces drawn taut with fear. Reticent, reluctant and crawling flat, they made it to the log. Ski briefed them on the suspected enemy location. There was no hostile fire. One by one they crouched just higher than the log. Suddenly they fled the cover, diving flat to the ground. They leap-frogged into a position exactly parallel to where the green tracers and devil voice had come from.

Still no contact. Could it be they were dead? Had the voice died?

The 79s prepped the area.

P.J. rose to one knee. The LAW fired true the first time. What luck, I thought.

THUMP... THUMP... THUMP, more blooie rounds. Another LAW exploded. Then like in some wild war story, the squad leader stood, yelled an obscenity while we laid down sheets of covering fire. One boy froze and shit his pants while the rest of the squad got on line, firing, rushing and assaulting their position.

The assault was an unanswered two minute barrage. The squad quickly overran the bunkers and fighting holes, and set up security.

P.J., Buddy, Ski and I put on our packs and walked by the kid who froze as he groveled and cried like a child. There were several fighting holes and bunkers. Frags were tossed into the bunkers just to make sure, but we had done the damage the night before. There were eight dead, and with the two by the trail that Rat had wasted, ten all told. They had lost chunks of heads and arms and looked like broken dolls. Blood trails indicated more wounded or dead had been dragged off or maybe buried somewhere. Two women were also found covered with brush, dead from multiple wounds. Another dead NVA had been chained to his machine gun, which in turn had been chained to a tree. His option was to fight until death. A draftee, I chuckled to myself. These few jerks were left behind to die. Left to slow our battalion up so that their main body of men would escape.

We had uncovered a large enemy camp, and a supply depot. It was obvious that we'd surprised them. Inside and outside of the bunkers, scattered throughout the encampment, were large bags of rice, stamped-out cooking fires, and small black pots. We had interrupted dinner. Rifles and boxes of ammo had been left behind during their hurried retreat. A sack of medical supplies and a North Vietnamese flag were left behind, too. And then we found a massive underground network of tunnels. In one cavern there were boxes of literature printed by our American "Students for a Democratic Society" and additional boxes of Mickey Mouse shirts, mailed from California. Another cavern held dozens of rockets and thousands of rounds of ammo. In a room off to the side of what appeared to be a hospital, were six army cots in neat order with dead Vietnamese, each shot once through the head.

As the day progressed we pulled the dead from their holes and searched their bodies. Then we straddled the dead enemy, laughed, and took turns pissing on them. We pissed and we laughed. I don't know why we did, it just seemed like the thing to do.

The C.O. came up along with those that made up the C.P. He surveyed the situation, told us all what a commendable job we had done, and had his radio man take pictures of him standing, smiling, next to the enemy dead.

I wanted to put a bullet in his head. Why wasn't he standing next to Rodo, or Rat, I thought.

"The C.O. says we get to move to the middle of the column," Ski said.

"What about Rodo and Rat?" I asked.

"Well, we have to carry them."

"Where?" I was stunned.

"Til we get to the top, or somewhere where we can blow an LZ. The canopy is too thick here to get a bird in, so we're stuck. We've got some wounded, too. One dude shot himself in the foot last night; wanted to go home."

The platoon that was behind us when we started on the Op

and the platoon behind them struggled up the hill and passed us, moving us to the middle of our column. We went down to pick up Rodo. Another squad would carry Rat.

In all the war movies I had ever seen, and in all the imagined battles I had ever been in, carrying the dead was nothing like this. There were no stretchers here. None. The Medics and Red Cross didn't suddenly appear on the scene, load up the bodies in a Red Cross marked truck and swiftly whisk the dead away. The dead stayed with us. We carried them, like drunks from an all-night party. P.J. grabbed one arm, I took the other. Buddy in front, with his back to us, held both legs in his arms. We took the poncho from Rodo because it was awkward and kept slipping off. Makeshift stretchers made from utility shirts or ponchos only worked in boot camp and movies. Here, in the bush, with the difficulty of the terrain, it was impossible.

So, we carried him. Arm in arm. Leg in arm. We carried him. His butt and back dragged the ground and his head hung limp, mouth open, eyes empty, staring up at me. Blood had dried and stuck to his lips and the sides of his face. The white thing that was hanging from the hole in his neck was longer, and dangled down, off to the side. I could see inside his throat; tiny pink and flesh colored vessels.

It was just one small hole. Not enough to kill, I thought. Now Jimmy, who took the wrong path, left much more lying in the dirt. He was shattered, yet he lived. It didn't make sense. A little hole, that's all. But a bigger one in back.

Rodo was white. Cold and heavy and white. At some time his muscles had given way, and like the kid who froze, he emptied his bowels all over himself. The smell and the expression on his face made me want to puke.

One goddamn little hole, that's all. If it had only been his leg or arm. Rat's head was half blown off, he wasn't even close to life. But Rodo... all he had was one little hole.

We alternated carrying his body. From arm to arm to legs and back to arms. I liked carrying his legs; I could lose myself in games. I was carrying my drunk cousin Rich home from a party. Or throwing Kristen into the river like I used to do. Or

I imagined it was me. Me being carried off the football field my senior year when I broke my leg. I concentrated hard, trying to detach myself. Yes. It was me being carried, I thought. Not Rodo. And all the kids were cheering for me. And later, when I came back from the locker room, and out onto the field, I was cheered again and again. It came into focus now, became clear. Yes. It was me. I was a hero and the crowd was acknowledging me. It was me.

But just when I would begin to drift, to shift back, an arm or a leg would drop or catch on a branch, bush or tree. Just at the moment I was home and Saturday's hero, just when my mind would let go to be free, we'd trip and fall and end up in a pile.

It was hard for us to keep up with the rest of the platoon. Fatigue overcame us and became as constant as our sweat and the stench of our dead friend. Our arms grew as heavy as his dead body.

We stopped to eat, dropping Rodo like a sack of grain.

"Boys, you'd want to be carried out if it was you," the C.O. said, coming back to us and then leaving quickly as if he were running from his conscience.

Bullshit, I thought. If I were dead and had shit all over me, and was thousands of miles from home, I wouldn't want anyone, let alone my friends, to see me this way. That's bullshit. I wouldn't care.

It was a younger man's war. How did it go? "Old soldiers never die, they just fade away." It's the young ones who die. They die and stink and bloat up and turn cold and white. Yes, that's it, I thought, that's it. It's the young soldiers who do the killing and the dying. The old ones start the wars, and write home about the dead. The young ones simply die. They die in spastic convulsions of uncontrollable pain. They die twisted, bodies ripped open and spilling life in buckets of fleshy pulp. They die screaming, raving, mumbling, and choking on their blood and spittle. And they die quietly, like Rodo, with only one small hole. Shit. What does the C.O. know? I wouldn't care.

We filed on, lifting, shoving, dragging and dropping Rodo. We struggled over fallen trees and up severe jungle grades of impossible-to-cut-through terrain. We battled with his weight, the heat, and insufferable bush. Our helmets fell over our eyes or dropped from heads, on to Rodo, and rolled to the side, off the trail. Packs slipped and rifles flew from shouldered arms. We'd let loose of one dead arm and a series of stops and stumbles sprang up like dumb comedy. If one of us faltered, we all faltered. It would never end.

The day went on and on and on, as he was dropped and carried, dropped and carried.

"Motherfucker," Buddy said, as we dropped Rodo hard. "You motherfucker," he cried, with tears in his eyes as he planted a boot on the side of the dead kid's head. And Rodo's head thumped and whipped to the side, not changing his face.

We weren't shocked. We weren't sad. We were tired. Our lives had changed so much in just a few hours. We stood over Rodo in silence, looking down. Then, not saying a word, we picked him up and moved out.

We settled in that night, set up a perimeter and sent out L.P.s. I dug my hole, made a tent with P.J., and finally ate. We moved Rodo away from our hole about thirty feet to the front of us. In the dark and with the dense thicket and natural slope of the land, he wasn't there.

I stood my watch, tired and drained. Morning came. Charges were set to trees and an LZ was blown. A Huey picked up Rat, Rodo, the Luey, and an assortment of wounded. They were going home. It was over for them.

We packed our gear and moved out.

> Dear Kristen,
> How you doing, babe? I am missing you so much, I can hardly stand it. How's Jenine? It will be so good to see her. I'll have the two best looking girls in town. I miss holding you. It's been so long.
> I don't know where I am. Somewhere in the mountains near the Ah Shau Valley. The Operation we are on has been long and hard this time. But not without its moments of humor. Every morning when light comes, so do the "fuck-you" birds. Yes,

that's right, the "fuck-you" birds. Please excuse my language. These birds, that I have never seen, only heard, screech loudly a sound like someone yelling, "fuck-you, fuck-you," in a falsetto voice. That's the truth. It's hilarious. Surprised I spelled that correctly, aren't you? I got hold of a dictionary. Look out, woman!

Ski was Medivac'd yesterday. He was getting really short and figured the best way to get out of the bush is pretend to get bitten by a rat. It's really common. You take a C-ration opener and prick your arm or leg with two tiny marks, then tell the Medic you were bitten by a rat. They Medivac you and it's back to the rear for a series of fifteen anti-rabies shots in the stomach. A lot of guys do that when they're getting short.

I am attempting to get transferred into a Combined Action Platoon. I've filled out a transfer request form, and I'm just waiting. I heard C.A.P. units are a lot easier. From what I understand, they live in a village and train the villagers to defend themselves. I think it would be an excellent opportunity. I would have a chance to live with the Vietnamese and get a clearer idea of what this war is all about. Most of the time I'm up here in the mountains and never have contact with the Vietnamese. We worked with an ARVN unit one day, but that's about it. The only Vietnamese I've seen up here are dead NVA soldiers. If I were transferred, I would be sent to Da Nang for three or four weeks to a special school. That would be great. From there I would head out to my new unit. I sure hope I get it. It would be safer, too, hon.

It's so strange out here. I've seen rats as big as small dogs. The other day, I was bitten on the hand by an insect that looked like a hummingbird. It made my hand swell up and a Corpsman had to give me a shot of penicillin in the butt. He was a real comedian. P.J. had to get a shot for cellulitis, so the Corpsman told him to drop his drawers and turn around. The Corpsman drew a circular target with iodine on P.J.'s butt and tossed the needle like a dart into the target. Later he stuck me there and said, "Just a minute," and pretended to walk away while the needle and syringe were still hanging there. I guess it sounds funny now, but it didn't feel funny then.

Your letters mean so much. When I read them it's almost like you're talking to me. And when I look at your picture, you are here, or rather I'm there. Sometimes I can see you rushing to the mailbox. Or I see you sitting in your mother's kitchen next to the window that looks out onto the back yard. I can see the apples fall and I can see you in my mind and in a million different memories. I love you and as each day passes, I love you more.

I feel sorry for some of the guys here. Some of them are so uneducated. A few can barely read or write. There are a couple of guys in other squads whom I help write letters home. I thought I had it bad with my family being so screwed up, but hon, some of the guys are really messed up. For them, the Marine Corps is a home, a place where they can belong. But I've got you, and that's the most important thing to me in the world.

How do they feel about the war back home? Are there many riots? I suppose it's different than in the larger cities. I really don't know. All I've seen is the mountains and all I want is to come home to you in one piece.

I dream of you. And I dream of the moment I'm finally home and you are there to hold me.

I love you, Kristen, more than I can ever express. I'll make it, hon.

Love,
Jack
October 1968

P.S. P.J. keeps bugging me. He still wants some of your underwear. He just says that to be bizarre. His whole existence is bizarre.

Dear Kristen,

It's me again. This is the second letter I've written you today. I'm just a little bit lonely, and I wanted to talk to you. This is the next best way. Excuse the condition of the letter writing gear. I used all of mine up, and I borrowed this from a guy I used to know.

It's an unbelievable night. The moon is so bright. I wouldn't even need lights to play baseball. This country is so different. Some nights I can't see my hand a foot away from my face. Yet other nights, like tonight, I'd swear the moon was a second sun.

I just finished the best dinner. I had my favorite, spaghetti and meatballs, peaches and pound cake. To top it off, I made a big cup of cocoa. Everybody is always trying to get me to reveal my secret cocoa recipe.

I make the best around. My secret is a pinch of salt, like you taught me.

I get so lonely for you. At night when I'm lying in my poncho tent and P.J. and I are talking about how it was back home, I tell him all about you. About how your mom used to worry about us fooling around and would yell from the top of the basement steps, "Curfew! Curfew!" and then flip the basement light off and on.

Remember when we made love underneath the pool table? Your brother and his friend walked in, played a game, but never caught us?

I think about how you and I, Rich and Gail, used to do everything together. Remember when the four of us took his old '53 Chev down to San

Francisco? You girls were so paranoid. You would both go nuts when Rich and I would swipe gas from parked cars. San Francisco was something. So many hills and faggots and prostitutes. And Haight-Ashbury, now that was different. I'll never forget that gal running down the middle of the street with nothing on and her body painted with flowers and butterflies. Or the Golden Gate Bridge. God, it was huge. I miss those times.

Well, I'm rambling on now, so I better close. I sure miss you. Tonight when I go to sleep I'll lay on my stomach and push the ground hard and think about you. I need you. Good night, hon. God, I love you. I miss you calling me "Papa Bear".

Love you
Jack
October 1968

Ten

MY ATTITUDE ABOUT COMBAT and the bush had changed. Tension and fear were replaced by fatigue and the overwhelming anxious hope of someday going home. I was no longer a boot or new b and had earned respect from my peers, if not for my strength and courage, then for having survived for four months in Vietnam.

We stayed deep in the jungle, high in the mountains for several weeks; blowing LZs, stringing wire, and digging in. Then leaving and doing it all over again. During the day we would run patrols off the mountain and at night we would send out ambushes with little or no contact with our elusive enemy. Charlie seemed to be always just one step ahead of us. One time we walked up on a group of five NVA as they were cooking rice and wasted them quickly, only to discover through documents that they were going on their R & R. But basically, life in the bush had become quiet and boring. Friendships were forged and strengthened by the shared burden of our environment and loneliness for home. When we talked it was always about how it used to be or how it would be when we got back to the world.

"When I catch the bird back to the world I'm going to soak in the tub for a week and have my ol' lady rub my feet and take care ah her ol' man, 'like the hero I is.'"

"Brother, you just be stone cold glad ta git out this shit."

We were dug in and socked in for several days now as P.J.

and I huddled under two ponchos forming a tent. The rain was hard and constant and the jungle was still. We had taken broad green leaves and scattered them on top of the dirt floor to help insulate against the wet rain and wind blowing cold across us. But we were still soaked and very hungry.

"Jackson, my man, I'm so hungry I'd give anything for just one bite of ham and motherfuckers," P.J. said, referring to the dreaded ham and lima beans. "That or I'm going to catch me a big-ass rat and do some serious barbequeing."

"How the hell are you going to catch a rat, Einstein?" I said. "Whistle him over here?"

"Why don't you just lie there and make like a big fat piece of cheese," he replied, "and when he starts nibbling, you can fart and gas him to death."

"You're the gas expert. Let's hear your second idea."

"We hear 'em all night. You do a pop-up and I'll level their ass with my E-tool. Comprendo, amigo?"

"Si, señor. I didn't pull straight Ds in Spanish por nada."

That night the rain slowed to a light sprinkle as P.J. and I waited for the rats to come out of their holes and hiding places.

"Jackson, I think I hear one," P.J. said anxiously in the dark from inside our tent.

"No, man. That ain't nothin'."

"You got your pop-up ready?"

"Right. Are you sure you want to do this? Rain has almost stopped. Chopper might make it in tomorrow."

"I got my E-tool ready. If we don't get resupplied you're going to beg me for a little of this rat."

"I'll starve and be six feet under before I eat any damn rat. You're outa your head, you know."

"Shhhh. Listen. I'm going out. Come on, be quiet and get ready to pop it when I say so. I hear one, Jackson. Now." I slammed the pop-up against my knee, sending the flare shooting up in the air, opening the night and lighting the jungle. P.J. ran and started to swing his shovel when he suddenly held up. Someone was bent over with his pants down and a handful of C-ration toilet paper in his hand. It was the new guy named St.

Lawrence. He forgot to tell us he was going out in front of the lines.

"I coulda killed you," P.J. whispered angrily. "I thought you were a rat."

"Do I look like a rat?" he replied, embarrassed and scared.

"Wellll."

"Well, fuck you." And as the flare drifted and landed in some trees, P.J. and I moved back to our hole.

"What a dumb ass. I wish Ski was still here."

St. Lawrence was assigned as our new squad leader, taking Ski's place. He was older than the rest of us, about twenty-six, and for some reason, he didn't seem to belong. He was different. He wasn't alive and free like Ski. He was methodical and military. He should have been an officer. That's where he belonged. He had a square-looking head and I'm sure his short hair wasn't worn much differently when he was a civilian. He tried to be a leader and he was calm under trying conditions.

Once when the C.O. inadvertently called gunships in on our own position, and several kids got it, St. Lawrence remained remarkably composed. The radio man from another squad had just taken a round through the jaw. St. Lawrence held his hand over the wound, trying to stop the blood, and at the same time, attempted to settle the kid down. Part of the kid's lower jaw and teeth were torn loose and hanging out, so St. Lawrence held them in one hand, pressed tight, while cradling the back of the kid's head with his other. Blood kept pouring and he kept soothing him by saying, "You'll be all right, kid. You'll be all right."

I admired him after that. I appreciated his capacity for compassion, a quality that seemed increasingly absent as the days wore on.

We were flown back to Stud for a few days and P.J. promptly caught the clap. No one knew where he got it, but we suspected the old woman with blackened teeth who wandered into camp one day to pick through the garbage dump.

A week later we went back to the bush, however we didn't go to the mountains. This time we were choppered into an area with terrain similar to that of my first few weeks. We landed in a valley outside of a village and were once again surrounded by mountains, only this time the mountains were several miles away.

It was mean and hot. The sun began to bake us, as it had the yellowish elephant grass. I hadn't felt well for the past couple of days and the diarrhea I had was coming more frequently, accompanied by violent pains in my lower abdomen. I was on an O.P. when it first started to hit me. I would get very hot, then very cold. And even though I had slept many hours the night before, I felt incredibly tired. The O.P. I was on was called in and we were told to get ready to move out. I was becoming increasingly tired and constantly having to relieve myself.

We were saddled up, waiting for choppers when it finally took hold.

"St. Lawrence," I said, barely able to stand under the weight of my pack and illness. "I..." and I could feel my face distort uncontrollably. "I... I'm sick." He looked at me and said something about dropping my pack and about walking over to the Corpsman. I was so fatigued I didn't think I could walk ten feet, let alone several hundred to a Corpsman. I dropped my pack with great effort, and then collapsed.

Images gathered around me. I was on my back. Faces, a swirling and melting, a blending together of backgrounds. Voices. I couldn't quite make them out. I had to sleep. My head was spinning. Drifting... drifting... about to lose images... voices... and one last sentence, "He's such a strong kid. I wonder what happened."

When I came to, I realized I was in a helicopter being Medivac'd out. I could feel my body getting heavier and heavier. I was tired, hot... dying? So tired, so tired... out again.

I came to again.

I'm in a bunker now. I'm naked, looking up. I can see the faces take shape. The faces look down at me as if I were in a football huddle looking up. They are talking and I can see them. One face is pouring something on me from a bottle, another is putting ice on me. I can feel it now. Ice on my balls. Ice on my face. Ice on my chest and stomach.

I can see a fan. The face pouring liquid on me is now moving a large electric fan over me. Another face. A voice. It sounds alarmed. "Shoot him up. Shoot him up." And now they are sticking me with needles. In one arm, the foot, the other arm, and the other foot. I'm freezing. What are you doing? I screamed and nothing more than spit and drool slid from my mouth.

I need water... water. What's happened to me? I try to rise.

"Hold on, tiger," a face with glasses said, "you're awfully sick. You've got malaria. Do you understand?"

I tried to nod my head.

"It appears you've had it for a couple of days. Your temperature is up to 106. We have been pouring alcohol on you and packing you in ice to try and bring your temperature down. You've got four IVs in you. You should have been in here a couple of days ago. You hear me? You hear?"

I drifted again... falling... spinning... and the faces turned to shadows and the voices faded weaker and weaker and finally disappeared. I was out again.

When I came to, no one was around me. I found it hard to focus. I was lying on top of the sheets, white sheets. A voice mumbled next to me. "Kill me, kill me, kill me," the weak voice said over and over. I could see clearly. I was lying in a bed, looking up at several rows of white fluorescent lights attached to a curved ceiling. The ceiling was shaped like a tunnel, only it resembled inflatable mattresses. An inflatable hospital. Shaped like a section of tunnel. Inflatable, the mortars and rockets can bounce off. I laughed a laugh even I couldn't hear.

I'm in a hospital. I've got malaria, I thought.

"Hey, fella, you decided to join the waking world, huh?" a face and voice appeared. "You have been out or delirious for three days. Let's check your temperature." The face stuck something in my mouth and waited. "Well, let's see," he said, pulling the thermometer from my mouth. "Just over 103. That's good. You're doing a lot better."

Just as he said that, I felt a sharp pain in my lower intestine. My bowels erupted and I couldn't stop. I knew I'd shit all over myself.

"Oh, man," the face said, "I'm getting tired of this." He got a cold wet towel and wiped between my legs and butt, and the insides of my thighs.

"Now that you're awake, here's your prognosis. Can you understand me?"

"Yes," I said, amazing myself.

"Well, you've got two types of malaria and a bad case of amoebic dysentery. For the next day or so, you will be shitting every twenty minutes. When you feel like you have to go, tell me, or whoever is on duty and we will help you out."

"Could I have a blanket? I'm cold," I said weakly.

"That's a negative. Your temp is still way up there. Now don't be moving around in bed, you've still got two IVs in you and I don't want to have to put them back in. We still aren't sure as to what one type of malaria is, so I'll have to take some more blood from time to time. Oh, yeah, the guy in the bed next to you has malaria too, in fact, that's what this whole ward is."

"Could I get some water?" I asked.

"Sure." He walked over to a green cooler and brought back a paper cup full of water. "Is that enough?"

"Yeah, thanks."

"No problem. From what I hear, you're lucky. They got you out of the bush just in time. If you hadn't been Medivac'd when you were or soon after, you'd be a dead dog. It's not over yet. You will be getting flashes of hot and cold for several days. In fact, you've got malaria so bad, I think you'll be Medivac'd down south."

"What do you mean?" I struggled to ask as my head started spinning again and a throbbing pain rushed up and down the back of my neck and head.

"They send the real severe cases down south to Cam Ranh Bay for a few weeks. Listen, you are a sick boy."

I felt myself draining of consciousness... growing heavy and slowly slipping into darkness.

The next few days were jammed together in hours and hours of sleep and wild dreams, scattered with moments of consciousness. When I was awake, I vacillated between being unbearably hot and thirsty, and long moments of extreme cold and chills. I dreaded the long hike to the three-hole outhouse. The pains that signaled each warning were deep and striking. I was being given inordinate quantities of medication, and my body was rejecting it. Moments after taking pills, I would vomit in dry heaves. After one heaving episode, I was told that they still were unable to control or contain my disease, and that I would be Medivac'd to Cam Ranh Bay. The next morning I was helped to a truck, taken to the Quang Tri hospital air pad, and loaded onto a cargo plane for my trip south.

Dear Kristen,

This is the first time I have been able to write you without anyone helping me. I hope the other letters I dictated did not scare you. I'm feeling much better now. I have been here at Cam Ranh Bay for about a week. Today I even got out of bed and walked over to the Mess Hall and ate lunch. They had fruit, meat, real food.

It's beautiful here. This base sits right on the ocean, and from the back door of the billet I'm in, I can see people sunbathing, swimming, even surfing. It's amazing.

Everything is so clean. There are walks leading from billet to billet. No dirt, trash or filth. It's like being home. It's another world. Many of the billets are equipped with TVs. There's only one channel though, and all they play are reruns of Bonanza or Gunsmoke. Listen to me complaining.

I'm sleeping in a bed at night, taking showers every day and even sitting on toilets that flush. They have some Vietnamese working here on the base and it's really crazy. I walked into the head yesterday and there was an old man and a boy, using two stools. Both of them were standing on the toilets. From what the boy said, it was their first time here, and they had never used one like that before. I cracked up, it was so funny. It's absolutely fantastic. I would love to spend my tour here. I was talking to a guy this morning at lunch, and do you know what he does? He's the beach lifeguard. No kidding. I met another guy who runs the gym and recreation area. I think I'll walk over there today.

The Corpsman who has been taking care of me during the day is a great kid. His name is Bob Babbington, and he has been really kind. He's in the Army. That's what this is, an Army base. In fact, the only other Marine I've met down here is the Liaison Officer. Bob says I'm a real rarity. He told me it is also an R & R Center for the Republic of Korea troops. The ROKs are all over this place. They are very friendly even though none of them speak English. Everyone calls them "Rocks."

Bob said tonight he would take me over to his billet and show me his stereo equipment. After that we are going to an outside movie. They show movies here every night. It's superb, but I still miss you more than anything. I will be here at least two more weeks. So, I'm really getting a rest.

Well, hon, I'm getting tired. I get tired so easily now. It was kind of tough for awhile, but now I'm skating. You know, it's so unfair that my buddies with Kilo have to go through all that shit and guys down here are watching TV and movies and living like human beings.

Well, I'll write again tomorrow.

Love you

Jack

November, 1968

P.S. I got so carried away about this place I forgot to mention my second sweetest lady, Jenine. Give her a hug for me.

I had just come back from chow and was resting, trying to digest my dinner. My stomach wasn't used to being full, and I felt bloated and uncomfortable. I sat on the side of my bed, took off my boots, lay back and began reading an old "Stars and Stripes" newspaper. I was skimming through the paper feeling a little bit better, when my Corpsman, Bob, flew into the room.

"Jackson, my man. What it is! What it is!" Bob exclaimed, extending his arm, slapping my palm. "How's my STARRRR patient?" Before I could respond, he interrupted me. "You are looking toooo good, toooo-night. Are you read-dy? We'll slide over to my place and listen to some good tunes. Maybe a little Jimmmmi!" He picked up a mop that was sitting in a bucket near the foot of my rack and began strumming his make-believe guitar, à la Jimi Hendrix. "Yes, sir, my man, we'll listen to some sounds and then get our heads all messed up and catch the flick. Sound like a plan?"

"I don't know about that, but I'll certainly check it out," I said.

Bob's living quarters were much different from any in-country military facility I had ever seen. Instead of bunk beds, or rows of single racks, each man had his own 10x10 living cubicle, most consisting of a bed, dresser, footlocker and three-foot high refrigerators. Some had TVs or stereos or both. Pictures of naked and semi-naked women covered all the walls. Bob's room had beads hanging down in place of a door. Inside, in addition to all the other amenities, he had a beautiful rocking chair and two-stool bar.

"Sit down, my man. Sit down," he said, motioning me over to his chair.

"A rocking chair, come on. Where'd you get this?" I asked, amazed and admiring the deep rich golden oak wood.

"Traded some Darvon for it."

"Darvon? You traded Darvon for a chair? What fool would want Darvon?"

"To get high, my man. To get high. What you do is break open one of these red and gray capsules," he said, reaching into his pocket and pulling out a handful. "Then you take out the little pill inside, swallow it, sit back, and BAM, you're loaded. It's a high, man. Does your head right in no time. We're always toking up and having Darvon parties. Here." He bent over his TV and began breaking one open. "Here you go, bud."

"No..." I hesitated. "I haven't taken any of that stuff before."

"It's cool. You're not in the bush. It's cool. We aren't gonna get hit. Man, no sweat. I was out water skiing during lunch today. I know it's hard to handle, but this is just like the world, only the dope is better and a hell of a lot cheaper. We ain't gonna get hit. I been here ten months. Don't even KNOW what incoming sounds like. It's cool, dude. No sweat. Come on." Reluctantly, I took the pill from his hand and slowly swallowed it.

"You got it, my man. You got it. I took three, but since it's your first time, you'd better stick to one. Listen, let's go get this buddy of mine and diddy bop on up to the hill and fix our heads, then catch the flick." He grabbed my arm and squeezed it, trying to generate excitement. "Come on."

We quickly walked over to pick up Bob's friend.

"Jackson. Meet my man, Stash. Stash has been here so long he's after my job."

Stash, nicknamed because of his thick, drooping moustache, was a platoon sergeant from the American Division and was at Cam Ranh Bay recovering from wounds suffered in a firefight near Na Trang. His unit, the "Screaming Eagles", was involved in one- and two-day helicopter assault operations in the flatlands, after which they returned to the rear. It sounded like a skate to me, compared to what I was used to.

We sat on top of a sandy hill overlooking the camp and the ocean and watched the sun slowly set.

The sun turned from a round glowing gold to shades of bright, vivid magenta and gracefully settled into the sea. It was a capsulation of all the dramatic sunsets I had ever seen. I milked the last precious moments before it passed to the other side of the world. I hoped Kristen would see the sun coming up. Maybe she would share its beauty and warmth, I thought. If the sun could speak, I would have it shout to her how much I missed her and needed her next to me.

Feeling at ease for the first time in months, I decided to succumb to peer pressure and get loaded.

"Here you go, my man," Bob said, passing me the joint. "Take a hit and hold the smoke deep in your lungs." I did just that. Bob was the reigning expert. "Go on, pass it to Stash," he said excitedly, obviously pleased that this was my first time. "Pass it to Stash." I took a long drag, held it deep in my lungs, and then exhaled it. Then I repeated the routine. The joint traveled from Bob to me, to Stash, back to me and then to Bob. I soon discovered that the middle seat is the best position to occupy when smoking dope.

"Look at this Bogart! This dude is in the middle, gettin' hit on both sides, Bogarting the shit outa this dope," Stash said.

I took my turn again and again.

"You gettin' a buzz yet?" Bob asked.

"Not at all," I lied. "Are you sure this pot is any good?" I asked, feeling as if my mind was slowly deteriorating.

"Hey, man, this is the best dope in the Nam," Stash said. "This is ass-kicking dope. It'll get you about six ways of fucked up."

We started grinning and laughing. Bob quickly and expertly rolled another number. He lit it up "Fire in the hole," and he passed it. "Watch this," he said. He rolled another joint, this time with only one hand. He quickly licked the paper and we were duly impressed.

"This ain't pot," I ventured, taking another deep hit. "I don't feel anything." My face tightened up as my brain dulled. "The dudes back at Kilo are going to crack up when they find out I smoke dope." I passed it and thought profound thoughts for awhile. Things quickly forgotten and never remembered.

"That pill you gave me. Uh. That pill. Right. Ain't no good, either." I laughed an embarrassed laugh.

We smoked and talked and laughed in deep, guttural sounds. Things were beginning to really slow down. Every word and sentence spoken became a burden. There were long periods of silence, smoking, and passing the joint.

Suddenly I spoke, "I'm hungry." And once again we cracked up, laughing our asses off. "I need food! I need a McDonald's double cheeseburger and a large order of fries.... Man, I'm so hungry I can't stand my own mind."

"Well, let's hit it," Bob said. We stood up in slow motion and stumbled down the hill, over to the flick.

We moved off the knoll like the Three Musketeers, dead drunk on mead, until we finally made it to the hot dog and sandwich stand set up for the movie. After taking what seemed like four hours to decide what to order and pay for it while trying to act straight, we headed back through crowds of people sitting in the sand. It was like LZ Stud, only everyone was clean and relaxed. There were no rifles and much more smoke. If you were discreet, the officers wouldn't hassle with you.

"Hold it. Hold it," I said. "Not too far from the hot dog stand," and I stopped, creating a Three Stooges collision of stonies.

"Hey, man, you're on my feet!" Bob said, pushing me. "Man, you're on my feet." We untangled.

"Let's have a contest to see who can sit down the slowest," Stash said brightly.

"All right! All the time..." My sentences were having an increasingly difficult time getting out. "All the time..." I could feel my head wobble. "All the time, I do everrrything... quickly. Let's-have-a-contest. Let'sssseeeee who can sit down the slowest."

It seemed like an excellent idea. I soon thought it was my own. But I was feeling twinges of paranoia. I felt like they were laughing at me. It was dark now as Stash spoke.

"Here's the rules," Stash announced. My mind seemed to clear. I was getting better, I thought. Understanding Stash with more clarity. "The last butt to hit the ground is the winner."

We laughed and shoved at one another. I said, "I'm cereal... I mean, I'm serious." Again, we laughed, bent over, still clutching our sandwiches. "Come on, you. Come on. I smoked your pot, you can play my game." I was thoroughly excited. "Come on," I said.

"My man's cheating. This funky dude is cheating," Bob said, referring to Stash. "He's got his hand on the ground." Stash moved his hand away quickly, gave us a dumb grin, and then gradually rolled back, flat, laughing at the stars.

Bob and I continued our battle and kept getting closer and closer to the ground, neither one of us giving up, each battling through the pot's potent kick, trying to be straight.

"Airborne all the way," Stash screamed as he got up from the sand and dove on Bob and me, knocking us to the ground. We laughed and laughed, and then finally sat up, munching dirty sandwiches.

A few minutes passed. "This dope ain't shit," Stash said, looking dumber than I thought I looked. "Hey, give me a bite of that hot dog."

I slept more deeply that night, my mind swirled with dreams. Pot was good, I thought. It freed my mind for silly thoughts and eased the trying days.

The next few days went quickly. My strength was rapidly returning and soon I'd be sent to rejoin my unit. In the mornings I would eat breakfast, fall out for P.T., and in the evening I would get stoned with Bob and Stash.

I began to adjust myself to my current living situation. But, still, I missed the bush. I missed the camaraderie, the intimacy and closeness we all shared, yet never spoke about. I missed my friends and digging in. The guys here at Cam Ranh were my pals. But the guys in the bush were my brothers. We were family, and I missed my home.

One night Bob asked me to walk over with him to the PX. When we got there, he told me that I could call home on the Mars Satellite Radio that had been set up. He had had his name in on a waiting list for weeks, but he wanted me to take his place. In a way, I knew he felt a sense of guilt for not having to suffer. He knew he'd never be one of "us" any more than I could ever be one of the skates back here. I couldn't believe it was happening to me. I was afraid it was a trick.

When I called home, Kristen's dad answered. It was about three in the morning for them. "Woody, this is Jack. I'm talking on a shortwave radio, can you hear me?"

"I sure can," he said excitedly. "Are you all right?"

"Oh, I'm feeling great. Get Kristen on the phone. I don't have much time, over." My heart was pounding and I was being overwhelmed. I loved her so much and after months of hell, I would be talking to my lady. I could hardly believe it. I was nearly in tears when she answered.

"Jack? Oh, Jack." She started to cry. "Oh, Jack..."

I could hear her trembling. "Don't cry, baby. I'm OK. Did you get all of my letters? Over."

"Yes, hon..." her voice cracked again. She sobbed and sobbed. "I have been so worried. For over two weeks I didn't hear from you and I was so worried. And when I did get your letters, they came all at once. I love you and miss you so much."

"You'll have to speak up. The connection isn't very good." I was straining to listen. Trying to capture each word.

"I love you, honey. Jenine is growing up so fast, and I can tell she's daddy's girl. She looks so much like you." Her voice brightened. "Just yesterday we were out shopping and I ran into some old friends of ours and..."

I couldn't hear her. I pressed the phone to my ear. There was only silence.

"Sorry, pal," the radio operator said, "the phone went dead."

And that was it. My connection to Kristen and to the world had ended, just as suddenly as it had begun.

I stood there for a long moment. Dumbfounded, crushed, staring, I went back to my bed, lay down, cursed, cried, and thought about home.

A week later I was choppered back to Stud and lifted out to the bush to join Kilo. I was back home again. Back where I belonged. Back in the bush.

I was choppered in to a firebase called Winchester Cathedral, named after the popular song. Later the same day, reporters from "Life" magazine were flown in and randomly interviewed some of the guys. P.J. was among those interviewed.

"How do you like Nixon?" the reporter asked.

"He's all right, but Wallace is my man."

"Do you think Governor Wallace would have a different perspective relative to our involvement here in Southeast Asia? And if so, what approach would he take?"

"I think old George would do what most of us here want to

do."

"And what is that? Please be specific."

"He'd say, 'If we're gonna be here, let's do it right and sweep the Nam.' We could be outa this armpit in thirty to forty-five days."

For the next few days P.J. was kind of a celebrity; however, being back in the bush was very difficult for me. I found the heat unbearable and on my first hump I nearly passed out.

"I'll carry some of your gear, Jackson," P.J. offered.

I said "no," I thought about what my high school coach used to say during football daily doubles when it was so hot that the sweat would make the jersey adhere to my skin and after practice someone would have to help me pull it off. I remembered him saying "Punish yourselves, men. It will be easier next time."

So I never gave up. I always pushed myself. I always punished myself.

As the days wore on we had an assortment of meaningless firefights with small enemy elements and on occasion watched napalm being dropped on suspected NVA positions. But mostly I was bored.

Thanksgiving came and went and soon dissolved to just another bleak memory. We ate turkey loaf that day and I had diarrhea. P.J. took an early R & R to Bangkok and came back just before Christmas with wild stories and pictures of his naked playmates. But things had changed. Bob, Stash and Cam Ranh Bay were soon lost history, swallowed by the rain and filth of each passing day. I found myself writing home more and more and saying less and less.

The bush that I had longed for in the hospital became drawn out, repetitive, and depressing. Patrols were sent out, and patrols came back. Food was dropped. Supplies were dropped. Soldiers were dropped. Beer was dropped... sometimes. It was always the same. The bush that I had missed was rapidly becoming the bush I could not stand. Yesterdays were soon forgotten, replaced by boredom or disastrous stupidity.

One night, three boots were on watch in the same hole at

the same time. As dusk approached, two went outside the lines to string a claymore. The one kid left behind had the hell box. The box was attached to the wire, the wire to the mine. He unwittingly pressed the lever, sending two more boys home in a thunderous flash of light and death.

I had not yet heard if I was going to be accepted into the Combined Action Platoon program and live in the villages. I wanted a change. A chance to be with the Vietnamese people and perhaps gain some insight as to what the war was really about. It was peculiar how the anti-war demonstrators that I would read about in the "Stars & Stripes" or in an occasional newspaper sent from Kristen seemed to believe that they knew so much about the Vietnamese people, what they wanted, and about the war. And yet, I was in Vietnam, and knew virtually nothing about the people. I saw very few Vietnamese and the NVA I saw were either shooting at me, or were dead, and I had not yet discovered a reason, if any existed, for being there.

In the Nam we had a motto: "War is Hell, but a Firefight's a Motherfucker." That's what Vietnam was all about. It wasn't war. It wasn't hell. It was worse. It was indescribable. It was a motherfucker, for no apparent reason. I had to find a reason. I had to find some sort of justification for fighting. I needed to escape the mindless nature of the bush. There must be a purpose, a direction, I thought. I felt I would have to live with the people to really understand. But I also just wanted out of the bush. During Christmas my chance came.

Christmas Eve day we were flown back to LZ Stud for a forty-eight hour cease fire. Our entire battalion was there. Tents were set up for each company's C.P., forming short rows like houses on a Monopoly board. Inside each tent were twenty military cots that were available on a first come first serve basis. Stacked in the corners of each tent were Red Cross packages and more mail than usual; dozens of red and green sacks full of letters from home. A string of colored lights hung along the poles of our tent, and someone was walking around in a Santa Claus suit wearing a 45 in a shoulder holster. The Santa was carrying a bottle of Jim Beam in one hand, saying

"Merry Christmas" and pouring shots to whoever had a canteen cup.

P.J., Buddy, and I had just left the large C.P. tent and were sitting in our private three-man hooch about twenty feet from the C.P.'s tent. We were B'S'ing, cooking chow and hot chocolate. We were going first class this time. We had made our tent with a wooden pallet floor. We sat on the pallets cooking in the mud as our legs straddled each stove. Light drops of rain were falling and spitting on our C-rat fires set between our legs. We felt good, except for Buddy.

"I sure as hell hate this cease-fire bullshit. Every time they plan one of these, the gooks go nuts and try to kick ass. Those gook mothers don't give a fuck about no cease-fire or no Christmas. Tet's worse. They go batshit. I don't know," said Buddy, shaking his head while breaking open a packet of dry cream and stirring it into his cup of cocoa. "I think it's crazy. I just wish I was home, plugging some ol' lady and drinking hot toddies."

"Hot toddies!" P.J. gasped. "Now, what the hell is a hot toddy?" P.J. and I roared at that one.

"Hot toddy?" we laughed. "Shit, get some. For Hot Toddy." We cracked up again, slapping each other's hand.

"Hey, man, hot toddy is a Christmas drink. You know, like eggnog. Come on. Hot toddy... you know what I mean?"

"I ain't heard of no hot toddy. P.J., you ever hear of a hot toddy?" I asked.

"Fuck, no," P.J. answered. "I knew a girl back home named Hot Dottie. Grrreat piece of ass. She loved carrots and the football team." We roared. For a few moments we were in harmony with each other. We were so close, it almost seemed like Christmas. "Hot toddy. Damn."

Then it came. Not in a sleigh pulled by eight tiny reindeer. And not in a helicopter or in a red suit and fake white beard to the grand opening of a new shopping center. It came suddenly and without regard for holiday happiness and good cheer. It came with no intention of peace on earth and good will toward men.

The first rocket hit the India Company C.P. tent with a loud shrill whine and a tumultuous explosion.

KABOOM! Christmas was dead and so were seventeen young men.

Another loud whine came, and another, and another, and another. We raced for cover. The screams began. The cease-fire was over. They violated the agreement, the newspapers would say. Maybe. That's all the papers or news reporters ever said. That's all anyone back in the world would read or want to read. Where were the news cameras now? Where was Jane Fonda now? The reporters would not even be around later for the party. The work party. The loading of the dead.

The rocket attack lasted but minutes. Not a very big violation by time standards. Hardly worth the print. Besides, back home, people would be much too worried about getting drunk or deciding which New Year's Eve party to attend. Or they'd be home safe in front of TVs and Presto Log Christmas Eve fires too busy to worry about a few dead Marines.

"Seventeen dead; cease-fire violated." Just five words in newsprint.

We loaded the bodies onto two separate flatbed trucks. The trucks drove off. I washed the blood from my pants, puked, and went back to my tent to write Kristen about the great cookies she'd sent.

On Christmas Day I received orders of transfer to the Third Marine Amphibious Division, the Second Combined Action Group.

"Are you going, Jackson?" P.J. asked.

"Fuck it. I'm gone."

Eleven

IT WAS NEARLY NOON as the jeep left the 3rd Mar Div headquarters in Da Nang to take me to the 2nd Combined Action Group Headquarters.

As we drove through the city the dusty road flowed with waves of motor scooters, bicycles and three-wheeled buses packed with Vietnamese women, children and old men. Their belongings were tied on top in neat bundles or hanging from the windows with strings of fish or an occasional caged chicken. Military trucks, jeeps, tanks, and ontoses would all jockey for position, horns blaring, drivers with their heads stuck out the windows screaming, "Move it, slope! Move that piece ah shit outa the road!"

Both sides of the road were lined with dirty little shanties and skinny little kids begging for food or cigarettes or offering to shine our boots or sell us a watch they had probably just stolen ten minutes earlier. When the jeep slowed to round a corner, the more enterprising kids would offer their sisters or pot. "Hey, Marine," they'd shout. "She number one boom boom," or "Dinky dau cigarette?" or "Hey, Marine, Coke! Only two dollar 'merican."

Once when the jeep stopped I could smell the strong odor of fish and shit that seemed to be everywhere. Then a small boy ran up. "Marine, buy Coke?"

I looked at the dirty brown kid with big oval eyes, dressed in a ragged shirt and shorts and gave him five dollars for the Coke.

"Keep it," I said as he tried to hand me back some change.

As we drove off, I didn't feel any better, I only felt despair.

Finally the jeep turned off the main road and wound down a narrow dirt street that was also lined with shanties, but little activity. We stopped at the entrance to the 2nd C.A.G. compound.

A gate thirty feet long, made of barbed wire and green metal engineer stakes formed in a row of X's was the only way in. On each side of the gate were bunkers large enough for several men and well fortified with rows of sandbags, worn heavy from the war. Sand from the battered bags blew into the air, dusting and blanketing the area. Each bunker had an M-60 machine gun guarding the road leading in, like giant stone lions protecting the entrance to an Egyptian tomb.

Armed and helmeted Marines stood at the gate checking anyone coming or going, while rows of concertina wire helped form a protective cocoon insulating the entry.

The entire camp was encircled with eight-foot-high barbed wire and chain-linked fencing. All four corners of the camp were guarded by twenty-foot-tall towers. They too were heavily sandbagged and mounted with M-60 machine guns.

Inside, the compound consisted of several cement block or adobe buildings, a few wooden billets with tin roofs, a small outside stage for USO shows and an outdoor area for playing basketball. Outside the perimeter, the camp was surrounded by a refugee village consisting of scores of shanties, made of discarded slats of wood, cardboard, and shiny military tin. It appeared that our clean compound had been dropped from the sky, smack in the middle of a filthy, densely populated, starving, grubbing Vietnamese community. We had an abundance of comfort, while the Vietnamese had overwhelming poverty and filth. I felt a shameful inequity.

With all the bunkers, barbed-wire and fired-on adobe walls, I also felt like I was in a modern day Alamo.

There would be no more mountains, jungles, and weeks and weeks of seeming aimless wandering. No more leeches or rancid, uncontrolled filth.

The guards directed me to the command building where I was processed, assigned a billet, given a bunk, and told that lunch was on. When I walked inside the mess hall, I was shocked and a little ashamed that I would be living so well.

Inside was a cool, clean cafeteria. The cooks serving food were pleasant looking Vietnamese women dressed in bright white aprons. They stood in line, behind shiny metal counters, smiling while scooping out large portions of meat, vegetables and potatoes.

I passed through the line, feeling like a child at a candy counter, admiring foods I had not seen since Cam Ranh Bay. There was a cooler for ice cream and milk machines with both white and chocolate. I drew some chocolate, downed it, and was ready for more. What a break, I thought. How lucky can a guy get? I was here for at least thirty days, and I was going to savor this. I wouldn't allow guilt to set in this time. I filled my tray and sat down at the table. I looked around realizing I was the new guy again, only this time I was the filthy one with caked-on dirt and the smell of war all over me. But I would enjoy this new beginning. Just as I settled in to eat, I heard a familiar voice from behind me.

"I'm a good looker, a high hooker, a lover, a fighter, a wild bull rider — I got a hard-on a yard long, and I'm looking for something to start on." I turned and standing in the doorway was P.J., grinning red-faced and wide, his mouth full of cigar. "You ol' donkey dick — you didn't think I was gonna let you skate none, did you?" throwing out his hand and sticking a cigar in my mouth.

I was speechless. "How the hell? What are you doing here?" I asked, flabbergasted.

"Sweetpea, I didn't want to lay it on you all at once. I wanted to surprise your dumb ass. Didn't think I'd get C.A.G., but my orders came the night you left. 'Bout shit nickels. I mean I was about six kinds of crazy. Caught a chopper outa

Stud, and here I am, Sweetpea — your favorite lover, fighter, and wild bull rider."

I stood and shook hands and hugged him.

"Jackson, we're gonna skate and stay high like the desert dogs that we are. We're gonna party hardy!" and we slapped a perfect diddy bop dap, shook hands, pounded a clenched fist in our chests and said, "Get some!"

"Forget that sentimental crap. Let's eat, I'm starved," he blurted, reaching down for my food.

"Hey, outa my tray, dog breath. In line," I said, motioning toward the cute, clean Vietnamese girl serving food. P.J. filled his tray, winked at the girl, and shoveled his food with his usual non-stop abandon. Looking up only to comment on how he'd like to "service that sweet lady with my sweet peter."

"As soon as you're done, let's go shoot some hoop," I said. "You saw the basket outside, didn't you?"

"Yeah. You know where we can get a ball?"

"I think the guard shack has one. Come on, let's ask around."

We dumped our trays, hit the screen door and, after asking around, located a basketball. Soon we were joined on the cracked cement court by a big tall hulking kid from Nebraska named Moose, and a tall graceful slender black kid who must have been born with a basketball in his hand. We played a little two on two: Moose and the black kid against P.J. and me. We got crushed! The black kid kept stuffing or hitting long arching jump shots, or spin moves to the basket, banking it softly. Moose just sort of occupied space. No matter, P.J. was his usual ball of energy. A head shorter than all of us, but always moving, smiling and chattering, with a cigar in his mouth and a big grin on his face. I just stood around yelling at P.J. to "Pass the ball, shorty, pass the ball!"

Our first night, P.J. scored a couple of numbers from the sergeant of the guard, and we found a safe place behind the head to smoke. We got high and spent hours talking about the world and what it would be like when we caught the freedom bird back to the States.

142

"Jackson, you dick head. Let me ask you one question," P.J. said, taking a heavy hit and holding the smoke deep in his lungs.

"Well, come on, P.J. What is it?"

"Jackson," his sentences were slow, deliberate and broken up with long pauses and exaggerated dull gestures. Each time he spoke my name it was as if he was oblivious to having spoken to me before.

"Jackson."

"Yes, P.J.," I answered, feeling somewhat removed because I knew I wasn't quite as stoned.

"Jackson, tell me." His eyes were reduced to little lizard slits and he was falling into a slurring stupor.

"What, P.J.? What do you want?" I was becoming humorously irritated.

"Jackson. What the hell is this all about?" he asked, regaining some clarity.

"What do you mean, P.J.? What's what all about?"

"I mean, I mean... sit-sitting here. Getting fucked up outa our minds on dope that's being sold by, by the same slopes we're gonna waste. I mean, I don't know. None of this makes sense. If I get wasted or blow a million of these slant-eyes away, what changes? Does the world stop rotating? Is anyone saved? What the fuck does it matter? When I go home, do you think anyone will give a damn about what I did? Hell, no. So, I'm gonna party this war out, kick ass, stay high, and try to go home in one piece with my dick hard."

Maybe P.J. had hit on it. Do my time, then sky out. But I wanted more to believe in. I still envisioned my being there as important in some as of yet inexplicable manner.

"P.J., I don't know anything about philosophy or political ideals. I still don't fully comprehend why we're here in this filthy little country. All I know is, I feel good when I toss cans of food to the kids. And I'd like to believe I'm helping out in some way. None of it makes sense. I want to go home, but I sure hate to think that this year here is being wasted. I'd like to believe I've done right."

"You're an idealistic piece of shit," P.J. scolded. "This war is some general's wet dream. That's all. It's not my war."

"But what about the kids? They don't know anything about Communism or Democracy. All they know is war and sickness and poverty and all they want is a can of chow. Let's just drop it. Here, look at these." In the moonlight I showed him some pictures of Kristen and my baby, Jenine.

"I've seen those about eight hundred times," he said. We smoked another doobie and talked some more before turning in. That night he moved his gear to an empty rack next to mine. We lay back in the dark for awhile, not saying anything.

"Jackson?" P.J. asked tentatively, and in a gentle voice I had seldom heard before.

"What, P.J.?"

"Oh, nothing." A few minutes passed. And then in a voice softer than before, he called my name again. "Jackson?"

"What, P.J.?"

"You know, you and I are like brothers. You know what I mean?"

"Yeah, I know."

"Good night."

In the dark I closed my eyes, and felt somehow safer than before.

The next morning P.J. and I ate breakfast and were in the classroom by 0730 for our introduction to C.A.G. The room was packed with well over one hundred other Marines. We sat at old grade school desks with collapsible writing tops. The arms swung up for writing and down for us to leave. The chairs squeaked when we moved and were tight for anyone over a hundred and fifty pounds.

In the front of the room was a wooden podium. On the wall behind it was a large blackboard and a three by five foot map of the Da Nang area with little red pin flags stuck in it.

We were given pencils and paper to take notes. As Marines around us talked and chatted freely, an unknown excitement seemed to permeate the air. Soon a Vietnamese man dressed in Marine Corps jungle fatigues walked up to the podium, placed some papers down and stood at parade rest. Silence now hung in the room. A few moments later, a spit-and-shine Marine Corps captain strode to the podium.

"Ten-Hut!" he shouted, and we all sprang out of our desks to attention. A colonel entered the side doorway, walking with long, powerful strides up to the podium. He was a strong, well-built man, over six feet tall. A prideful career man, in his mid-forties, I guessed.

"At ease," he said, as the captain stepped next to the Vietnamese. "Be seated." He placed a thick black leather notebook on the podium's slanted top. He paused, then opened it.

"Good morning, gentlemen. I'm your commanding officer, Colonel Davis. Welcome to the Third Amphibious Marine Division, the Second Combined Action Group. You men will be staying here for a duration of approximately thirty days, at which time, upon completion of training, you will be assigned to Combined Action Platoons in the I Corps area. Gentlemen," he continued, "I am now beginning my forty-eighth month in country."

The figure staggered my imagination. Chairs stirred noisily.

"I know what the Nam is. I'm not a boot luey, or an office pogue. I have been in the shit." He paused, reached beneath the podium and pulled out a book, placing it in front of him. "Most of you joined our Combined Action Group with the belief that you were going to skate. You volunteered for this duty because you felt that anything was better than the bush." Again, a long pause.

"You are in for a big surprise. A Combined Action Platoon consists of ten enlisted Marines and a Navy Corpsman. You will be working with local Vietnamese militia called Popular Forces. You will live and work and fight, and in some cases, be wounded or die alongside the Vietnamese people. It will not be easy. Many of you will be assigned to C.A.P. units that are confined to compounds located miles and miles from any other military support. These are stationary units. Others of you will become members of mobile C.A.P. units, moving constantly, covering a specified tactical area of operation. You will set-in every morning and move every night."

"You will run patrols and ambushes. You will stand guard for villagers while they harvest their crops. You will help build schools and you will provide medical aid."

"This is not a skate." Pause.

"During the time you are here, the three of us will be your instructors. Each day you will be given classes in Vietnamese history and culture by Chaplain Reynolds, and two hours a day will be devoted to learning the Vietnamese language. Lieutenant Nyugen Win Hieu will cover that portion of your study. Every morning when you first arrive in the classroom, a summarization of each current C.A.P. unit's previous night will be reviewed."

He then proceeded to read the reports from the night before.

"C.A.P. 2-1-1, light contact, one KIA, two WIAs"

"C.A.P. 2-1-2, no contact."

"C.A.P. 2-1-3, three KIAs, three WIAs" I could hear people stir again as they had earlier.

"Eight enemy dead and three captured, six assault rifles, eleven Chi-coms and two hundred rounds of ammunition captured." The list went on and on, and as he spoke I thought what an absolute dumb shit I was. I was looking for a reason to fight, not necessarily the opportunity to get my ass kicked.

"C.A.P. 3-1-3, no contact."

"C.A.P. 3-1-4, two KIAs..." He covered every Combined Action Company and their platoons.

As the colonel continued, my mind raced. My God, what if I got stuck in the middle of nowhere with only a handful of other Marines? Jesus, at least in the boonies with Kilo I had tons of guys around me.

P.J. elbowed me, interrupting my train of thought. "Jackson, I think we fucked up!"

One night when the moon hung round and bright, three of us crept through the dark on our way to the latrine to get loaded. P.J., Moose, and I fired up a joint and listened to some tunes on Moose's cassette tape player. We sat with our backs against the latrine wall, talking above the toilet's flush and Moose's tape of The Doors. The pot was sweet and smooth.

"This is good dope, Mooser!" P.J. said, taking a deep hit and passing it to me. I took one, then two tokes, and held it in for what seemed like a long time, finally passing it back to P.J. He toked up again.

"Damn! This is some good dope, Mooser!"

"Yeah, I know. I scored a party pack from some dude at the Supply Building."

"What dude?"

"You know, the guy who got the hole in the chest," Moose said.

"Right on!" P.J. asserted. "I hear ya. The strange dude who fogs out and looks like someone took a big hunk out of the front of him and didn't bother to fill it back up. He's hurtin' for certain."

"Yeah, that dude is double fucked up," Moose continued, "His C.A.P. unit got overrun and everyone was killed except him and a splib who pretended he was dead."

"Right on," I added. "I guess the Supply dude was shot two or three times and was leaning up against a bunker when one of the gooks came up, pointed his AK at the dude's head, then moved it and fired into his chest."

"Bet he was shitting," P.J. interjected.

"You bet," Moose said, "and I heard the gook what shot him wasn't much over twelve or thirteen years old."

"Damn!"

"What C.A.P. unit was that?"

"Hell if I know. But it was one of those stationary units."

"God, I hope we go mobile."

"Yeah, me too."

Dear Kristen,

Tomorrow we graduate from C.A.P. School. It's so cool here.

I just can't believe my luck. I told you things would be better if I transferred to a C.A.P. unit. P.J. and I have been assigned to the First Company. The Command Post is located at Hue Duc, I don't know any-thing about it, but it's close to Da Nang. I think it's a mobile company.

My letters almost seem repetitive. All I can think of is you. You and Jenine. I miss and love you so much.

A sales representative from General Motors stopped by our compound the other day. He was selling cars and Bibles. Or he could even order you a suit from Hong Kong. Anyway, I didn't quite understand how he did it, but apparently if I were an E-4 or above, he could arrange for the purchase of a new car over here, and it would be waiting for me when I got home. A lot of guys went ahead and signed up, and their pay is automatically deducted.

I'm not an E-4, of course, but it sounded like a great idea. I bought a Bible instead. It has a family tree and it's done up in gold. It's really beautiful, and I can pay on time. I've never owned a suit, but that can wait. You need the money. That sixty-five dollars extra you get because I'm in combat helps, I hope.

I'm putting in for my R & R for Hawaii. I should get it sometime in February or March. You are going to have to write and find out the cheapest accommoda-tions you can find. Even though they fly us free, I still worry about your not having much money.

Anyway, Hawaii and the end of February should be our goal. From now on, try to save everything I send home. We'll need the money, that's for sure.

Hawaii will be tremendous. I can see us at night on the beach, alone, making love in the sand. Remember when we went to the coast with Rich and Gail that time and found the hidden cave? Maybe it will be like that.

How's my baby Jenine? I can't wait to hold her. I go crazy showing everyone the pictures of her you sent me. I even show them the one that you sent of you in your slip, giving Jenine a bath in the sink. God, I miss you so much. It gets even worse when I start to write you a letter.

Good night. Sweet dreams. When I think of you and all you've been through, it makes me realize we really will make it. I love you. And carry you in my heart wherever I go.

Love you

Jack

January, 1969

P.S. I'll write you as soon as I reach my new unit.

Twelve

P.J. AND I GRABBED a ride on the back of a half-ton truck leaving the C.A.G. compound heading for our C.A.P. unit at Hue Duc. As we drove, the road was busy with motorbikes and their white-shirted drivers scurrying madly about. The day was hot and dust was thick as we followed a convoy of green crushing tanks and trucks.

Once we left the city with its rows of shanties, the convoy turned off. The road now divided miles and miles of rice paddies, villes, and isolated grass huts accustomed to despair. Pagodas, cemeteries, banana trees, distant mountains and a small river bordered the road on one side, while more villes, more cemeteries, and more brown people consumed the other.

The Vietnamese traveling the road looked aimless, detached, like cattle being herded, seemingly not thinking, from point to point. I could see they were losing their identity. They were experiencing an historic death. The Vietnamese countryside, once a grand expanse of endless rice paddies, and farmed primitively with water bulls and stooped conical-hatted farmers, was being overwhelmed with modern trucks and jeeps and tanks, or literally being destroyed by massive bombers. The people didn't seem frightened by this intrusion; they appeared to be numb.

Along the road, at the outskirts of each tiny ville, were checkpoints. Little stations where Vietnamese Military Police were placed to monitor all civilian traffic flowing to and from the villes. Each station stopped a collection of three-wheeled and four-wheeled buses, jammed full of Vietnamese families and their belongings. The riders were detained and searched. Questions were asked, identification cards were shown. Silly smiles were flashed and either they were gestured on or held for further questioning.

The road was the lifeline. The giver of breath and the perpetrator of death; and at night the road died.

P.J. and I sat on the back of the truck for miles, taking in the sights and throwing cans of C-rats to the "Gimme chow" kids.

We ate the red dust, wiping sweat from our eyes and swore at the driver for hitting every chuckhole he could find. We passed an area called Dodge City, slowed as we scooted by Hill 10 and turned a short mile up the road toward the company C.P., Hue Duc, which was set on a hill located several hundred yards from Hill 10.

Hill 10 housed the First Marine Division, artillery support, mess halls, E.M. and officer's clubs, a small underground hospital, and all else that normally accompanied a divisional support base.

Hue Duc, however, housed next to nothing. It was literally dwarfed by Hill 10, like a marble sitting next to a baseball. As our truck approached, I could see several rows of concertina wire, badly in need of repair, encircling the perimeter. Worn and shabbily bagged M-60 machine gun emplacements were situated in three corners of the compound and an unmanned .50 was guarding the gate. Inside the wire fighting holes were dug and ran together, connected by shallow trenches.

In the center of the perimeter was a two-room stucco building, home of the Second Combined Action Group, First Combined Action Company. We had been briefed earlier at C.A.G. Headquarters that four platoons operated from Hue Duc with the help of local Popular Force soldiers. Usually, a few Marines would be staying there, waiting to leave for R & R or to rotate home.

As we entered the compound, the gate entrance was not being guarded. The truck stopped and P.J. and I hopped down, grabbed our packs and rifles, and watched the truck pull away.

"All right, God damn you, bring your gear and follow me inside." I was stunned. It was our boot camp bad dream, the Mexican Madman, Sergeant Garcia — without the riding crop. In its place was a wooden cane and a noticeable limp. We heard later that Garcia had apparently latched on to some tequila one night and became very drunk by himself. The last person to see him said he was babbling about "Gooks all over the goddamn place." Supposedly, he passed out on his cot, came to in the middle of the night and fired on a sinister gook trying to sneak up on him. In his drunken stupor, what he mistook in the dark for an evil enemy hand coming up from the floor, over the bed, to do God knows what, was his own bare foot. He promptly blew a hole in it. His version, of course, was not nearly as humorous. When asked "What happened to your foot, Sarge?", his reply was short, curt and to the point.

"Listen, God damn you. God damn you, I got shot. I got shot." Then he would storm away or send you on a work party.

"Oh, boy," P.J. said under his breath, making sure Garcia didn't hear, "boot camp in Nam. That's all we need. But, I tell you, he fucks with the kid, I'll make tortillas outta his ass."

We followed our moustached cartoon into the small building and threw down our gear. "I know you girls. You two were the Communists trying to infiltrate my boot camp," Garcia said with an over-zealous grin.

"You fuck up here, you're dead men." And he laughed out loud, bringing back memories that seemed like vivid dreams.

"Captain Dunn will be along in a minute. You two just hang tight," Garcia added as he limped out of the room.

A moment later the captain, unsmiling, entered from a curtained doorway. I recognized him immediately from back at the training headquarters. He was a paper shuffler. I guessed he was in his late thirties. He reminded me of the kind of person who show up at a twenty-year high school reunion and no one remembers him, or wants to. They must be short of C.O.s, I thought. This was probably his first command. He stood and looked at us, shaking his head. He projected a condescending attitude; he was unfeeling, aloof, a lifer all the way. Then he smiled like a used car salesman trying to unload a lemon.

He sat his soft body down at the desk, sifted through some papers, and looked up. "You're at attention," he ordered.

We snapped to. Not crisp like in boot camp. We snapped to... pissed.

"You can stand at ease now," the captain said, not looking up from his paper work. He rifled through a stack of manila folders for a few more minutes. Finally he stopped what he was doing, leaned back in his chair, and clasped his hands behind his head. His armpits were dark with sweat pouring through his skivvy shirt. His belly hung over his belt like rolls of bread dough. He rocked back against the wall for awhile, smiling at us with a silly grin, looking very resolute, and enjoying his position as Commander.

Suddenly, throwing himself forward in his chair, and slapping the desk with both hands, he snarled, "I won't allow shit-birds in my company." Then he leaned back again, smiling his sickening smile and looking smug. "Things are run a little differently around here than out in the bush," he said, making sure each word was clearly understood. "We are on display all of the time. We are representatives of the American people around here. We dress like disciplined soldiers. And we act like disciplined soldiers. Do you understand what I'm saying, BOYS?"

Boys? I thought. What was he doing calling us boys? Boys were back home playing ball.

"Listen, boys... there are **four** Combined Action Platoons in our company. We have a specified tactical area of operation to cover. No more, no less. Do you understand what I'm saying, boys?"

Sure. Asshole, I thought.

"When one of our C.A.P. units gets hit, we get artillery support from Hill 10 and if need be, air support from Da Nang. We also help each other out. Last night, the Combined Action Platoon you two are going to went to help another platoon.

They got their ass slapped. Each C.A.P. has ten Marines, a Navy Corpsman, and anywhere from eight to twenty Vietnamese Popular Force soldiers. Some of the PFs are good, some are bad, just like Marines. I assume you have already met Sergeant Garcia."

"Yes, sir." He seemed droll and functionary as he rambled on.

"Sergeant Garcia will ride with you out to your C.A.P. unit. You're both assigned to C.A.P. Two, which operates in the Ti Lon One and Two villes. Your address will thus read, 'The Third Amphibious Marine Division, Second Combined Action Group, Combined Action Platoon 2-1-2.' Is that understood?"

"Yes, sir," we said.

"You better write that down," he added. "We have three mobile units and one stationary. You will be going to a mobile C.A.P. Any questions?" We shook our heads. "All right, then. You will be going out on the chow run, tonight. For now, put your gear in the corner, and you can go out back and work on my bunker and latrine facilities." He pointed to an open doorway. "And let me give you boys one piece of advice. You fuck up here and you'll be going home in a body bag. And it don't mean a rat's ass to me. Now get outa here and start shoveling."

We walked out of his office through a small supply room, and out back where we saw two Marines digging knee-deep in dirt. The reddish clay hole they were standing in was about twelve feet by twelve feet. Off to the side of the large hole was the beginning of a smaller hole. The smaller hole was probably the start of the captain's private latrine. His own special one-hole outhouse.

"I wonder if he's holding a big turd back until his hole is ready for his fat ass," P.J. remarked.

The two Marines kept the dirt flying. One Marine had a shovel and one had a pick. The one with the shovel was wearing a cast on his right arm running from the wrist to the elbow. It reminded me of the scar on P.J.'s arm. I had a feeling the cast resulted from something less heroic than combat.

"What's happening?" P.J. asked.

"It's all happenin' right here in this fuckin' hole," the one with the cast said, stopping and leaning on his long shovel. The diggers both had their shirts off and were washed with sweat. The midday sun was draining them, squeezing them dry as the beads of perspiration gathered on their skin.

We stepped down into the hole and were just finishing getting acquainted and going through the grunt's special handshake when the captain appeared in the doorway, holding a can of beer.

"What do you think this is, a circle jerk? I want to see assholes and elbows. Get yourselves a shovel and go to it." He disappeared back through the doorway.

"That Dunn is later," P.J. complained. "I mean, that punk is all kinds of fucked. I'd like to blow his shit away," he said as he picked up two shovels and tossed one to me.

"You got it, pal. He's only been here a few days and he thinks he's a goddamned super hero or some sort of Smidley Butler or Chesty Puller," said Jimmy, the kid with the cast on his arm. "Well, he ain't shit to me. I told him so, too. No shit, right to his face. I mean, like you know, what can they do? Bust me up and send me to the Nam? I mean, fuck it, man, I was a private when I got in the crotch, I'm a private now, and I'll be a fuckin' private when I get out. I mean, like it don't mean a fuck to me. You understand where I'm coming from? Making us dig his bunker and shit house. Mannnn," and he shook his head and went back to shoveling.

We nodded and agreed that the captain should be fragged.

Dirt flew from the hole in slow, methodical scoops full of resentment. P.J. and I soon took off our shirts and settled into the rhythm of the moment.

"What C.A.P. you with?" Jimmy with the cast on his arm asked.

"I guess we'll be with the 2-1-2," P.J. said.

"Great one," Jimmy said. "I'm in Two. It's all right." The other digger didn't say much, he just kept digging. "I used to be in Four, they got a compound with a shower and everything. But when I got busted, they sent me to Two."

"What did you get busted for?" P.J. asked Jimmy.

"Well, I got a little bit high and was riding on a gook's Honda when I blew a turn and crashed into the side of a hut in the ville. Broke my fuckin' arm. Bummer, man!"

"Tough break," P.J. chuckled.

"Bad joke."

"What I want to know is, why are we digging his bunker?" P.J. asked.

"Tell you why," Kentucky said, speaking for the first time. He had a slow, lazy southern drawl like he was talking about half-speed. "Tell-you-why. 'Cause the Cap is too damn lazy to dig it himself." Kentucky was hot about that. He went on to explain that he was the captain's driver, and that he drove the chow run, too.

For the next few hours, the four of us tossed dirt and leaned on shovels. We were interrupted only by the arrival of Captain Dunn's outhouse. It came via helicopter and was lowered into the compound by cable. Dunn made a big production out of the arrival of his sitting room, directiing the choppers, lowering and making sure wasn't damaged.

It was a typical-looking one-hole outhouse, made of a thick green plastic like you'd find at construction sites. It was lowered into the hole so that during use, the captain would be sitting slightly below the ground. Added insurance against a sudden attack.

An "Officers Only" sign was placed on the door, as Dunn smiled with approval. We kept digging in the larger hole.

Sergeant Garcia came limping up from out of view, looking annoyed. "All right, God damn you, out of the hole. Kentucky, get the wagon and bring it up front. You jokers get cleaned up and your gear gathered."

The truck left the compound with Captain Dunn standing in the doorway of his outhouse, grinning his arrogant smile. P.J., Jimmy and I rode in the back, sitting on the side bench, hanging onto the rails and trying not to fly out. We sped past small groups of Vietnamese and were soon pulling up to the back of the mess hall of Hill 10, where we exchanged empty green food vats the size of picnic coolers for full containers. A case of milk, a sack containing several loaves of bread and four cases of C-rations were also tossed into the back, along with a mailbag and ammo supplies.

"Chow runs like this every night. I mean like I almost never eat the shit," Jimmy said. "I mean, like it's the same shit every night. Cheap meat, watered down potatoes and sour milk. The only thing worth eating is the bread and C-rats."

We left Hill 10 and hit the road in a hurry.

"They call this section of the road 'Freedom Road,'" Jimmy said, yelling above the roar of the speeding truck and waving his broken arm in a parallel direction. He continued to explain how Freedom Road ran in a north-south direction and what the main points of interest were. "Da Nang, you know the big gook market, city and shit. Dog Patch, lots of pussy. There's Freedom Hill, where the PX and flick are. Across from it is an air base or some shit. I don't know for sure. They won't let Marines in 'cause they say we're too dirty. Further down the road and off to the side are some villages that are called 'Dodge City.' Beaucoup booby traps around there, let me tell you." Jimmy was really enjoying the old-salt role, telling us anything and everything; some of it we already knew.

Kentucky slowed the truck down and pulled to the side of the road. A couple of black Marines were waiting to pick up C.A.P. Four's supplies. Both wore flak jackets and no shirts. Neither wore a helmet, and the taller of the two had a silver cake cutter stuck in his hair. They seemed more pissed than pleased at having to meet the truck.

"Kentucky," the one with the cake cutter asked, "they got the same ol' funky grits tonight?"

"You got it, bro," Kentucky said, handing down a green vat.

"That's bullshit. That's fuckin' bullshit. I can't stand that nasty ass stuff." Then he broke from his complaining and turned his attention to P.J. and me. "Hey, we got some new fools. Happenin', Chuck?" and we exchanged a few brief words.

"Got to hit it," Kentucky said, climbing from the open bed back over the front seat to the open cab. A few minutes later we again pulled to the side of the road. This time we were greeted by a small welcoming party consisting of two Marines, several young Vietnamese boys and a taller, well-built older boy. The group was clustered together like relatives at a family gathering, each one talking, no one listening, and everyone was reaching for something coming off the truck.

"This is it, guys. This is C.A.P. 2-1-2," Kentucky said.

"Hey, Water Bull. Water Bull," the older boy said, smiling and grabbing my arm as I stepped down from the truck. "Him Water Bull," he said again, pointing at the embarrassed me. The kids laughed. "You strong like water bull," he laughed out loud again, causing everyone to join in.

"Come on, grab the rest of this," Kentucky said. "Gotta get outa here."

I towered over the tall older boy, as would anyone who was six feet tall and weighed 190 pounds. To the Vietnamese I was huge. The boy was about seventeen or eighteen and had probably been fighting the Viet Cong and NVA for many years. He was constantly talking and constantly smiling. It was easy to tell that he was a leader and that the kids and the other Marines enjoyed him.

We were introduced to Tyus from Georgia who had facial features like an ugly bird. He had a hooked nose, pocked face, and crooked teeth. His accent was thick and heavy, and even slower than Kentucky's country-boy southern drawl. He looked simple-minded, but seemed honest and sincere. "Shorrr am glaaad ta meet Y'all," he said to P.J. and me, drawing each word out.

"And I'm Corporal Morgan, but you can call me Mouse," the other Marine said, shaking our hands. "And that loudmouth is Ta'," he said, pointing to the tall Vietnamese. "He's a PF."

Mouse seemed like a nice guy. He was plain and unassuming, the kind of guy you might see on your way to work every day for years and say "Hi" to, but never take time to know. Then maybe one day you find out he owns the building you work in.

"You guys pick up your gear, the kids will carry the supplies and we'll head over toward Ti Lon One where we're set up."

I had a wonderful sensation when I picked up my rifle and pack to follow Mouse and the others. I felt like I was joining a friendly community of different cultures. The environment was no longer hostile nor foreign. It was a blessing compared to the bush. Then, during those first few moments, I felt that perhaps there was a purpose, a meaning, to all of the insanity I had been a part of. I felt a direction. I could almost sense an emerging self-worth, as though I was appreciated and in a place I belonged.

We walked along the road that ran along the outside edges of the small Ti Lon One hamlet. As we walked, I joked with P.J. and Ta' and the kids that carried our chow vats.

The road leading into the hamlet was well worn from years of pounding feet and hooves and rolling oxen-pulled carts. It cut through rice paddies on one side and a river on the other. The first signs of the ville were the gray headstones of an old, untended graveyard with little temples and broken pedestals in remembrance of the dead. The graveyard carried a history of firefights, illustrated by headstones riddled with bulletholes.

Past the graveyard was a cement building with a thatched roof. Next to it was the beginning of a gently ascending knoll. The knoll was dotted with several dozen connected grass and cardboard huts that looked as if they would come crashing down like a house of-cards if a shack was pulled from the base of the knoll. Some of the shacks were patched with the same tin and flat C-ration boxes that characterized most refugee villes.

The river and the road paralleled the back of the shacks while to the front of the shacks and halfway down the knoll, stood the remains of a never-completed stone schoolhouse. Parts of four walls were all that had survived the rockets and mortars and machine guns of many bad nights. To the sides of the schoolhouse and inside its walls, fighting holes had been dug. To the immediate front of the schoolhouse was a smaller bare hill and rice paddies. To its right side at the opposite base of the knoll was another graveyard, only this one was well tended. Each grave had a stone or rock marking of some kind. Vietnamese graves differed from the traditional American graves. Each individual Vietnamese grave was laid in a circle like a mud pie, with twelve- to eighteen-inch-high mounds marking the burial location. From the graveyard edges the knoll melted into tree lines that hid isolated huts.

From these huts, the road that divided the hamlet from the river narrowed to a path, more huts, thick foliage and banana trees, forming another little hidden community. The other side of the hidden community led into dense jungle and the base of the foothills leading to towering mountains. It was from the foothills and their sister mountains and back along the river side of the road that the NVA and Viet Cong found sanctuary.

Our area, as I was later to understand, took in Ti Lon One and Ti Lon Two and the Hoa Hong hamlets. Each consisted of a few dozen families at most.

We stopped at the first house that led into the hamlet. Like most huts, it was built up on layers of dirt to prevent being swept away during monsoon flooding. Tall banana trees and bamboo shoots nestled the hut, giving it shade from the sun and protection from the monsoon winds and rain.

To the front of the house was a dirt patio, used by the Vietnamese for their everyday living activities. At this particular house, a food stand had been erected on the patio and it was now being tended by a young girl with one arm missing. It reminded me of a Kool-Aid stand I once set up in front of my house when I was a child. The owners of the stand sold Cokes and a sweet juice, or colored ice, like a snow cone. The girl had soft dark eyes and straight black hair that touched her shoulders. She was dressed in a clean, white blouse and dark loose-fitting pajama pants. She smiled as we walked up.

"Marine buy Coke?" she asked shyly. I was overcome by her gentleness and amazed at how she could keep so fresh looking in this heat and filth.

"Uh, yeah, sure," I stammered, looking at her stump. "How much?"

"For Number One Marine, I souvenir you Coke. 50 P."

"Get back, Jack," Jimmy interrupted, grabbing my arm with his cast.

"You got to watch Susie. The girl be doing a number on your head. Cokes only cost 20 P."

I dug through my fatigue pants and produced two rumpled up notes of ten M.P.C. and handed them to her. She quickly produced a cold bottle of Coke from a styrofoam container, put the neck of the bottle in her teeth and swiftly pried the cap off. Then she started to close her stand, obviously not pleased with the way Jimmy had handled things.

"Now, that is my kind of girl!" P.J. remarked. He was duly impressed with the way she popped that bottle cap.

We quickly drank the Coke and walked over to four Marines who were sitting on the ground playing cards on a bamboo mat. Two of the Marines were black.

"'Bout time you ladies showed up," the larger of the two black Marines said. "'Bout fuckin' time." Then he stood up and slapped hands with us. He was well over six foot two, had an athletic body and a friendly way about him. His head was almost egg shaped and he had a severe scar running around one eye that gave him the appearance of having a much larger eye. When he looked at us his bad eye seemed to wander in the opposite direction, as if attracted to something else.

"Name's Hodges. The brother's Bingham. And that's Red and that goofy-lookin' other chuck is Charlie."

We spent a few minutes introducing ourselves to Hodges.

"Hey, Oreo. Get your head outa your ass and back in this game," Bingham said, addressing Hodges, annoyed at our interruption.

"Get some big bloop. Kick ass and take names."

Hodges said, throwing a trump on Bingham's ace, "Black Beauty strikes again!"

"Shit!" Bingham exclaimed. "God damn if you're not a sorry son-of-a-bitch."

"Darn it," Charlie said, "Darn it," shaking his head as if he was being careful not to swear. His accent was heavy and thick like Tyus but he seemed to have a gentle touch. His adam's apple stuck out and when he spoke it looked like a ball was bobbing up and down in his throat. "Glad to meet you fellas."

Charlie introduced the other guy playing cards. "This here's the dog handler, Red."

Red was obviously nicknamed for his hair, which was a faded orange, and a face full of freckles like Tom Sawyer.

"Red and King have been temporarily assigned to our C.A.P. to help smell out them North Vietnamese," Charlie added. "But don't ask me how he does it. Back home ah hound dog go plum crazy tryin' to smell out them VC. Damn near like trying to smell out Democrats or Republicans."

The card game concluded and the players stood up and exchanged a round of "How do you do's" slaps and handshakes. "Any you guys from Philly? Huh? Damn, ain't nobody from Philly," Hodges said, shaking his odd-shaped head and walking toward the chow.

"You guys beware," he then directed to no one in particular. "I'm six-feet-four, two hundred pounds of Black Beauty."

"You may be black, but you shore ain't no beauty," said Bingham.

I found out later that Bingham was from Alabama and had been raised very poor. He was short and thick and was so dark-skinned that he made Hodges look almost like light milk chocolate. He seemed like he was pissed off all the time. Not about anything in particular. He was just the kind of guy who was always complaining.

Like Bingham, Charlie was from the south. But he was a nice guy whose tall, slender frame was in need of about twenty pounds. Charlie had extended six months in the Nam and was in the first month of his second tour. While he was back in the world on his thirty day leave, he had married his high school sweetheart. His extension bonus was one thousand dollars, which he was going to use as a down payment on a farm. He was a good ol' country boy, always polite, kind, and never complained or had a bad word. He claimed that he came back to the Nam for the bonus money, but everybody knew it was because he liked it here.

Charlie possessed an inner strength which seemed to radiate at times, especially when playing with the Vietnamese children. He loved the grubby little kids, running up to him and wrestling with him like he was their father. During his first tour he had helped a village woman deliver her child. Doc was at Hue Duc at the time, and the village midwife, the only other one who could have helped, was down with malaria. After that he was kind of the ville's local hero. To the Vietnamese in the area, and to all of us, Charlie was special.

Corporal Jensen was the C.A.P. unit commander. I found out quickly that Jensen was loud, outspoken, and more than aware that he was a corporal and we were privates or PFCs. He wasn't like Mouse or Charlie, he didn't relate well to us and was never well liked. Even the PFs spoke disparagingly about him. "Him fucked up," Ta' used to say. "Him Number Ten."

A few minutes after P.J. and I met the C.A.P. members, their medic showed up. "And, here's Doc Mayham," Charlie said, putting his arm around the shorter, moustached man. "Ol' Doc here's been out on MedCap. Either that, or he's been down by the river skinny dipping and drivin' all the mamasans wild. Ain't ya, Doc?"

Doc turned red, and searched to find an answer. "To tell you the truth, I have been over at Ba Sat's eating noodles and treating a few of the villagers."

As we were finishing chow, the other PFs began arriving. Ta' was directing, laughing and taking over, introducing P.J. and me to each and every new member.

"Water Bull, this is my brother Tinh." Ta' called everyone his brother. It was a custom that I never quite understood. "And this is our Bac Si," Ta' said, introducing us to their Corpsman.

These PFs we would be fighting and living with wore all sorts of uniforms and carried varying degrees of combat gear. Some wore uniforms too small or too large and wore green Army baseball caps that didn't fit. They carried old M-2 carbines or double barrel shotguns that looked like they'd never fire, and one old man even carried a cross-bow. The younger PFs brought newer weapons. Ta' had an M-16, Bac Si a well-cared-for Thompson submachine gun, and Hein carried an M-79. From time to time weapons were exchanged or upgraded when weapons were captured.

The PFs also had a diminutive radio man who had a 45 tied to his radio. I could just imagine him trying to untie his gun in a firefight.

And we met Porky. Porky was round-faced, incredibly stocky for a Vietnamese and had to be several inches short of five feet tall. He was married, as were most of the older PFs, had many children, and was perhaps in his early forties. He spoke only one word of English and coupled with his round little body and round head was a perfect caricature of Porky the Pig. No matter what we'd say to him, he'd always smile and nod his head and say, "Yes."

"Hey, Porky, you wanna get naked and hammer on Red's dog for awhile?" Hodges asked, and Porky would nod, not understanding, smile and say, "Yes, yes."

Ta's good friend, Hein, who carried the Blooper, was intense, had a gold front tooth, and was well built. Like Ta', at five foot seven, he was taller than most of the PFs. Hein, Ta' and Bac Si were the teenagers and unmarried. They grew up with the American presence and were thus influenced by the language, the mannerisms, humor, and cultural nuances. They spoke broken, but clear English. They liked to listen to our rock music and get loaded with us. They used the same slang terms we did and shared many of the same attitudes.

Unfortunately, the PFs even developed a prejudice against blacks that was regrettably prevalent in military life. It was a prejudice that was, for the most part, buried by the rigors of shared everyday survival, but it was indelibly a part of their lives. "Soul brother, Number Ten," Ta' once told me. "He fuck Vietnamese girl and give baby. Black Vietnamese baby, beaucoup Number Ten." That was the structure of the caste system in Vietnam. The mixed White-Vietnamese child was an outcast, but the Black-Vietnamese child had no acceptance at all.

The leader of the PFs was Sergeant Trao, who, like Porky, was probably in his forties. I learned from Ta' that Trao had been a soldier for many years, fighting first against the French, and now against the Viet Cong. As Ta' so wisely put it, "Sergeant Trao, he no like the war. He fight so he can grow rice and work the water buffalo."

We were a collection of misfits. Eleven Americans and fifteen South Vietnamese. Given my immediate viewpoint, I wondered if we could fight off anyone.

P.J. and I played with the kids for awhile until Charlie said "Diddi mau, diddi mau" to the three little guys who were still hanging around. We finished chow, checked out our weapons, and got ready to move out. Darkness would soon be our brother, and it would come soon. We gave the mamasan who allowed us the use of her home during the day our empty chow vat can and a case of C-rats so we wouldn't have to hump them at night. In exchange for her hospitality we "souvenired" her several cans of ham and motherfuckers, which she appreciated greatly.

As was the case every night, we would leave our day position and set up in a predetermined night ambush position. Every other day, one of us would have to carry overlays to the Hue Duc compound, marking the coming two nights' ambush positions. This was necessary to prevent patrols from Hill 10 or other C.A.P. units from wandering into our ambush.

As we packed up and moved out with the PFs down the road that ran in front of the hut, I felt a sense of purpose and meaning to this war. I felt like I was protecting the little kids and helping the old men who came to fight with us.

The biggest difference from the bush was seeing the people and knowing that the PFs who were with us lived and worked and fought and died in this little section of the world that I had come into. They were born, raised, got married and had children here. They had identities and a special affinity for the ground they patrolled and ambushed. It was their home. They could not remove themselves from the war.

Dear Kristen,
  I have been with my new C.A.P. unit for just a couple of days now, and already I love it. It is without a doubt a much safer and desirable environment. Except for the flies. God, there are flies all over the place. They just seem to collect and stick to me when

I sweat, which is *all* the time. But it's beaucoup better than the bush.

In the morning, after our nightly ambush, we gather up our gear and migrate over to a hut to spend the day. It's just outstanding.

There's a little eight-year-old Vietnamese kid named Frenchie who does everything for me. He's my boy. He washes my clothes, goes to the ville for Cokes, and even offers to clean my rifle for me. He is twelve years old, and is so bright. He speaks French, Vietnamese and English.

I pay him, of course, and he works for other Marines, but he's basically my boy. His father was killed in last year's Tet. And his mother was killed by the NVA for helping Marines. He hates the VC and NVA.

He has a little sister who is eight, and they stay with relatives. They are sort of passed along.

Frenchie is always trying to go out on ambushes with us. I really like the kid. He's like a little brother, or like my child to me.

I even get on him for smoking. It's unreal. As soon as the kids can walk around here, they are smoking.

Ta', a PF I met, and I are becoming fast friends. He's always calling me Water Bull because I am so much bigger than the Vietnamese.

At night, before we go out to set up our ambush, I wrestle with Ta' and Hein, or two or three other PFs. They gang up on me like a bunch of kids.

Of course, there are older PFs, but we really get along best with the younger ones.

It's really unusual around here. During the day the Vietnamese tend their crops in one area and at night the women and children and their animals move to another area, which is considered safer, to sleep.

I almost melted the other day when an old Vietnamese man came up to me and kissed my hand because I had given him some of my C-rations.

The Vietnamese are really an affectionate people. It is customary for men to walk around holding hands. In the morning, I often see the kids on the way to school, the boys hand in hand. The older Vietnamese and even some of the younger PFs we work with are amazed that I, as well as other Marines, have hair on my arms and chest. Another thing they do is smell me. It's a way of saying "Hi." This little fat PF named Porky and several other PFs are always coming up to me, hugging me, and burying their head against me, as a sign of affection.

From what I have heard, many of the PFs are the best fighters you will ever find. They differ from the ARVNs. The ARVNs are usually made up of draftees who were taken from the area they were born and raised in, and end up fighting hundreds of miles from their homes.

Anyway, it's really quiet around here. So don't worry.

How's my baby girl? I miss her and I haven't even seen Jenine. In her pictures she looks so clean. Some of these little kids and babies look so bad. Lots of the babies look sick with sores on their heads. I've gone on MedCaps with Doc and I feel so sorry for them.

But, listen, girl, your man is missing you. It becomes more intense every day. I can hardly wait until our R & R in Hawaii. I think I will invent a few new and different approaches to our lovemaking. Hey, now, I know you let Gail read my letters, but don't let her read this.

Well, my little Sweetie, let me know how the world is, and I will be writing to you soon. I love you, honey. Nothing will keep us from being together—

Love and lots of kisses and hugs and ?????

Jack

February 1969

P.S. P.J. sends his love.

Dear Kristen,

Me again. Today, without a doubt, was the best day I have yet to spend in Vietnam. Last night we stayed up on the knoll near the old schoolhouse. It rained, but we stayed inside the huts that are strung together, so I woke up dry. That started my day off right.

It was a beautiful day. Not too warm or humid. Even the flies that seem to be everywhere, in the food, on our clothes, and constantly on us, were almost absent. I think the rain has something to do with that.

I fixed myself some hot cocoa for breakfast, and my boy Frenchie showed up with some tiny, very sweet bananas and a bag full of incredibly delicious bread cookies. They look like miniature muffins. They tasted so good. After we ate, we moved to another location for the day, and Ta' wandered over.

P.J., Ta', Frenchie and I then went down to the river. P.J. and I got naked and went swimming. Then we got dressed and went fishing. We stood on the banks of the river and took hand grenades and tossed them into the water. When they exploded, the fish were stunned. Frenchie would dive in and swim out to gather them as they floated to the top.

People from the villes came out of their huts or left the fields to see what we were doing. Any leftover fish that Frenchie couldn't corral were caught by them.

It was so ironic. Here there were people tending their fields, plowing with big water buffaloes like they have for centuries. And there we were, on the banks of the river, crossing time, fishing by exploding hand grenades.

I have only been here a few days, but I have had more good times already than I did during my six months with Kilo.

After we went fishing, P.J. and I played cards in the C.A.P. Back Alley Tournament (it's like Hearts) and we won, hands down. We crushed Bingham and Hodges in the final match. Boy, did Bingham go nuts. First he started complaining about P.J. and me cheating, and when he couldn't prove that, he started in on Hodges, his partner, claiming they were losing because Hodges was playing the wrong way.

Anyway, we won three bucks, and Hodges and Bingham have got to go meet the chow truck for a week straight. Boy, were we hot.

Today would be complete, though, if only I were there, with you.

When I was in the bush, it was so far removed from home and you and what living is supposed to be like, that it was easier not to miss you. But here, with the kids and the PFs with whom I live, and with the relaxed atmosphere, I'm constantly drawn back to you.

We could share in this experience. We could live and learn about a different world, a different people. There is so much good to be done by being here.

I really feel as if the Vietnamese want us to stay, even after the war is over... if it ever ends.

Baby, I love you so much. I wish I could take home all the good memories and give them all to you. I love you and Jenine.

Be with me in your dreams

Jack

February 1969

P.S. Be sure to check out the Hawaii situation.

Thirteen

THE RIVER THAT RAN along the Ti Lon One hamlet filtered out the sticky heat, and with shade as its comrade, made life and living bearable.

We were on the river side of the road that ran through Ti Lon One. We had set up in a small hut, fighting the flies which would be with us as usual until nightfall. All of the PFs had either gone home to tend their crops, off to the village marketplace, or to Da Nang. It was midday as Corporal Jensen pored over his map and overlays at a wooden table inside the hut, while Mouse slept in a hammock strung between the center posts that held up the hut we were staying in. The rest of us were outside on the dirt patio cleaning our weapons and listening to Hodges' tape blast out, "Hey, Mr. Tambourine Man, play a tune for me..."

"Damn, I need some boom boom," P.J. complained. "The kid's got a hot rod," he said, rubbing his crotch. "I'm ready to mount a water bull."

"Jimbo," Charlie intervened, "we ought to take these here boys into the ville to meet Ba Sat. She might even have a little poontang for you all."

P.J. was sitting on his haunches, flat-footed, like the Vietnamese customarily sat, stirring a can of ham and motherfuckers, occasionally licking off the white plastic spoon. "I could go for some pussy action," he said, not looking up from his food, or missing a stroke.

171

It never ceased to amaze me how P.J. was forever eating, and then, just to be weird, he would snatch up a couple of bugs crawling around and stir them up in his food. "Protein," he'd say. And everyone would shake their heads.

"Let's hit the road," Charlie said.

Suddenly Jimmy kicked an empty C-rat can, apparently angry. "Charlie, ya know I can't go. The C.O. banned me from the ville," he said, kicking another can vehemently. "Shit. All I did was get a little drunk and ride a motorbike. Damn."

"That's right, partner, I'm sorry," Charlie said, trying to console Jimmy. "I just plumb forgot. Yer 'bout like a rooster in an empty hen house. Y'all don't get pissed now, ya hear?"

We talked to Jensen and told him we were going to the main ville. He reminded us not to hitch rides on gook trucks or Hondas and not to get deranged on dope or Tiger Piss.

"What's Tiger Piss?" I asked naively.

"That's gook beer," Charlie responded. "It's terrible. Y'all wanta stay cleara that stuff. It'd make my Daddy's home brew taste like some fancy French wine."

We strapped on some ammo, threw on our flak jackets, and grabbed our helmets and rifles.

"We're gonna sky outa here. Be back in a couple of hours or so."

It was about a half mile from where we had set up to Freedom Road and another mile to the main ville. It was hot and sultry as we tried to hitchhike, but were unlucky and ended up walking all the way. As we humped along the main road, I felt like I was back home with my buddies, hitching to the gym to shoot baskets or over to some friends' just to screw around. As we walked, I wasn't worried about mines or booby traps, and didn't really have to be. The stretch of road we were on was swept every morning by soldiers from Hill 10 and if it was mined, they were pressure release devices that would only go off from the weight of a truck or tank. Mines were usually placed more to the center of the road, but just to make sure, we walked on the shoulder.

The road was well traveled. Honda motorcycles zipped by while heavily burdened carts and three-wheeled buses sput-

tered behind, packed with too many Vietnamese and too much
junk.

We flipped the bird to half-ton trucks for passing by our
thumb, yelled obscenities when one truck stopped as if to pick
us up, but then pulled away, the driver laughing wildly.

The road to the main ville powdered us with red thick dust
as it did the few trees and scattered wooden shacks that bordered it. There was an empty history on this road. No remnants
of ancient Asian culture. It was just a road, long on dirt, dust
and misery. From the road I could see past the shacks out into
the rice paddies and beyond to the mountains, some ten miles
away.

From the doorways of the straw or clapboard huts, old
women smiled at us. In their customary, squatting position,
surrounded by flies, they tossed and swirled rice in round flat
baskets, while spitting betelnut in snake-like spray. Kids in
shorts would run to greet us, begging chow or cigarettes with
hungry eyes and outstretched arms, "Marine gimme chow," or
"Marine fuckin' Number Ten." We would run after them, but
only a little way, because they knew and we knew we were
both only kidding.

Leading into the ville was an old cement archway once
painted white with red letters that spelled out Hue Duc. The
wind and rain and probably the years of war had harshly
punished it. The arch was cracked and chipped. Hue Duc was
now Hue Du, and in need of paint. Inside the archway and off
to the right of the road leading to the heart of the ville was
Ba Sat's.

"Y'all don't get excited now," Charlie directed, "but here it
is. This is Ba Sat's. And this is the road into the main ville."

"I'm askin' for it, beggin' for it, and I'll be willin' to pay for
it," P.J. remarked.

"P.J., I know you're like a stud bull in heat, but cool down,"
Charlie warned.

Ba Sat's home had been ravaged by the war. What once had
been a fine French home, by Vietnamese standards, was now
four cement walls, with a tin roof, surrounded by gray and
green sandbags, some of which were tattered and torn. Her

home had once been painted a pale pink with white trim around glassless windows that would close up at night with wooden shutters. Now the pink was dull, faded and chipped. Huge chunks of wall had been blown from its side and never replaced and the wooden shutters were old and worn. But it had survived. It had survived the French Occupation, and it would survive the American Occupation. It had experienced a bellyfull of war and had taken rockets, mortars and machine gun fire, but it had survived.

Ba Sat greeted us before we made it to her doorway. Smiling, clad in black, loose fitting pants and white top, she was excited as she spoke: "Cha-lee! Cha-lee! Long time no see, Cha-lee! Ba Sat think Cha-lee go 'nited States. No pay Ba Sat!" She ended with an exaggerated frown.

"Yaaall knowed I wouldn't run out on my favorite girl," Charlie said, putting his lanky arm around the diminutive Ba Sat and giving her a hug. She was embarrassed by the attention he showed her, but it was easy to see they were friends.

"Cha-lee Number Ten, no pay Ba Sat," she said, shaking her finger at Charlie and scolding him like a favorite child.

"No sweat, Ba Sat. I got your money right here," Charlie said, patting his shirt pocket.

Ba Sat smiled and said, "Cha-lee Number One." We then followed her inside her home.

Ba Sat's age was hard to determine. It was somewhere between thirty-five and fifty-five. I suspected that at one time she had been a very beautiful woman. She had long, dark hair that was always rolled up in a bun, and straight, white teeth. Her dark eyes were alert and sensitive and, despite the war and loss of wealth, she had maintained a sense of dignity.

Inside her home, we sat at either wooden benches and tables or on plain bamboo mats spread out across the cement floor. On the walls were a figure of Christ and a picture of Ba Sat holding a child. She kept old, five-gallon tin ammunition cans full of water, chunks of ice and Cokes. In front of the long, open window that opened to the road, were wooden shelves. The shelves held watches, rings, packages of noodles, and plastic dolls clothed in bright Vietnamese female dress.

There was an old Kodak Instamatic camera and a beat-up pocket-sized transistor radio. There were cans of C-rations and packs of Kools and Lucky Strikes.

Ba Sat made her living by selling Cokes from Da Nang, cigarettes, noodles and whatever else she could get her hands on. It was several miles to Freedom Hill PX, so the Marines in the area were her main clientele.

She had long ago figured out the pay schedule of the C.A.P. units, and so, to keep business going, she had come up with the enterprising idea of extending credit. She only gave credit to those she knew and liked, and only after they had signed their name in a notebook and written down what item had been purchased and its price. More than once, she had gone up to the company compound, waving her book and complaining in broken English and loud Vietnamese that "Marines Number Ten, no pay Ba Sat." Sometimes the new Marines would try to cheat her by signing names like Richard Nixon or Zorro, but sooner or later, Ba Sat always got paid.

"We'll take three Cokes and three noodles," Charlie said, "Y'all like noodles, don't ya?" We both said yes. Ba Sat left the room, disappearing behind a blanket drawn across a doorway in the back, then a minute later, she reappeared.

"You new Marine," she said, looking at P.J. and me.

"No, I Viet Cong," P.J. said. And laughter followed. "Yes, I new Marine, and so is Jackson. We're new to here. We both been up in the mountains."

"You want maybe watch or ring?" she asked, quickly moving over to the shelves next to the front window. "I give for you good deal!"

"No, thank you," I replied as graciously as possible. "But, I will take another Coke."

"You want cigarette American?"

"No. No, thank you."

Then the blanket in the back of the room moved and from behind it stepped a beautiful young girl, maybe fifteen or sixteen. She walked toward us, carrying three wooden bowls on a wooden tray. She had rich, long black hair that hung down to the middle of her back and cascaded across her front. Light from the windows caught her hair just right, shining from it like the light that radiates from figures in religious paintings. She had big round dark eyes like a doe and she approached us shyly. She looked part French. Her lips were thick and wet, and her breasts were curved and full beneath her clean white blouse. She smiled at us while setting down the tray. Then she turned and walked back behind the blanket.

She looked like a woman to me. Her face, her hair, her full breasts, and the gentle way she moved made her seem so much a woman, and so unlike a child.

"She's really beautiful!" I said to anyone who would listen.

"She's Number One, that's for sure," P.J. said, grinning from ear to ear.

"Y'all keep your hands off that stuff. That's Ba Sat's niece, and she's off limits. Ain't that right, Ba Sat?"

"She go to school. Do much work. Number One girl," Ba Sat stated proudly.

"She got some everything," P.J. joined.

"Come on! Y'all," Charlie said, interrupting. "Let me show you guys the rest of this here ville." We finished off our noodles, paid Ba Sat and left.

"Charlie, Ba Sat's niece has got some tits. Jeez, she's just beautiful! I'll bet she's part French," P.J. said. "God, she's beautiful and so clean. I'd give up religion for some of that action."

"Keep your pecker in your pants, boy. You're liable to get it cacadowed," Charlie said.

We walked along the road that ran through the ville. Kids were everywhere, running up and following us around. In the center of the town was a small open marketplace. Villagers were gathering, exchanging, bartering or buying rice, fish, bananas, cloth, or bowls and baskets woven from bamboo. To the side of the main market, a calf was being slaughtered and everywhere, kids or PFs were squatting in the dust around the ville, playing cards and gambling.

"There ain't really no whores in the ville, guys. You want pussy, we got to have a PF bring it in or go to Da Nang," Charlie said and we walked along.

The ville was like Ti Lon One only with a much greater population. There were also more cement and tin homes, and more sandbags and bunkers.

At night hiding was a way of life, so for every hut, hooch or home, there was an underground bunker. When darkness fell, most of the ville went underground because anything moving after dark was free game.

We walked around the ville, talking with everyone and meeting friends of Charlie's. On the way out we stopped by Ba Sat's, downed another Coke, picked up one for Jimmy, and then headed back.

We stood by the side of the road leading back to our area. This time we were lucky and were able to hop on the back of a crowded three-wheeled bus, knowing that if we got caught, we'd be in trouble.

"Damn," P.J. said disappointedly as we hung on to the back of the bus, "I mean to tell you, that Ba Sat's niece is double cute."

"Patience, P.J.," Charlie added, "there's always your right hand."

P.J. and I did everything together. We were undefeated Back Alley Champs. We went on chow runs together or hitched rides to the main ville. We went swimming or fishing at the river and took bucket baths from deep water wells. At night we ran two-man killer teams checking out the villes for VC. We had become inseparable. On those evenings when we sat up on the top of the knoll near the old schoolhouse, we would lie back and talk about home. We shared such closeness, such understanding. P.J. told me everything about his life, his hopes and his dreams. He told me about back home and the first girl he ever had, and about the time they made love and how his brother stuck a hose through the bedroom window and sprayed them with water. We talked about taking long hot showers and clean sheets and how good it would feel to sleep in a bed.

"Jackson," he said one night as we lay back looking up at the stars, "when we get out of this war and we're back home, we'll start some kind of business. Hey, maybe we'll be heroes and be in the movies."

"Yeah, you can be Lassie's double," I joked.

"Seriously, I want people to be proud of me," he said, speaking in a gentle tone. "I want to do something important. If I have to be here, then I guess I'll do my best. I'm really not... well, hell, you know I'm not really crazy," he continued, searching for words. "Heck, I even like these damn slopes. And listen, about Ba Sat's niece. If I was back home, I'd... I'd... well, I'd just like to see her. Not like a whore... Oh, you know. Oh, forget it." And then, softly, "I mean, she's just like a regular girl." We lay, cooled by the night, sharing a poncho, and drifted off to sleep.

The days came and went peacefully. We went through the month with little contact other than killing two VC, caught on a night rice run.

One afternoon P.J. and I were bored, so we grabbed Ta' and walked over to Ba Sat's. We were sitting there drinking Cokes, admiring her niece's beauty, and examining a Viet Cong flag Ta' had liberated from a dead NVA, when a patrol of Marines from Hill 10 happened by. A couple of them came inside and bought Cokes and remarked at how they wished they had a flag like Ta's. Then P.J. came up with a brilliant idea for making some quick cash. "Hey, dude," he said to one of the Marines who was particularly interested in the flag, "you want one of these? Jackson here's got all sorts of that stuff!"

I looked at him, wondering what he had in mind. He gave me a "Be cool, don't blow it, I'm talking," look and went on explaining. "This is the straight scoop. We got all sorts of this stuff. Partner, we got some everything! We got beaucoup flags, sandals. We got anything a VC ever had!" The kid who had so admired the flag was duly impressed.

In grunt units, such as the ones that operated from Hill 10, any enemy gear found had to be turned in, or was confiscated by the officers. Conversely, in a C.A.P. unit, we could keep anything we found.

"Can you get me a flag?" the kid asked.

"Sure, no sweat, but it will cost you some money. I'm talking about twenty bucks."

"Twenty bucks!" the kid said, "That's awful steep!"

"We got overhead, my man," P.J. said.

"Overhead? How about ten? If you get me a flag, I'll give you ten bucks, OK?"

"It's twenty big ones or it's no dice!" he said with a cocky grin, winking at us again. The kid thought about it for a minute and said he'd be down tomorrow and would meet us at Ba Sat's place.

"I... I can't make it tomorrow," P.J. stammered, buying time. "Tell me what billet you're sleeping in and we'll slide on up in a couple of days." He told us and left.

"What you do? You no sell Ta's flag!" Ta' said.

"No sweat. We don't have to," P.J. assured.

"Well, then, how are you going to come up with another North Vietnamese flag?" I asked.

"Simple, donkey dick, we'll have Ba Sat make us some. We'll sell them to those lame ducks on the hill." It was a brilliant coup.

We had a half dozen made up, blew a few holes in them, and splattered them with chicken blood. We went from unit to unit on Hill 10, hawking our wares. The wilder the story and the bigger the holes, the more money we made. P.J. was in his element, wheeling and dealing, talking like a big shot.

"Pal, I took this one off an NVA captain. Killed him with my bare hands."

"No shit?"

"No shit!"

We sold out, placed orders, and sold out again. "Partner, we're just a couple of entrepreneurs!"

The next few days were spent much as the last few. The only real responsibilities we had were radio watch during the daylight, and our patrols and ambushes at night. On occasion we would send out two- or three-man killer teams at night, to creep around the huts and try to catch VC or NVA who came down from the mountains to steal rice. The Mad Mexican, Sergeant Garcia, came out with us one night, fell into a fighting hole and broke his already bad foot. Captain Dunn shipped him home. But basically, it was just dull. Our unit established excellent rapport with the people in the area and we soon found out who were the good PFs.

Our ambushes moved smoothly and efficiently. We would receive Intelligence Reports over the radio daily from the company compound. They advised us what was to be expected during the night. The reports focused on enemy troop movements or suspected attacks. More often than not, they were wrong. The only true indication of enemy troop movement came when the VC or NVA were there firing at us or walking through our ambushes. But when reports came in that six hundred NVA would be passing through our area, the tension was dramatic.

On the night of February 20, we were set in an ambush position in Ti Lon One, in back of the schoolhouse by the river side of Ti Lon One. We dug in at one of the several predetermined spots we had used before. Five NVA walked in front of us carrying rifles and sacks of rice. We opened up. Volumes of tracers and several bloop rounds tore through the darkness, killing them almost instantly. It was all over in two or three minutes. Pop flares were fired, silhouetting their bodies as we prepared to search the dead. But then something unusual happened.

"I killed this gook!" Hodges said. "See the row of sixty holes through his chest?" he added, pointing at the body.

"No way! No way! I blew his ass away," P.J. said.

We argued and fought over our fallen prey, each claiming a specific kill.

For a moment I thought I was crazy and felt dirty fighting over dead bodies. But feeling that way was uncomfortable, so I pushed it out of my mind.

The next morning we took turns taking pictures of the dead, propping them up against rice dikes and putting cigarettes in their slack mouths. We even put our arms around them and helmets on their heads. They were dead clowns. Our slant-eyed, slope clowns. We took Chui Hoi pamphlets, little pieces of white paper stating American policy that had been dropped across the countryside from airplanes, and stuck them in the holes of their bodies. Just a reminder, we chuckled, that this was our area and they had better stay clear. We were on a roll now. Good hunting ahead. A feeling of power was surging in us.

The night we killed the five NVA, the other C.A.P. units in the company also made contact. That was very unusual. One or two C.A.P.s might get hit, but not four at a time. It was a sure indication that enemy activity was increasing.

The Vietnamese celebrate the New Year at the end of January. It is called Tet. In 1968, during Tet and on into February, there was a major enemy offensive launched which resulted in some of the bloodiest battles of the war. Both sides sustained heavy casualties but it was the opinion of our Military Intelligence that there would not be a 1969 Tet Offensive. Although we were well into February, we began to worry that history would repeat itself.

Reports began coming in daily of suspected enemy strength passing through our small area. The estimates were of hundreds.

The NVA and the Viet Cong appeared to be moving down from the mountains, preparing to launch a major attack against the city of Da Nang. To do that, however, they had to first pass directly through our area, the Quang Nam Province. It was the responsibility of our company's four Combined Action Platoons, as well as elements from Hill 10, to crush their efforts.

Almost overnight, tension grew dramatically. Even for the slow pleasant pace of hamlet life, the days were eerie and still. The ambush of a few nights before and the early morning excessive elation was rapidly waning and being replaced by subtle resolution and a mixing of excitement and impending doom. The morning villagers, who normally tended their crops, had mysteriously and ominously disappeared. Groups of children who used to hound us had all but disappeared. The Popular Forces elected to stay with us during the day, milling around, pensive and alarmed.

Orders from the C.P. that we were to be "on one hundred percent alert" added to the tension.

"Water Bull," Ta' explained, "there much VC. Old men, old women hide. VC come at night, no sweat. VC come at day, Number Ten!"

It was midday as we set up by the schoolhouse on the knoll in Ti Lon One. Our perimeter expanded to the graveyard and circled back around the front of the row of shacks facing the road. From our position we had a 360-degree view of the immediate rice paddies and distant tree lines on one side and the hamlet, road, and river on the other. The sky was clear and there was a welcome breeze as holes were dug, machine guns placed, and fields of fire agreed upon. We were being cautious and much more professional.

"There beaucoup VC!" Ta' said again, his voice and face devoid of the usual high pitched animation.

He asked me for an extra frag, and we both walked over to the beginning of the graveyard, away from the walls of the schoolhouse. Our backs were to the huts. We met Sergeant Trao, who was studying the rice paddies below, visually scanning the wide expanse and the distant outer edges of Ti Lon Two and the Hoa Hong hamlets.

"What's up, Trao?" Corporal Jensen asked, walking over and joining us. His face showed great concern and suggestions of fear. "Do you think there's VC?" he asked. "What do you think, Trao? What do you think?" His questions were quick, desperate for answers. "I mean, all the villagers have skyed out of here. There ain't even any water bulls in sight."

Trao thought for a moment, still looking out across the paddies and down into the hamlets. "There VC," he finally said, his expression of studied quiet not changing. "There NVA. Maybe too much NVA."

In the distance, we could hear firing from the direction of C.A.P.s One and Four. Apparently, they were making contact.

Jensen ran over to Tyus, who was monitoring the radio, and made contact with the C.P. A few moments later, he came back. His speech was breathy and rapid as he spoke. "Sergeant Trao, I just got word from the C.P. They want us to sweep Ti Lon Two!"

Trao calmly acknowledged that he understood, and told Ta' to alert the other dozen or so PFs. We left three PFs, Tyus, Mouse, and Doc with one of the radios to stay behind on top of the knoll. They would cover our rear, watch our packs and set up for possible Medivac. Then we started down the hill, with Red and his dog, King, at point. Ta' then followed, P.J., me, Hein with his .79, Hodges and Bingham with the 60, some PFs, Charlie with the other .79 and Jensen and Porky. We reached the top of the graveyard and immediately started taking rounds from across the paddies in Ti Lon Two, some one hundred and fifty yards away. It was of short duration, meant more to slow us down than to kill, but P.J. and I dove behind separate gravestones and looked over at each other.

"We're gonna get some today!" P.J. said, with a light-hearted grin. The he moved to another gravestone, closer to me, as a round of bullets followed him, kicking up dust and impacting in the side of the hill and the front of the headstone he was crouched behind.

"You're zeroed in." I said, concerned. "You best keep your ass down!"

"No sweat," he said with his usual confidence. Then, rising, he quick-stepped and short-rolled two gravestones further down the hill, toward the paddy area. He looked like something out of a John Wayne movie as he did the same thing again, drawing fire. He joined Red and King, who were safely hidden behind several protective stones.

Our PFs then opened up with volleys of rapid fire while Charlie dumped a couple of .79 rounds, tearing into the tree line and huts facing us across the paddies.

More rounds flew back. We, in turn, responded with dozens of semi-automatic bursts. Several figures could be seen running near huts inside the tree line, so we concentrated additional fire power in that area and leap-frogged down through the graveyard, ready to advance. We were still at a slightly higher angle than the level rice paddies and the banana trees bordering them, giving us a good field of view. I took one of the three LAWs I was carrying and tossed it over to P.J. I still hated the damn things and decided that getting rid of them now

183

would be a good idea. P.J. and I were safe behind separate little walls of bullet-proof stone. We raised and fired once, twice, and three times, into the huts that marked Ti Lon Two.

To my surprise, the three fired and exploded on contact, ripping huge holes in the huts, throwing up dirt in violent sprays and starting smoky shallow fires. We thought we heard moans, so we unleashed a stationary, long thunderous assault. It was recon by fire.

We spread out as a unit on line, crouching down behind the last of the gray headstones before beginning the sweep across the paddies through the tree line and into the tiny cluster of huts.

Behind us, Jensen clung to the radio, explaining our progress to the C.P. "They're all over the place," he yelled frantically down to us. "God, they're everywhere!" I looked around and saw that the PFs were scared and reluctant to involve themselves in the sweeping action, so Sergeant Trao, Ta' and gold-toothed Hein encouraged them to move with the threat of a rifle butt to the back.

First Red, Ta', P.J., then Hodges and Bingham and I left the safety of the graveyard and ran about fifty yards, while Charlie and Hein popped 79 rounds over our heads and into the tree line. We received little resistance. We then continued the same procedure. First the six of us, then the rest of the Marines and PFs. We were yelling just like in boot camp. Running and yelling and whooping it up.

My heart was pumping and I was wildly excited. It was an adventure. We were on line kicking ass. I had no thoughts or fears of death or injury. It was a frantic, insane dash for the treeline, with non-stop firing. About twenty yards from the treeline, we all stood up as a unit and began assaulting the position. Ignoring the rounds coming at us, we screamed obscenities at the top of our lungs, firing from the hip. Charlie thumped and then switched his 79 to B-Hive rounds.

Hodges, his black arms strained and well-defined from holding the weight of the heavy gun, looked awesome, powerful, blasting short belts out of his 60, held tight and strong against his waist. Sweat poured as he released round after round. We were blasting away, P.J., Ta', Hodges, Bingham, and me, in a deafening surge of relentless firepower.

Ten yards shy of the huts, the tree line opened up. We ignored it, blending together as an unstoppable force. We were invincible. I could see bodies running and falling among the huts and trees and broadleaf plants.

I felt an unparalleled surge of adrenaline. I felt like I couldn't be stopped. Nothing could stop me. Bullets would bounce off me. I felt this even as two PFs dropped to the side, wounded or dead. We charged in like supermen, catching tan-clad NVA still in their spider holes. Several more were running in all directions.

We were uncontrollable now. We were plugged in, electrified, getting higher and higher, like being shot up on fast dope. We blew the enemy away and pumped rounds into their freshly dead bodies. It was a wild rush of screaming death and energy. We hard rocked right through, killing everything. Pigs ran scurrying across our paths. We killed them. Chickens and stray dogs, too. Everything got caught up in the madness, howling, squealing, dying. We walked through the huts firing, shooting up walls and religious shrines, laughing and shouting to each other.

"Charlie, bloop that hut!" Hodges yelled, stopping for a moment to load another belt in his gun. "Blow the shit out of that mother!" It was done.

"Look out over there!" someone shouted, and we all fired at whatever was in front of us. We sped through, magazines dropped and new ones snapped into place. Huts were fragged and blown apart.

"Dong Li. Dong Li!" we screamed at several escaping black-clad VC. Then we pumped them in the back.

It was TV, the movies, boot camp and all our euphoric dreams of kicking ass rolled into one. No one was in control and no one wanted to be.

The months of frustration poured from my barrel and the only thing I felt was the recoil.

The PFs stopped firing, but we continued, locked in on the crazed moment.

"PULL THAT BITCH FROM THE HOLE!" Hodges yelled crazily, standing over a bunker.

"DON'T SHOOT HER!" Charlie screamed. "She's just a kid!"

"She PF sister. No VC," Ta' said.

Hodges held up.

"Jackson," P.J. yelled at me from about twenty yards away. "I'll circle around the back of this hut. You cover me."

I was high and ready, ready for anything.

P.J. ran to my front, circled in behind the huts, hopping over a two foot high garden fence made from planted wooden stakes and strung with tight thin wire. "OH, SHIT!" I heard him yell, and froze thinking he was in trouble.

Suddenly he came running around from behind the hut like his ass was on fire. He ran across the garden, hit the wire fence and went flying through the air, his rifle lost in flight. Tumbling to the ground, he swore, got up quickly, and kept running.

Charging right behind him was a massive, snorting water buffalo. Frothing, its head and horns down, the water bull hit the fence, soared and flipped in slow motion, crashing to the ground, shaking the earth with an enormous tremor. I took careful aim at the bull as it struggled to get up, front legs first, shaky, like a newborn calf. Then I emptied the rest of my magazine into him. The bull slowed, swayed, and veered to the right, disappearing into the heavy thicket.

"Partner," P.J. said, panting, "I was ALL KINDS of scared! You saved my young butt! That bull was after my sweet ass!"

The rest of our unit came up from behind, loud, laughing, and grabbing ass.

"I got me a purple," Hodges said, showing us his hand and a small cut on it, bleeding red on black.

"Shit, the damn fool cut it on the gun, changing belts," Bingham said.

"Well, it's blood. Whatta you want? My whole damn hand?"

"You sorry sonofabitch," Bingham said disgustedly, shaking his head.

"Where's Jensen?" P.J. asked.

"Beats my ass," Hodges replied, still looking at his hand.

Ta' came up to join us with Hein right behind.

"You looked too good on that 79!" I said to Hein, **and** he returned a gold-toothed grin.

"We kill VC!" he said with a proud smile.

"Those aren't no VC, Hein," Charlie corrected, "they's North Vietnamese Regulars."

But it didn't matter to Hein or Ta' or the other PFs. The enemy were all VC to them.

"Ta', you seen Jensen?" I asked.

"Him way back in rice paddy. I think maybe him run, I don't know. Him Number Ten. I think him Number Pa-two-ie!" he said, spitting on the ground. We doubled back to the beginning of the treeline and began searching for the dead NVA. By this time, everyone who had begun the assault was there.

Every one of us, that is, except Jensen. He was still out in the rice paddy, standing over some wounded PFs. I walked back to him with P.J. and Charlie. "What are you doing?" I asked, annoyed.

"Why, I stayed back to see if we needed artillery. And besides, I have to call in a Medivac for these PFs."

"BULLSHIT! I OUGHT TO KICK YOUR ASS!" I screamed. I was enraged and probably would have kicked his ass if Charlie and P.J. hadn't stopped me.

"That's bullshit! You aren't going to call artie in while we're sweeping the treeline. You're FUCKED! You better get your ass home!" Then I stormed off, back to the dead bodies.

We searched the dead and found a few rifles, some ammo and an NVA flag. P.J. took the flag and I took some sandals which I later sent home to my brother. He'd be a hit on the beach.

"I told you we'd GET SOME!" P.J. said. "There's nine, count them, nine big ones," he said, holding up his fingers to illustrate the count.

I didn't care about the total. It could have been nine or ninety, it didn't matter much to me. Besides, more of them were probably buried or dragged off somewhere, I thought. I was still high, though, and upset with Jensen.

Fighting continued in the distance. The other C.A.P.s were making heavy contact. The PFs who were wounded were taken back to the schoolhouse to have Doc look after them until their Medivac truck came.

We went back to the graveyard and ate dinner, sharing what we had with the PFs. We waited for dark. There was no chow run that night.

The Tet Offensive had begun.

Fourteen

ON THE MORNING of the second day of Tet the sun burst over the horizon in a brilliant display of gold incandescent light. Birds were back in the trees and as the sun rose I felt glad to be alive.

I stood on top of the knoll next to the broken-down walls of the former schoolhouse, watching over the rice fields and distant hamlets that were the scenes of yesterday's battles. It had seemed so easy yesterday, and so we had spent the night dug in around the schoolhouse and shacks, almost hoping we would be hit.

I walked over to where Ta', Hein, Hodges and Tyus were sitting. They were gathered in a tight circle in front of a shack, eating and bragging about how fierce they had been.

"Ta' cac a dau VC," Hein said proudly as sunlight glanced off his gold front tooth.

"Ta' cac a dau VC my ass," Hodges interrupted. "Hein, you were A-fuckin' Number One with that bloop," he said, causing Hein to break out in a full-faced grin. "You did a number on those motherfuckers."

Then Hodges stood up, danced around, and said, "Hein, you was popping those bloop rounds in sooo sweet. Reminded me of how I used to shoot baskets back in Philly when I was king ah the court." And he proceeded to shoot a couple of imaginary baskets. "Swish. Swish. Got two from downtown!" Then he turned back to Hein, and said, "You keep that shit up and we're liable to let you be a real Marine."

"Why not, Beauty?" Tyus cracked, "You sho' ain't." "You gotta cut Beauty here some slack," Charlie said sarcastically. "He's a hee-ro. Why, he got himself a purple yesterday. Next thing he'll be puttin' himself up for a silver star."

This made us all crack up. Even the PFs slapped hands and said, "Get some, Char-lee!"

Hodges stood there in front of us, his bad eye wandering, trying hard to keep from smiling. Then he let go and joined in with the rest of us.

We were all alive, healthy and fresh from sleep and pumped up about our combat performance. I felt we would crush any enemy who dared come through our area. We had a great advantage. The NVA were coming down from the mountains and entering turf that we knew, like a tongue knows the inside of a mouth. We had covered every inch of our area and covered it continuously. We knew the open spaces and where they led, as well as the closed, unseen portions of the hamlets. They could come. We were ready.

"Hey, Beauty," P.J. said, walking over while stirring a cup of hot cocoa. "You were awesome on the .60 yesterday! You were just all kinds of bad!" Hodges flashed a big, toothy grin. "You had that bitch smoking, babe!"

"I was kicking ass! Like Smedley Butler! Can you dig it? Semper Fi, Do or Die! All right!" He laughed out loud and bent over to slap Red's hand. Red was sitting on his pack brushing his dog King.

"Now, why don't you have that funky ass dog of yours run on down to Ba Sat's and pick me up a couple of Cokes, and a pack of do-bee?" Hodges asked, jokingly.

"Well, I tell you, I would, but old King here is about ready to run up to Freedom Hill and fetch me a couple burgers!" Red laughed and snorted at his joke.

"You think that dumb ass dog know what a VC is?" Hodges asked.

"Hey, now, don't you go insulting King. He's liable to take a big bite outa your black butt!"

Hodges quickly clenched his fists, shadow boxing, going into his Muhammed Ali routine. "Tell that sucker to get up! Come on! Tell that funky ass dog I's ready to throw some hands! I'll whip that dog so bad he'll wish he was back in the world chasing cats." Hodges threw a couple more punches at the air, did a poor imitation of Ali's fancy footwork and almost fell on his face.

"Watch him, King!" Red said. Immediately the big German Shepherd hopped to all fours, growling at Hodges with white fangs showing and his nose crinkled up, ready to attack.

Hodges backed up quickly and fell over his M-60 in a frightened swirl of tangled feet and settled square on his butt. "Call him off, Red! Call him off! I was only foolin'," Hodges pleaded, throwing up his hands in a defensive gesture. By now, those who weren't listening at the beginning of the exchange were gathered around and watching with great delight.

"First, you have to say, 'I'm sorry, Mr. King. I'm sorry I offended you.' And don't forget to call him Mr. King!"

"Come on, Muhammed, let's hear it!" Jimmy yelled.

"I'm sorry I offended you... Mr. King," Hodges said, with obvious difficulty.

"Make him kiss that dog's ass," P.J. shouted.

"That's better," Red said. "Down, boy." King lay back down on the ground as if nothing had happened. "Good boy. That's a good boy," Red went on, carefully brushing and petting King.

Toward noon a call came down from the C.P. that our C.A.P. unit was to join forces with C.A.P. Four, east of the Hoa Hong hamlet. We were to link up as blocking action. Apparently a company of NVA were dug in and around the Hoa Hong hamlet. We packed our gear and stored it in the huts around the schoolhouse and moved out. The sun was high and hard and the sky was clear and blue when we met up with C.A.P. Four at the ruins of an old French mansion. It was similar to the schoolhouse in Ti Lon One, with broken walls and bullet holes. The rise we were on looked down and across rice paddies and into a treeline that marked the Hoa Hong hamlet. The NVA were supposed to be dug inside the treeline and occupying Hoa Hong.

Approximately 100 feet to the front of the French mansion was a long, three-foot-high cement wall. It was thick and sturdy and ran some 200 feet before stopping at a short cliff. The wall reminded me of the stone fence that surrounded the downtown Post Office and Marine Corps Recruitment Office back home.

From our position, and with the protection of the wall, we could look down and see any movement coming into or out of the area. If NVA were dug in there, it would be a slaughter. With Hill 10 at the backside of the Hoa Hong hamlet, the NVA could not escape. It appeared as if the NVA had moved down from the mountains during the night, passed through the tree-line into Hoa Hong and had dug in. They had probably hoped to make an assault on Hill 10 and support additional units in attacking Da Nang.

We dug holes behind the wall and placed rifles in the open gaps that occurred every two feet in the wall. A .30 machine gun was mounted on a tripod, extending just up and over the wall. Two M-60s were placed at opposite ends and a vintage World War II B.A.R. was set in the middle. Four or five M-79s and at least ten or twelve LAWs were available. M-16s and M-14s and a collection of carbines, shotguns, a Czechoslovakian S.K.S. and even a crossbow were strung along the wall.

The atmosphere was festive. We would simply open up and bury the surrounded enemy below. "We got us a damn turkey shoot," Charlie exulted. Word came down from the C.P. that Hill 10 would prep the area with artillery and that air strikes would follow. We, the blocking force, would fire into the area some one hundred meters away at our discretion. There would be no escape.

Before the artillery began, Huey gunships flew over the target area, warning villagers by loudspeaker to leave because of the impending airstrikes. One of the choppers was quickly shot down. The villagers meanwhile had already moved, couldn't move, or had been killed by the NVA. The common practice of our adversary from the north was to come out of the mountains and into a hamlet area to take whatever they wanted or needed. If the residents resisted, or attempted to warn the PFs or Marines, they were butchered. One time, in an area that C.A.P. Four patrolled, an entire family, except for the mamasan, was butchered because cases of Marine C-rations had been stored at the family's hut. The children were shot and disemboweled in front of their screaming mother. The mamasan was allowed to live, so she could tell other Vietnamese families what would happen if they helped Marines.

After the Huey was shot down the remaining choppers raked the area, then flew off as artillery began. The guns from Hill 10 boomed, sending rounds ripping through trees, crashing through thatched roofs, destroying huts, and shooting up volcanic-like sprays of dirt. Movement could be seen, figures were running, half flying, or were reduced to piles of human debris.

Then our two units opened up as one. Tracers shot out in solid lines, marking and strafing the treeline. Bloop rounds popped, arched, and exploded with incredible rapidity, blasting more holes in the already burning huts. LAWs flashed and roared as entire huts were demolished. Alarming resistance came flying back at us but impacted harmlessly against the wall. A squad of enemy was buried in a hail of fire as they broke from the treeline.

We fired and fired and argued over who got a chance to shoot the .30. We exchanged weapons like kids exchange toys at Christmas. We were wild and ecstatic, pouring hundreds of rounds into the treeline. Bullets flew like steel sheets, relentless and designed for slaughter. Moans and screams could be heard coming from the trees, huts, foliage, and the squad of NVA lying helplessly in the paddies. Suddenly P.J. ran to the wall, dropped his pants, turned around and flashed a quick bare ass. The PFs were stunned. But for us it was a wonderful joke. I couldn't stop laughing. It all made sense, because nothing made sense any more.

We covered the area, blanketing it with fire for over thirty minutes. It wasn't a firefight. In a firefight, the enemy shoots back. This was a kill. A remorseless destruction of those who would have, given the chance, done us equal harm.

Finally we received the order to cease fire. A few minutes passed and then from out of the bright aqua sky, came the jets. They soared and sliced through the sky like majestic eagles, swooping the area once, making a pass to determine their target, then swooping down again, firing rockets into the treeline and few huts. Then they circled around and passed over, dropping silver canisters of napalm. The tubes fell casually from the planes in seeming slow motion, tumbling end over end, until disappearing from sight before finally reappearing as huge exploding balls of violent orange fire. We whistled and cheered, "Get some for a fat man! Get some!!" A pig, flaming, followed by four NVA, also on fire, appeared at the treeline. A quick, concentrated burst of PF and Marine rifles and machine guns stopped the running fires and left them dead and smoldering. We were high! Getting stoned on death.

"Get some rocket action!" P.J. screamed.

After several more canisters, accompanied by our cheers, the party was over. We'd won. We'd crushed their asses.

It was midday and our spirits were high when we split from C.A.P. Four and rallied back at the schoolhouse. We had just spent a couple of hours involved in punishing and destroying a trapped enemy force.

"All right, guys," Jensen said, trying to sound authoritative. "The word is, we are supposed to sweep Ti Lon Two again. Red, you'll be up front with King. Jackson, you're next. Hodges, you're behind Jackson."

"Wait a minute," P.J. said, interrupting Jensen. "I'm going to walk behind Jackson." There was no argument. I felt secure walking next to P.J. We were best friends and knew what to expect from each other. We were confident and felt we could not be defeated.

Once again our C.A.P. unit, led by Red and King, left the schoolhouse. The sun felt good on my face and the air smelled of napalm and burning flesh as we wound down through the graveyard to the borders of the rice paddies. We jogged left, and got onto the well-traveled trail that ran along the outside edges of the huts and paddies of Ti Lon One. Every day, the inhabitants of the various hamlets in the area walked the trail, carrying heavy bamboo baskets, full with rice, shouldered and balanced on the ends of long poles. To the left and right were straw huts hidden from first view. Often there would be a break in the thicket that landscaped the edges of the living area, then it would open quickly to a hut on another trail leading out to foot-high dikes that sectioned wide open fields of rice paddies. From the trail villagers walked the three-foot-wide connecting dikes to other hamlets or tended their fields.

We were moving smoothly and confidently, when suddenly King darted from the path, pulled Red and ran through a dry field of rice paddies for a hut and treeline approximately one hundred yards away. They had twenty-five yards on P.J. and me and had crossed over a rice dike when the distant treeline erupted in small arms and light machine gun fire. Ahead of us Red suddenly pivoted and jerked spastically. Then he crumbled to the open ground, dead.

As Red fell, I hit the ground while Doc, who had been close behind us when we first entered the open paddies, ran past me into the field. "Doc!" I screamed. "Get down!" As the last word sounded in my mouth, a burst of fire from the treeline knocked him to the ground just short of a rice dike.

"P.J.!" I yelled over the now constant shooting from the treeline. "Are you OK? Are you hit? P.J.? P.J.?"

"I'm fine," he shouted from a prone position. "I'm pretty sure Red's bought it and Doc's been hit, but I don't know how bad."

The firing ceased. Everything grew quiet. King didn't move. He sat in the middle of the open field, next to Red's body, his head up, his mouth open and his tongue hanging out from the midday heat.

P.J. was a few yards off to the side of Red and King while Doc was in between P.J. and me, moaning, "I'm hit! I'm hit! Oooohh, God!"

"Jackson," P.J. yelled back to me. "I'll lay some rounds in the treeline, you crawl up to Doc."

Just then Tyus ran past me toward Doc, carrying the machine gun. The treeline opened up again and Tyus made a guttural sound, spun around, and fell a few feet short of Doc.

The firing stopped. I crawled up to Doc and Tyus, and P.J. crawled near us.

Doc had gotten hit several times, in both legs. He had made a tourniquet on one leg just above the knee from a battle dressing, while the other leg pumped blood freely in little red spurts like Jimmy's had back at Kilo.

He'd shot himself up with some morphine, but the pain didn't understand, and he mumbled and spit and clenched his fists and cried, "Oh, Jesus, Oh, God, hit me up. Come on, hit me up."

"Doc," I said, "take it easy. We don't want you to O.D. on drugs." I wanted to get his mind off what was happening. "Here, I'll give you one more hit." I took out another stick of morphine and fixed it in his leg.

There was still no firing, and in the momentary silence, I began to feel detached, separated from myself. I felt as if I were floating outside myself, watching me and having no ability to control my destiny. I couldn't just leave, just walk away. I was trapped in the field and trapped in a moment of time. I thought about Red and I thought about being dead, alone and thousands of miles from home.

While I was with Doc, P.J. started crawling over toward Tyus. "No sweat," Tyus shouted while lying on his belly, ten or fifteen feet away. "Just got me ah million dollar nick."

He was lucky. He'd be going home.

P.J. crawled back to me and Doc, dragging Tyus' machine gun. "He's all right, flesh wound. Just a round through the arm."

"You guys all right?" someone said. Startled, I rolled to my side quickly and looked back at Mouse standing bent over above me. I started to yell, "Get down!" but the treeline e-rupted again, and Mouse crumpled to the ground.

The rounds were flying over our heads again, with nothing to protect me, Tyus, P.J., Doc or Mouse, but staying lower than the dike just a few feet in front of us. The rounds whizzed and twanged, inches from my ears, and impacted in the dike to our front.

"Oh, God, it's over. I'm going to die," I thought. "I'm going to die." However, P.J. didn't seem to be concerned with the fire and so he raised to one knee and opened up with Tyus' machine gun. I found my composure and crawled to the dike and fired over the top of it. We concentrated fire into the treeline, killing trees and huts and suppressing the enemy. I wasn't sure we had hit anything, but at least P.J. and I were keeping the gooks' heads down.

I crawled back to Mouse, who was alive, but clenching his hip and bleeding profusely. "Hurts like a bitch. I am such a dumb shit. You got to get us out of here, or we're in a world-a-hurt."

I did my best to patch him up, then yelled back as loud as I could that we needed some support. But I received no response from our treeline. Where the fuck were they, I wondered.

Meanwhile, P.J. opened up with the machine gun again, firing non-stop, yelling in Vietnamese, "Up your ass, luke. Your mama sucks dick, slope fuck!"

Whenever we started to move, the treeline would zero in on us with quick bursts. Mouse had the radio, but was in no condition to help out, so I tried to contact the C.P. for a Medivac. Both Doc and Mouse were losing lots of blood and needed immediate medical attention.

I was lying on my side, trying to raise the C.P. on the radio, when the firing started again. One, two, three explosions came. Oh, God, I thought, they're firing rocket grenades. More firing impacted against the dike. Please, God. Please don't let it hit me. My heart was quick as the rounds and sporadic explosions continued. Finally I got the C.P. on the horn.

"WE NEED A MEDIVAC DOWN HERE FAST!" I yelled. "WE'RE PINNED DOWN. RED IS DEAD. WE GOT THREE WIAs AND TWO ARE ABOUT TO DIE."

"State your position," the radio said unfeelingly.

"We're in the middle of the FUCKING rice paddy, near Ti Lon One and Two."

"What are your grid coordinates?" came the mechanical reply.

I was enraged. "I don't know what the damn coordinates are, you son of a bitch. Get a Medivac and some support here!"

"Locate a map," the radio said.

The treeline erupted again, this time louder and more concentrated, forcing me to hug the ground even closer. I screamed into the horn again, "I don't have a map! Get a fucking chopper. We're getting our ass kicked. We're pinned down!"

P.J. was back up on one knee, firing into the treeline as rounds flew around him. Then he stopped and lay flat again. "Jackson, I'm out of rounds," he said, looking at me with a face full of confusion. "Those slopes must be eatin' this lead."

"I'm down to a few magazines," I told him, "I'm trying to get a Medivac in. Hey, where the hell is Jensen and the rest of the squad?" I asked. My mind was swirling. Everything seemed to be happening at once, and nothing was getting done. The C.O. knew where we were. We were here every day. I got back on the radio, "ARE YOU GOING TO GET THAT MEDIVAC?" I screamed into the receiver.

"We're trying," the radio said. "We're trying. Calm down. Hold it!... C.A.P. Two, word just came in. Medivac Bird on the way. Switch to Medivac frequency."

Rounds started coming in once more from the treeline. Doc was moaning again, Mouse had lost consciousness and was bleeding badly, and Tyus was quietly going into shock.

"Your frequency for the Medivac chopper will be 17/35," the radio said.

I flipped to the frequency as the firing stopped. P.J. crawled closer to me. "I'm about ready to check out of this fucking war, partner. I can handle getting shot at, but all this crawling through buffalo shit is double fucked, ya know? I mean, shit everywhere!" he added, almost comically, as he wiped his face clean. I looked at him and thanked God for my friend. I loved him and was close to him in a way only those who have ever shared great danger could ever hope to understand.

We waited and waited... maybe thirty minutes, receiving no fire. Finally we heard a Huey gunship and a C-130 Medivac overhead. I picked them up on the radio.

"All right, guys," the radio said. "We got you spotted down below. We'll do a little work with the Huey. Where are your friendlies?" the chopper's radio asked.

"I don't know. Just blow up the treeline in front of us!" I yelled.

"Roger."

I liked the voice on the radio. He was calm and reassuring. If I got out of this, I would buy him a drink, I thought. I'd thank him and he'd be my good friend. Yes, I liked the voice. I liked him even more when the Huey swooped close to the treeline firing mini-guns and rockets. He tore up the hut and banana trees for several minutes.

"I can't see any VC down there," the radio said. "I think they're dead or skyed." Firing from the treeline had not been heard for a long time. I was still worried about getting up, though. They could be dug in, just waiting.

"LISTEN, what's your name down there?" the radio asked.

"My name's Jack, but my friends call me Jackson."

"Fuck the formal introduction, my man," P.J. blurted, "tell him to get his ass down here. Tell that bird ta git me back ta the world!"

"Yeah!" Tyus yelled.

"Jackson," the radio said, "the Huey will make one more pass. As it does, you guys get your ass out of there. Then we'll land the Medivac to your rear. How's that sound?"

My confidence went up, but it certainly didn't soar. Especially since I knew we would have to get to our feet to move Doc, which meant leaving the protection of the dike in front of us. P.J. and I paused for what seemed like several minutes until he said, "Let's do it. We're burning light."

The Huey made a sweeping pass, lower than before, blasting the area. "Tyus, get your Kentucky ass ready to move," P.J. said. P.J. and I picked Doc up, each under one of his arms, and ran toward our treeline, with Tyus sprinting ahead under his own power. The Huey mini-gunned and rocketed the enemy position.

No fire came back from the treeline.

We placed Doc near the path we'd left when we entered the field. Hodges, Bingham and Jimmy came out of the treeline and rushed to help Mouse as the Medivac hovered fifty feet above, waiting for us to pop a green smoke canister to mark an LZ near our treeline.

P.J. and I left Doc and went back across the open field to pick up Red's body and call to King. As we were crossing, I felt myself drifting again. Drifting out above myself. I had no sensation of fear. I was experiencing a moment of total reaction unassociated with premeditated thought. I felt I was finally going to make it out of the moment that I had been frozen in.

Corporal Jensen appeared from behind some PFs who had come up alongside the path that bordered the field. He took a green smoke, popped it, and threw it into the field about forty feet from Doc and the path.

The huge double-bladed Medivac chopper landed in the paddy parallel to the enemy treeline. Its back door opened, flattening the knee-high grass. The door gunner smiled wide under his helmet and dark glasses as he directed us in.

Bending over and ducking the blades, Tyus ran inside the chopper, holding his arm, while Mouse limped up the ramp, clutching his hip. P.J. and I carried Doc aboard. As we crossed inside, the treeline exploded violently in a barrage of small arms fire, riddling the chopper. We dropped Doc. Immediately, Tyus was shot through the back, the front of his chest spraying small chunks of flesh and thick matted blood all over me. At the same instant, as I turned to dive from the chopper, the smiling door gunner's head burst wide open, sending parts of his brain, skull, and helmet flying, as the rest of his head banged against the inside of the chopper wall.

I dove outside and it seemed to take forever to hit the ground. P.J. was next to me, and we landed low in the green fading smoke. I gagged and vomited in deep, heavy convulsions, bringing up nothing.

The chopper lifted and engulfed us in a wash of whipping wind as it rose to escape the raging rounds.

I couldn't move. I was spent. As the green smoke slowly disappeared, so did the firing from the treeline. I pushed up to my arms and looked over at P.J. through the last wisps of smoke, then I passed out.

"Yackson! Yackson! Big Water Bull all right?" I came to with Ta' pouring water on my face. P.J. was standing over me, his helmet and flak jacket gone. He was shirtless and smeared head to toe with dried blood.

"Ta' and Hein helped me drag your ass over here." P.J. said as he extended his arm down to me. I grabbed hold, as he and Ta' helped me to my feet. "You sissy ass. You OK?" he asked, grinning.

We were off the path, in a cluster of bending, broad-leafed banana trees. Like P.J., I was shirtless and caked with red reminders of Tyus and Doc.

"Thanks," I said. "I just kinda blanked out."

"Ta' and Charlie and the rest of the PFs were kickin' ass while we were in the field. But we got to sweep through the other paddy over here," P.J. said, pointing to another section of paddy that was on the safe side of the treeline. The grass in the paddy we were going to sweep was tall and swayed like wheat from the late afternoon breeze.

"I'll tell you straight, my man, that was a bitch in the chopper," P.J. said somberly.

"Tyus die. Red die. Fuckin' VC," Ta' said.

"What I want to know is, while we were out there getting our ass shot off, where the hell was Jensen?" Just as I completed the question, Hodges walked up.

"That chuck fuck, Jensen," Hodges said, "He been in the hooch, jerkin' off with the PF's radio, hidin', cryin'. Went in and slapped that jive muther's face. He best haul balls outta here most ric-a-ti-tic or he'll be suckin' the end of my 60!"

P.J. attempted to cool down Hodges. "Listen, Beauty. We'll fix that dildo later. Let's sweep the paddy before it gets too dark."

We swept the field that Charlie and the PFs had battled in, firing at will, at nothing. We found a young girl dressed in black, lying dead with an AK next to her. Ta' grabbed the AK and spit on her.

I came across an NVA with his leg mangled, almost blown off, sitting up against a dike, smoking a cigarette. He had tied off his shattered leg and stopped the blood from pumping out.

He showed no emotion, and no sign of pain. The frustration and flashbacks of Tyus and the gunner's head exploding drove me wild.

I swore long and loudly, pointed my rifle at him and kicked him in the side. "I'LL GIVE YOU SOME HURT. HERE, EAT THIS!" and I kicked him again, perfectly in the mouth.

P.J. found two more wounded NVA hiding behind another dike, both nearly dead. Charlie captured another two as they attempted to crawl off. We questioned them as to troop movements and I lost control and smashed one in the face. Then Sergeant Trao took his .45 and shot him neatly in the back of the head for coming up with all the wrong answers. Correct responses from the other one came more freely after that.

As darkness approached, a small contingent of machine gun-mounted personnel carriers full of Marines and PFs barreled down from Hill 10 to pick up the Marines from our C.A.P. unit and the wounded NVA. I was exhausted as we walked to the road to meet the carrier. Captain Dunn accompanied the column.

"Where's your helmet and shirt?" Captain Dunn asked me irritably as he jumped from the top of the carrier onto the dusty road. He had the same arrogant smile on his face that he always wore, accompanied by the same official tone in his speech.

"I don't know. I lost the son-of-a-bitch somewhere!" I was tired and in no mood to listen to his bullshit. I yelled obscenities at the wounded gooks as we loaded them into the belly of the personnel carrier for transport back to Hill 10 and eventual interrogation.

"MOVE IT, YOU FUCKIN' SLOPE!"

"Don't talk to them that way!" Dunn bellowed, "They might be able to give us some information. We don't need YOU scaring them. Now get it together, Marine."

If we had been in the bush, I would have blown him away. I hated him. I was so tired and emotionally drained that if it were at all possible, I would have blown him away.

"You Marines hop on board," Dunn said, climbing up the side of the big rectangular shaped carrier. "You'll be staying at the C.P. tonight," he added, as if he were doing us a favor.

"Big deal," P.J. said, "Big fuckin' deal. All he wants is us to help take care ah his ass! He's a worthless piece of human garbage."

"I hear you talking," I said, as we climbed aboard, sitting next to a gook we had shot just an hour or so before. I looked at the gook's face as he stared blankly ahead. I wanted him dead. I wanted him to die slowly so that I could watch.

We made the quick trip to the Hue Duc C.P., and jumped off at the gate while the wounded NVA continued on to Hill 10. P.J. and I took a shower under the makeshift rain barrel.

Standing under the shower, letting the blood and smell from Tyus and Doc and Red and the wounded NVA rinse off my body, I noticed a gash about three inches long and an eighth of an inch deep on my left side. I must have scraped myself on something. I dried off, put on clean fatigues and picked up my flak jacket. In the back of my jacket was a small hole where a round had obviously passed though. Probably, I guessed, when I crossed the rice paddy where Red was killed, a bullet from the treeline had gone though the front of my open flak jacket, grazed me, and passed out the back, causing the hole. I'd been so pumped up I never even noticed it.

"You're one lucky donkey dick," P.J. exclaimed, examining my cut and the hole in the jacket. "You got someone watching over you. That's for damn sure! Let's go suck down a beer."

We copped a brew from some Army dudes who were temporarily staying on the hill and hung out with some new guys who were flown in to replace the ones we lost earlier that day. I didn't pay attention to who they were, and later split with P.J. to find a bunker to get high and crash out in. We settled on a hole that was crowded with PFs. Ta' and Hein were there, talking and laughing as if the day had been spent at the river fishing.

"Water Bull," Ta' said, acknowledging me as we walked up. "Kill beaucoup VC Number One! Charlie kill VC boom boom boom!" He grinned and imitated the firing of Charlie's M-79.

I liked Ta' so much. He and Hein and Sergeant Trao and Porky were loyal and courageous. We could always count on them. I'd rather have those guys backing me up than any squad of Marines I'd ever met.

Even though we lost Red, Tyus, Doc, and Mouse, the day had been very successful from a military standpoint. We demonstrated we could hold our own, and dominate well-equipped troops. For P.J. and me, confidence in how we could perform under combat conditions soared. We were tired, of course, but we felt we could withstand anything. We shared a feeling of power and I felt protected by God. We were young, strong Americans who could "kick ass on those slant-eye fucks," as P.J. would proclaim. That night, before I turned in, I didn't think in terms of right and wrong, or in terms of Communism versus Democracy. I didn't see us as divine entities protecting the South Vietnamese.

I thought of what we'd done that day in terms of winning. That's all, winning. We had survived, P.J. and I, and the rest of the Marines had survived, and therefore we'd won. Living was a victory. I thought about living. But mostly, I thought about Kristen and Jenine and home and getting some sleep.

P.J. and I slept close to each other that night, stealing Captain Dunn's Snoopy and heavy blanket from his cot and sleeping on them "I hate that Dunn—harassing you," P.J. said. "I think I'll blow his shit away."

"Lighten up, P.J., he'll get his."

"We're gonna get some tomorrow, Jackson, we're gonna get some."

The night was uneventful. We could see tracers from brief firefights in the distance, motivating Dunn to hide in the bunker his Marines had dug. Just before morning, P.J. snuck over to Dunn's prized private outhouse and tossed in a grenade and blew the hell out of it. Within seconds the entire camp was up running. P.J. came bolting back to us laughing, "I told you I'd blow his shit away." Dunn went crazy and was still ranting when P.J. deadpanned, "It must have been sappers, sir."

It was already hot as we left the compound later in the morning with the new Marine replacements and our PFs.

Captain Dunn was rambling on as we left, "I'll find out which one of you destroyed government property. I'll find out!"

The early part of the morning was spent sweeping through and around Ti Lon One and Two, searching for dead bodies and finding a few more wounded NVA. When searching through Ti Lon Two we found a PF's wife and mother tied together with wire and their throats slit. Apparently, they were unable to get out of the area in time and the NVA found them, tortured them, and killed them silently at night.

We found twenty-five dead enemy left behind, most stripped of their weapons. The heat of the day had already settled into their bodies, causing them to swell and stink. We also located shallow fresh graves where two and three, sometimes four, bodies were buried. Many we had killed in random fire; many, I supposed, from the gunships. Dead animals, including the water buffalo I had shot two days before, had been strung across the paths leading into the hamlets or were lying stiff with rigor mortis in clumps of bushes. Pigs and NVA that had been caught by the napalm lay burned, black and bloated to the point where their bodies had begun to split open. Straw huts were destroyed with only family underground bunkers remaining intact. There was no sign of village life. As P.J. and I cautiously searched some huts we came across an old papasan, shot dead, lying on the floor under a religious altar. The papasan's shrine was complete with white wax candles and a tray full of banana offerings.

Stepping carefully over him, we ate the bananas.

It was just past noon when word came from the C.P. that we were to link up with elements of a Marine patrol from Hill 10. The patrol was pinned down in rice paddies bordering the Hoa Hong hamlet. When we arrived, the situation was similar logistically to that of yesterday's battle, except that the enemy treeline was extended in an inverted L shape.

There was no firing as we approached. An overweight Army captain was clumsily attempting to rescue some Marines.

"What's going on?" I asked the pudgy captain, not bothering to consult with Corporal Jensen.

"Some of your Marines are trapped out there in the rice paddy," he replied, as he crouched behind a tree and pointed. I looked into the field and saw a Navy Corpsman about 75 yards out, lying wounded next to the intersection of two dikes. Beyond the dike another twenty yards and facing us was a collection of straw huts, banana trees, and dense thicket while the adjoining dike ran back to our treeline. The Corpsman was lying close to the dike parallel to us and on the right side of the dike running back to us. Six or seven Marines were also pinned down on the left side fifteen or twenty feet from the dike running back to our treeline.

I didn't like the way the captain explained the situation. It was as if it were a Marine Corps problem because the Marines were out there, not an American tragedy because Americans were trapped.

"Were you linked up with the Marine patrol when they got hit?" I asked.

"Well, uh, yes, we were. But they were ahead of us," he said, redefining his right to be safely hidden back in the cluster of trees and bushes. "We have to get out of there soon, or the Corpsman out front is going to die," he concluded.

That was an astute observation, I thought, for someone 75 yards away from a man who was, in addition to being wounded, almost hidden from view.

"How did the Corpsman get way out front of the rest of the patrol?"

"Our point was hit and he went up there to administer First Aid. The Doc yelled back after he got hit that the point was dead."

I walked over to corporal Jensen, who was, as usual, as far as he could get from the battlefield. "Well, what do you want to do?" I asked.

"There is nothing we can do. I'm not about to send anybody out there. The gooks would love it. They'd pick us off from the treeline one by one. No way I'm going out there. That's suicide!"

He made me sick. I wanted to kick his sissy ass! He was a one-way motherfucker, as far as I was concerned. If it were

Jensen out there, spilling his life on the ground, he'd sure as hell want someone to do something.

I walked back and asked the captain again what he thought we should do.

"I suppose we'll have to send someone out to get the Corpsman and direct the others back here," he said with a considerable amount of apprehension in his voice. "I guess I'll go. What do you think?"

"Sure, go!" I was surprised that he would even ask for my suggestions. "We can lay down some covering fire for you," I said. As soon as my words left my mouth, his face took on a look of fear and second thought.

"You know, I would go but I... well, I'm not sure now. Let's think about this for a few minutes. Maybe there's some other way."

He was disgusting! He was just like Jensen. I could see by the look on his round red face that he wasn't about to go out into the rice paddy. I yelled back to P.J. who was talking to one of the new men and, explaining the layout, asked him what to do.

"Partner, let's just do it," he replied. "We're burnin' light. But we'd better take off our helmets and flak jackets so we can move quicker and get closer to the ground."

We didn't take our rifles, as they would have slowed us down, and there was no need for them because of the firepower we had protecting us from our treeline. It was simple. We'd crawl along the edge of the dike which would protect us from fire on our right flank until we reached the Corpsman where the dikes intersected.

In case the NVA were dug in close to the Doc, we stuffed several flags into the side pockets of our utilities, along with a couple of battle dressings.

The PFs, the Army unit, and the rest of the Marines began a flood of fire on the treeline. It was a long, murderous assault, followed by deafening silence. I looked at P.J. as his eyes met mine.

"One thing I'd like to know, Jackson, before we run out there," he said seriously.

"What?" I replied, concerned by the expression on his face.

"Why hasn't your old lady sent me a pair of her under-panties?"

The sky was clear as P.J. and I ran out of the treeline and dove to the ground. We crawled four or five yards through the knee-high rice shoots until we reached the wounded Corpsman. We crawled another forty feet out and met up with a black Marine, and three white ones, too scared to move.

"Hey, guys," P.J. said reassuringly. "No sweat. Just stay low, and follow the dike back to the treeline. Most of the gooners are in that far treeline. It's OK. Don't worry, you'll be all right." I could hear P.J.'s words, but couldn't see his face because I was crawling right behind him, looking at the black waffled soles of his green boots.

He reassured the Marines and again we crawled on. It was easy, I reasoned, to stay low and don't worry. We had the L shaped protection of dikes and not one shot had been fired. We snaked along, about twenty-five more yards, staying close to the dike. As we moved, I could smell the stench of buffalo dung used to fertilize the fields. It reminded me of how farm fields smelled back home when the wind shifted just right.

We crawled on in silence, receiving no fire, until we met up with another Marine, who was on the same side of the dike as we were. He was curled up almost in a fetal position.

"Hey, slick," P.J. said calmly. "How you doin'? You OK? You going to be all right?"

"I'm scared. I'm scared," the kid said. "Doc's on the other side of this dike, up about ten yards and out about ten feet," the Marine said. "He's hurt awful bad."

"Are you hit?" P.J. asked.

"Nope, I'm OK, but I'm afraid to move."

We crawled up just a few feet past him. We could hear the Doc moaning in low, short, guttural sounds on the other side of the dike.

"Doc, Doc, you all right?" P.J. asked.

"Get me out of here," he said, pleading with us, "Oh, Jesus, please, just get me out of here. Please! Help me, help me," he cried.

"Where are they dug in?" I asked the Marine, crawling back closer to him.

"They're dug in about twenty yards out on the other side of this dike in front of us," he said calmly, "and off in that far treeline on the other side of this dike." He pointed to the treeline about fifty yards away on our right. "There's a bunch of them, and they're dug in good."

"Listen, slick," P.J. said to the Marine, "we'll roll over the dike and get Doc. On the way back, we'll have to raise up, so you have to give us some cover." The Marine agreed and P.J. and I rolled over the dike quickly, in perfect unison, receiving no fire. We crawled to the fallen Corpsman. He was lying on his back, softly groaning.

"Doc, what's happenin'?" P.J. asked in a high-hearted voice, trying to be light. Blood had soaked through Doc's pants and his legs looked like they had been ripped off and then put on backwards.

"What do you want to do,, P.J.?" I asked.

"I'd like to take a piss and go home and get laid. I — Oh! Come on. Let's roll on our backs and frag the hell outta the treeline in front."

But just as P.J. finished his suggestion, one, then two chicoms flew from the treeline to our front and exploded harmlessly about fifteen yards from where we lay.

"Oh, God... get me out. PLEASE get me out," Doc moaned. P.J. and I took turns flipping frags, listening for the explosions, and hoping for screams. We had to hurry and drag Doc over to the dike and get out of there. The NVA were closer than we had anticipated and if they left the treeline we would be defenseless with only our treeline to stop them.

Doc was on his back as we crawled to the dike, each of us pulling one of his arms. The explosions had stopped. The only sounds were those of our breathing and Doc's gentle sobs. A breeze came up, cooling us and reminding me of those late hot summer days back home during football practice, when sprints were done and I used to lay down on the grass next to the goalpost, with my helmet off, thankful for a gentle breeze.

"Jackson?"

"What, P.J.?"

"I think I'll quit!"

"What are you talking about?"

"I think I'll just quit this fucking war," he said, fighting apprehension in his own personal manner.

As the breeze disappeared, tears began easing their way to the corners of my eyes. Fear began to edge its way into my mind. Not in pictures, but in overwhelming feelings of dismay. I thought about my child and I wanted to be home, that's all, just home.

"Sweetheart," P.J. yelled to the Marine on the other side of the dike, "when we say 'now', you open up on the treeline to the front and keep 'em busy. We're coming over with Doc."

We rolled Doc onto his stomach and I put his right arm over my shoulder. P.J. got under his left. We braced ourselves, our three heads almost touching the dike, ready to move.

"You ready, Doc?" P.J. asked. "In a few minutes you'll be Medivac'd and in a little while you'll be going home. You're gonna skate, partner. You're gonna skate for a fat man."

"Ready, Jackson?" he said, looking across Doc's drained face. For a brief moment I saw a tenderness in him I had seldom seen before. Then he covered it up and yelled, "Let's get some! Now!"

The three of us began to stand and at the same time the Marine on the other side of the dike opened up on the treeline to our front with what seemed like polite fire. We struggled to our knees, lifting the cumbersome weight of Doc's body between us. As we pushed up, time began to slow. Each movement was exaggerated and heavy, like we were trapped in individual time frames. Once again, for the briefest of moments, I felt outside myself, looking down. It was as if all my life had led directly to this moment.

We made it halfway up, and were starting to dive, when the treelines erupted.

As we dove face first to the other side of the dike we were caught in criss-crossed U-shaped fire. Firing was coming from three directions, pounding where the dikes intersected.

The first burst hit P.J., Doc, and the Marine. It continued as we fell into a heap on the other side of the dike. The rounds raged, blended together, and came like flat heavy monsoon rain, ripping and tearing into their bodies.

I knew I would die. I knew it was over. I knew that a round would enter my head and tear through my brain and explode out the other side, just like what I had imagined a hundred times before. I wondered how it would feel, and what it would sound like. And if I would have a moment of memory to recall its impact.

The fire kept coming from all sides, impacting into P.J., Doc, and the Marine. As the rounds hammered their bodies, I knew soon I would be hit. Soon I'd be just another dead, dumb son-of-a-bitch. I'd be history, bagged up and dumped on the back porch of America. Please, God, I pleaded over and over again, please take care of my Kristen and Jenine.

The bullets poured on and on, kicking up next to me, around me, above me. They sliced into the boys on my left and right.

"OH, JESUS... GOD... THEY'RE KILLING ME!" Doc screamed in a voice known only to the dead.

"I'M HIT! I'M HIT!" the kid screamed next to me.

I could hear our treeline opening up, and could feel the rounds spraying just inches above me.

If I can keep my head close to the dike. If I can avoid being hit in the head or neck, maybe I could survive. My body is big and strong, I can take several bullets in my body, but not my head. I have to keep my head close to the dike. But the firing wouldn't stop.

"I'm hit! Jackson, I'm hit!" P.J. groaned, not like a boy hurt, crying from pain, but like a hero, with dignity.

"Oh, PLEASE sweet Jesus, help me! Help me! They're KILLING me! HELP me!... Help me!" Doc cried.

The firing slowed. I crawled to P.J., shaking uncontrollably, thinking I might live. He was lying face down, unturned from the dive. His head was turned to the side, his mouth open, with thick red spittle easing along his lips and down his chin. His left forearm was shattered in the middle. A four-inch chunk of bone and muscle was chiseled out in jagged fashion.

Blood flowed from broken arteries where his flesh had exploded in a rent of ravaged skin, muscle, and tendons. Flat on the ground, his forearm bent in the center from its devastation.

"I'm hit in the chest," he said, not crying, almost calm.

"No, it's your arm. It's your arm," I told him, ignoring the blood dripping from his lips.

Doc kept crying, "Get me out... get me out..." He'd been hit again, several times.

The Marine crawled quickly past me on his hands and knees, dragging his foot that was almost severed, then collapsed about five feet away. The fire continued, randomly, impacting into the dikes and cutting overhead.

I'd used my last battle dressing on Doc, so I took off my boot and used my sock to tie P.J.'s arm back together. As I finished, the firing subsided. I listened for the round that would hit me.... A few minutes passed... only quiet crying from Doc. I noticed the grass that P.J. was lying in was wet. I felt its warm stickiness. He had been hit in the chest. I started to look for the hole, but before I could turn him over to try to dress his wounds, all sides opened up again, more violently than before. The firing was continuous. I sucked the earth, crying to myself and flashing back home.

"Oh, Jesus, get me out of here!" P.J. said, now pleading. He had been shot again, lying next to me, our bodies touching. This time it was through the buttocks. "Oh, Christ, Jackson, they're cutting me up."

Doc kept moaning, while the kid was quietly crying.

But I was alive.

The firing stopped.

I was alive. I wasn't hit. I was alive. I was out of my mind, but I was alive.

P.J. and Doc and the kid all wanted out, and I wasn't hit. I was alive.

"Get me out, please, Jesus, please... get me out," Doc kept crying, while the kid said nothing.

"Jackson," P.J. said, suddenly calm, "leave me. Get out of here!" Then his voice dropped lower. I could sense he was about to die. "Go home with my body."

I was alive. I wouldn't let this happen. I turned P.J. on his back. He had been hit twice in the chest and once in the shoulder. Once in the arm and once in the butt. Five times, and I wasn't even scratched. We were touching or at the most, inches apart, and I wasn't even grazed.

Doc, P.J., and the kid had been hit repeatedly and I wasn't touched. I was crazy and I wasn't touched.

I placed P.J.'s sock-wrapped arm across his chest. I took the plastic wrapping from a battle dressing he had and bandaged the gaping hole in his chest. Then I crawled to the front of him and began pushing myself backwards, toward our treeline, dragging him with his good right arm.

"Leave me... leave me... just go home with my body." I could feel his spirit and life drawing away.

"Come on, what are you talking about, you told me we were gonna party stateside. You told me! Don't you check out on me. Don't you die on me!" I pleaded.

"Go on... save your dumb ass," he said, spitting out blood and starting to lose consciousness.

"Don't give me that. Don't you die on me. You're going home, skate! I'll be knocking on your door come August or September, we're gonna party and we're gonna be together. Get drunk and.... Come on, P.J., don't do this."

I wanted to cry, but I couldn't. P.J. was my friend, I could tell him everything. I could count on him in anything, he couldn't leave me now. We had come too far for this.

The fire started again in sporadic bursts.

I swore and pushed and pulled, scraping along the side of the dike, trying to crawl inside it.

"I can't make it. I can't make it," he groaned, rocking his head slowly from side to side.

"No, no, you're my brother, you're my brother," I pleaded. "We'll make it. We'll make it."

The firing stopped and in its silence I could feel P.J.'s life and my humanity draining from me. I could feel myself change, knowing it was my destiny to live.

Finally, we reached the edge of the dike, just feet from the safety of our treeline. "We made it, P.J., we're home free," I said. "Can you get to your feet?" He rolled awkwardly to his belly, rose to his feet, and we staggered with the help of Ta' and some PFs into the safety of the trees.

I picked him up and carried him to the rear of the treeline, next to a hut, and laid him down on a bamboo mat that Ta' brought over. I ran back to the edge of the treeline. Rage was beginning to swell and spill out of me.

"Why the fuck didn't you get your fat ass out there with someone to help us!" I yelled at the Army captain. Grabbing him by the shirt, I screamed at the PFs, "Where's my rifle! Where's my fuckin' rifle!?"

I went back to check on P.J. He was lying motionless, his eyes closed, his mouth open, not breathing. He was dead, he was fucking dead. I exploded in anger. I ran back to the treeline and grabbed a rifle from a PF. "Give me that!" I shouted angrily.

God had cheated me. I had worked so hard to save my friend. P.J. had endured so much and now he was gone. Taken from me, in a last cruel moment. I was a madman. I raved. I swore. I jumped out in front of the treeline screaming, "MOTHER-FUCKERS!" I unloaded a magazine in the treeline ahead. "YOU MOTHERFUCKING GOOKS!" I cried, tears streaming down my face. Why had they taken him away? I ran back to the treeline, found a LAW, quickly extended it, and fired where I knew some of them were dug in. It didn't explode.

I was insane, erupting in rage. I broke the LAW on the ground and flung it as far as I could. Anger consumed me.

"Water Bull, Water Bull!" Ta' yelled at me. "P.J. OK! Him Number One OK. Bac Si help!"

I rushed back to where P.J. lay. He was alive! He had only passed out. I couldn't believe it. I thanked God again and again. I talked to Kristen out loud. I bent down and held P.J. in my arms, crying.

I had snapped. I couldn't stand it anymore. The pressure I had not let myself feel in the days before rolled over me in a wave of relentless emotion. I wanted to go home. I wanted to be safe. I couldn't take it anymore. I cried and cried, and I held P.J.

Ta' stood over us and placed his hands on my shoulders. "Water Bull, Number One. OK now. No cry," he said, holding my head next to his leg, like a father comforting his child. "Water Bull OK."

At dark, a truck came and took P.J. away. He was going to live. He was going home. I would stay behind.

Doc and the kid made it out too, only they had to endure a bit longer. A spotter plane blasted the treelines with rockets, and they were eventually pulled out safely.

That night on the radio, the C.P. said my orders for R & R in Hawaii had come in. A week later I was on a jet, on my way to a seven-day stay in Hawaii.

The plane lifted from the runway, leaving my heart and soul behind.

Fifteen

AS THE PLANE MADE a gentle descent toward the Honolulu Airport I knew that it would be different. I knew that I had changed. For months I had dreamed of holding Kristen, loving her and being safe. I had fantasized about how she would look and smell, and how it would feel to take her in my arms and be gentle and kind. As the plane banked over the ocean I was nearly delirious with joy and anticipation of seeing Kristen and holding her. In a few moments I would be with my wife and for the first time I would see my baby, Jenine.

The city below grew closer as I tried to recall how it felt to be gentle. I wondered if I had had a tender, caring moment or thought in the last several months. I was sure I had, but now I couldn't remember one. Maybe the night I talked to Ro-do. Maybe then I had been kind. My mind began to race as I thought about breaking Smitty's fingers so he could go home, and how the door gunner's smiling face had looked as it exploded. I wanted to love my new baby and I thanked God for letting me live.

As the plane made its final approach the cabin seemed to grip with tension. I glanced across the aisle at the young Army captain who had a patch over his eye and his arm in a cast. We hadn't spoken. I'd talked to no one on the flight over. I felt guilty, as if I were stealing something. I had been lucky to live and wished I'd been shot and had suffered more pain. As I looked at the captain, I was almost ashamed that I still had both eyes.

The sign above my seat flashed "Fasten Seat Belts. No Smoking." As I buckled up, I felt like I was strapping on magazines for a night killer team. I was scared. I was afraid that Kristen wouldn't love me anymore. It had been so long since I had seen my young wife. So long since I had felt safe or secure.

The pilot's voice came over the intercom. "On behalf of United Airlines, I hope you men enjoyed the flight," the voice said. "And the next time you fly, I hope you'll consider the friendly skies of United." The plane's cabin stirred as if to laugh, but like the flight over, remained silent.

The plane landed smoothly, coasted to a stop and I fought the crowd to move down the aisle and out the door. Fifty feet down the ramp I reached an opening where dozens of families were frantically waving and calling out names, trying to catch a first glimpse of their husbands or lovers or friends.

As I moved into the crowd, an arm reached out, grabbing me. "Jack! Jack!"

I turned and looked into Kristen's face and the first thing that entered my head was how white she looked. I threw my arms around her, feeling detached, yet holding her tight, still thinking to myself how white she was and wondering why I was feeling no emotion. Her whiteness confused me, but then I hadn't seen a white woman since I'd arrived in Vietnam.

We parted just enough so that I could kiss her mouth, long and without reserve. I loved her mouth. It was clean and pure. I could feel myself slowly drifting into her. I began to feel love again. She was my woman, my lover, my wife, and the mother of my child. Yes, I could feel love.

"Oh, Jack. Oh, honey, you're here!" Her eyes were wet and happy. "Come here, honey," she said, holding my hand and leading me through several people to a baby stroller a few feet away. "Here's Jenine."

Jenine. My child. I was nineteen, married, and the father of a beautiful little baby girl! My child! My baby! I was overcome with emotion. Emotion that still wouldn't show.

I bent down and picked Jenine up carefully. She was clean, beautiful and soft, so unlike the hollow-eyed, scabbed and scarred children of the Nam.

I looked into her eyes and at her nose and mouth to see if she looked like me.

"I'm your daddy. How's my little girl?" For a moment her smooth round face looked confused until I kissed her nose, then she waved her arms and gurgled a smile.

She was so much bigger than I remembered from the last pictures Kristen had sent me. I held Jenine with one arm and tickled her tummy as her mouth rounded into a big toothless grin. "Your daddy loves you, baby girl."

For the past several hours I'd felt ashamed to be alive, now I felt embarrassed, dumb, and fiercely proud.

It was a beautiful, sunny, clear day as we left the airport receiving area pushing Jenine's stroller and began our walk to the motel. As we walked down Honolulu Boulevard I began to feel a sense of culture shock. I had slept in holes and on dirt floors for months. I had lived in a jungle and I had killed and watched others be killed. Suddenly, I was here in Honolulu with my wife and child, dressed in clean, pressed khakis, walking past lush green parks, coconut trees, the ocean, and unbelievably tall buildings. I was surrounded by people in brightly colored shirts and bikinis, carrying picnic baskets or surfboards. There were old people, young people, babies in their mothers' arms, and children in short pants laughing and playing in the parks and along the ocean shore.

There was no bomb-pitted countryside dotted with peasant Vietnamese or rifle-toting American boys.

I was among young men my own age who weren't counting their days, but were running on the beach, playing football, tossing frisbees, drinking beer, or chasing beautiful young girls.

The human crush of excitement seemed to pour all over me. It was an outrageous change from the river, the villes, the filth and the half-naked brown children with swollen bellies.

I felt the glaring imbalance of good versus bad, poverty versus wealth. It was undeniably commercial and distorted, but it was safe and it was clean. It was loud with taxi cabs and honking cars, and scores of shoppers, but it was America and I loved it.

I devoured everything I saw. I marveled at the bewildering collision of tall towering motels overlooking a beautiful blue sea. It was everything P.J. and I had wanted and dreamed of, from the white rippling waves carrying swimmers and surfers, to the get-down-and-party atmosphere and McDonald's.

"Babe! Look! McDonald's!" I said excitedly, pointing across the street. I could taste the french fries. "I can't believe it! I have been dying for a plain double cheeseburger and a large order of fries! We used to joke about it back at Kilo." Laughing, we hurried across the street.

Several cheeseburgers later, we left and walked to our motel. Over twenty stories, and with an ocean view, our motel was perfect. Each room had a balcony that overlooked the motel's swimming pool or looked out on the beach a short distance away.

"How do you like it?" Kristen asked, throwing her arms around me and giving me a quick kiss and smile as we settled into our room

"It's outstanding! It's really too much!" I beamed, uncoupling her arms from around my neck. Then I picked Jenine up from her crib and walked through the sliding glass door that led to the balcony and looked out on the ocean. "It's fuckin' great!"

"Jack!" she said.

"What, babe?" I asked, turning from the ocean and people hurrying below.

"Did you hear what you just said?"

I stepped from the balcony, rocking Jenine to sleep in my arms. I was puzzled by Kristen's comment, but ignored it. "Let's take a nap," I said, smiling.

"What are you grinning at, Papa Bear?" Kristen asked, looking very sexy as she turned the corners of her mouth into a smile.

"It must be the jet lag," I said, winking at her. "I'm sooo tired." I placed our sleeping little girl back in her crib and then fell onto the bed in an exaggerated display of exhaustion. "I think I will take a nap."

I pulled her down on top of me. She was soft and warm, and

the weight of her body on top of me felt good.

"I love the way you smell and how you feel. It's been so long." I undressed her slowly, tenderly. We crawled between the clean, cool sheets and made love desperately, sweating, until we finally fell asleep.

I felt a kiss on my cheek. "Wake up, sleepy-head," Kristen said. "You've been snoozin' for hours." She stood above me, then walked to the mirror and began combing her hair. "I gave Jenine her bottle, but I'm starved," she said, looking over her shoulder at me. "Don't you go to sleep now," she playfully scolded me, turning back to the mirror and combing her long, clean sunshine-streaked brown hair.

It felt good to lie there, looking up at her sleek body. Her white slip clung to her, accentuating her round firm backside, making me want her again. Somehow, she, too, had matured, from the seventeen-year-old girl who wore knee socks when we met in high school, to a woman, mother, and my wife. I loved her even more than I did when we parted.

We dressed and left the room, spending the rest of the day and early evening walking up and down the boulevard, pushing Jenine and shopping for some civilian clothes for me.

I was out of place in my uniform. The short hair was bad enough, but the uniform was too much. My uniform didn't make me feel special, it made me feel out of place. I wanted to blend in, to become anonymous.

It seemed as if no one on the island knew that there was a war going on, and I felt as if they were looking at me like I reminded them of something unpleasant.

The first night set the pattern for all the other nights. Unable to sleep, I got up, put on my pants and walked to the balcony. I stood there for a long time, looking out through the palm trees across the sandy beach, into the ocean. The moon was full and bright, casting soft light on the water. Except for a couple walking hand in hand, the shore was deserted. As the waves kept running in and drawing back, I thought about how my life seemed like a dream.

I thought about P.J. and how we'd shared our food and intimate thoughts and I wondered if he'd ever be able to use his left arm again. I missed him and how we used to fish with hand grenades in the river. I stood watching the waves and reconstructed how we'd cheated death.

After awhile, Kristen came up to me in the moonlight. "Jack-o-lantern," she said, tenderly putting her arms around me from behind and hugging me.

"What, hon?"

"Why are you up?"

"I couldn't sleep."

"Why? What's wrong?"

"Oh, nothing. It's... nothing," I said, trying to keep what I was thinking from her, trying to protect her from all the pain I was feeling.

"Come on, Papa Bear," she said gently, coming around to face me, her back to the railing. "Come on, now, tell me what's bothering you."

"I was just thinking about P.J."

"What about P.J.?"

"Well... I was thinking about how he looked when he was lying in the middle of the field, all shot up." I felt dazed. I could feel myself fading from her and passing back to that moment. "I wondered what the pain was like." The image of him dressed in blood had come back, clearly. His red spittle rested in my mouth.

"Oh, Jack, I don't want to hear stuff like that," she said. "It's our vacation. Why don't you just forget about that and come to bed?" A soft breeze came in from the sea, and Kristen, shivering, left the balcony for the warmth of a silent bed.

I stood alone for a long time, drifting, wanting to cry, and not knowing why. Nothing made sense to me anymore. I had no idea where my life was headed and wondered if Kristen could ever understand how I felt. So I gathered up P.J. and the rest of my bleak history and went to bed.

Over the next few days I tried desperately to teach Jenine how to talk and I changed her diapers regularly. The three of us swam in the pool or ocean and played along the beaches.

One day we visited the zoo. I lifted Jenine from her stroller to see the bears.

"See the papa bear, baby girl? And there's a momma bear and a little bitty baby bear."

I carried her on my shoulders to feed the elephants, grin at the monkeys, and growl at the cage full of tigers.

After the zoo, Kristen and I took turns trying our luck at surfing, with me, the supposedly finely tuned athlete, being thoroughly shown up by my wife. I would paddle out on the surfboard, turn to face the shore, and stand up whenever I pleased, trying to defy the strength of the waves to knock me down. I never won. Kristen, on the other hand, would paddle out, turn, and wait to flow in with a wave, staying on her feet more often than not. I supposed there was a lesson to be learned, somewhere.

The next day we picnicked at a park near the beach, where I slid down the slide and swung on the swing with my "darling pie" little girl.

As we walked through the park I carried Jenine on my shoulders while Kristen pushed the empty stroller. A warm breeze with the smell of salt rushed in as clouds gathered in the sky. Suddenly a tropical shower came and we ran for cover into a grove of coconut trees that bordered the ocean.

"Is the rain like this in Vietnam?" Kristen asked as she took Jenine from my shoulders and placed her in the stroller, covering her from the rain.

"Well, not exactly. It comes fast and hard, but usually the sky is almost black and you always feel depressed."

"I know what you mean. Sometimes when Jenine's crying and I think I'll take her for a walk and I look outside and it's raining I just get really depressed," Kristen said, trying to console me and at the same time wanting to be consoled. "This whole Vietnam business is so confusing. Half the time I don't even know who you're at war with," she added. "But I try not to let it worry me. I know you'll be home soon."

I looked at her and I loved her, but she knew nothing about what I was doing or how I felt. She thought I was simply stuck somewhere I didn't belong or want to be, just as I knew death in a way she couldn't comprehend. I lived on the edge every moment of my life over there. One wrong move at the wrong time and I could be dead. Or even all the right moves couldn't stop a stray bullet from slicing through my brain. Vietnam was a crazy nightmare that fired energy through my soul. I loved it and I hated it and as she spoke I wished I were there....

On our last night we arranged for a babysitter through the hotel so we could have a night out alone. It was a warm night with a comfortable breeze coming in off the ocean as we left the motel, hand in hand. The streets were busy and the sidewalks crowded. With no definite plans we decided to catch a movie first, and then go out for dinner.

"McDonald's?" I said as we walked from the theater lobby back into the bright lights and noise on Honolulu Avenue.

"Absolutely not," Kristen frowned. "I want some place nice."

We found a fun-looking Polynesian restaurant not far from our motel. Wooden pagan statues greeted us at the entrance. Once inside we were surrounded by grass skirts, exotic shells, and tiny fake palm trees. Native masks amid spears adorned the restaurant, and a huge silver swordfish was affixed to one wall. Every third table or so, a flaming dish was being prepared.

The head waiter showed us to our table on the balcony overlooking a circular pool with a miniature volcano and running waterfalls. We looked over the rail, down at the diners tossing coins into the pool, eating, drinking, and enjoying their evening.

"I'll bet I can sink a quarter from up here, with no sweat at all!" I said to Kristen, reaching into my pants pocket for a coin and starting to stand up.

"Jack, sit down. Everyone's watching. You're embarrassing me," Kristen complained, reaching across the table to stop me.

"Let them watch. What's wrong?" I asked teasingly. "I'll make this shot with no problem at all." I started once more to stand.

"Jack, honestly. Can't you act like an adult?" she said, again reaching across the table for my arm. "You can't be trying to toss money from up here. What if you missed and it landed in someone's soup or something? Now, wouldn't you feel foolish?"

"You're right, hon, I would feel foolish..." I said, reassuringly.

"That's better."

"...if I missed!"

I stood up quickly and shot an arching underhand toss toward the pool and the tiny fake volcano below. Then I watched in horror as I saw it land short, right in the middle of a group of four heavy-set middle-aged ladies in bright flowered dresses and straw hats who were eating huge chocolate desserts.

They looked up, shocked, and I sat down quickly, assuming a look of innocence and nonchalance, appearing to be involved in an intimate conversation with Kristen.

"Oh, Jack," Kristen said, trying to hide her face, "you're impossible!" She started to laugh, and we both peeked up over the balcony to survey the damage.

"Look," I whispered, trying to suppress my laughter, "the one in bright pink, with the miniature Budweiser can on top of her hat, is trying to pick the quarter out of her food." As we both started to laugh, the waiter came up.

"Would you like a cocktail before dinner?" he asked, hovering over us, sounding very official.

"Yes. Yes, I believe we will," I said, in my best imitation of a composed, responsible young man. "I think maybe I'll have one of these," I said, picking up the beverage list and pointing to the picture of a tall red Singapore Sling tossed with fruit and a tiny American flag. I was proud of my quick decision.

"Fine. However, I'll have to check your I.D. first," the waiter said, offsetting my festive mood. I felt stupid and offended. I wasn't old enough to drink. Maybe he wouldn't say anything, I hoped, if I showed him my military identification. I'd just show him my pink I.D. proving that I was defending our country and he would overlook the fact that I was only nineteen.

"I'm sorry," he said impassively, handing back my I.D.

"Hey, I'm on R & R from the Nam. All I want is a drink. Come on, I won't say anything."

"I'm sorry, but you're under age."

"Now wait a minute!" I stood up, starting to get upset.

"If you have a complaint, I'll get the manager."

"Do that!" I demanded, becoming more and more annoyed.

"Sit down, Jack," Kristen said. "Come on, honey, sit down." She tried to console me.

"What do you mean, sit down? I've been fighting in a damn war for months, and I take a few days off and I can't even get a drink. That's bullshit!"

A moment later a rotund man, about forty-five, appeared, peering over glasses too small for his face. "What seems to be the problem, sir?" he asked politely.

"Listen, I'm on my R & R from Vietnam, and I just wanted to have a quiet drink with my wife. The waiter says he can't serve me because I'm under age."

"If that's the case, I'm sorry, we can't serve you alcohol if you're under age."

"Listen, all I want is one drink," I said, not wanting to lose my temper.

"I'm sorry, it can't be done."

I wanted to frag the place. I wanted to open up with my M-16. "Look what the fuck's the problem?" I asked.

The manager's face and tone of his voice suddenly shifted. "I'm sorry, sir, but I'm going to have to ask you and your wife to leave."

"Leave? What the fuck are you talking about?" I asked, about ready to explode.

"Yes, leave. I told you twice that we couldn't serve you and you've refused to listen. I'm asking you to leave. Now! If you don't, I'll be forced to call the police!"

I wanted to put a .45 to his head and show him what I was old enough to do. I grabbed Kristen's arm and left the restaurant. The manager muttered something about all Marines being animals.

Outside, I became enraged. "God damn it, what's wrong with these people? All I wanted was a drink! Jesus!"

"Calm down. Come on, calm down," Kristen said. "That's no way to act."

"Calm down? What do you mean, calm down? They treated me like dirt." I took a couple of deep breaths and tried to relax, wishing I had some pot. I paced back and forth.

"I'll be all right," I said, forcing myself to control my rage. "I'm sorry if I embarrassed you."

We ate dinner at another restaurant, making sure not to order drinks. Later, we stood outside a grocery store and asked an elderly man to go in and buy us a six-pack of beer. Then, beer in hand, we walked down to the beach to be alone.

We took off our shoes and carried them, walking along the edge of the water, our feet grazed by little lips of foam that rode the small waves. A breeze scented the air with clean, sweet fragrance, and cooled us as we walked. The night felt gentle and calm.

"I wonder if we can see the Big Dipper from here?" Kristen asked, letting go of my hand and staring up at the stars. "I know it's hidden somewhere. I'll bet it's over there," she said, pointing and turning slowly. She looked and sounded like an innocent little child. "No, it's not there. But I know it's somewhere," she added with undaunted optimism. "What are the stars like in Vietnam?" she then asked, sounding once again like an inquisitive little girl.

"They're just about like here," I said, "only brighter and more intimate."

"More intimate? What do you mean? I've never heard of that before."

"Well, they're like friends. They're someone I can talk to. I even made up a game," I said.

"What kind of game?"

"Well, at night, when it's quiet and safe and I don't have to worry about what's in front or in back of me, I look up at the stars and sort of talk to them. I lie on my back and find the ones I have seen before and talk to them." I was feeling foolish.

"About what?" she asked.

"Oh, I don't know. You must think I'm crazy. Mostly I talk about you and how much I love you, and what a good life we will have when I get home. I know it sounds kind of silly, but it relaxes me. It takes me away from what's happened that day, and helps bury the loneliness." We walked along the beach holding hands, not speaking, until I stopped and turned to her.

"Kristen..."

"Yes, Jack."

"It's only been a week or so, but since P.J. left, I can't seem to relate to anyone. Do you know what I mean?"

"I think so," she said, stopping to pick up and examine a tiny seashell, then placing it back in the water.

"Oh, I talk to people, all right," I said, watching the water at my feet. "But not like with P.J. I guess I'm afraid to." I kicked the water and hung my head, pausing for a moment. "I guess I'm worried that I will get close to someone like I did to P.J. and then lose them. Oh, I don't know."

I wanted to change my train of thought.

"Anyway, the most important thing to me is that we are together and that I love you." I pulled her to me and we wrapped up in each other's arms.

"I have a surprise for you," I said.

"What's that?" she beamed.

I reached into my pocket and pulled out a folded gum wrapper. "Last night when I couldn't sleep, I got up and looked at you for a long time. You were lying naked with just the moonlight covering you. I found a pen and wrote this for you," I said, as I unfolded the green gum wrapper.

"Read it to me," she said, turning to me and looking up at my face.

> *Sweet Lady*
> *Curled up in your embryo sleep*
> *You seem so childlike and lovely*
> *Breathing, breathing*
> *Next to me.*

I stopped. We looked at each other for a long time.

"Papa Bear, I love you so much," she said, holding me closer.

We walked along the beach and I lost myself in thoughts of her. I loved her so much. She gave me a reason to survive, a comforting clarity to my life. I was secure in her arms, protected and important.

For the first time since I had left Vietnam, I could feel

myself shedding and forgetting where I had just been. I was drifting into Kristen, losing myself in passion for her.

We walked on further down the beach until we reached an area of secluded coves. No one was in sight.

"Over here, babe," I said, leading her by the hand over some rocks and onto a hidden little beach. It was like a cave with the stars as our ceiling. We were alone, far away from the noise and the smell and the color of the crowd.

We looked at each other for long moments. I wanted her so much. I pushed back her hair with my hands until it dropped away from her face and rested on her shoulders. The moonlight played on her cheeks and brightened her eyes. I cradled her head and turned my face down slowly, running my tongue on her lips, once, twice, then kissing her full-mouthed.

I stood back not speaking. The moonlight was breaking on the water and showering me from behind. I stepped from my clothes.

Enjoying her eyes gazing at me, holding me, I could almost feel her heart beating in mine. Then Kristen slipped from her clothes, slowly, teasingly, exposing her firm breasts until, finally standing naked in front of me. Her body was pure, lovely. I wanted her and went to her, holding her around the waist with one hand and cupping her breast with the other. She felt soft and tasted clean.

"I love you," she said, encouraging me, "I love you more than I can say."

Her words rang and rippled through me, shaking me as nothing else could. "I love you," I said. Then she ran into the waves and I followed, the two of us laughing and splashing each other. I found her with my hand, beneath the water. She moaned softly and held her head back, eyes closed, taking me.

We left the ocean, laid my shirt out flat on the sand, and made love on top of it. It was much more than sexual fulfillment. I felt as if we had touched the center of all life, as Kristen made love to my soul. For a few moments, we were inseparable. For a few minutes, I was home.

The next morning I flew back to the Nam.

Sixteen

On the back of the chow truck headed over toward C.A.P. Two, reality finally caught up with me. The road was the same, the shacks were the same, the hungry kids were the same. Nothing had changed. I was back.

My hopes of the war ending while I had been gone were dashed at the sight of a jeep blown off the road lying on its side, twisted from the explosion. It must have happened recently, I thought, the tires were still on. No bodies, though.

The truck slowed and pulled to the edge of the road, where Ta', Frenchie and two Marines met us. I jumped off the back with Happy, whom I had met back at the command post.

Happy joined our C.A.P. when Red and all the others were wounded. He had very dark hair and a matching moustache that turned down from the corners of his mouth, just enough to give him the appearance of never smiling, hence the nickname "Happy." He was a lance corporal and had aspirations of being promoted to corporal and running his own C.A.P. unit. He was, consequently, impeccably squared away. His hair was trimmed short, his moustache neat, and his uniform remarkably clean.

"Water Bull, you come back," Ta' said, smiling, as I slapped hands with the new guys. "You get Number One boom boom from mamasan?" he asked, punching me on the arm and giving me a hug.

"Come on, Ta', knock it off." I grinned, embarrassed, but very happy to see him. "My ol' lady is beaucoup Number One."

I walked over to my boy Frenchie, who was smoking a cigarette and looking a little pissed. "How you been," I asked, putting my arm around him.

"Got no money. You owe 25P," he frowned.

"Oh, so that's it. You didn't miss me, huh? All you want is money. And I thought you were my Number One boy," I said, trying to look sad.

His expression changed immediately. "I sorry. You pay later. You for my brother."

"You got it, bud. Here's 30P," I said, reaching into my pocket and handing it to him. He took the money, counting it twice. "Water Bull, you for my. You Number One fuckin' good. I carry rifle, OK?"

"Sure, and stop your swearing and smoking." I grabbed the cigarette from him. "Listen, I have some presents for Ta' and you when we get back to camp."

"What you get me, Water Bull?" Ta' said excitedly. "You bullshit Ta'."

"No, Ta', I bought something for you when I was in Hawaii, and something for Frenchie."

We picked up the chow vats and case of C-rations and started down the trail leading to our encampment.

"Jackson," Happy said, "I almost forgot. I've got some good news for you. Jensen's gone. He's back in the rear. Suffering from combat fatigue," he said, rolling his eyes.

"Combat fatigue!" I said, disbelieving. "Well, that chicken... He makes me want to puke. Well, I'm glad he's gone. Who's taking his place?"

"His name is Swan. Seems like a good head. A little naive. Thinks that all the gooks are gone. He figures that since Tet is over, there's nothing to worry about. He's a transfer from C.A.P. Three."

We reached the area we had set in for that day. It was on the far end of Ti Lon One. It was warm and the flies were out swarming in groups of five or six to each Marine. Fortunately, the hut and the thick foliage cut the sun's heat and provided shade. With the hut's wide shutters opened up and out, we had plenty of room to lay our gear down, play cards at a table or sleep.

Charlie, Jimmy, whose cast was now gone, Hodges and Bingham were there waiting for us. We dropped the green chow vats and exchanged handshakes.

"So, you're back from the big island!" Corporal Swan said, getting up off the ground from a game of Back Alley with Charlie, Hodges and Bingham. "Glad to have you back."

"Can't say I'm too thrilled about being back. But it is good to see some of these bums again. Even sourpuss Bingham," who brushed away a couple of flies from his face, but didn't bother to move or speak. I turned toward a smiling Hodges. "How you doing, Black Beauty?" I asked.

"Just looking sweet as ever," he said, looking up from his cards. "Gettin' ready to do dirt to Bingham."

"Charlie, Jimmy, you dudes are looking sooo ugly!" I joked.

"This here's Doc Franny," Charlie said, standing up and ambling over like a country cowpoke. "He's a regular Florence Nightingale."

It was good to see Charlie. "Doc Fanny," I said to our new Corpsman, offering him my hand and purposely making fun of his name.

"That's Franny!" he said, correcting me while shaking my hand vigorously. "Almost everyone I know calls me Fanny, but I really prefer just plain Doc."

"Touchy, touchy! Then, Doc it is."

He was handsome and well-built. He had thick dark hair, striking brown eyes and a well-manicured, but dominant moustache. His teeth were unusually white, and when he smiled, his face creased with perfect dimples. I liked Doc.

It felt good to be back.

After we finished eating, I walked over to my pack, with Ta' and Frenchie's eyes following me closely in anticipation of what I had brought them. "Come here, Frenchie," I said to my scrubby little friend. I reached into my pack, taking out a black New York Yankees baseball hat, and pulled it over his head. It was much too big. The sides dropped down, past his ears, and the brim dropped over his eyes. But he loved it.

"Number One! I do everything for my!" he smiled and

grinned and a couple of other kids ran up, trying to snatch it from him and place it on their heads.

"And to my Number One Friend, Ta', this is for you." I pulled a light-blue T-shirt from my pack and handed it to him. He looked at the front of it and laughed. It had a picture of a can of Primo beer on it and the words, "Primo Beer" above the can. Then he turned it over and I could see he was fighting back tears. On the back, in big letters, were the words, "TA' NUMBER ONE." We looked into each other's eyes, past our cultural barriers, and spoke no words. From that day on, he wore that shirt nearly all the time.

It was a shock to be back in the villes, so the first few days seemed to drag on slowly. I missed my wife and child terribly and was afraid that I would never see them again. But after awhile I adjusted to the fact that I would be here for a few more months and would do my best to tough it out.

The collection of new guys, Corporal Swan, Recon, Duck, Happy, and Doc Franny, seemed to blend in well with Hodges, Bingham, Jimmy and Charlie. They appeared to enjoy the daytime kickback attitude that accompanied the life in the villes and weren't too concerned about the threat of violence that crept in with the night.

Corporal Swan ran our C.A.P. with a carefree attitude that fit well with the new guys but sort of bothered me. He'd smoke dope with us in the day and let us stay in hooches at night and not bother to dig a hole. He was just an average type of kid who, at seventeen, mistakenly signed up for four years in the Marines instead of two, like most of us were doing. Now, at twenty, he had eight months in country and was resigned to "skating these last few months out like a big dog. You don't mess with me, I won't mess with you."

Recon was a transfer from Third Reconnaissance whose idea of a perfect day was to stay high and eat everything he could get his hands on. Without the hard humping he'd had in the bush, he'd become soft and fleshy and double laid-back. He was the exact opposite of Duck.

Duck was a wild man. He'd been in the Navy for a couple of

years and had traveled all over the world, and in every port he landed he'd "Get a goddamned tattoo. I got thirteen of these motherfuckers," he said to me one day as we took a bucket shower from a deep water well.

"Got this baby in Singapore," he said, pointing to a snarling bulldog on his arm. "Got my first case of clap there, too," he added proudly. He had a "Grade A Inspected Meat" tattooed on his ass and his personal favorite, Donald Duck, was tattooed on his calf. "After I got Donald in the Phillipines, everybody started calling me 'Duck.' And it stuck."

The Navy just wasn't exciting enough for Duck and so after two years he transferred into the Marine Corps "when I was young and dumb and full ah cum." At twenty-two he seemed much older than most of us. If Duck wasn't trying to win somebody's paycheck playing cards, he was trying to figure out how to get laid. He was basically a good soldier and probably the only thing that kept him from being promoted was his "repeated cases of venereal disease," as Doc once told him.

Out of all the guys I liked Charlie the most. He never had a bad word for anyone. He was always giving his C-rations to the kids or wrestling with them. In the early evening when it was cooler and just before we'd move out, he and I would often take on Frenchie and a couple of his pals. Invariably, Ta' and Hein would jump on top of us and we'd have a free-for-all. I was stronger than the other Marines and was naturally stronger and of course, much bigger than the PFs.

It was almost like wrestling with children. They'd laugh and jump all over us, yelling "Get Charlie. Get Water Bull!"

The villagers and the PFs loved Charlie, and he seemed to love them. He was good working with his hands so he'd carve Frenchie a flute out of bamboo or make whistles for the other kids who hung around. One time he even helped Porky build a table and showed Trao how to firm up the foundation on his house. Charlie and I made a pact that when we got out of here we'd see each other again, so at night especially, we both made sure we were prepared. We dug holes while the others didn't and we never got stoned.

Overall I liked the Marines in my C.A.P., the PFs and the

villagers, but I guess I especially cared for Ta'.

One day as I was going through my pack, sorting out socks and other gear, and Ta' was by my side in his Primo T-shirt, cleaning his rifle, I came across my high school graduation picture of Kristen. Ta' knew I was married, but he had never seen any pictures of my family.

"Well, what do you think of my lady?" I asked, carefully unwrapping the photograph from a piece of white cloth Ba Sat had given me. "Isn't she beautiful?"

Ta' took the color picture from my hand and studied it for a few moments. "I know her," he claimed, as if trying to pull together a memory. "She before my lover. She Number One!"

"What are you talking about? That's my wife!" I said, enjoying his fantasy.

"She my lover. One time I go 'nited States. I see her. She say I plenty good looking."

"Where did you see her?" I questioned, playing along with him.

"I see her in big market," he said grandly. "We ride stairs that move up and down. She my lover for long time. She buy me watch. She buy me ring. She buy me everything."

He was really rolling now.

"How long ago was that?"

"One, maybe two year ago," he answered.

"Now, wait a minute, Ta'. Don't tell me you were seeing my wife before we got married. Didn't she tell you about me?"

"She tell Ta'. She say she got big dumb Water Bull. She say Ta', you Number One lover!" Then he broke out in laughter while I wrestled him to the ground. "Water Bull VC!" he yelled as I pinned him beneath me. "Water Bull VC!"

As the last days of May approached, an unimaginable and extraordinary calm settled over the area around C.A.P. Two. We were happy with the way the war was going, there was no war, and I was learning about life in Vietnam from a different perspective.

The villagers were at peace, and the rich, fertile fields were being worked again. We helped build a foot bridge over a stream, held MedCaps for the villagers and visited the orphanage to distribute food and clothes.

It was hard to feel sorry for myself, especially when the war was so hard on the children. The orphanage was always overflowing and the few things we brought were gratefully received. The children loved us and clamored about as if we were Santa Claus and saviors, all in one. They collectively hated the NVA and VC and that gave us a sense of hope. Hope that maybe our being here was good and right and appreciated.

Of course, there were moments of incredible loneliness and longing for my wife and daughter. During remorseful periods I would write long letters home or go down by the river and watch the sampans and fishermen glide by.

The river was peaceful... smooth, always flowing, never stopping, and never turning back. As I would sit on the bank staring at the river, my mind would wander or focus on the unequaled beauty and momentary calm of the countryside. There were times, especially at dusk, when the sun would be settling in a flood of brilliant red hues, and the people would be leaving the river, walking home to cook the day's catch, when I would feel as if I belonged by the river. In those moments Vietnam would cease being my prison, and instead, became my home.

Often my little friend Frenchie would come sit with me beside the water. He'd have his Yankee hat on, pulled sideways so that he could see, and he would ask me questions about my home, or dream about what he wanted to do when he grew up.

"Frenchie, you'd better start heading home," I told him one evening. "Soon it will be dark."

"I go soon. Tell me more 'bout 'nited States."

"I've told you so much already," I said, tossing pebbles into the water and watching the ripples form, then disappear. "I'm not sure I have more to tell."

"Tell me one more time about white rain!" he asked excitedly.

"You mean the snow?"

"Yes. Snow and babysans that go swoosh, swoosh," he said, gliding one hand downhill. He looked at me wide-eyed, with his hat on sideways, and such an engaging grin that I could almost believe he had seen no pain.

"When I was about your age, Frenchie, we used to go to my grandfather's home in the winter. He lived by himself in a great big beaucoup house with fifteen rooms. During the winter, when it snowed, we would go outside and slide down hills on truck tire innertubes that were as big as we were. My grandfather's dog, Charlie, would chase after us, barking and falling into the snow. Charlie wasn't like any of the dogs here in Vietnam. He was what we call a basset hound. Charlie had big ears and a big nose; a long body and short, stubby legs. His ears almost touched the ground when he ran, and he was always getting lost because he'd follow his nose on the ground."

"You tell me truth?" Frenchie asked, not quite believing, but wanting to; listening so intently.

"I tell you the truth," I said, reassuring him. "We had so much fun! Then, after we'd play, my grandfather would call us inside and we would eat many different foods."

"And milk?" he asked, hopefully.

"Lots of milk. Then we would sit by the fire and tell stories."

"No VC come and shoot?"

"No, Frenchie, there were no VC... ever."

Dearest Kristen,

These past weeks have been the best since I've been here. Ta' and I are constantly together and Frenchie isn't far behind. During the day we rest or go down to the river and fish with frags. I'll toss a grenade in and the concussion stuns the fish and they float to the top of the water. Frenchie and his pals dive in and gather them up. We go to Ba Sat's for noodles and hang around the main ville. It's almost like when you and I would hang out at Arctic Circle after a football game, talking to friends and drinking beer in my car. I miss those times. I miss parking on Rocky Butte and steaming up the windows. I miss you and worry about you and Jenine.

Hey, here's a funny story.

One day I gave my PF friend, Porky, an air mattress, we called them "rubber bitches." Anyway, that same night, we set up in an ambush position along a tree line, facing out into some rice paddies. It was very dark and spooky. I was making sure the PFs were set in correctly, when I heard a loud huffing and puffing and low, audible Vietnamese swearing. As I got closer to the noise, the breathing and blowing and swearing got louder and more pronounced. I crept closer, disturbed at the noise and fearing it would give away our position to any VC close by.

I spotted Porky. He was attempting to blow up his "rubber bitch," which was bad enough, but you won't believe this. Little round Porky was lying on his mattress, oblivious to the world, trying with all his might to blow it up. He didn't figure out that it would be impossible with him lying on it. I about had a cow. He cracked me up. It took a great effort on my part to try to keep from laughing my head off. Here we were, in the middle of a potentially dangerous ambush, and he was lying on his mattress trying to blow it up. But I like Pork and am helping him learn English.

The new guys here are pretty cool. But I really like Charlie. He's so kind. Right now he's working on a little, swing set that Porky's wife can swing their baby in.

Things are slow and that's good. I do love you, but wish you could find time to write more. I know you're busy with the baby, but it scares me when you don't write.

I'd better close now.

                                   Your Jackson
                                   May, 1969

Seventeen

THE YEARS OF HER LIFE were etched on the old mamasan's face, like thin dry streams in a river bed. Her eyes were sunken deeply and covered with cataracts. Clear sight had become another memory. She chewed betel nut vigorously, turning her head to spit, then turning back to smile at us through blackened teeth. Hers had been a long war. She walked slowly, bent over from years of working the rice paddies or carrying rockets. Beside her was a little girl, perhaps six or seven years old, holding the hand of a smaller boy. Both children were dirty, dressed in torn clothes, and shoeless. It was approaching darkness as they walked up to us. All three seemed frightened and hungry.

"What's your need, Mamasan?" Hodges asked, walking up, acting real cool and real loose. "You want to go dancing tonight?" We laughed, they didn't. "What you need, old woman?" Hodges quickly asked again when a response didn't come. "Now if you is asking for a handout, you is shit outa luck. The meal train just blew town," he said, kicking the hollow chow vat.

"Cheiu Hoi," the little girl said.

"Cheiu Hoi?" Hodges said, flabbergasted that the trio wanted to surrender. "Cheiu Hoi, the little one says. You dig this shit?"

"Cheiu Hoi!" she said again, clenching tight the old woman's hand and holding fast to the little boy.

We were nearly ready to move out to our night position, when the unusual trio showed up. Most of the PFs were standing ready as the last few Marines packed up. Ta' walked over in his Primo shirt and questioned the old woman and kids in Vietnamese for a few minutes. By then I was familiar with most of the people in our area, but I had never seen these three. None of us had.

"She say VC take her and daughter and babysans to mountains from village far away. Her say VC rape and kill daughter and make mamasan and babysans do work. Carry rice, cook for VC," Ta' explained in his broken English.

"Well, how the hell did she get here?" Corporal Swan asked, suddenly becoming attentive and walking over to face the three.

"Her says them run away at night when VC sleep. Walk two, maybe three nights in mountain. Sleep in bush all day. You first Marines they see."

"Why didn't they stop and stay with some other Vietnamese family in a village somewhere?" Swan inquired, puzzled.

We knew, but Swan just wasn't using his head.

"Her say she afraid villagers tell VC, or maybe villagers VC."

Swan thought a moment, cursing out loud and to himself. The solution was obvious, but it would take him a couple of tries to come up with it. "Jimmy, get on the radio and contact the C.P. Tell them we have an old lady and a couple of kids who want protection, and ask them what we should do. See if they can stay here," Swan ordered, thinking he'd come up with a profound revelation.

The word came down from the C.P. Jimmy relayed it to our leader, Swan. "What? They want us to take them with us on our night ambush? And keep them until morning? That's crazy! What if they're VC? Shit!"

"Y'all calm down, now," Charlie said, walking over to Swan, Ta', and our three new arrivals. He handed the mamasan and two kids each a can of chow and an opener, then turned back to the thoroughly perplexed Swan. "We used to do it all the time," he said, putting his hand on Swan's shoulder like a father would his son. "Just like keeping the chickens from the fox. You been over in C.A.P. Four, in the compound where nothing happens. Heck, y'all might jest as well been staying at Freedom Hill." That brought a snort from Swan and a chorus of laughs from the rest of us.

We fed the three, and moved out with the mamasan and her two skinny kids tucked safely in the middle of our column, right behind the radio and directly in front of me. They spent the night with us in our ambush position. Nothing happened.

As the days passed, the only thing that disturbed the calm was my growing concern over our setting up in the same place every night. I would complain but Corporal Swan would respond, "I mean... check it out," he'd tell me. "There's no gooks in the area. Lighten up, huh?"

But I worried. So did Charlie and Ta'. It was frustrating, though, because no one else seemed to care. But it ate at me. It was quiet, too quiet. I could feel something was about to happen, so I began to carry more gear; flares, a claymore, extra frags, and I started wearing a shoulder-strapped 45 like the big guy I saw eating Eskimo Pies when I first arrived. I cleaned and oiled my 16 almost fanatically. With God watching and a clean 16, I felt I could make it.

At night when we set in, only Charlie and I would dig holes or stand watch. The others would sleep and give cans of C-rations to the PFs to stand their watch.

Two or three nights in a row we set in on top of the knoll in Ti Lon One, next to the schoolhouse. It was during this time that something happened, though I couldn't quite put my finger on it. Duck was spending his days hanging around a new Vietnamese girl who had moved to Ti Lon One. Ta' told me she was rumored to have been a prostitute in Saigon and that she moved north because of problems with the Military Police.

It didn't bother me that Duck was seeing her. What disturbed me was that she would show up at night on the knoll or first thing in the morning at our day position. Duck must have been telling her where we were setting in at night so she could meet him. I mentioned it to Swan, but he shrugged it off as "Duck's horny. No sweat. No problem."

"Jackson," Duck said one time as he, Happy, and I walked along the dirt road on our way back from Ba Sat's, "I like you, but you ain't got no animal in you."

"What do you mean by that?"

"Well, like Ba Sat's niece back there, wouldn't you like to get into that?"

"Sure, if I wasn't married and didn't love Kristen," I said, thinking about the promise I had made to myself and to God. I knew I had survived so far because there was a special reason. The simplicity of staying lower than the log had not explained my surviving when P.J. got hit. So over a period of weeks, I had developed a more expansive personal philosophy as to why I had survived. I wasn't important, but my wife and child were, therefore God would let me live to go home and take care of them. But I couldn't tell Duck or Happy that. They would think I was crazy. I just felt I had to be faithful and pure. So I was.

"I'm married, too," Duck said, "But I still get a hard-on and have to knock off a piece once in awhile. Shit, you just ain't got no animal in you."

We moved out that night and set in on the knoll just above the ruined one-room schoolhouse. At night there was a policy forbidding light of any kind. But on that particular night, Duck's girlfriend showed up at the shacks, started a small cooking fire, and cooked several bowls of noodles for him, Corporal Swan, and Hodges. I ate some, too, but felt guilty because of the fire.

I dug my hole about fifty feet down the knoll, next to a partially destroyed wall of the school. From down in my hole I could stand up and see inside the ruined schoolhouse, and out the other side where parts of walls and foundation still stood. To my front was a shallow valley about fifty yards wide that led to another gently sloping small hill. The other small hill was the only thing standing in the way of seeing the main road leading to Da Nang, some five hundred yards away.

If we were ever hit, I had the protection of the wall to my left, the valley and hill to my front, and the rice paddies and semi-open graveyard to my extreme right. I had a fairly good field of fire. The only problem defending my position was if the VC came up along my backside by the shacks, or possibly through the graveyard.

I argued with Swan again about coming back to the same location, and couldn't understand why he didn't think it was important for the others to dig fighting holes. I opposed the gun staying inside with the rest of the gear and not outside to the side of the string of shanties, covering the graveyard. His response was the same. I was paranoid. "There ain't no gooks! Lighten up!"

I strung out my claymore and trip flares and stood my watch by my hole, more alert than usual, and then moved inside the shacks to the dirt floor to join the others. Again, I could not sleep. For me the tension was growing.

Ta' and gold-toothed Hein slept to my left, in an adjoining shack. The three of us, as was our custom, shared watch.

I felt the same eerie emptiness that I had experienced the night P.J. and I slept in the very same spot. It was the night he had talked so vividly about his home. It was the night before the first day of Tet.

The night passed slowly.

As morning broke, most of the PFs scattered out to the fields, or town, by the time all of C.A.P. Two's Marines were awake. We packed up and moved about three-quarters of a mile toward Ti Lon Two, with Bingham bitching about the long walk. Captain Duck meanwhile talked about his new true love, while Corporal Swan smiled arrogantly.

"I told you so!" he said. "Look out, Jackson, the VC are after your ass!" He laughed with mocking pride. "You carry so much fire power with you, you'd think you were one man army or some shit."

I was in the last ninety days of my tour and began to wonder if maybe I was paranoid. But I decided to ignore Swan and some of the others and dig my hole at night, string my flares and claymores and be ready if the darkness opened up.

We threw our packs down on the dirt patio of the small grass hut. The others started cooking while I laid out and organized my small arsenal.

"I be gettin' sooo short, I'll be home before the Phils finish spring training," Hodges said to anyone who would listen. "Yes, my man," he said, walking over to Duck, who was lying on the ground, shirt off, like a human comic strip, with his hands clasped behind his head. "Yes, my man, Mr. Duck, I be home takin' care of your old lady where Jody left off!"

"Hodges!" Duck said, sitting up, "my old lady takes one look at your black dick and she'll be thinking E-mag-i-nation! 'Cause that's all you got!"

Charlie walked over, hands deep in his pants pockets. "Hey, y'all want to go to Freedom Hill with me today?"

"Not me," Duck said, "I'll be takin' care of business today, while you boys is talkin' about it!" he added, in reference to screwing his prostitute.

"Hell, no!" Bingham said. "You think I want to walk my ass off, after walking all the way over here? You know how hot it's going to be. Come on. You some kind of fool! Walk to the Hill. You gots to be crazy!"

"OK! OK, Bingham," Charlie said. "I hear you. Heck, you'd complain if you was hung with a new rope!"

"But if you're going," Bingham added, "Could you pick me up some smokes at the PX? Oh, yeah, and how about some peanuts? You know those little cans of peanuts. Not the ones with the stuff on the outside. You know what kind I'm talking about?"

"Yes, I know."

"Charlie, listen, I'll go," I volunteered. "But I want to catch the flick, OK?"

"Fine with me."

I strapped on my .45, picked up my rifle, and we set out for the main road leading to Freedom Hill. Bingham was right, it was a scorcher. The sun blazed in a cloudless sky as we stood alongside the road thumbing for a ride, getting caked with red thick dust by passing trucks. Finally a military half-ton flatbed truck geared down to a stop, spraying us with another powdered shower of red dirt. The driver stuck his arm out the window, motioning for us to hop on back.

We had just started to roll when we spotted Ta' and Hein up ahead, dressed in their green PF uniforms. Charlie banged on top of the truck's cab, yelling for the driver to stop. "Them's our special Vietnamese interpreters, Captain Ta' and Lieutenant Hein," he lied. It was hard not to laugh. The driver pulled the truck to a stop and I jumped down and ran over to Ta' and Hein.

"Listen, you guys, want to ride to Freedom Hill?" I asked.

"No can ride on Marine truck. PF no can do," Ta' said.

"No problem. Just don't say anything. Charlie and I got you covered."

When we arrived at the PX, I told Ta' and Hein to wait outside for us. We went in, and while I purchased the things Charlie had come for, Charlie went over to a glass showcase and asked the corporal behind it for a set of captain's and lieutenant's bars.

"Listen, fellers," Charlie said to Ta' and Hein when we got back outside, "put on these here officer's bars and we'll tell those slick-lookin' MPs you fellers is Special Vietnamese Interpreters assigned to our Combined Action Platoon."

"No can do. Beaucoup trouble," Ta' said.

"There's no problem," Charlie said, trying to reassure them. "If they give you all any trouble, just hightail it outa here. Ta', you never been in a movie before. It's OK! Like my daddy used to say, 'Get what you can.'"

We pinned the captain's bars on Ta' and the lieutenant's bars on Hein.

"Now act like you all are officers," Charlie said.

We set off for the theater with Charlie and me walking a few steps behind Ta' and Hein. As we approached the massive tin building, I ran ahead to hold the door open for the new officers. Ta' walked proudly and confidently. Hein wasn't quite as brave.

From just inside the doorway, a U.S. Air Force Military Policeman stepped out to greet us, his M-16 pointing straight up in front of his body at port arms.

"Halt!" he said sternly as Ta' approached. "This theater is for authorized U.S. military personnel only."

"Hey, pal," Charlie said, "these here are interpreters, assigned to the Marine Corps. They's officers." Then, trying to bluff his way, Charlie turned to Ta' and said, "Excuse me, sir!" as if to apologize for the inconvenience. The MP looked at Charlie and me standing at attention, then put his rifle to his side and snapped neatly to attention and threw Ta' a picture-perfect salute. Ta' and Hein both returned the MP's salute, and Ta' added, with perfect aplomb, "At ease, sol-yer."

Once inside and at our seats, we rolled with laughter.

"Water Bull and Charlie beaucoup dinkey dau," Ta' said, snickering.

The inside of the theater was better than some of the ones I had been in back in the States. The concrete floor was clean and felt smooth under my feet. The chairs were comfortable and reminded me of sitting in a theater back home.

"Water Bull, what that?" Ta' asked, looking at the screen showing a picture of a tub of popcorn. I explained, and he replied, "Maybe Number One! You buy Ta'?"

Although I didn't particularly care for the movie, Ta' and Hein loved seeing *2001: A Space Odyssey*. We caught a ride back to the C.A.P.

"You get my peanuts?" Bingham asked when we arrived back at the day position. "And how about my smokes? Damn, you guys been gone all day."

"Here ya go," Charlie said, tossing him his cigarettes and peanuts. Then, as we packed up and readied ourselves to move out, Charlie detailed in his down home country way what had happened. "You all won't believe what we done at Freedom Hill. We made Ta' and Hein officers. Then we took 'em into the flick!" Hein grinned infectiously.

"Y'all shoulda seen it! We had that old boy standing at attention and saluting Ta' like he was a damn Christmas turkey!"

Everyone got a kick out of that, even Bingham.

But darkness soon put an end to our conversation. It was time to move. Ta' walked point in his Primo shirt and I walked ten yards behind with my 16.

It was warm and moonless and though the lack of visibility

always heightened my apprehension, it did not hamper our movement. We were confident as we walked over frequently traveled trails and across familiar rice paddy dikes, crossing back in a circle toward Ti Lon One. Again we were to stay on the knoll near the schoolhouse. As we settled in, I immediately moved my gear down by my hole, next to the schoolhouse wall. I strung out trip flares from familiar bushes and hid my claymores on an approach to a trail that ran down in front of my hole some twenty-five feet away.

I placed several bandoliers of magazines and six frags along the front outer edges of my fighting position, hoping I would have no use for them. It was so dark that I couldn't see the small hill to my front, and could barely make out the narrow short gully that separated both hills. The graveyard to my right and the distant paddies were empty black space. Making sure one last time that everything was neatly in place, I finished setting up my position.

At the opposite end of the ravaged schoolhouse, Ta', Hein, and Charlie and a couple of other PFs dug in. Behind me, the shacks were candle-lit and conversations could be heard. Behind the shacks and graveyard's end were the rest of the PFs, including Porky, Bac Si and Sergeant Trao. We totaled nine Marines, one Navy Corpsman, and fourteen PFs. But as usual, I felt alone.

I was friends with the other Marines in the unit, and I felt close to Ta', but since P.J. left, nights had a way of compounding my loneliness. Alone with my thoughts, I drifted to Kristen and wondered why her letters seemed so trite, or why they didn't often come. Maybe I was becoming overly paranoid. I grabbed my rifle and an extra bandolier and walked back up to the shacks, promising myself that I wouldn't worry about home or mention my concern over coming here again.

Duck, Swan, Hodges and Bingham were sitting at a small wooden table playing cards and Recon and Happy were eating when I walked in.

"Did you get your little fortress all set up?" Swan asked, looking up from his cards, his voice laced with sarcasm.

"I'm ready," I replied. Not wanting to get into a hassle, I

changed the subject. "Duck, where's that gal of yours? I could sure use a bowl of noodles."

"You got me. She wasn't feeling too well today. Said she might not make it. She said I was too much boom boom," he boasted proudly.

I wanted to tell him he shouldn't have told her where we were setting in, but I figured, what was the use? Besides, maybe there weren't any gooks around. We hadn't been hit in a month, and after all, after our initial losses, we'd cleaned house during Tet. I heard that we killed and captured more enemy than the entire First Marine Division.

I walked over to Doc Franny, who was sitting on the floor, fumbling through his medical bag. "What you lookin' for, Doc?" I asked, sitting down next to him.

"Those damn tubes of morphine. Oh, here they are," he said, pulling them from the bottom of the bag, studying them carefully, and then placing them in the top pocket of his utility shirt. "I always keep three or four of these babies with me in case we get hit and I don't have time to reach my bag."

"That's a good idea." It made me feel better that someone else was prepared for the worst. Especially someone like Doc, who was virtually boot to the Nam, and hadn't even been through a firefight yet.

"Either of you girls want to play cards?" Duck interrupted, walking over to us, shirtless as usual. "You ain't too timid for some blackjack, are you?"

"Yeah, too much action," I said, and stood up, walked over to my pack, and brought back a can of fruit.

"You want to play, Doc?" Duck asked. "I know Jackson ain't got no animal. Come on, how about it Doc? You up for some back or black?"

"OK, I'll play for awhile," Doc said, somewhat reluctantly.

I ate my peaches, then pulled out my poncho and Snoopy from my pack and made my bed on the floor for the night. From where I lay, I could see outside the hut's wide open door that swung up and was propped by a pole. As I lay back the candlelight flickered and danced against the inside of the tin and straw roof and out across the bamboo walls.

I took out Kristen's picture and spent a few moments gazing at her and then at the light and shadows bouncing off the walls. I put her picture back neatly into my pack. Hawaii had come so slowly and gone so quickly, I thought. Maybe that was only a fantasy. It was easy for me to mix up reality with illusion, especially when I was lonely. Maybe tonight was a tired old dream.

I lay back for awhile, thinking about Kristen and what it would be like when I got off the plane, when I arrived home.

I had it all planned in my mind, how she would run and greet me when the plane landed. She would throw her arms around me, just like in Hawaii, and hand me our baby. This time, though, it would be much more important. At last, I would finally be home. My mother and father might be there, waiting, maybe even my sister and brother. Kristen's best friend, Gail, she'd be there. I'd be home.

One card game died down, erasing most of the flickering shadows on the wall. I looked up through the dim light and noticed for the first time how the primitive thatched and silver-gray tin roof was constructed. Thick yellow bamboo poles that formed the ceiling beams were tied with thin strips of bamboo. On top of the beam was the metal covering. The square above me had been stamped with the words, U.S. Army. That was somewhat ironic, since the Marine Corps was protecting it and sleeping under it. But it was a good roof, and somehow sleeping under it made me feel better about the night.

The other card game soon ended. The candles were blown out, and the night enveloped us with darkness. We were spread on the dirt floor of the one-room shack like kids at a slumber party. Voices tracked back and forth, slicing through the lightless night, finding their way to whoever would listen.

"Yes, I be gettin' sooo short, I'll be poking Duck's lady before the summer's through," Hodges said, loudly enough for Duck to hear.

"Beauty, one more word outa you and I'm gonna take a big bite out of your black ass!" Duck said, not angrily, but with stern intonation, and I imagined in the dark Hodges' bad eye wandering.

"Whooooee, get some for Captain Duck!" Charlie said.

"Hodges, you got the gun set up out back?" Swan asked.

"No. Recon will put her up when he goes on radio watch."

"Well, make sure you do. You know Jackson will be on your ass."

The PFs were positioned outside while we were to monitor the radio inside, which meant about an hour watch for each one of us and lots of sleep. I relaxed and closed my eyes, thinking of Kristen and Jenine and bringing home Ta' if I could. I woke up later to nightmares of P.J. I closed my eyes again, uneasily, and finally fell into a shallow sleep.

"Water Bull! Water Bull!" Ta' said softly, with enormous distress wavering through his voice. "Water Bull! VC! VC! Beaucoup VC!" he said, shaking me awake.

My mind cleared instantly. I stood up, strapped on my shoulder holster, grabbed my rifle and wrapped a bandolier of magazines around my waist.

Ta' walked through the length of the row of dark huts, stepping over warm sleeping bodies, saying "VC! VC! VC!"

As I made my way toward the open doorway to my hole, I heard Duck say disgustedly, "Shit, there ain't no fuckin' VC!"

Three quick steps through the doorway, and the war came back in a spontaneous, relentless eruption of small arms and quick explosions.

The firing came in flashes from the opposite hill a hundred yards away, flashes and green tracers from the graveyard, and explosions from the shanty's rear. It flowed all at once, in deadly streams, concentrating on the still sleeping huts.

I fell to the ground, crawling frantically for the safety of my hole. Bullets followed me, cracking and kicking up dirt. Head down, I found my hole and slid safely below the rounds. My trip flares popped as silhouettes ran up the hill. I blew a claymore and two bodies hurtled into the air as if jerked by a hook from the sky.

Explosions flashed and ripped into the string of huts, spraying hunks of shrapnel. The huts were being ravaged, destroyed.

The firing raged as Corporal Swan ran out, shirtless,

catching a rifle round that splattered into his bare chest. He screamed, "Oh, God!" as the round hit and another flash lit up his twisted face. He had no time to grab his chest and clutch for life. The round hit him square and knocked him back, falling flat. He didn't move or groan. I knew that he was dead.

Doc Franny followed less than a second behind. He made it one step further than Swan before being blown off his feet, his leg torn and broken by another rending explosion.

I took my M-16 and raked the hill in front of me, firing long rapid blasts, dropping a magazine and snapping one in place. From the hill and graveyard came back a violent assault of overwhelming fire.

I cowered at the bottom of my hole, wishing it were deeper. Rounds tore into the dirt and smashed the wall. I realized they could see my flashes.

Doc lay ten feet from my hole, crying in anguish, "I'm hit! I'm hit!" moaning in a high shrill voice like a run-over dog. "Ooooh! Ooooh!"

While Swan lay dead and Doc was dying, the huts were taking round after round. In the back and to the side of the schoolhouse came the welcome sound of PFs screaming in Vietnamese and firing back.

I wasn't cool or composed. I wasn't a tough Marine. I was scared. I couldn't see them firing at me. They were all around but all I could make out were muzzle flashes and broken lines of green and white tracers. It wasn't just a body or bodies to kill, it was the darkness opening up. We were surrounded and being slaughtered by the darkness. The once sleepy shacks had become fiery tombs of inescapable death. Screams of "Marine Die!" came nearly as often as the rounds, louder and more terrifying than the explosions of earth. I heard the PFs yelling and fighting and knew the VC were on top of us.

"GET THE GUN UP!" I yelled, ignoring Doc's pleas for help, hoping the .60 might keep them off us. "GET THE GUN UP!" I screamed again, as loudly as I could, at the shacks. "GET THE GUN UP, JESUS CHRIST, GET THE GUN UP!" I screamed, tossing a frag.

Suddenly I remembered Doc lying just outside my hole,

crying for help. I forced myself to leave the safety of my hole and crawled to him. As I reached him an explosion came, lighting us up. In the light I could see that one of the bones in Doc's leg had ripped out through the skin and torn through his pant leg. It was sticking out just below the knee like the end of a broken baseball bat. As I frantically pulled Doc into my hole on top of me the firing resumed. Suddenly a figure burst from the darkness, firing on Doc, then standing above our hole. I could see his bayonet and I could feel Doc's body jerk and convulse as he whined, "Oh, Jesus, God! They're killing me!"

In the same instant I could see the look of fright in the wild eyes of the VC boy as I fired my .45 and blew his face away. The force of the round knocked him back down the hill.

I pulled Doc to the side, letting his head and shoulders and upper body fall and bleed into the safety of the hole. I threw three frags down into the small valley and out toward the graveyard. Oh, Christ what is happening to me? I didn't want to open up again and give the darkness a flash of light to concentrate their aim on. I was rabid with fear, screaming.

"HODGES! GET THE GUN UP!" I yelled back at the shacks when the firing and blasting started to wane.

"Duck, get the gun up!"

"He can't, his head's blown off!" Hodges moaned from the shack in a sickening rage of hate and fear.

"Happy! Recon! Jimmy! Where are you?" I screamed. Time began to swirl and confuse me. Doc was crying for morphine.

"Shoot me up! Jackson, please. Shoot me up!"

Hodges was crying, "Oh, Jesus, they're dying!"

The hole was so cramped I could hardly move. I was on one knee, afraid to rise above the hole, while the upper half of Doc's body was still draped over me and his legs hung out in a mangled, twisted heap. I could feel his blood all over me. Doc, crying, Hodges, crying, everyone was crying and dying.

Ta' ran up to my hole and crouched down. "Cha-lee dead!" he said in broken, frightened English. Hein followed behind.

"Cha-lee shot in throat! I carry Cha-lee!" Ta' pointed back to where Charlie lay. And as he pointed, another explosion came and in its light I saw several rounds rip into Ta's Primo shirt and knock him violently back. Dead.

Unbelievably, the firing stopped. From nowhere, Bingham was suddenly next to my hole. He was completely out of control, while I was shaken with grief.

"They're shot! They're all shot! We got to get them out of here. They're all shot! We got to get them out of here!"

"Cha-lee dead! Ta' dead!" Hein cried.

"PLEASE! OH, PLEASE!"

"Come on, we've got to get them out of here!"

"I'm hit! Jackson. Please. Morphine. Please."

"OOOHHH! Help me! OHHH! I'm hit!"

All the voices seemed to come at once, pounding at me... pounding and pounding and battering me like a heavyweight beating on a man against the ropes and Ta' was lying dead next to me. I was losing my senses and yet trying to think straight.

"We got to get them out of here! Come on! Come on!" Bingham kept yelling and pleading.

"LISTEN, YOU ASSHOLE," I screamed, "get up to the huts and start moving them out of there. I'll shoot up Doc and then I'll help. And call in a Medivac!"

Bingham left. Hein quickly dragged Charlie over toward my hole. Charlie wasn't dead, but his throat was ripped open and he soon would be dead unless we got him out on a chopper. He mumbled blood as I wiped and cleared his mouth with my hand. I glanced at Ta' and then moved to Doc.

I fixed Doc with two hits of morphine and he calmed down. He helped me tie his legs together with battle dressing and my utility shirt. Ta', my broken friend, was beyond help.

In the faint light from a dying pop flare, I could see Hein running and yelling something in Vietnamese and pointing toward the hill. He opened up with his M-79, then fired a LAW. A brief scream followed the blast from somewhere in the night. There were only a few PFs left in back of the huts. The rest were either dead, wounded or had run down to the road and hidden somewhere. Hein, Bac Si, Sergeant Trao and Porky came to the school and fired on the hill and across at the graveyard and out into the open paddies. Hein never stopped firing his blooper. Sometimes he turned and fired it over the shacks, crying.

I went over to Bingham, who was between the shacks and the schoolhouse, to help with the wounded. Then I went inside one of the shacks to look for a radio. When I stepped through the doorway, I saw a figure move and throw something at me. Turning, I emptied my M-16 as an explosion knocked me down, the brunt of it catching a table before tearing into my holster and my side. I was hurt, but not badly. I found the radio I had sent Bingham for, and crawled out, ignoring the warm, wet blood running down my side. I tried to call in a Medivac, but the radio wouldn't work. It was shot full of holes.

The firing began again, coming in brief combinations of rapid fire and explosions. I had to get things done now. I knew we were about to be hit hard again. It would be just like Tet. The gooks would wait and wait until the rescue chopper landed. Then they'd blow us all away. Bingham didn't understand that. He hadn't helped P.J. and me during Tet.

I crawled back inside the huts and found the other radio and made it back to my hole.

"We got to get these guys out!" Bingham bellowed again in my face, his eyes wide open. I couldn't figure out why he hadn't gotten hit. He was the only Marine who wasn't hit. We had all been wounded and virtually everyone had to be Medivac'd, except me, Hodges, who had a minor back wound, and Bingham. I was finally able to raise the C.P. As the firing stopped, I pleaded for what seemed like an eternity. Finally, choppers were heard overhead above our smoldering huts.

I argued and screamed that we needed them to drop in now.

The Medivac was worried about taking fire.

I raved and swore and told him we were down here with men dying.

The Medivac questioned our position. I cursed and tried to be calm, but couldn't. Bingham kept screaming advice. The others who were wounded moaned to God. Charlie gurgled and choked. Doc was starting to come down from the high, and Swan and Duck lay silent, not breathing.

Hodges staggered over toward Duck and then as he knelt down and touched Duck's half open head, he lost all control.

He got up, ran and screamed, "He's dead, he's dead! His brain's on me! Jesus God! He's dead!" He ran to Swan's dead body, crazed, frantic.

"Swan's dead!" I yelled, then turned back to the radio, begging for help.

"No, no, he's not!" Hodges said, unbelieving, and desperate for Swan to live. "He's just passed out! That's all! He's not dead! He's not! I tell you! He's not!"

Another explosion came with enough light to illuminate Hodges as he knelt over Swan's dead body, kissing his lips, trying to blow life back in.

"Hodges, he's dead!" I yelled. "He's dead!"

But Hodges wouldn't listen. He hovered over Swan, shaking his head slowly and muttering in disbelief. "No... No!" and he kept blowing air and spittle into the dead Corporal Swan, saying, "No... No."

After long minutes of discussion and arguing, the Cobra gunships that accompanied the Medivac passed over us and anxiously radioed back to me. "They're still all over the place!" the radio shouted.

"WELL, BLOW THE FUCK OUT OF THEM!" I screamed. Rockets and long lines of tracers, and automatic M-79 rounds began erupting from the chopper and hammering the distant hill and rice paddies, while in my mind I could see and hear Ta' greet me at the chow truck that first day. "Hey, Water Bull. You Water Bull."

Then the gunships pulled back and the Medivac chopper landed in the dark on a flare in the shallow valley to the front of the schoolhouse. I pulled a crying, hugging, emotionally collapsed Hodges off Swan's body and made him help carry Doc on board. I was so exhausted I didn't care if I got hit. I knew we had to get everyone on board quickly.

"Come on out, Hodges!" I yelled into the chopper, but he wouldn't come back out. He cowered in the corner of the craft. His big body could still function, but his mind couldn't.

Bingham was bitching orders that no one heard, as he helped Happy and Jimmy on board. We finished loading the wounded and dead. The PFs who had been wounded were not allowed

257

aboard the chopper. They were not Medivac'd, even though there was room and even though they were dying. It was regulation. Only U.S. military personnel.

The chopper lifted off and received no parting fire. The VC hadn't waited for the final kill this time.

The sound of the Medivac's blades slowly faded, the lights disappeared, and it was gone. When the sun broke and settled on the row of shacks and the school, the game was done.

Eighteen

I SAT ON THE EDGE of my hole next to the schoolhouse wall, dangling my feet and feeling the warmth of the morning sun on my neck and bare back. The blood from last night's wounds had dried and scabbed on my skin. I picked several small pieces of once hot stinging metal out of my arms, left leg and side. Hardly worth a purple heart, I thought, especially when compared to dozens of other wounds I had seen. My ears felt stuffed and there was a ringing in my head. I was too tired to eat and too tired to feel bad. All I could appreciate was that I had survived.

The young VC I had killed was still lying down the hill in front of my hole, being sucked on by the morning flies. I felt no anger or remorse. Looking at him was like looking at a dead stray dog dumped by the side of the road.

Ta's mother and grandfather kissed my hand when they came to take his body away. I gave them my money and stupidly thought that it would ease their pain. I simply didn't know what else to do.

Aside from my hole, Hein and the PFs were the only reason I had survived, or maybe it was God. I just didn't know. Perhaps some day, years later, I would be able to come back to the scene of last night. If I could, I would sit in the same place that afforded me my life. I would sit, look across to the other hill and think and cry and remember what happened, and be so glad that I had lived.

Hein and the other PFs who had stayed to fight mingled with Bingham back at the row of grass shacks. Then they reluctantly dragged off the body near my hole and searched the graveyard for more bodies, but none were found.

I thought for a long time, while sitting in my hole. I thought about what had happened and how I had been graced to live a few more days. I thought about not being dead, but then not really feeling alive. I thought about Ta' and wondered where I had placed my grief. I guess I just didn't care anymore. Maybe I was crazy. I didn't know.

I stared out across the small valley where the Medivac had landed and wondered why the darkness had not opened up on us as the choppers were being loaded and swept us all away to death. Could Charlie live? I could see him in my mind, mumbling red bubbles. Old Duck, I shook my head. Hodges, Recon, Jimmy, Happy, they might be back since they walked onto the chopper. Doc, on the other hand, might never walk again. Corporal Swan... I didn't like him, but what bad can be said about a twenty-year old kid who died in Vietnam?

I filed that night away in my depository of nightmares, and drifted off to Kristen and seeing my baby daughter again. I wouldn't allow myself to be caught in grief. I would only think of Kristen now.

I stood up and walked back to the hut that housed my gear. Everything inside had been destroyed. I sifted through broken tables and stepped in sticky pools of Duck's or Charlie's or someone's blood. I found what was left of my pack. I withdrew Kristen's picture, which, like Ta', was reduced to just a memory. I was too spent to be enraged.

I would have cried for a long time, but I was drained of tears. Instead I found a can of pound cake and sat down amid the rubble and tried to eat. Bingham walked in, interrupting me.

"The C.P. called and they're on their way down here, and they're bringing some V.I.P. They got some new men with them. There's going to be an investigation or some shit about how we got our ass waxed. You gonna go meet them down at the road or what?"

"Sure. I'll head down there when I'm done eating."

"You'd better hurry!"

I would have said, "Fuck you!" but I was too tired. I finished my cake, wiped the blood and excess dirt from my rifle, threw on a flak jacket that was still intact and left the hut, heading for the road. Along the way, I saw Porky and asked him if he wanted to join me. "You and Hein kill VC. Save Marine," I said as we approached the road leading in and out of Ti Lon One.

"Beaucoup VC," Porky said. "Marine sleep. Die," he added, shaking his head and recalling Ta's warning from last night.

We reached the end of the road that ran the length of the hamlet as a contingent of Marines approached us. We stopped and waited at the first hut that led into Ti Lon One. Captain Dunn was leading the group, and striding powerfully and pompously. He looked like he had put on some weight, which bulged over the holster belt of his 45. His arms swung back and forth as if he were a fat tin soldier marching off to war. As he and the rest of his entourage drew closer, I could see he was not smiling. He walked up to us briskly with the V.I.P., Colonel Davis, and several other, unfamiliar officers.

"Marine," Dunn said, staring at me, anger in his voice, "where the hell is your utility shirt? Marine, you'd better get your ass at attention, and I best see a salute."

I snapped to and threw a salute, wanting to throw a punch and hoping some far-away VC could see this lame fuck and tap him right between the eyes.

"Now where's that shirt?" Dunn asked, somewhat satisfied.

"I used it to tie together Doc's leg."

He didn't have a reply. He looked stupid. I wished him dead.

Porky and I led the investigation team back up to the shacks and schoolhouse. Along the way, a young blonde second lieutenant, who was acting as interpreter for the group, stopped to question several of the peasant Vietnamese who lived in the hamlet. The lieutenant was a boot, I thought, since the Vietnamese he spoke was very poor. He might have been a whiz at Interpreter's School, but the peasants couldn't understand a word he spoke. They'd look at him, puzzled, and say, "Cum bic?" while shaking their heads, not understanding.

When we reached the ambush site, the colonel asked me what happened. I explained the situation, noting our repetitive routine and hinting that perhaps Duck's girlfriend had set us up, knowing in my heart that she had.

The colonel yelled and screamed about, "Fuckin' tactics, Marine, fuckin' tactics," probably for the benefit of the new men who had come along to replace the old ones who were killed and wounded.

While Dunn and the brass looked around the area, I went back down to my hole by the wall. A few minutes later, one of the new replacements came down and stood over me. "Boy, you sure look beat," he said, dropping his pack next to my hole. "What happened?"

I looked at him, studying his face for a moment. He looked so young. So much younger than me. He was just a kid. "What's your name?" I asked ignoring his question.

"Now don't laugh," he said, smiling cautiously. His teeth were straight and white and his eyes were bright blue. He was clean and fresh faced. "My name's Weldon."

It was fitting. He was a perfect portrait of the All-American Boy with rosy cheeks and blonde hair. I looked away, detached and exhausted. His being here was a mistake. He should have been back in high school sitting in some English class writing poetry to his girlfriend. Not here, in the Nam. He was the kind of kid, I imagined, who'd never had a fight, and always kissed his mother before he left the house. He seemed gentle, almost angelic. Even his uniform didn't look right on him.

"Weldon," I said, turning back to him. "Before we continue any kind of conversation, we have GOT to change your name." I thought about his gentle manner and almost virginal look, and it struck me.

"Cherry. Cherry is your new name."

He wasn't about to argue with me, I guess having sensed what had gone on during the night.

"OK. That's fine with me," he said in a most agreeable manner. "But what's your name? And Geeze, what happened?"

I studied him again, flashing back in my mind across months of war.

"Cherry," I said, trying out his new name, still avoiding his question, "my name's Jackson."

"How do you do?" Cherry said, shaking my hand straight and firm like a kid shakes a grown-up's hand. He was a nice kid and I imagined half his face blown away. He was probably the same age as me, but after last night, I had suddenly grown old. The intensity was over, I was tired, and wanted so much to close my eyes and race in my mind back home.

"I don't mean to bother you," he persisted, "but you and those other two are the only ones left." His voice was guarded as he spoke, hesitant, polite, and full of fear.

I looked at him and he at me. Our eyes touched. It was a meeting of the old and the new. "Cherry, we just got our ass kicked. We lost. That's all."

Dunn's team of specialists bitched for awhile, and talked with the PFs who had stayed and fought. The interpreter walked around trying to figure out why no one understood his classroom Vietnamese. When they left, I took off my flak jacket, used it as a pillow, stretched out and went to sleep.

The next day the Military Police came to the ville and picked up the body of Duck's dead girlfriend.

Quietly and unknown to all the rest, I'd walked through her doorway and emptied a magazine into her fucking head.

Dear Kristen,
    Time has stopped. I need you. Each day away from you seems like a lifetime. The days we shared in Hawaii are distant dreams, but they are the only thing that keeps me going. That and looking forward to being with you when I get home.
    It was rough for awhile, but things seem to have calmed down. We have a bunch of new men in our unit. They have only been in country a couple of months. I guess the policy has changed from when I came to the C.A.P. unit. I had to have at least five months' experience in country.
    They are a strange assortment of guys, but all right, I guess. The only one I have had a chance to get to

know is a kid named Weldon. I nicknamed him Cherry, and can you believe this, he has never been with a woman. He really is cherry! He's from a small town called Homedale in Idaho. Isn't that fitting? Anyway, I like the kid.

Happy finally got promoted. He's in charge now.

We have a new Corpsman, Doc Patman. We call him Fat Man. He is fat compared to all of us. He's a boot, only been the Nam for a few weeks. The other new dudes are Grubs, Big John, and a Mexican we named Taco. I don't want to talk about them.

Tell your parents I appreciated the packages of Kool Aid they sent me. And that I look forward to any more they might decide to send. Ask Woody about his golf game, and tell your mom she better stick to that new diet.

Those last pictures you sent of Jenine were outstanding, especially the one of her standing, holding on to the coffee table. I wish that I could be there when she stands alone, or when she takes her first step.

God willing, I will never have to miss another of her birthdays or Christmas! I'm at the point where I'm considered to be "getting short." I want you to write more. The last few weeks I've hardly heard from you. Anyway, Cousin Rich finally made it out of Flight School and is in the Nam, huh? I'm glad you sent me his address. I'll write him when I get a chance.

Well, it's time for me to get a move on. I have to go meet the chow truck. I sure miss you. I love you so much! In fact, I'm way over into the area of too much.

Love you,
Jackson
May 1969

P.S. I hope you like the flicks I'm sending. The little fat guy is Porky and the PF with the gold tooth is Hein.

P.P.S. There are times when I wish I could pick up the phone and call you. I'd give anything just to hear your voice or even listen to you breathe. I love you so much, but I've run out of poetry.

Nineteen

A FEW DAYS AFTER the Ti Lon One ambush by the schoolhouse, a new PF joined our C.A.P. unit. He was a very impressive looking Vietnamese. He was nearly six feet tall, weighed about one hundred and sixty pounds, and looked like he was part French. He was incredibly well developed, with sharp muscle cuts and definition. He had several scars, apparently from bullet wounds, including one through his nose. But he had a handsome face and a beautiful body that gave him a striking appearance. His name was Sergeant Whin, and he was one bad dude.

Immediately upon taking command of the PFs, he gathered together those who had run from the VC the night we got hit and beat the hell out of several of them. He punched them and kicked them viciously when they fell to the ground. He screamed at them in Vietnamese and cursed them in English. As I watched, I was worn out and felt nothing about what he did. They had run, but so what? Soon I would be gone and they were stuck here forever.

I found out later that Sergeant Whin was twenty and had been fighting the VC for five or six years, since the night they came to his village near Hue and rounded up and massacred over twenty of the villagers, including his parents, two sisters and two brothers. He had been shot several times, but escaped death by lying under his father's body, pretending to be dead.

With Sergeants Whin and Trao in charge, the PFs soon

became more bold and aggressive in their desire to fight. Although Whin spoke little English, we understood each other and held mutual admiration for one another. We were both physically stronger than our peers and we were survivors. As time passed Whin showed me how to spot hidden bunkers and how digging in next to trees and bushes would conceal my position and still allow me a clear field of fire.

Whin would sometimes get wild and drunk during the day and arrange for prostitutes to come out for the other guys. But at night when we dug in he was the best.

> Dear Kristen,
> Just a short note to let you know that you and Jenine are in my heart and soul every minute of my life. I'm getting short and I can't wait to be with you. I know I've changed, but I will try to be the best man I can.
> In your last letter you asked me if I had killed any children. No, I haven't. In fact, I went on a MedCap with Doc today and helped deliver a baby. It was dead, though, and I had to go behind the shack to cry. I don't want to kill anyone. I just want to come home.
> > Love you
> > Jack
> > June 1969

I sat along the bank of the river as I had so many times before. Sampans were gently gliding up and down as conical-hatted fishermen pulled aboard their newly caught fish. I waved to them, and they to me. As much a part of the river and country that the Vietnamese were, I, too, had developed an affinity with the place where I now lived.

The relationship I had with the PFs and hamlet peasants was a communion of pleasure, coupled with sympathy and sorrow. I understood what they were fighting for.

Sergeant Trao exemplified the spirit of resistance. For years he had worked and saved money so that he could buy materials to build his home. Not a humble peasant hut, but as he said, "a fine home... three rooms, strong with stone." During the day he worked hard on his new home and I watched with admiration as his dream neared completion.

One night we set in at an ambush position adjacent to his home. A small NVA force swept down from the mountains to steal rice from the villagers. When we opened up on them, they ran into Trao's new home to hide and fight. We were reluctant to fire on Trao's house, for fear we would damage or destroy it. I looked into his face and saw no sorrow, only hate for the invaders. He swore in Vietnamese and fired a .79 round into his home. We all followed his lead and opened fire. His house was nearly demolished. The next day and for several days thereafter, all the Marines in our C.A.P. unit spent time helping Trao reconstruct his home.

As I sat there on the river bank, I thought about the messages that the media had projected through the *Stars and Stripes* and what I saw on television in Honolulu. I understood how Americans back home could be influenced and persuaded to believe all sorts of distorted, twisted stories. And I could understand why the ARVNs and some PFs were portrayed as poor fighters. During the Tet of February and the year before, hundreds of ARVNs had deserted their posts and fled back to their homes. But, then, I would do the same if a war were going on back in the States. I'd race back to wherever my wife and child were. I'd do anything to protect their lives. The Vietnamese were no different. The PFs who had run the night we were hit at the schoolhouse were cowards to a certain extent, but even if they'd fought that night, there would be another fight to fight and another and another. There would be no rotation back to the world. Nothing to look forward to. My tour was thirteen months; theirs, an entire lifetime.

A new man came to our unit. He had transferred in from riding gunner on truck convoys. His name was Mike. He was a very young eighteen, practically a baby. Mike wanted to be where there was more action, and he figured C.A.P. units might be the answer. He arrived on the evening chow run. I took him under my wing and we shared watch together that first night. The next day Mike and I went to Da Nang to the big PX. On the bed of the truck he told me about his home.

"I'm from Carbondale, Illinois, and I tell you, it's a pretty town! When I get out, I'm going to open up a head shop with two of my buddies back there. With all the dopers and druggies, we'll make the bucks."

I liked Mike, and was humored by his dream. On the way back from Da Nang, we were standing along a stretch of road that was lined with shacks full of prostitutes. Two came up. I said no, and Mike said yes. I waited outside with his rifle and hoped God was taking note of my loyalty. A little while later, he came out. "Damn! That was good!" he said, smiling. "You got it made here. Why didn't you get any boom boom!"

Not answering his question, I said, "Come on, let's go." I stuck out my thumb and handed Mike his rifle. We caught a ride and I drifted in silent thought to Kristen.

That night we set up in the graveyard next to and below the schoolhouse. We got hit. Mike was killed before he could get his boots on. The VC who shot him ran toward my hole, firing. I blew his head off with a 79. The next morning, I moved up to my hole by the school, while the other Marines examined the dead VC. I was eating peaches when Cherry came running up. He was winded and excited from searching the dead gook's body.

"Don't you want to see the VC you killed?"

"No, I just want to eat."

Later, Mike was bagged up and flown out. I watched the chopper grow small. "Fuck it," I said as it disappeared into the sky. The head shop would wait forever and I finished my peaches.

Routine, routine, routine. Everything had become routine. The people, the filth, the food, the new Marines coming in, getting killed and bagged up and flown out, and the new Marines flown in to take their places. Everything repeated itself... routine. We would set in at night, and maybe we would get hit and maybe we wouldn't. It was all the same. I was getting tired of the Nam. There wasn't any glamor or excitement to it all. I wanted to go home. Catastrophic occurrences meant nothing anymore. I wanted to go home.

Four Marines from Hill 10 sat alongside the road between Da Nang and Hue Duc. They were resting. Two young boys pedaled up on old bicycles with styrofoam carriers hanging on each side of the bike's back wheels. They stopped in front to the Marines. "Marines want Coke? Marine want Coke, twenty piasters."

The Marines were hot, thirsty, and tired from walking in the midday heat. "Sure, kid, here you go." They all took Cokes from the two boys and went back to sit down. The boys put the money into the other foam box. They reached down and pulled out handmade chi-coms and hurled them at the unsuspecting Marines. The one Marine who lived told how it happened. His story wouldn't hit the papers back home.

Ba Sat's pretty niece was working in the rice paddies and stepped on an old land mine. Her left leg was blown off, her face destroyed.

Nothing was shocking or repulsive anymore. Bingham rotated home. Frenchie was kidnapped by the VC and I never saw him again. Sergeant Trao was a hero. After killing Viet Cong who walked in front of his hole one night, he hacked their dead bodies with a machete.

One night a Marine patrol wandered into our ambush. When we stopped firing, two of them were dead.

Cherry finally got laid by a prostitute and then cried when the PFs killed her. "She VC," Trao said. Before they took her away, they raped her, stuck a pop-up up her cunt and fired it. Her body wasn't human any more. But then... what was?

It was another beautiful, serene, sunny morning as we packed up, covered in holes and prepared to move to our day position. The day was fresh and clean, with bright calming light. The countryside was waking. The night before I had dug my hole deeper than usual, anticipating, for some unexplainable reason, that we might get hit. We didn't. But I was getting short, very short, and couldn't afford to become complacent.

As we settled in a hut facing the river in Ti Lon One, Porky came up to me.

"Water Bull, go Da Nang? Can do?" Porky asked me as I threw my pack off and lay down. I was in an unusually mellow

271

mood. We had not made contact for over a week and very soon I would be rotating back to the real world. Going to Da Nang sounded like a good idea. Maybe I'd take Cherry with us. I liked Cherry, but I was careful not to get too close to anyone since P.J. or Ta'.

"Sure, Pork, I'll take you to Dả Nang," I said, pleased with his improving English.

"We take Hein? Can do?" he asked. He looked so eager, I nearly laughed. "Sure, Pork, whatever you want."

"You Number One Water Bull," he said, grinning happily.

But orders came down from the C.P. I was called to the rear. I was so short that they would have made me stand guard duty at C.A.G. Headquarters, so Porky, Hein, Cherry, and I didn't make it to Da Nang.

I never saw them or the others again.

It was over, that's all. Just over.

Twenty

THE PLANE LIFTED from the runway, pushing me gently back into my seat. I could hardly believe that at last I was going home. After waiting for hours at the Los Angeles Airport for a military standby flight, I was finally on a late night flight heading home.

After being shot, sick, confused about everything... I was going home.

Wild, disjointed thoughts ran through my head in conflicting scenes of joy and dread. One minute my mind would take me home to Kristen and lying next to her... the next minute, I'd be in the middle of the rice paddy with P.J. shot and crying, "Get me out! Get me out!" As fast as my mind's eye took me from the seat of the plane to the airport with Kristen waiting with open arms for me, I'd flash back to Jimmy in Kilo who took the wrong path or Ta' lying dead right next to my hole.

I couldn't slow my thinking down. My brain pumped out images as fast as blood pumped from all the shattered bodies that I had seen. My mind's eye was a collage of shattered arms, legs, faces and the thin white thing that hung from Rodo's neck.

The pot, Cam Ranh Bay, the villes, the weeks of malaria and shitting all over myself. I saw Kristen running to me through a field as I stood over dead VC, emptying magazines into their already dead bodies.

I could see it and feel it. I was sweating and nearly delirious.

I felt my mind slipping. The woman sitting next to me, the middle-aged woman... the handsome woman... she could tell I wasn't sitting there next to her. Only my body was. She could see the perspiration on my forehead.

She thinks she knows what I am, I thought. She thinks I could go berserk and stand up and blow this fuckin' plane apart or I can drop what I'm thinking, without thinking, like I dropped dead boys' bodies on a flatbed truck. But I have a gift, I thought. No one on this plane could ever really understand my gift. I could retract, withhold and conquer all emotion.

After a year of mind-numbing emotional pounding, I had evolved to the point where I couldn't feel anything at all. I'd become a genius at recycling remorse and turning it into nothing.

The only feelings I would ever experience were those of loving. I would never, could never, be hurt. It all made so much sense to me on the plane.

As the flight neared its end, I lost myself in the long recorded mental image of stepping off the plane and having Kristen and Jenine there to love me.

The pilot announced over the intercom that it was time to fasten our seatbelts for our descent and that the arrival time would be 2:12 a.m. Like C.A.P. 2-1-2, I thought. The passengers were anxious, talking about being home. I was the only Marine on board. I looked good, I thought, in my clean, freshly pressed khakis. I hoped Kristen would be proud of me.

I felt proud. I had seen my way through an incredibly trying project and was approaching the end, just minutes away.

I hoped that Kristen would have on the dress that I had bought her in Hawaii. But it really didn't matter, as long as she was there.

The plane descended over the airport, circling lower and lower. It was raining, the pilot announced, but the city lights shone clear and bright below.

We landed and I sighed relief. Wouldn't it have been ironic, I thought, if the plane had crashed and I was killed on my way home.

"You have someone meeting you?" the woman next to me asked.

"Yes," I replied proudly, deciding that maybe she didn't know what was going on in my head after all. "My wife and daughter, and probably some other friends and relatives," I added with excitement.

"You must be happy to be home," she said, as the plane rolled up to the unloading ramp.

"Yes, I am," I said, fighting back tears and suddenly getting a wild rush of adrenaline from the expectation of feeling Kristen in my arms.

"Good luck!" the woman said, standing up from her seat and moving into the aisle in front of me.

My heart was pounding wildly as I crowded off the plane.

The walk down the narrow hallway ramp seemed longer than when I'd boarded several hours before. The glass walls, backed by night, reflected, and I stared for a moment at my much older image walking down the ramp and into the receiving area.

My long awaited, prayed-for moment was about to come.

My ordeal was over.

Past the gates, the passengers in front and in back of me were quickly surrounded by handshaking, backslapping, hugging, and kissing relatives. People laughed and some cried. All of them looked happy and tired.

The crowd thinned.

Where was Kristen?

Where was my moment?

Families and friends left the receiving area. The crowd diminished to four or five, and then to just me.

Where was Kristen!

I stood alone waiting.

I put the image of me stepping off the plane into her loving arms away and drew a new one in my mind. She would be up at the ticket counter. Of course, that's it. She would be there. I knew she would be there.

I walked and ran along the colorful hallway, past the bag-toting people, until I reached the ticket counter.

No one was there.

Where was Kristen? What had happened to her? Why is my moment being taken away?

"Excuse me, but is there a message for me?" I asked the ticket agent in his dark blue suit and tie.

"What's your name?"

Feeling stupid and lost, I told him my name.

"Yes, here's a message," he said, fumbling through some notes. "You're to call your wife at this number."

I took the piece of paper and walked to the phone booth.

What's happening to me? Why, after all I have been through, must I lose my most important moment? I want my dream. I dialed the phone. It rang several times.

"Hello."

"Is Kristen there?"

"Oh, Jack, this is Gail. Yes, just a minute, I'll wake her." The phone was silent.

Wake her, I thought. She knew I was coming. She knew I would be at the airport. What was happening? My moment! My moment! What was happening to me?

"Jack, you're home," Kristen said over the phone.

"Where are you? Where are you?" I stammered, crushed and devastated by her not being there.

"I got tired so I came to Gail's. What's wrong? I figured you could just catch a taxi here, then we could go over to your mom's."

I could not understand. I stared at the phone and then blankly at a couple walking by. What was happening? I felt destroyed. Nothing I had believed in made sense anymore. I had survived, I had been saved for my moment, and now it was a mockery. I tightened up inside. I wouldn't let her know! I wouldn't let anyone know!

I closed off. "I'll be there," I said.

"OK, honey," she answered and hung up.

I listened to the dial tone for a long time, thinking it sounded as good as her voice. Then I hung up the receiver.

I stood and walked from the phone booth across the long airport lobby and out into the pouring night. Alone I watched cars and buses being loaded and unloaded. I flashed back to P.J. and Rodo and black Jimmy. I knew my moment was gone.

Finally I waved a taxi down and tossed my bag ahead of me into the back seat. As we moved slowly away from the airport it grew darker and the rain beat down even harder.

"Where ya headed, pal?" the driver asked.

"Home," I said. "I'm just trying to get home."